# Unicorn
## of Many Hats
### Another
### Phoebe and Her Unicorn Adventure

## Dana Simpson

Andrews McMeel
PUBLISHING®

# Hey, kids!

Check out the glossary starting on page 172
if you come across words you don't know.

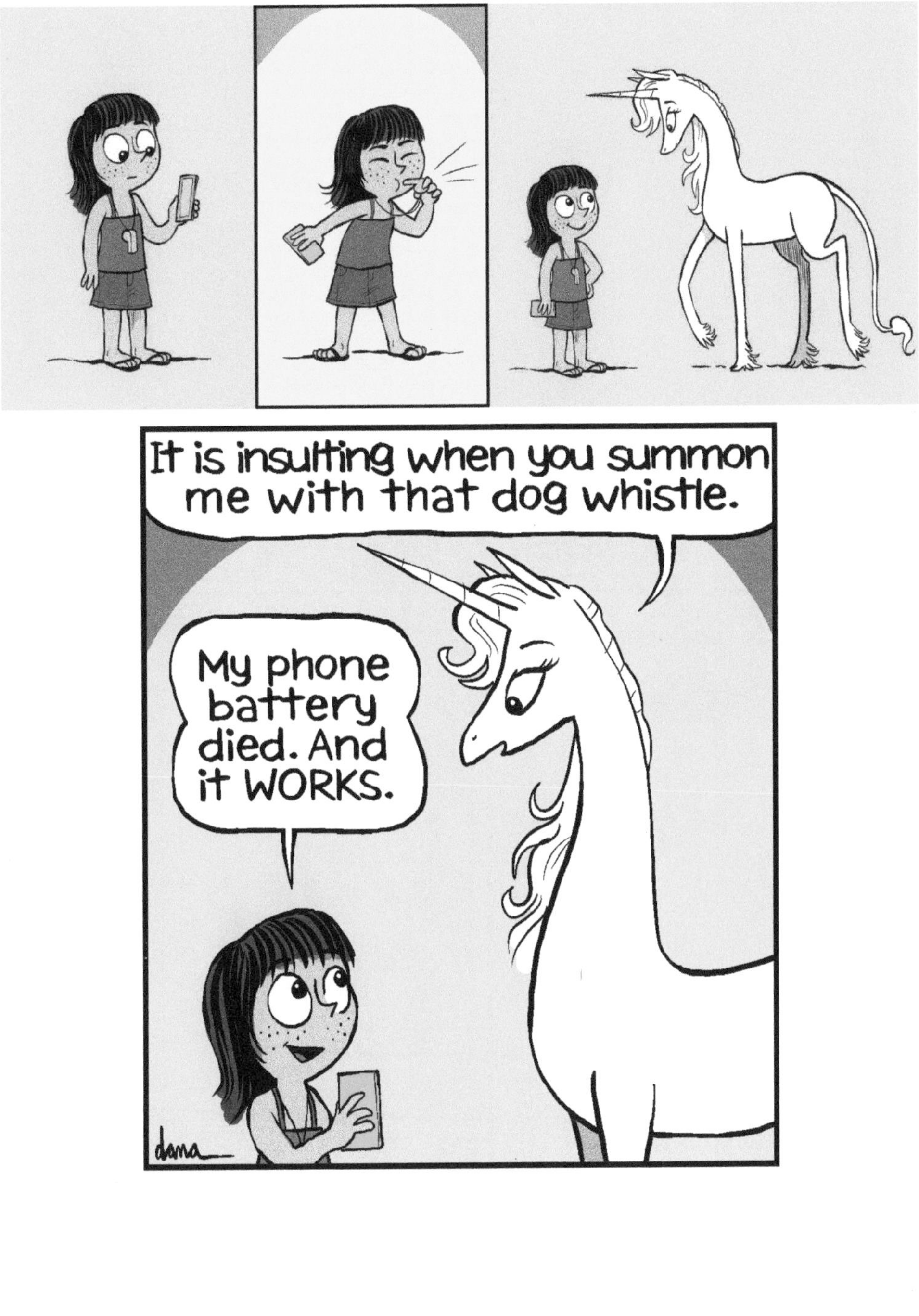
It is insulting when you summon me with that dog whistle.
My phone battery died. And it WORKS.
dana

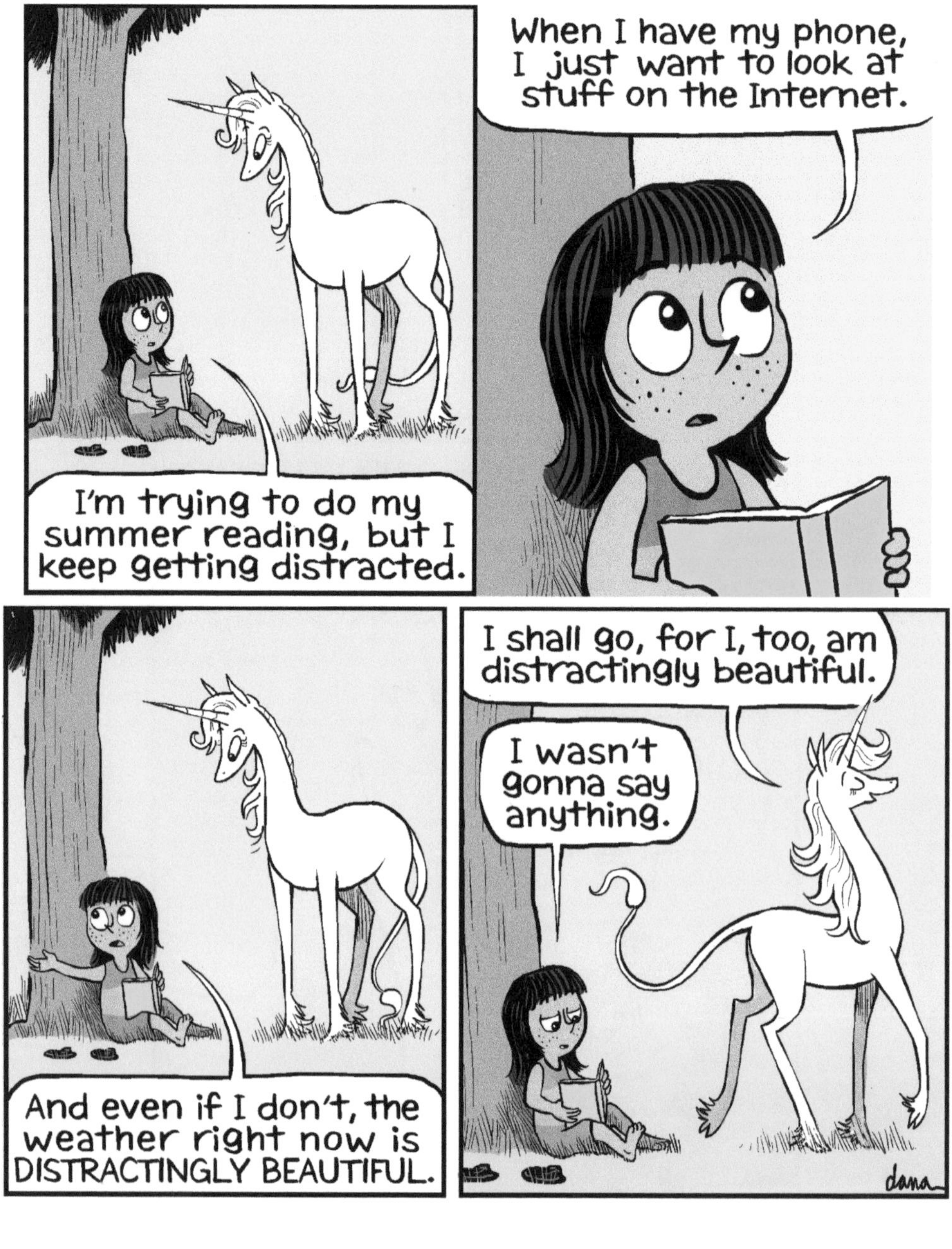
I'm trying to do my summer reading, but I keep getting distracted.
When I have my phone, I just want to look at stuff on the Internet.
And even if I don't, the weather right now is DISTRACTINGLY BEAUTIFUL.
I shall go, for I, too, am distractingly beautiful.
I wasn't gonna say anything.
dana

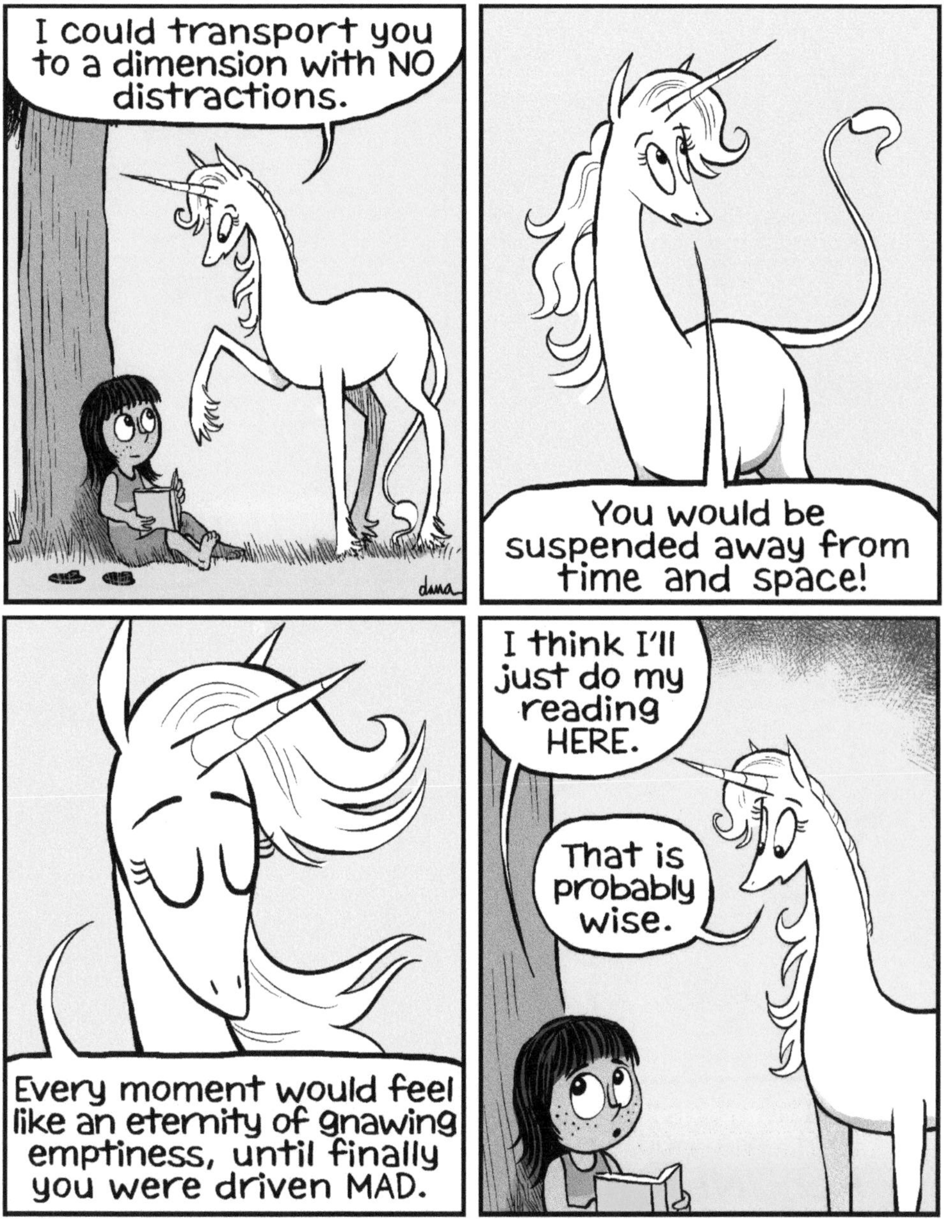
I could transport you to a dimension with NO distractions.
dana
You would be suspended away from time and space!
Every moment would feel like an eternity of gnawing emptiness, until finally you were driven MAD.
I think I'll just do my reading HERE.
That is probably wise.

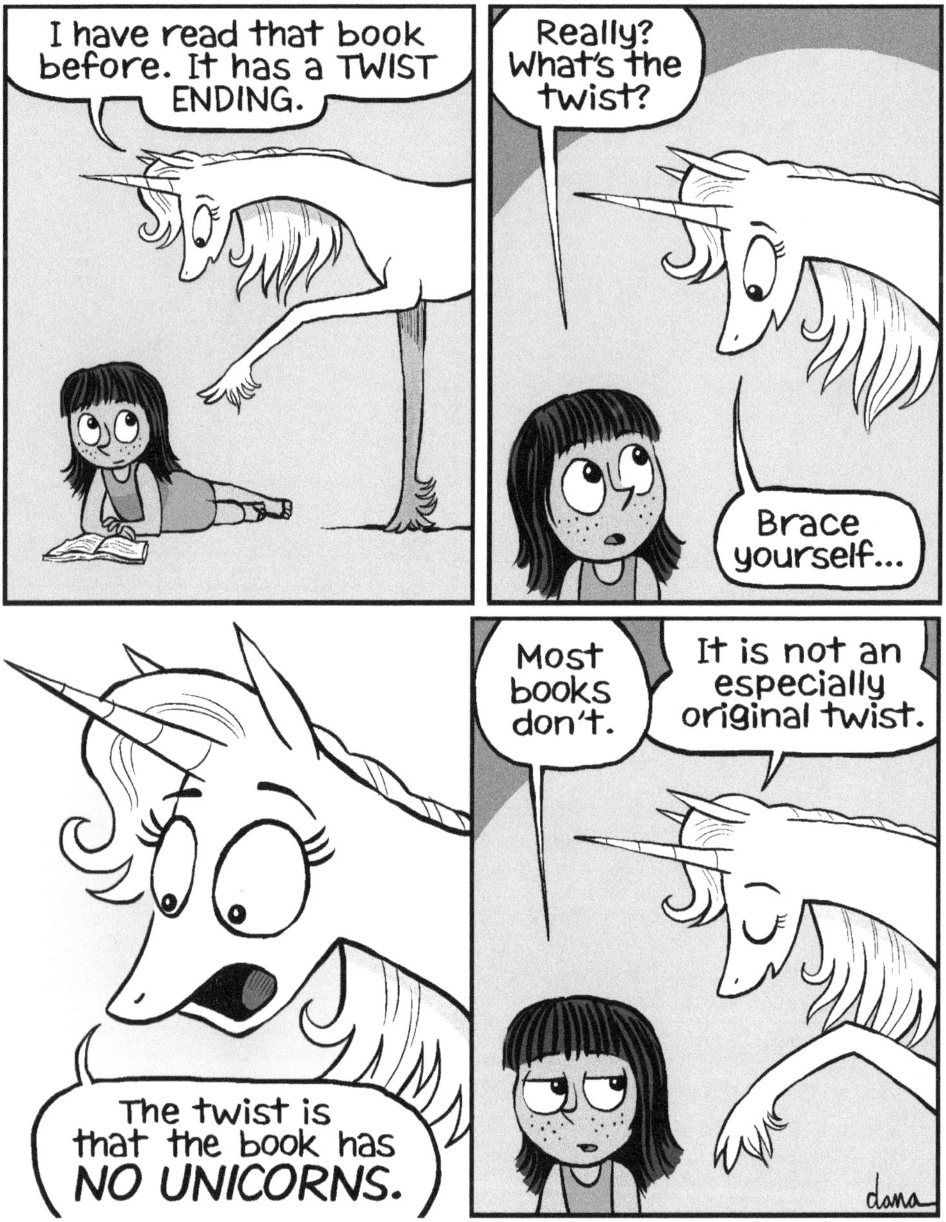
I have read that book before. It has a TWIST ENDING.
Really? What's the twist?
Brace yourself...
The twist is that the book has NO UNICORNS.
It is not an especially original twist.
Most books don't.
dana

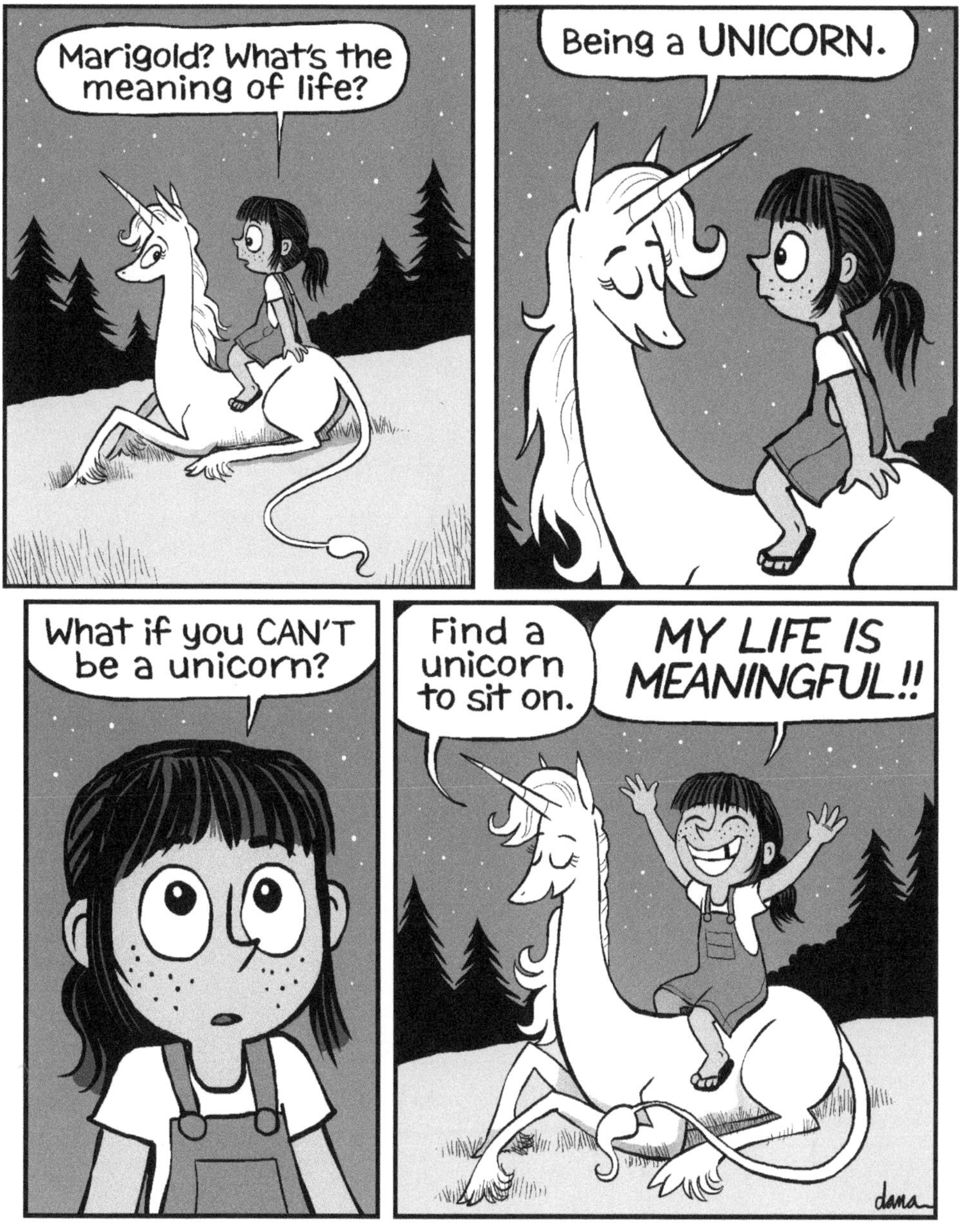
Marigold? What's the meaning of life?
Being a UNICORN.
What if you CAN'T be a unicorn?
Find a unicorn to sit on.
MY LIFE IS MEANINGFUL!!
dana

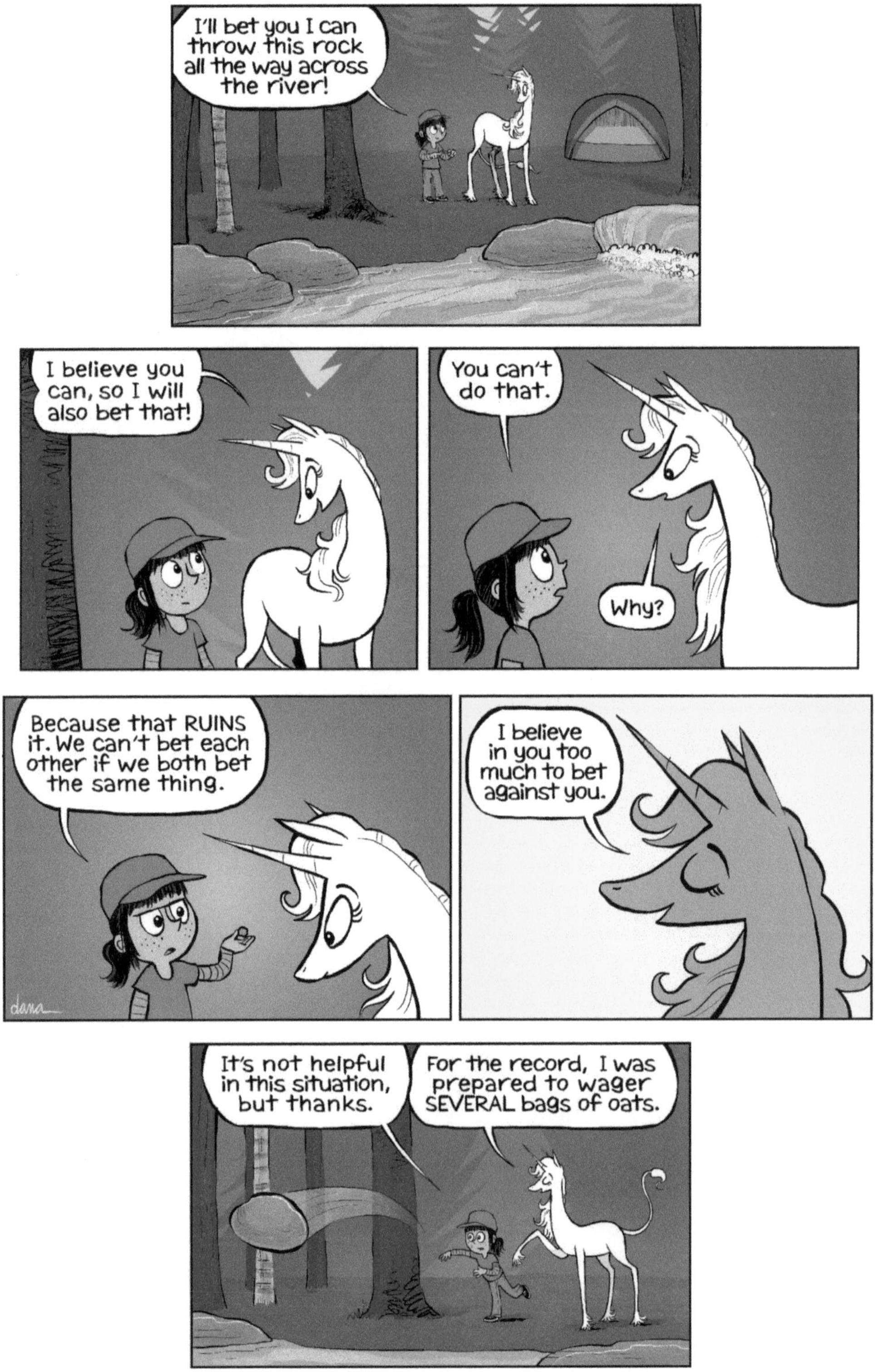
I'll bet you I can throw this rock all the way across the river!
I believe you can, so I will also bet that!
You can't do that.
Why?
Because that RUINS it. We can't bet each other if we both bet the same thing.
I believe in you too much to bet against you.
It's not helpful in this situation, but thanks.
For the record, I was prepared to wager SEVERAL bags of oats.
dana

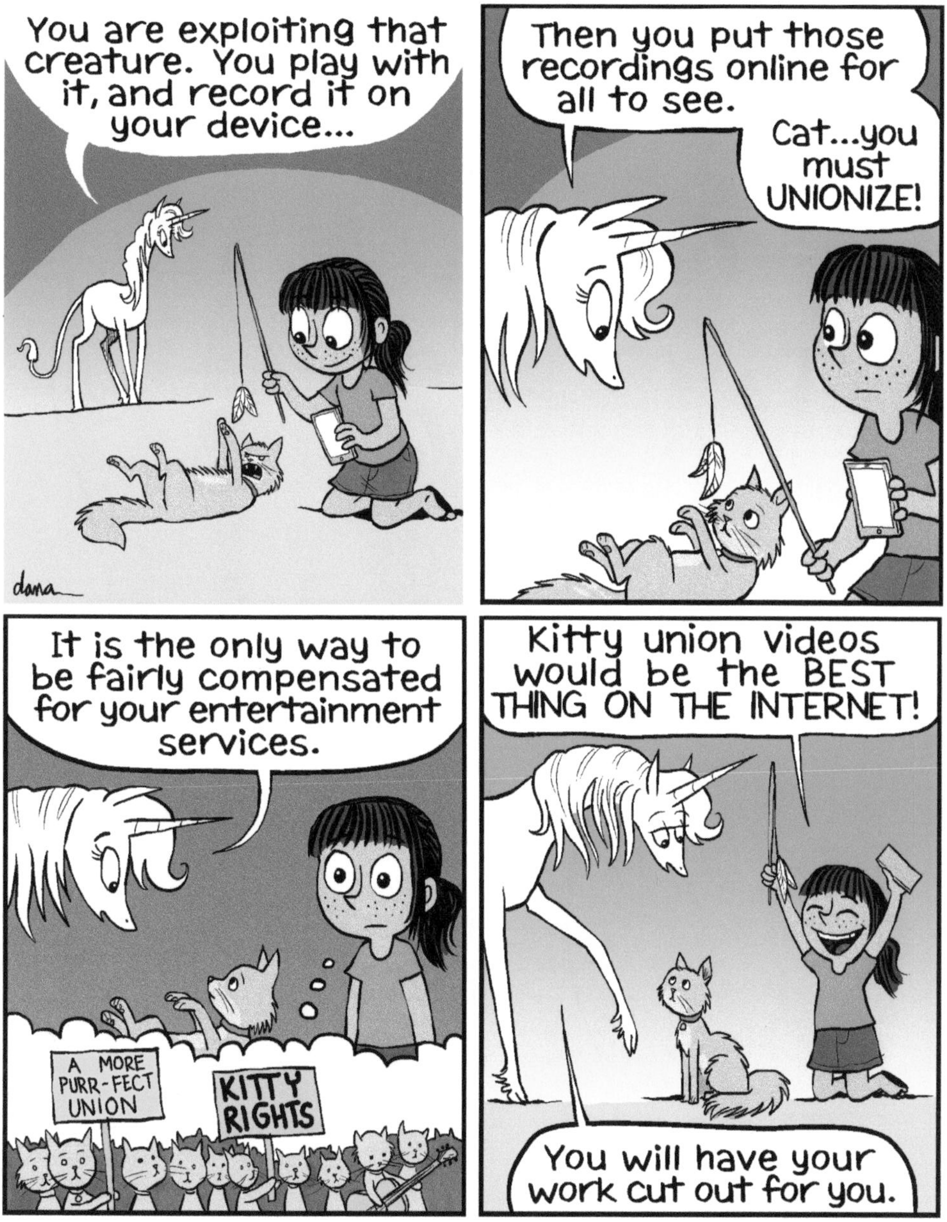
You are exploiting that creature. You play with it, and record it on your device...
dana
Then you put those recordings online for all to see.
Cat...you must UNIONIZE!
It is the only way to be fairly compensated for your entertainment services.
A MORE PURR-FECT UNION
KITTY RIGHTS
Kitty union videos would be the BEST THING ON THE INTERNET!
You will have your work cut out for you.

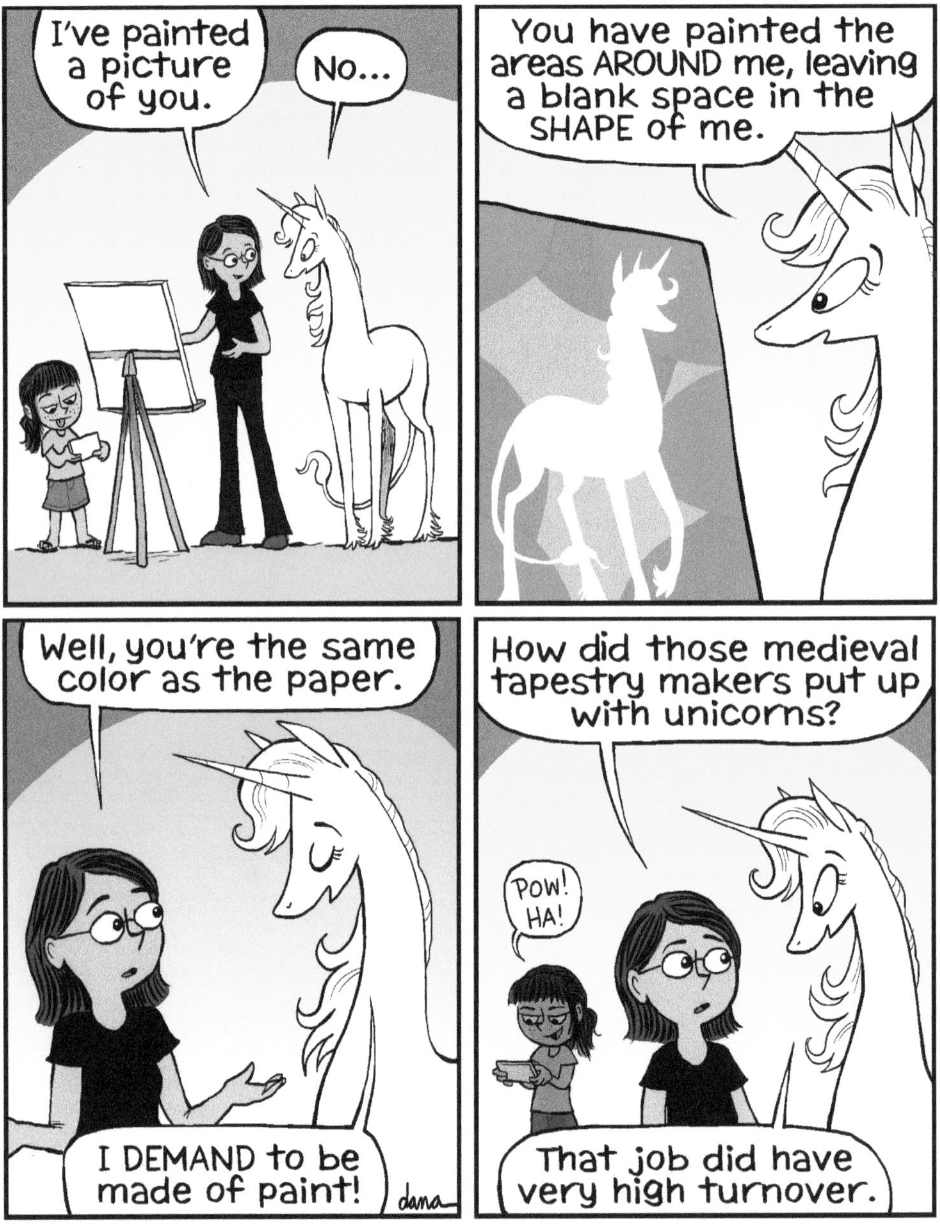
I've painted a picture of you.
No...
You have painted the areas AROUND me, leaving a blank space in the SHAPE of me.
Well, you're the same color as the paper.
I DEMAND to be made of paint!
dana
How did those medieval tapestry makers put up with unicorns?
POW! HA!
That job did have very high turnover.

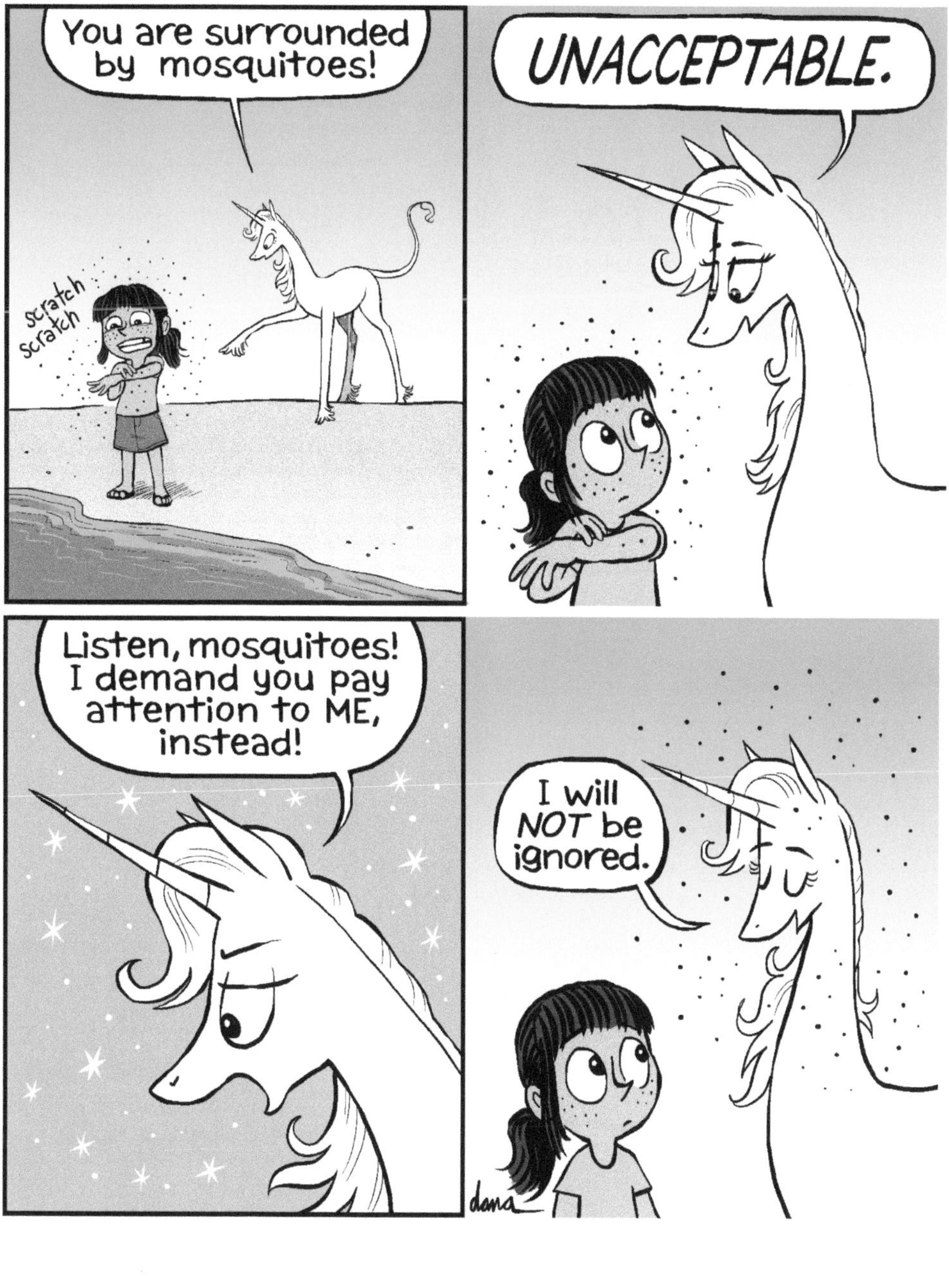
You are surrounded by mosquitoes!
scratch scratch
UNACCEPTABLE.
Listen, mosquitoes! I demand you pay attention to ME, instead!
I will NOT be ignored.
dana

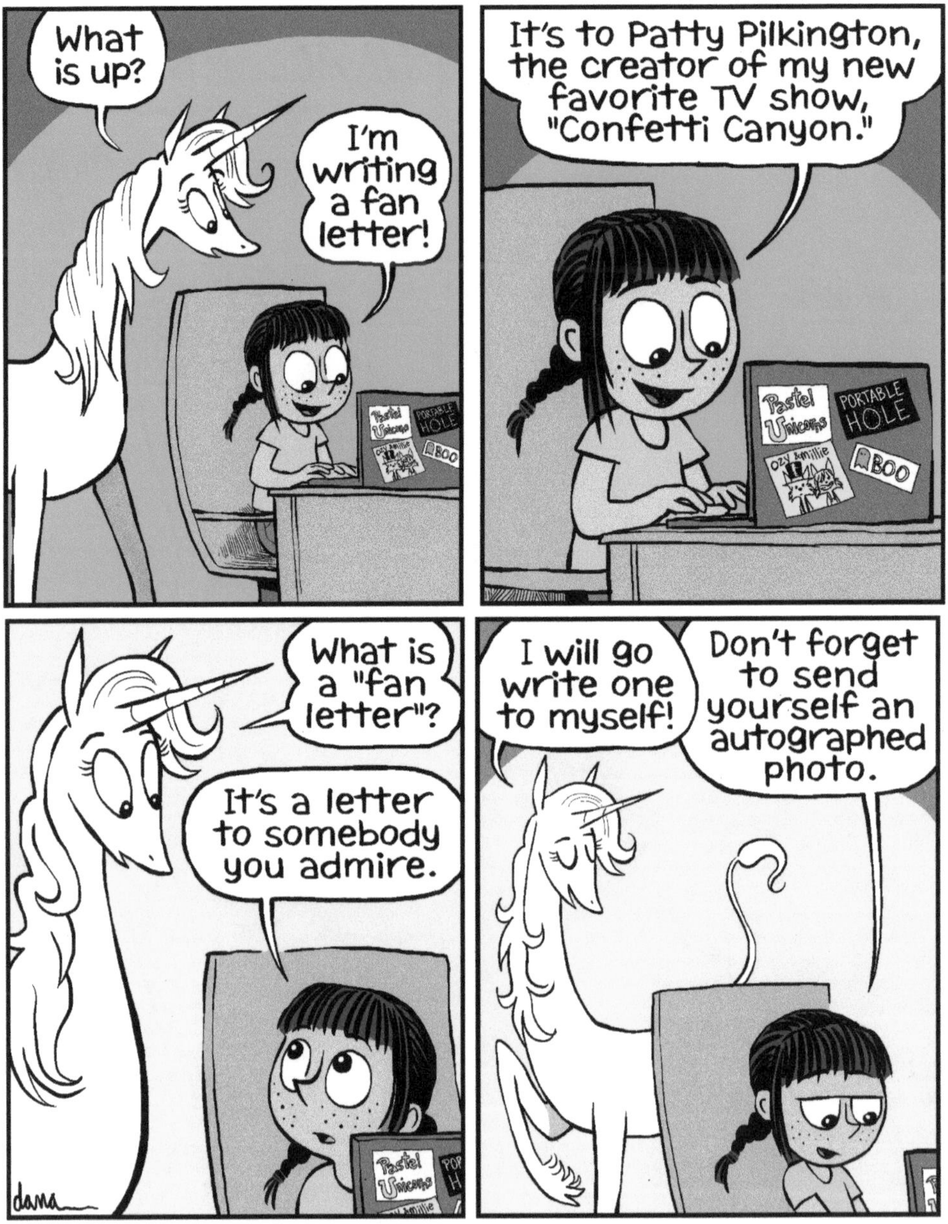

What is up?
I'm writing a fan letter!
It's to Patty Pilkington, the creator of my new favorite TV show, "Confetti Canyon."
Pastel Unicorns
PORTABLE HOLE
BOO
What is a "fan letter"?
It's a letter to somebody you admire.
I will go write one to myself!
Don't forget to send yourself an autographed photo.
dana

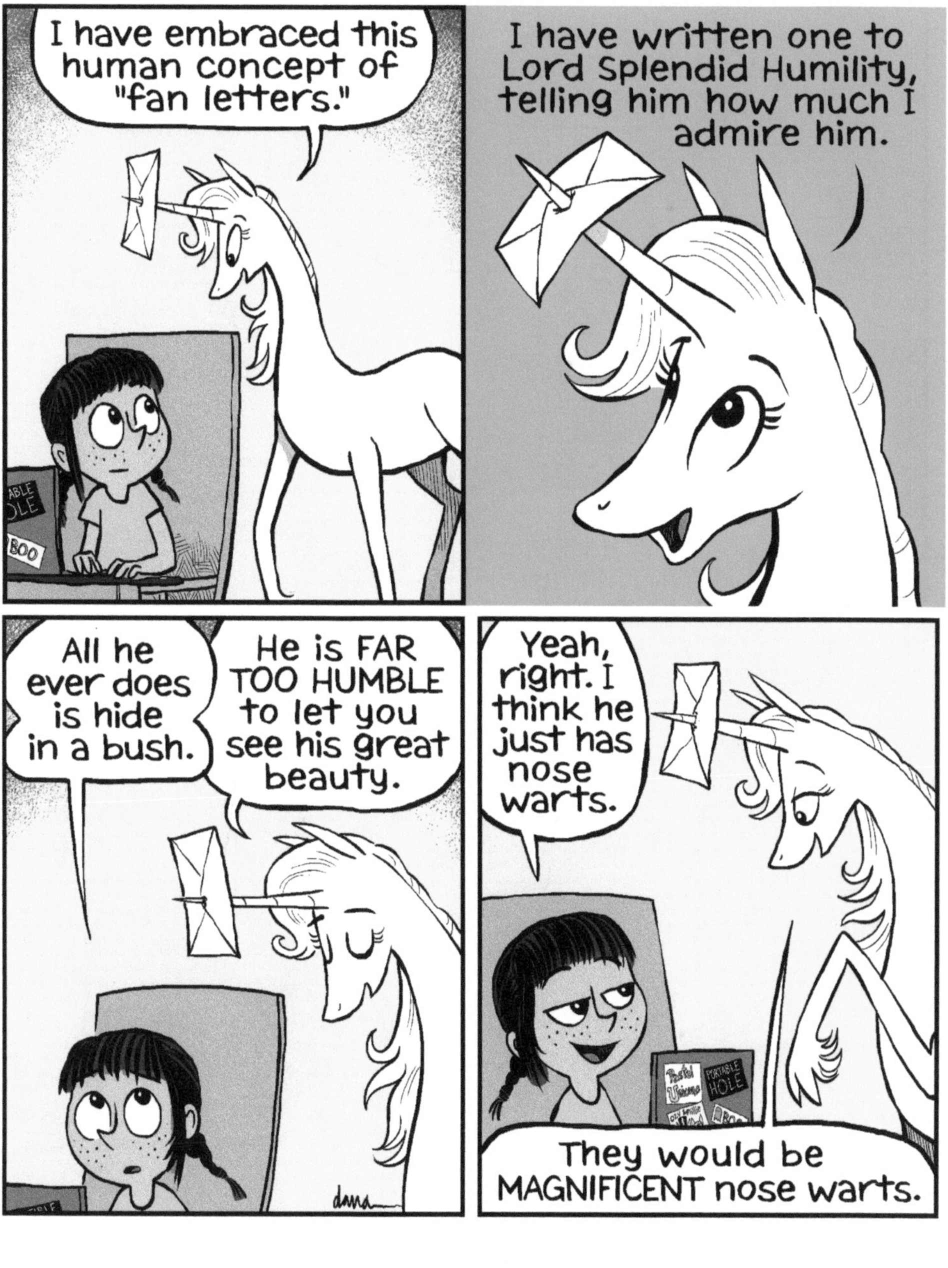
I have embraced this human concept of "fan letters."
I have written one to Lord Splendid Humility, telling him how much I admire him.
All he ever does is hide in a bush.
He is FAR TOO HUMBLE to let you see his great beauty.
Yeah, right. I think he just has nose warts.
They would be MAGNIFICENT nose warts.

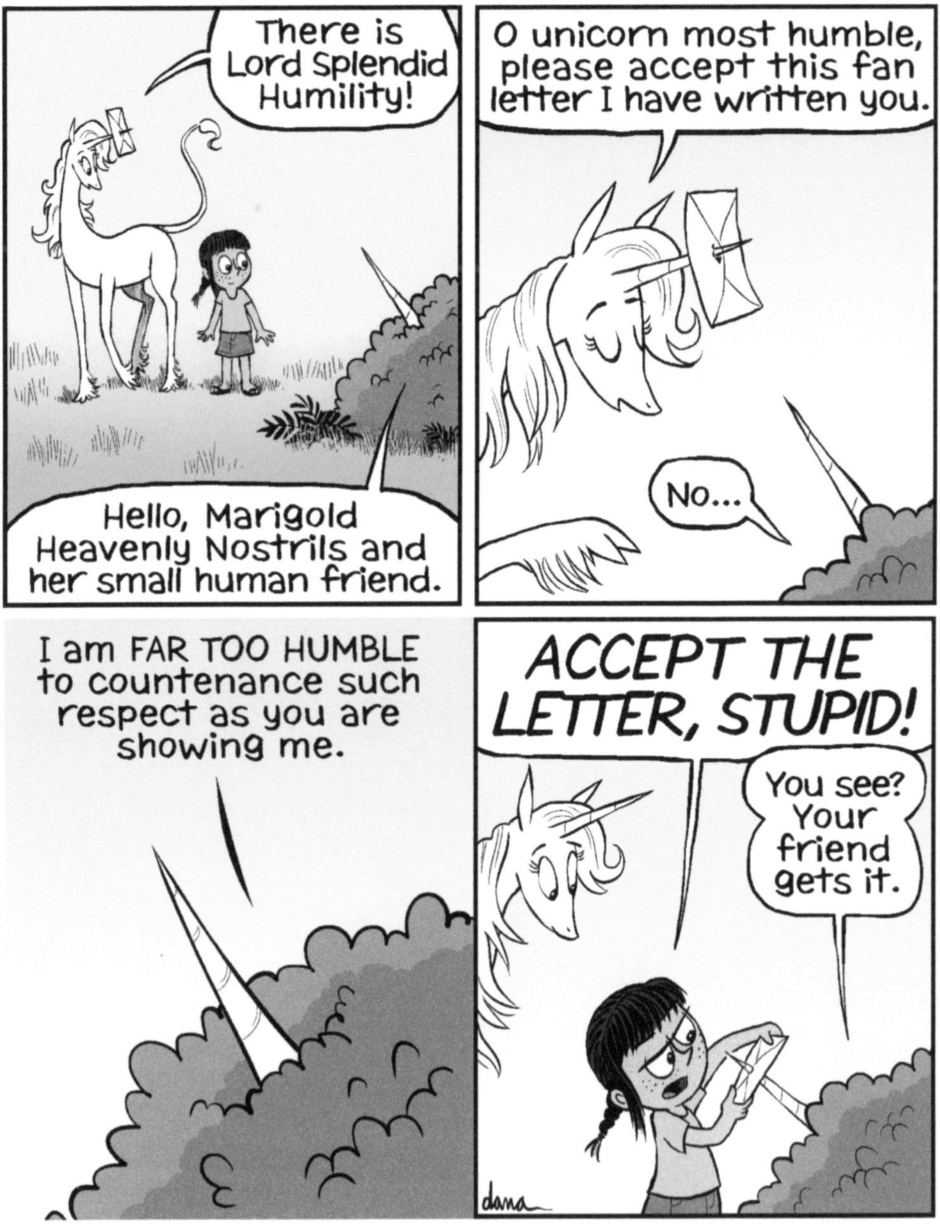
There is Lord Splendid Humility!
Hello, Marigold Heavenly Nostrils and her small human friend.
O unicorn most humble, please accept this fan letter I have written you.
No...
I am FAR TOO HUMBLE to countenance such respect as you are showing me.
ACCEPT THE LETTER, STUPID!
You see? Your friend gets it.
dana

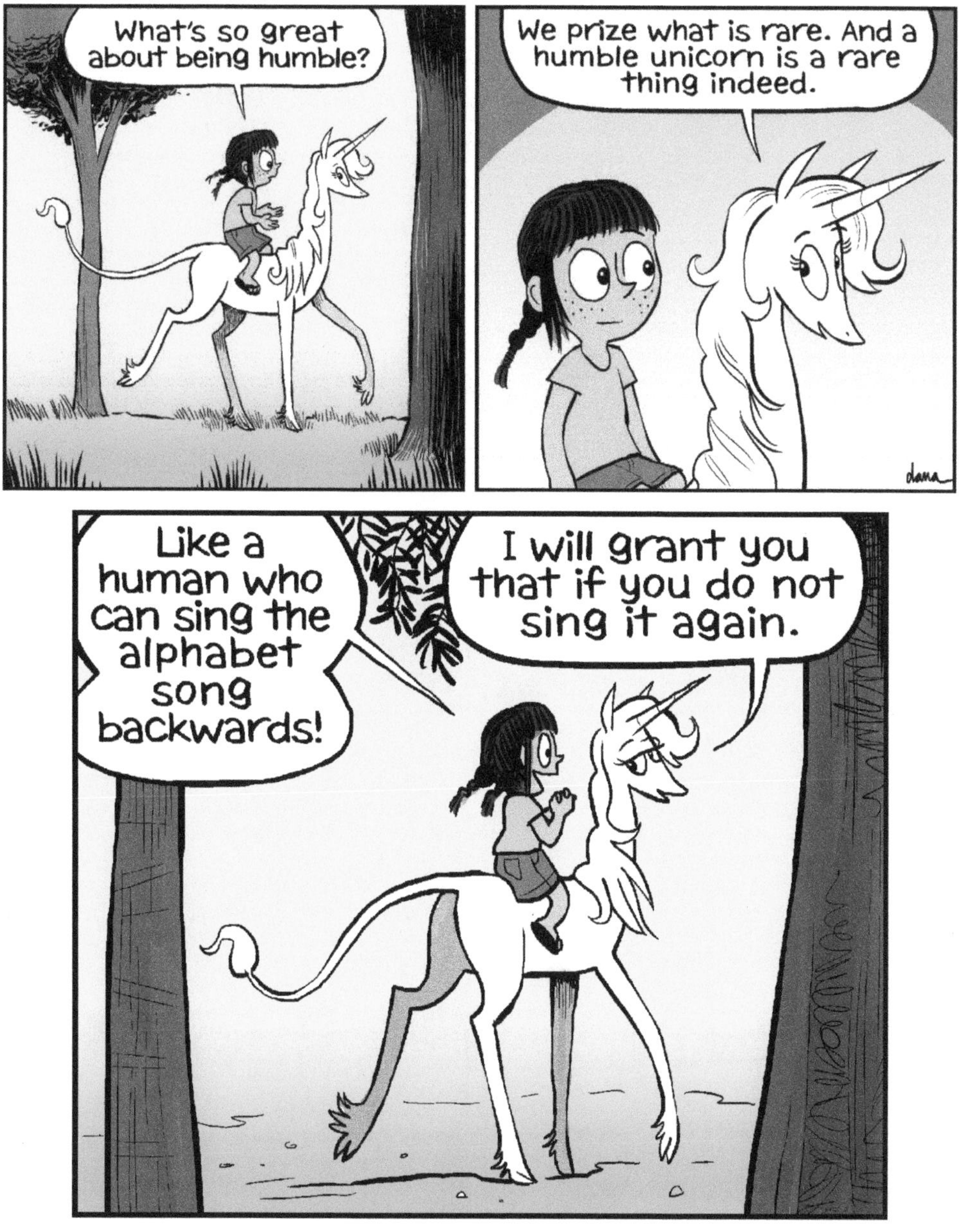
What's so great about being humble?
We prize what is rare. And a humble unicorn is a rare thing indeed.
dana
Like a human who can sing the alphabet song backwards!
I will grant you that if you do not sing it again.

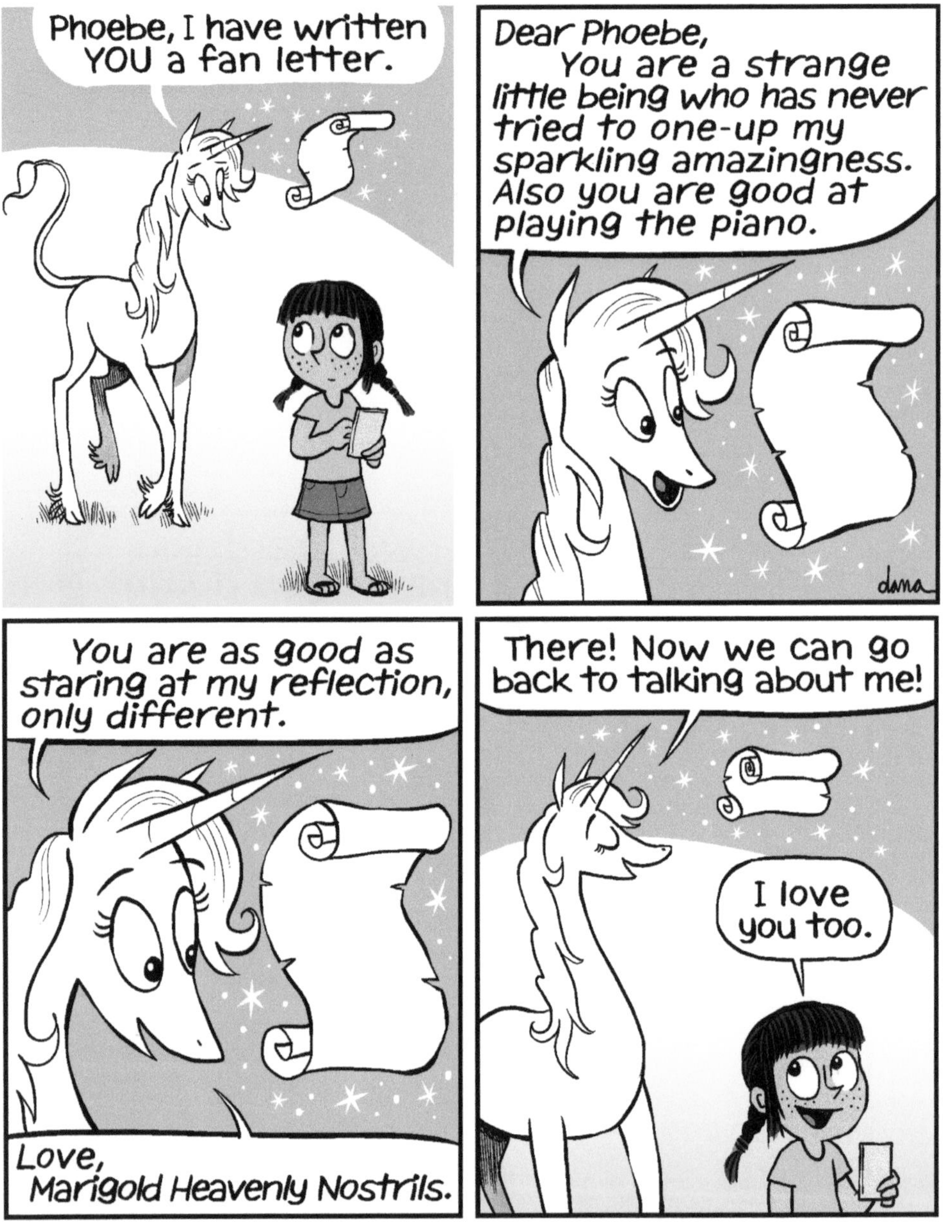
Phoebe, I have written YOU a fan letter.
Dear Phoebe,
You are a strange little being who has never tried to one-up my sparkling amazingness. Also you are good at playing the piano.
dana
You are as good as staring at my reflection, only different.
Love,
Marigold Heavenly Nostrils.
There! Now we can go back to talking about me!
I love you too.

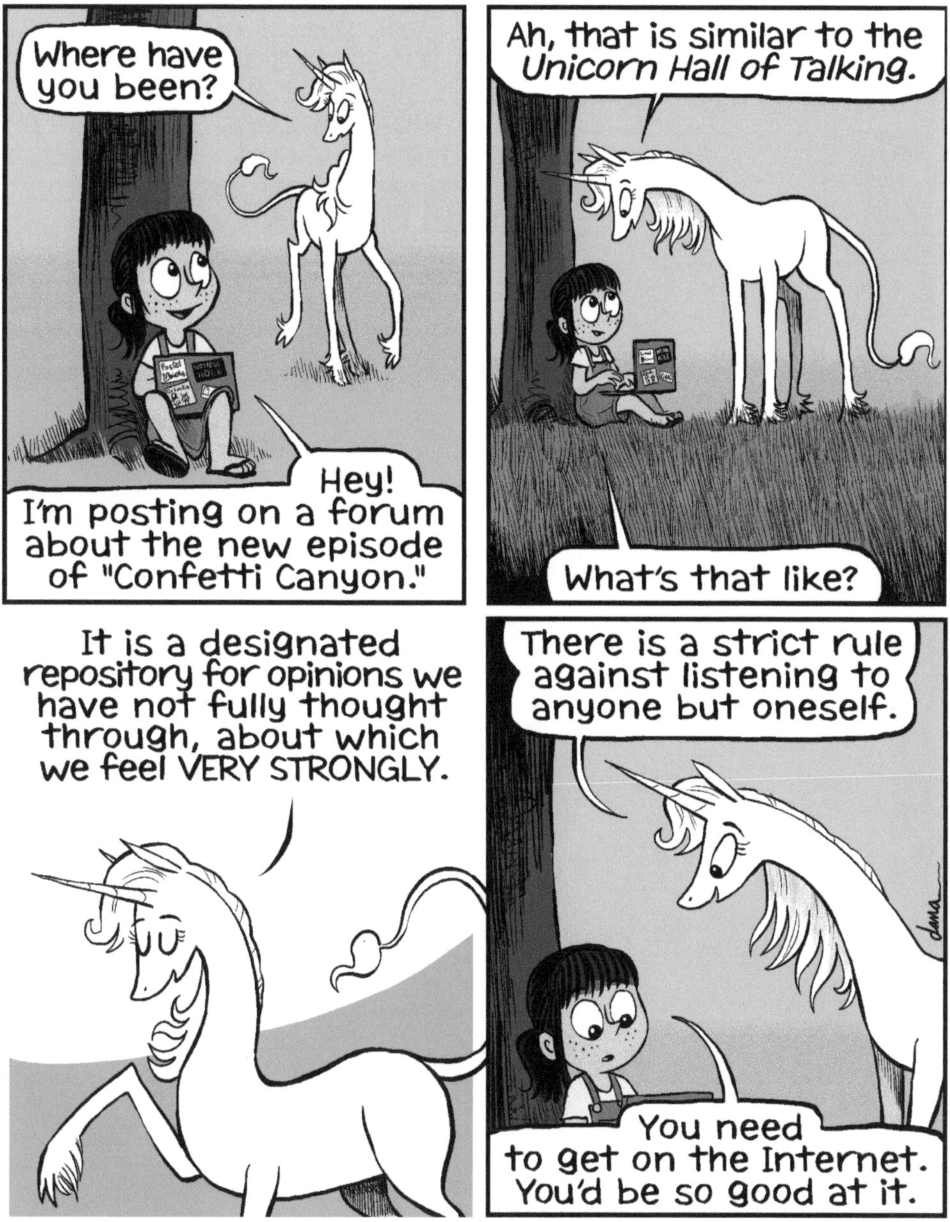

Where have you been?
Hey! I'm posting on a forum about the new episode of "Confetti Canyon."
Ah, that is similar to the *Unicorn Hall of Talking.*
What's that like?
It is a designated repository for opinions we have not fully thought through, about which we feel VERY STRONGLY.
There is a strict rule against listening to anyone but oneself.
You need to get on the Internet. You'd be so good at it.

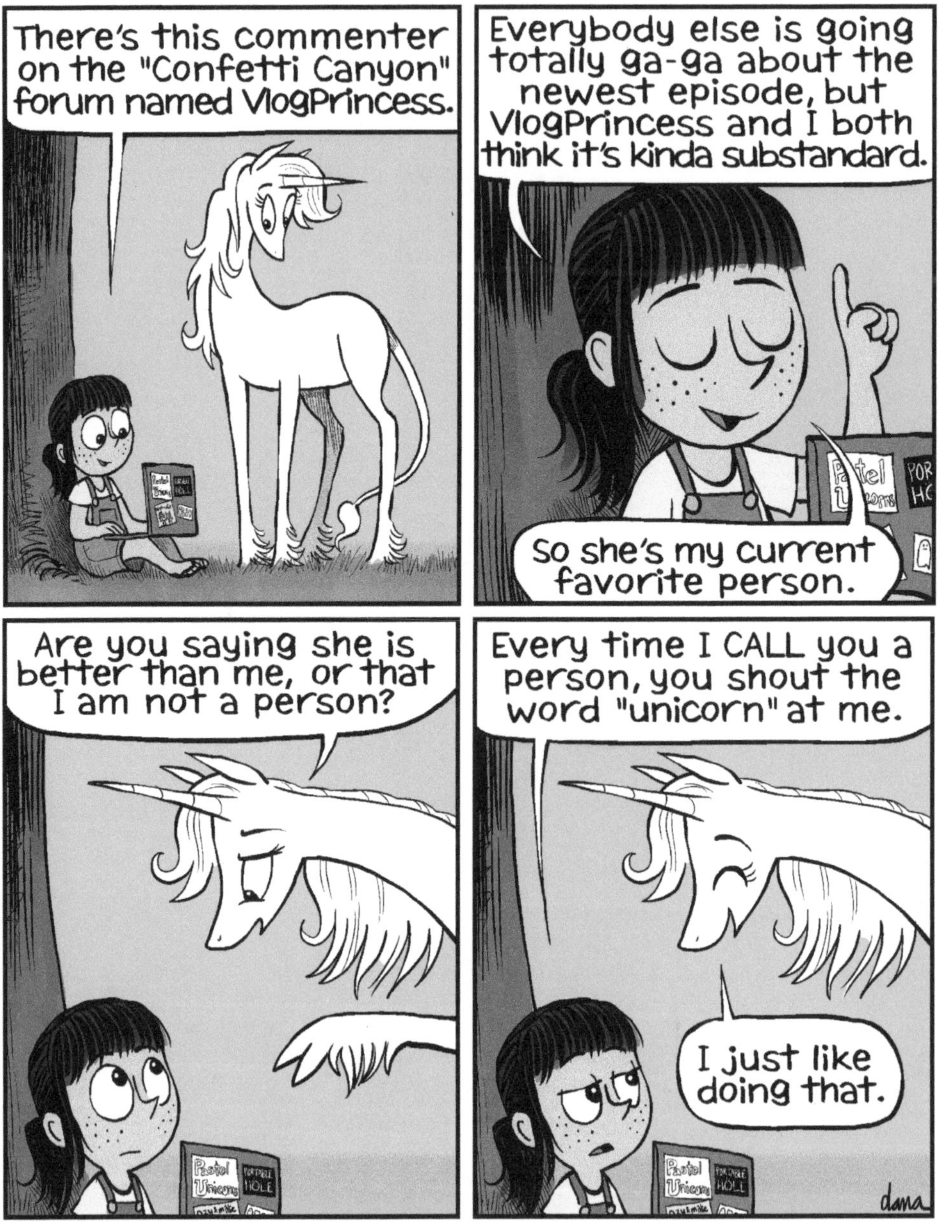
There's this commenter on the "Confetti Canyon" forum named VlogPrincess.
Everybody else is going totally ga-ga about the newest episode, but VlogPrincess and I both think it's kinda substandard.
So she's my current favorite person.
Are you saying she is better than me, or that I am not a person?
Every time I CALL you a person, you shout the word "unicorn" at me.
I just like doing that.
dana

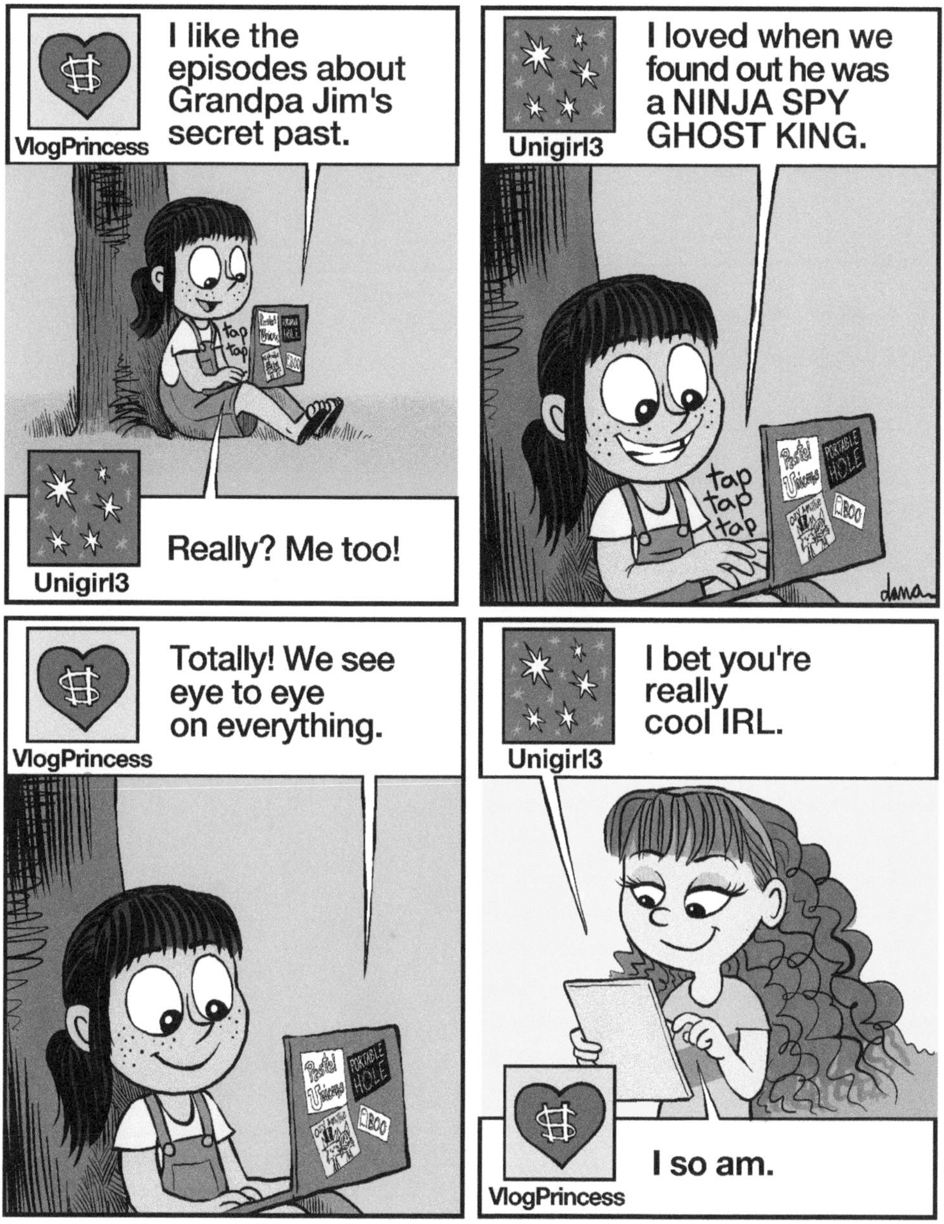
VlogPrincess
I like the episodes about Grandpa Jim's secret past.
tap tap
Unigirl3
Really? Me too!
Unigirl3
I loved when we found out he was a NINJA SPY GHOST KING.
tap tap tap
VlogPrincess
Totally! We see eye to eye on everything.
Unigirl3
I bet you're really cool IRL.
VlogPrincess
I so am.

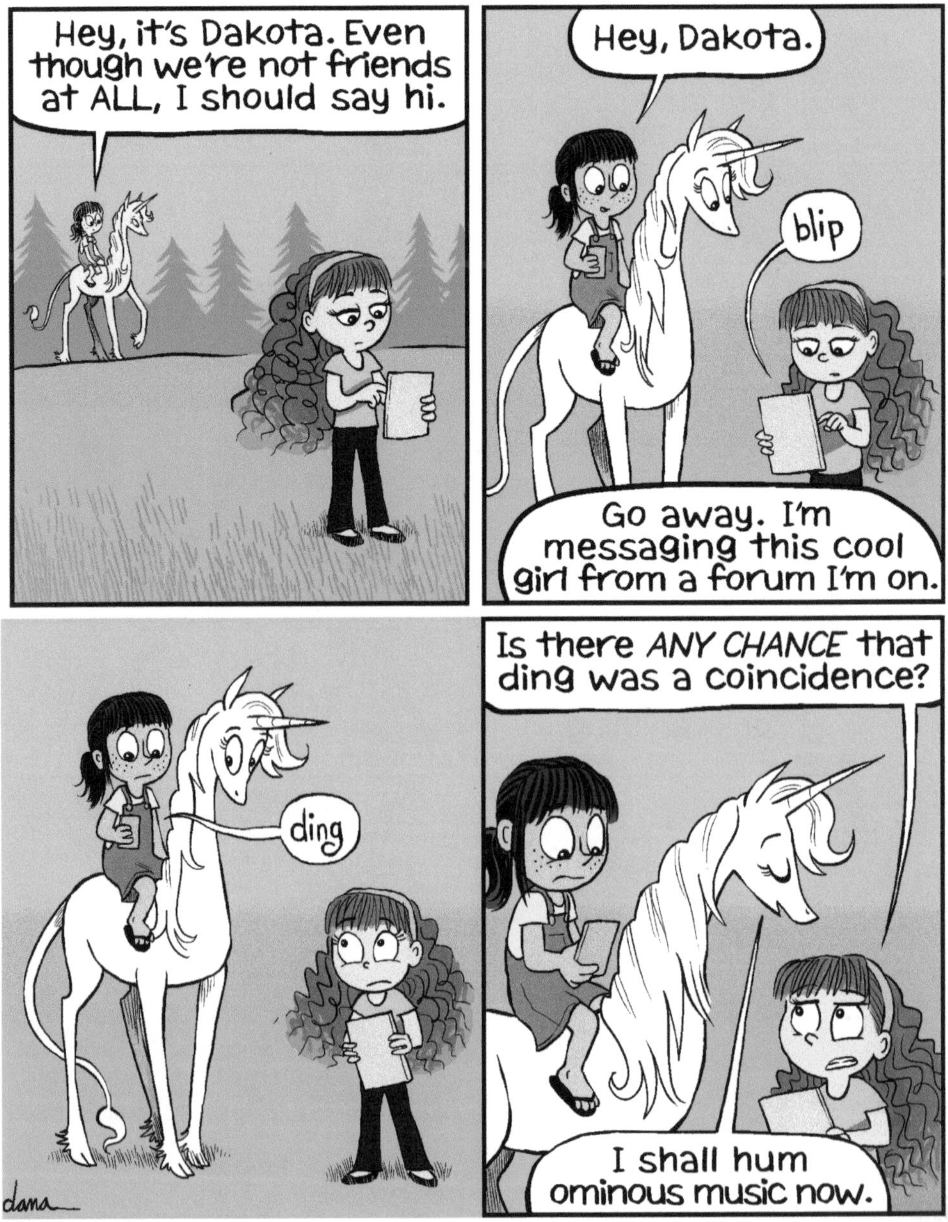
Hey, it's Dakota. Even though we're not friends at ALL, I should say hi.
Hey, Dakota.
blip
Go away. I'm messaging this cool girl from a forum I'm on.
ding
Is there ANY CHANCE that ding was a coincidence?
I shall hum ominous music now.
dana

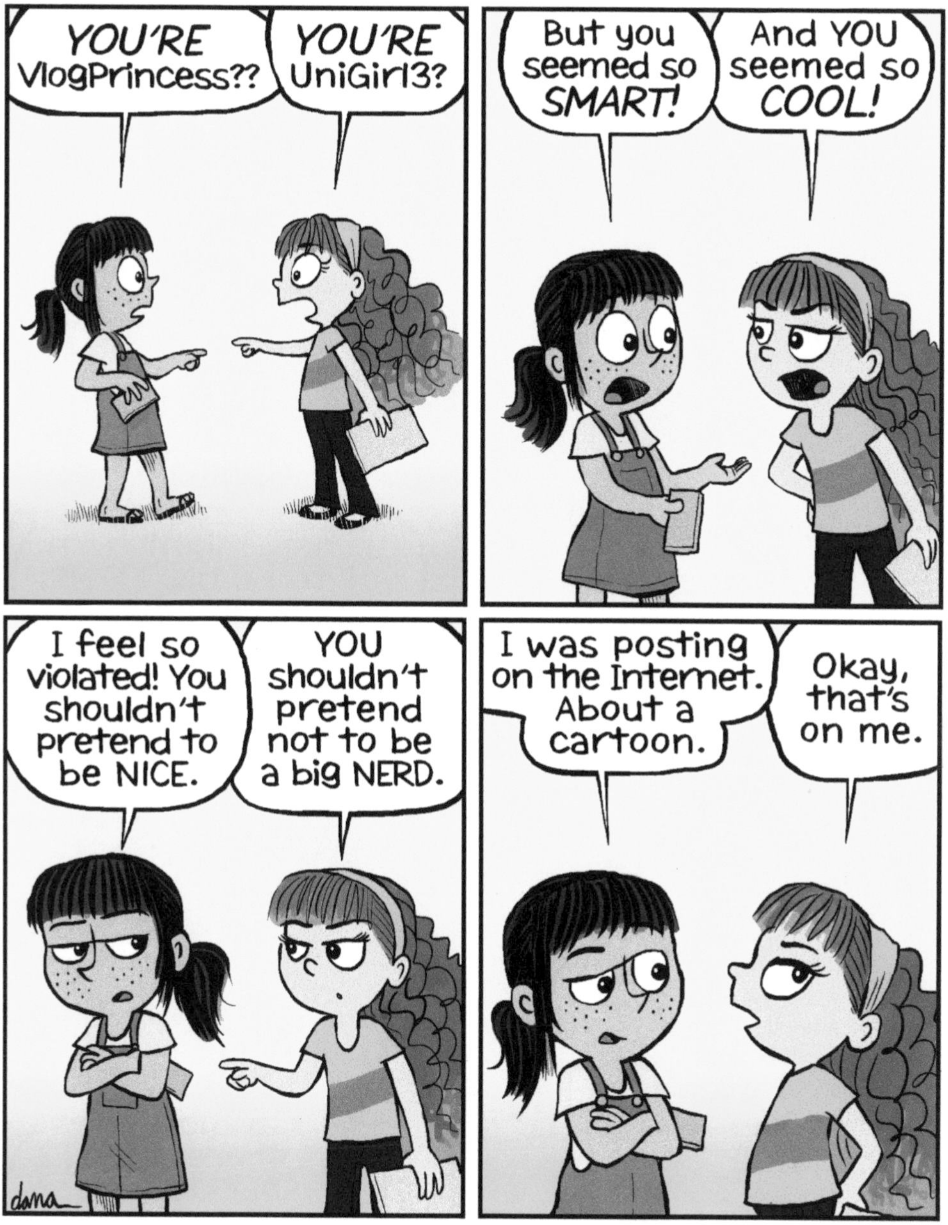
YOU'RE VlogPrincess??
YOU'RE UniGirl3?
But you seemed so SMART!
And YOU seemed so COOL!
I feel so violated! You shouldn't pretend to be NICE.
YOU shouldn't pretend not to be a big NERD.
I was posting on the Internet. About a cartoon.
Okay, that's on me.
dana

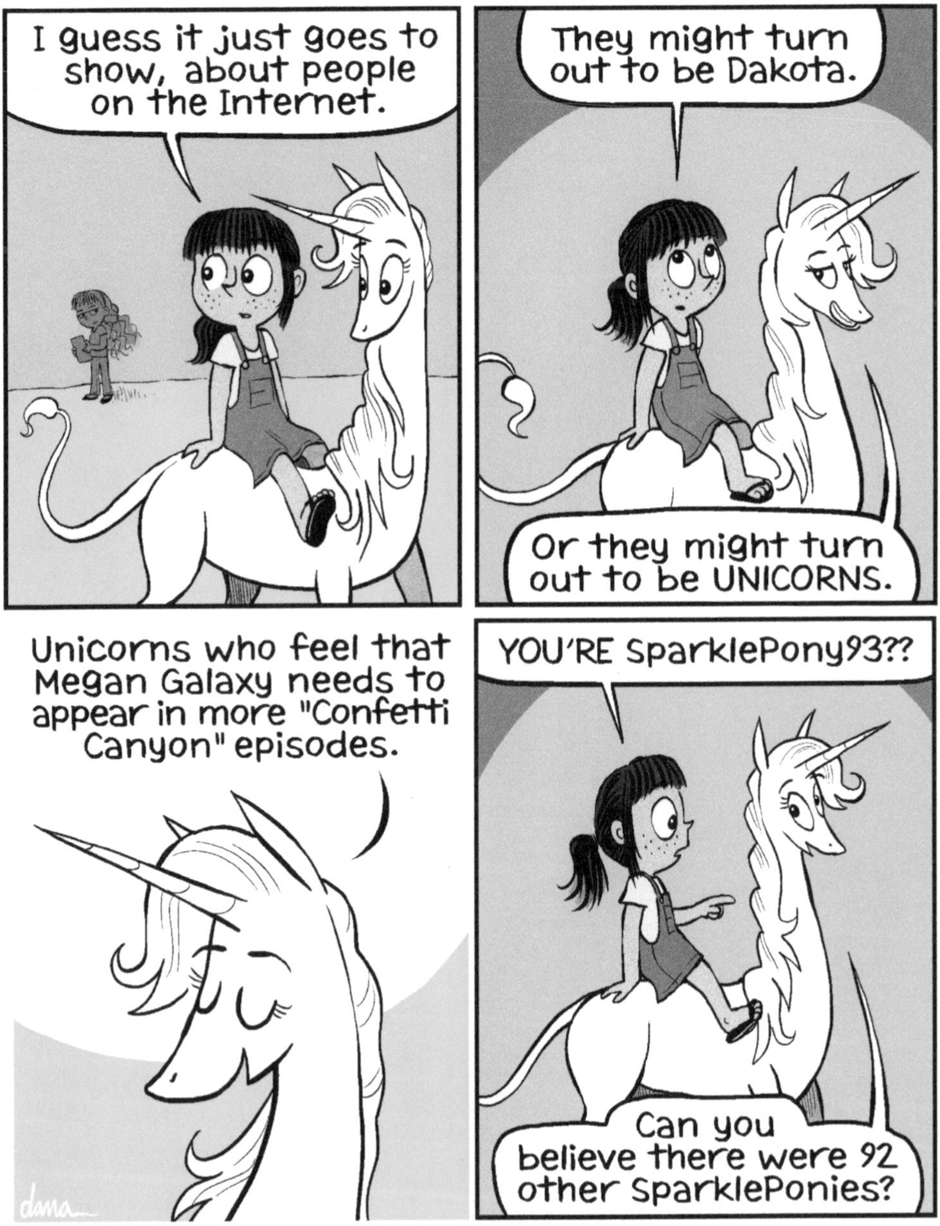
I guess it just goes to show, about people on the Internet.
They might turn out to be Dakota.
Or they might turn out to be UNICORNS.
Unicorns who feel that Megan Galaxy needs to appear in more "Confetti Canyon" episodes.
YOU'RE SparklePony93??
Can you believe there were 92 other SparklePonies?
dana

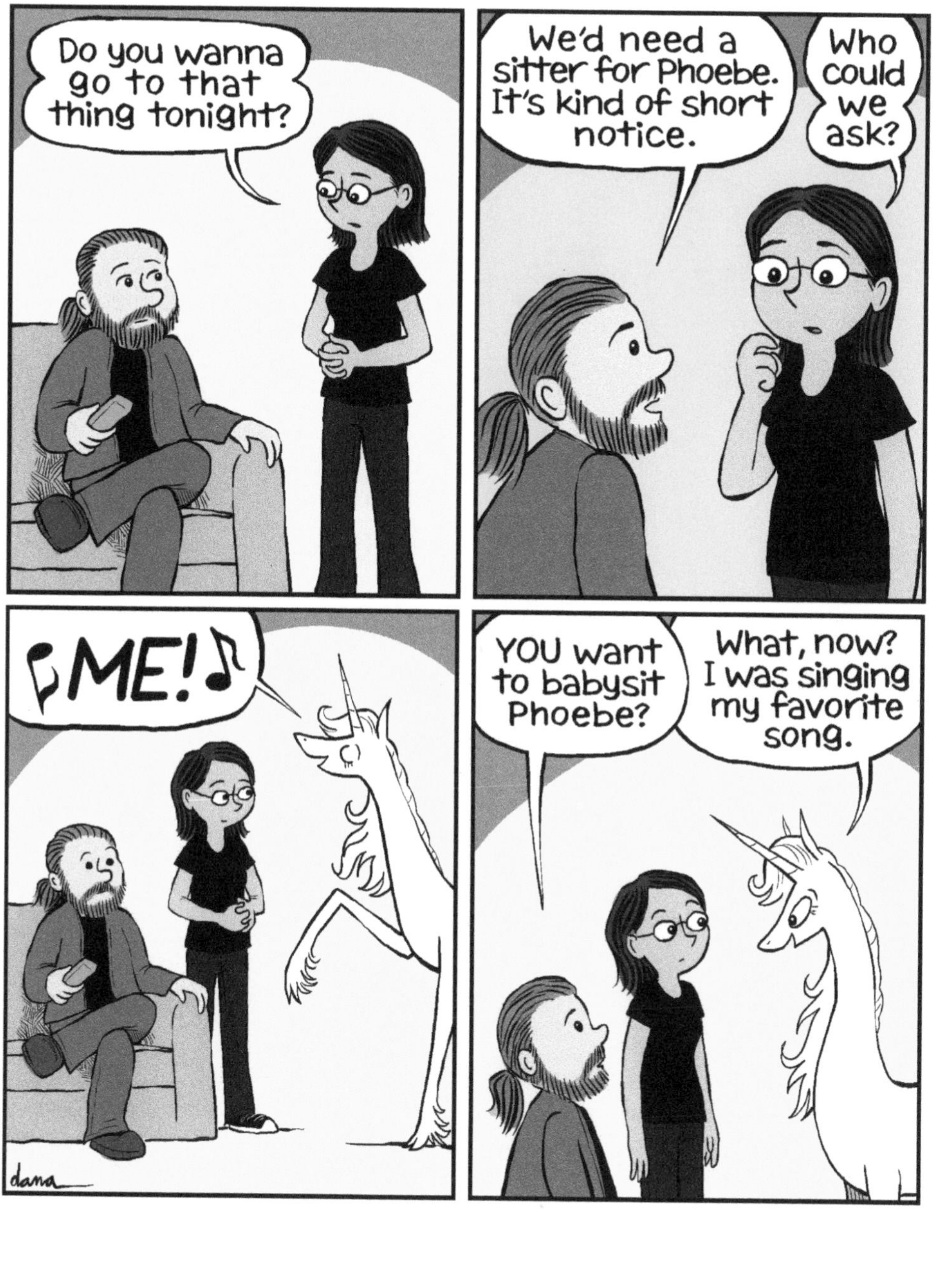
Do you wanna go to that thing tonight?
We'd need a sitter for Phoebe. It's kind of short notice.
Who could we ask?
ME!
YOU want to babysit Phoebe?
What, now? I was singing my favorite song.
dana

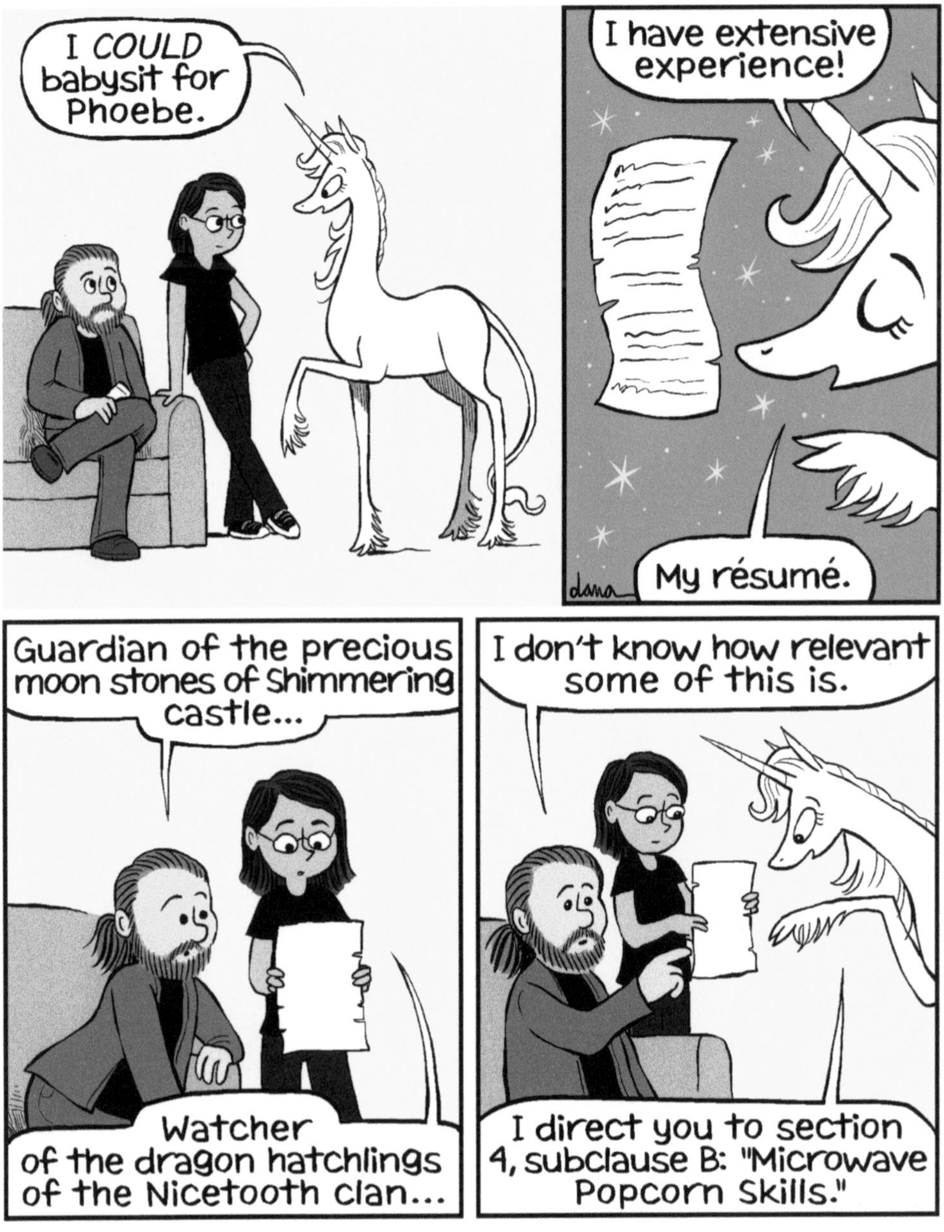
I *COULD* babysit for Phoebe.
I have extensive experience!
My résumé.
dana
Guardian of the precious moon stones of Shimmering castle...
Watcher of the dragon hatchlings of the Nicetooth clan...
I don't know how relevant some of this is.
I direct you to section 4, subclause B: "Microwave Popcorn Skills."

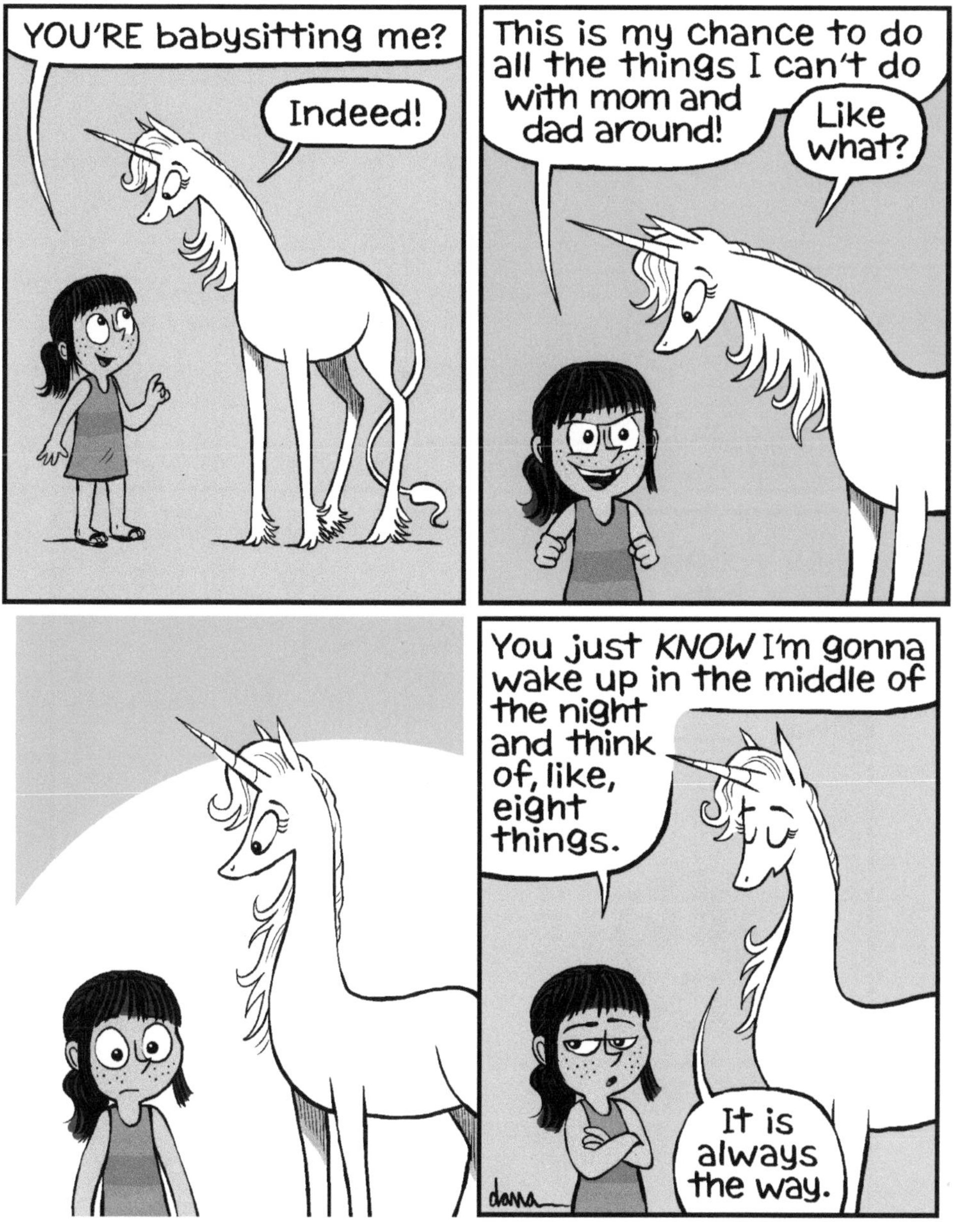
YOU'RE babysitting me?
Indeed!
This is my chance to do all the things I can't do with mom and dad around!
Like what?
You just *KNOW* I'm gonna wake up in the middle of the night and think of, like, eight things.
It is always the way.
dana

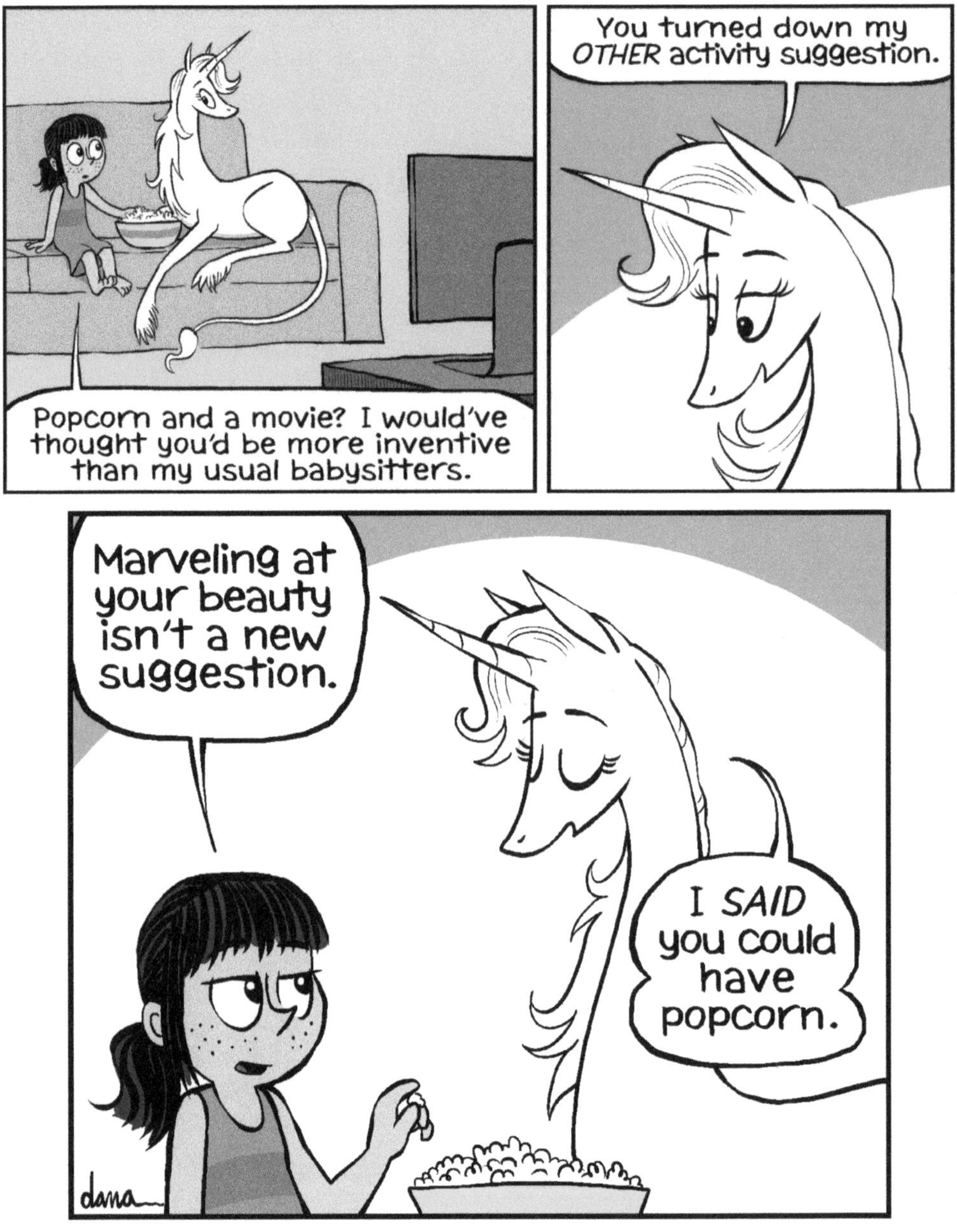
Popcorn and a movie? I would've thought you'd be more inventive than my usual babysitters.
You turned down my OTHER activity suggestion.
Marveling at your beauty isn't a new suggestion.
I SAID you could have popcorn.
dana

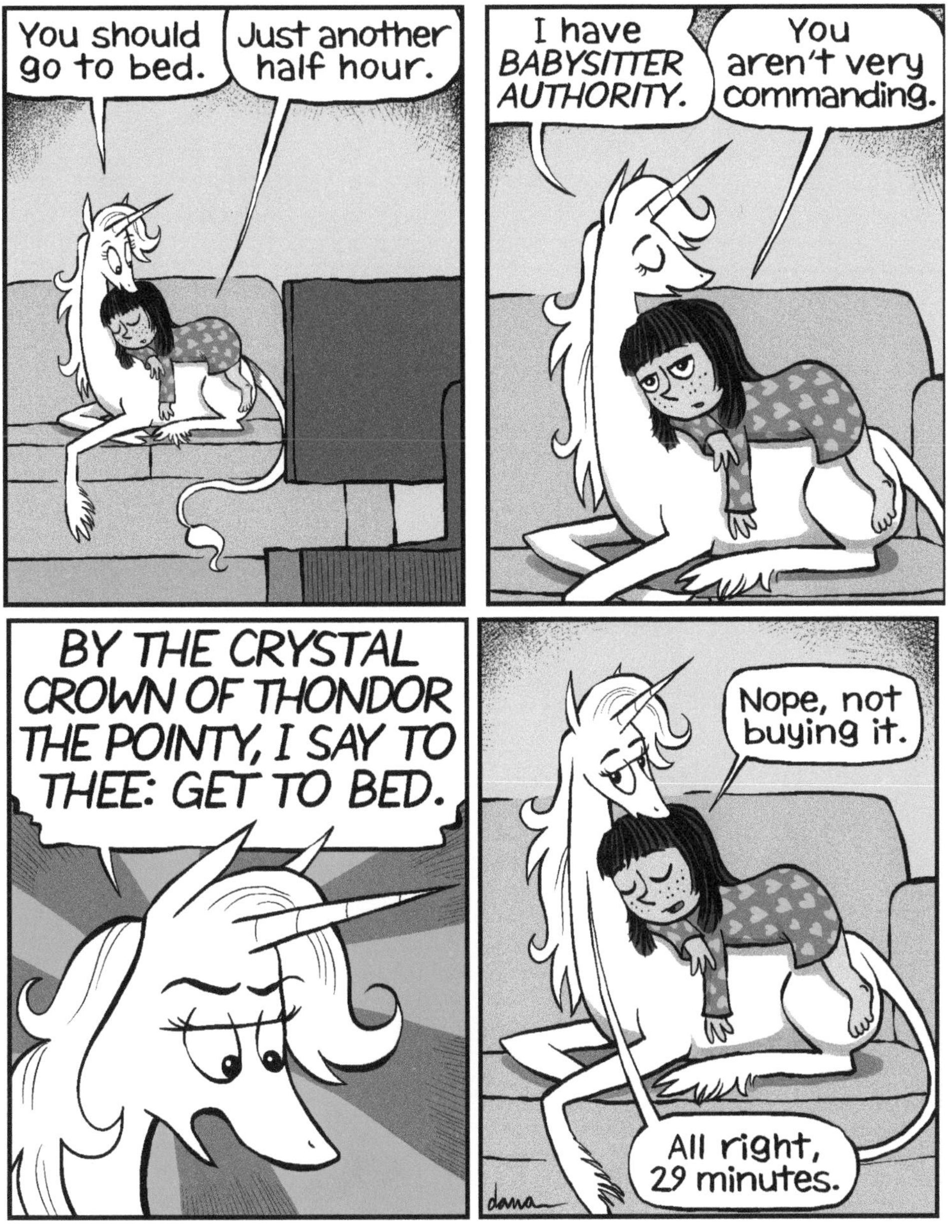
You should go to bed.
Just another half hour.
I have *BABYSITTER AUTHORITY*.
You aren't very commanding.
BY THE CRYSTAL CROWN OF THONDOR THE POINTY, I SAY TO THEE: GET TO BED.
Nope, not buying it.
All right, 29 minutes.
dana

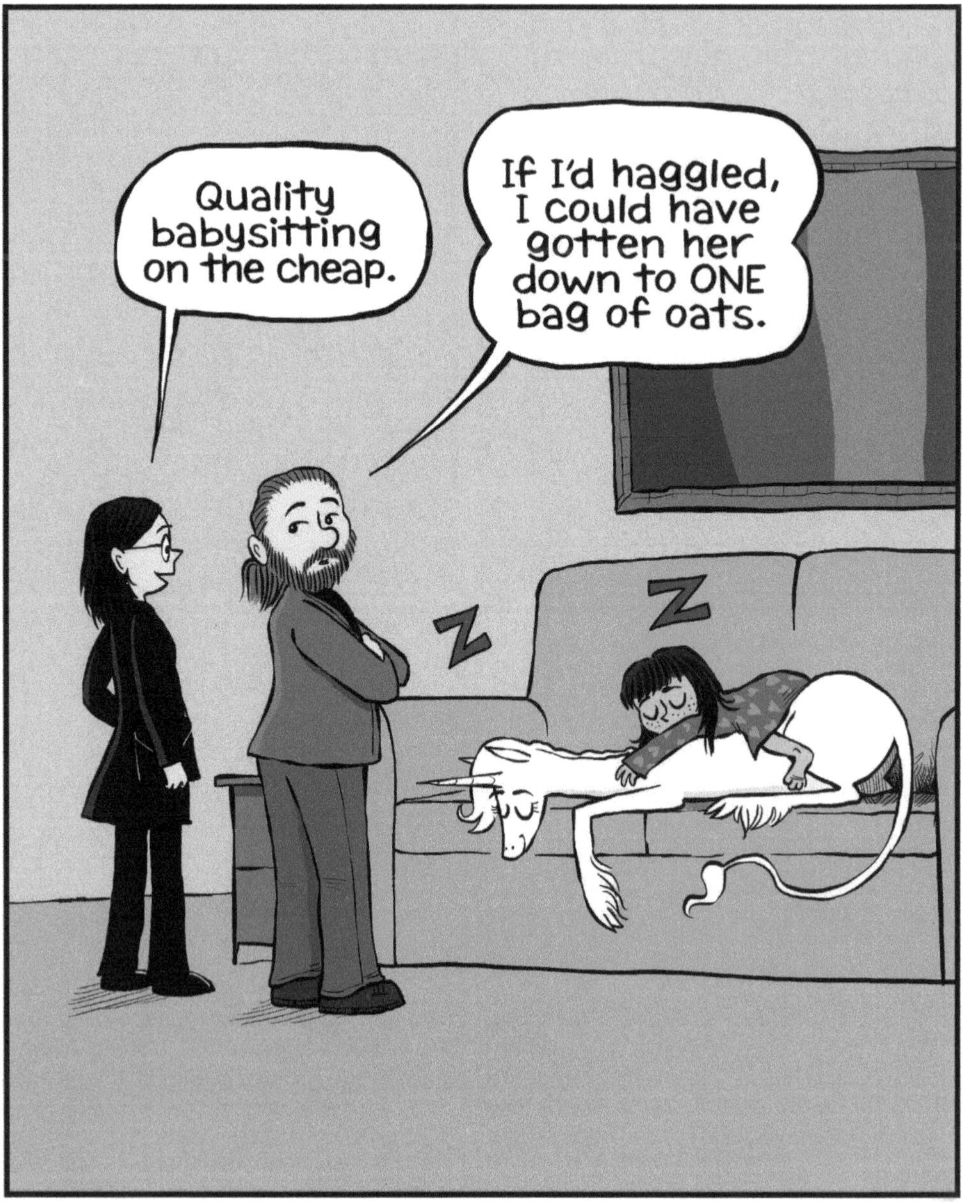
Quality babysitting on the cheap.
If I'd haggled, I could have gotten her down to ONE bag of oats.
Z
Z

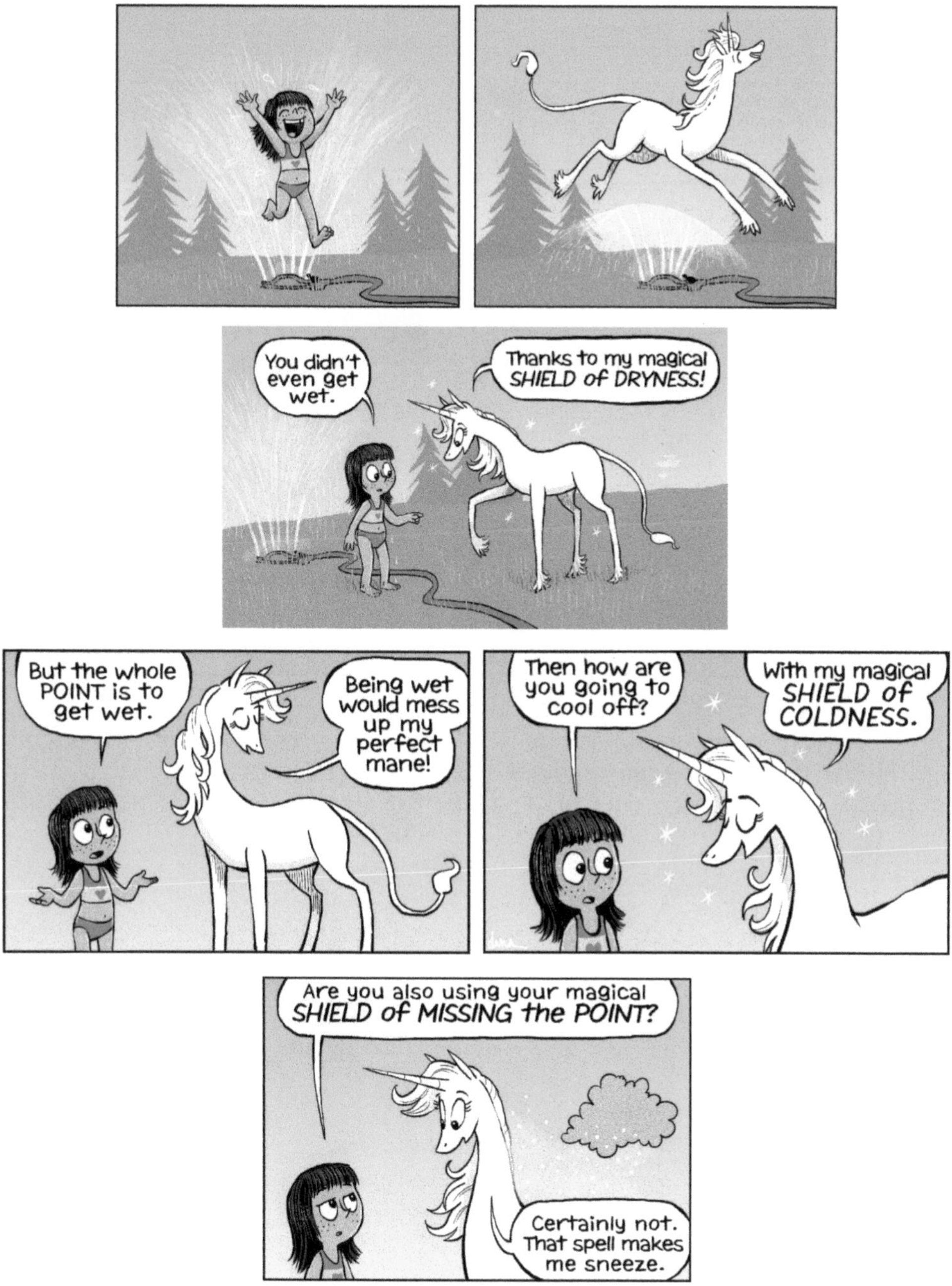
You didn't even get wet.
Thanks to my magical SHIELD of DRYNESS!
But the whole POINT is to get wet.
Being wet would mess up my perfect mane!
Then how are you going to cool off?
With my magical SHIELD of COLDNESS.
Are you also using your magical SHIELD of MISSING the POINT?
Certainly not. That spell makes me sneeze.

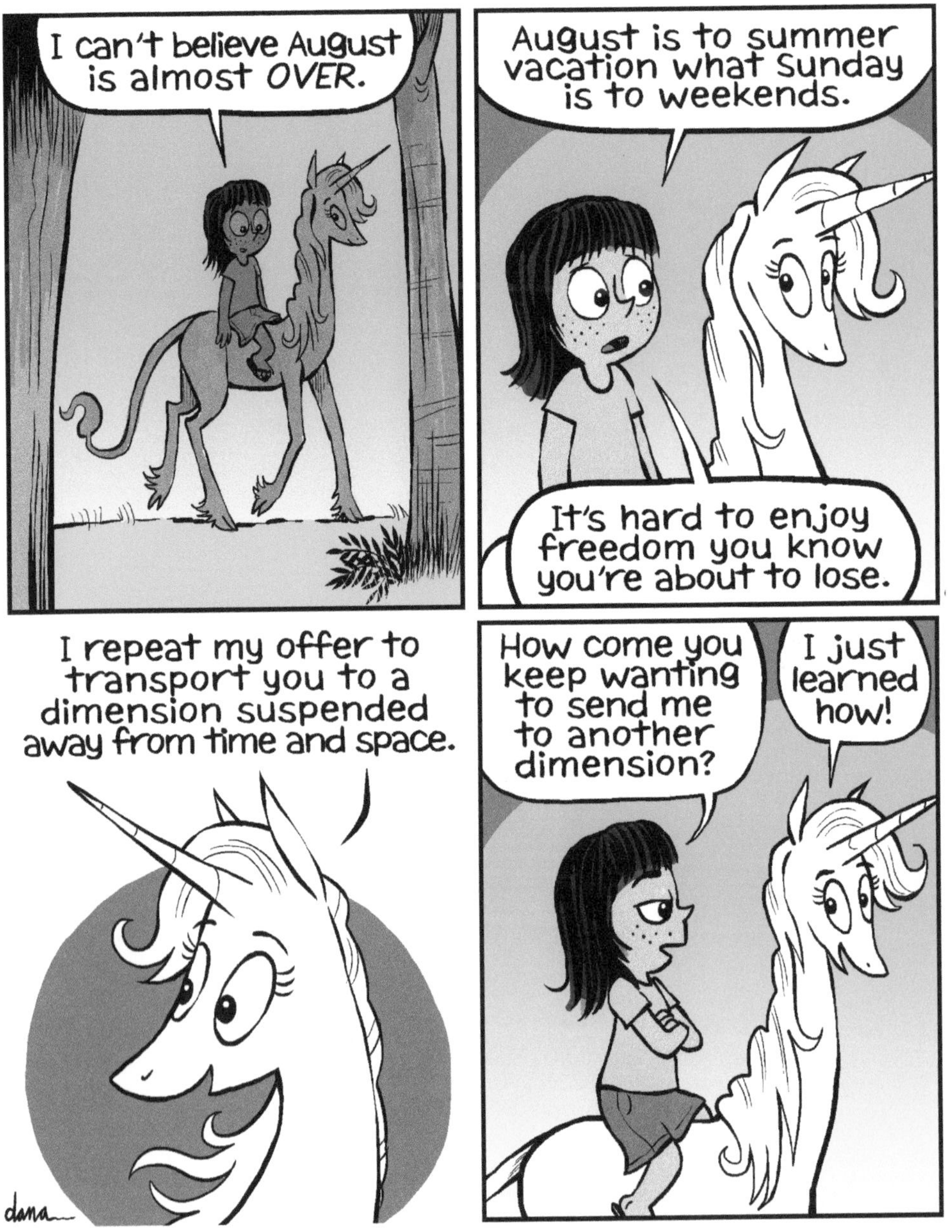

I can't believe August is almost OVER.
August is to summer vacation what Sunday is to weekends.
It's hard to enjoy freedom you know you're about to lose.
I repeat my offer to transport you to a dimension suspended away from time and space.
dana
How come you keep wanting to send me to another dimension?
I just learned how!

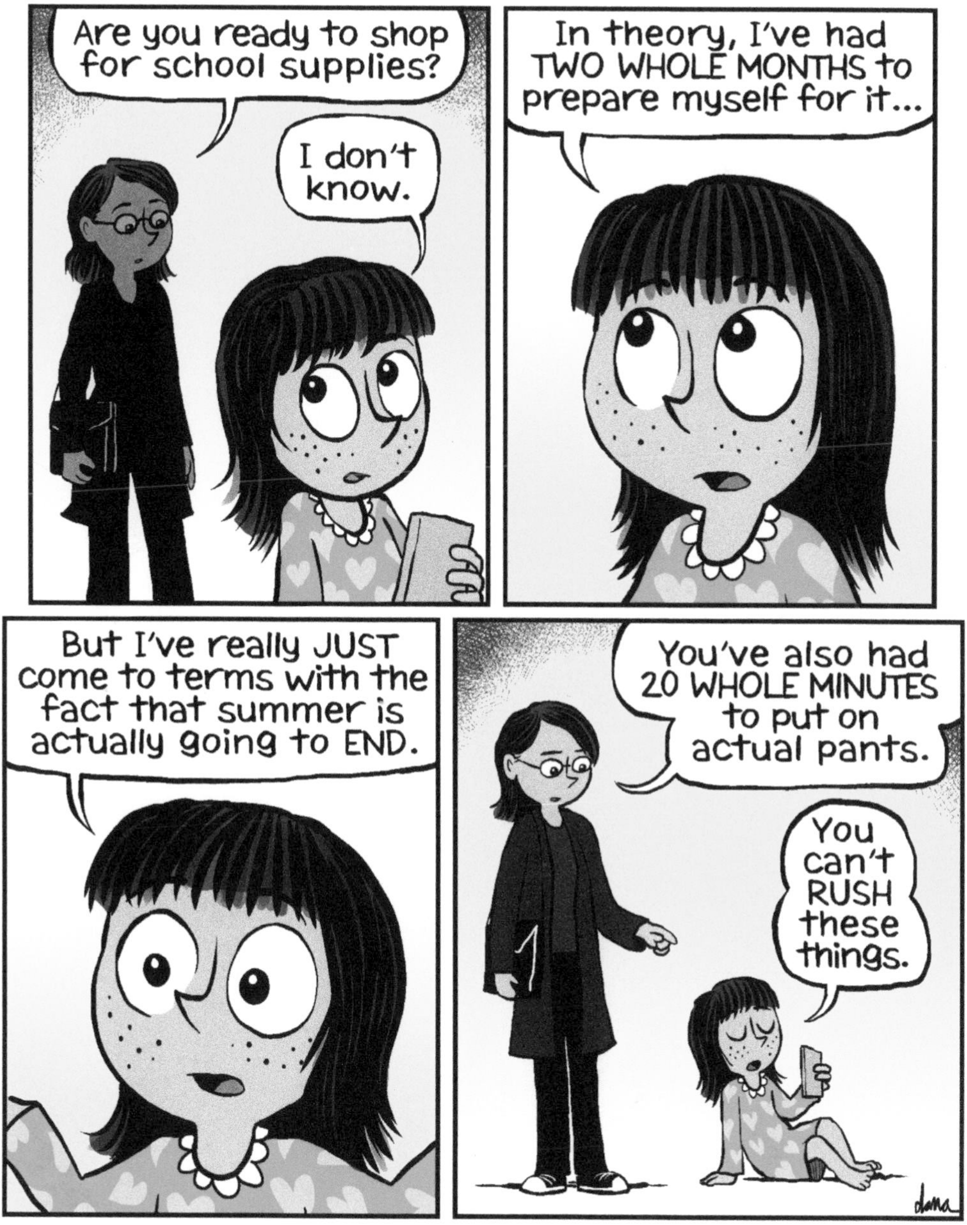
Are you ready to shop for school supplies?
I don't know.
In theory, I've had TWO WHOLE MONTHS to prepare myself for it...
But I've really JUST come to terms with the fact that summer is actually going to END.
You've also had 20 WHOLE MINUTES to put on actual pants.
You can't RUSH these things.
dana

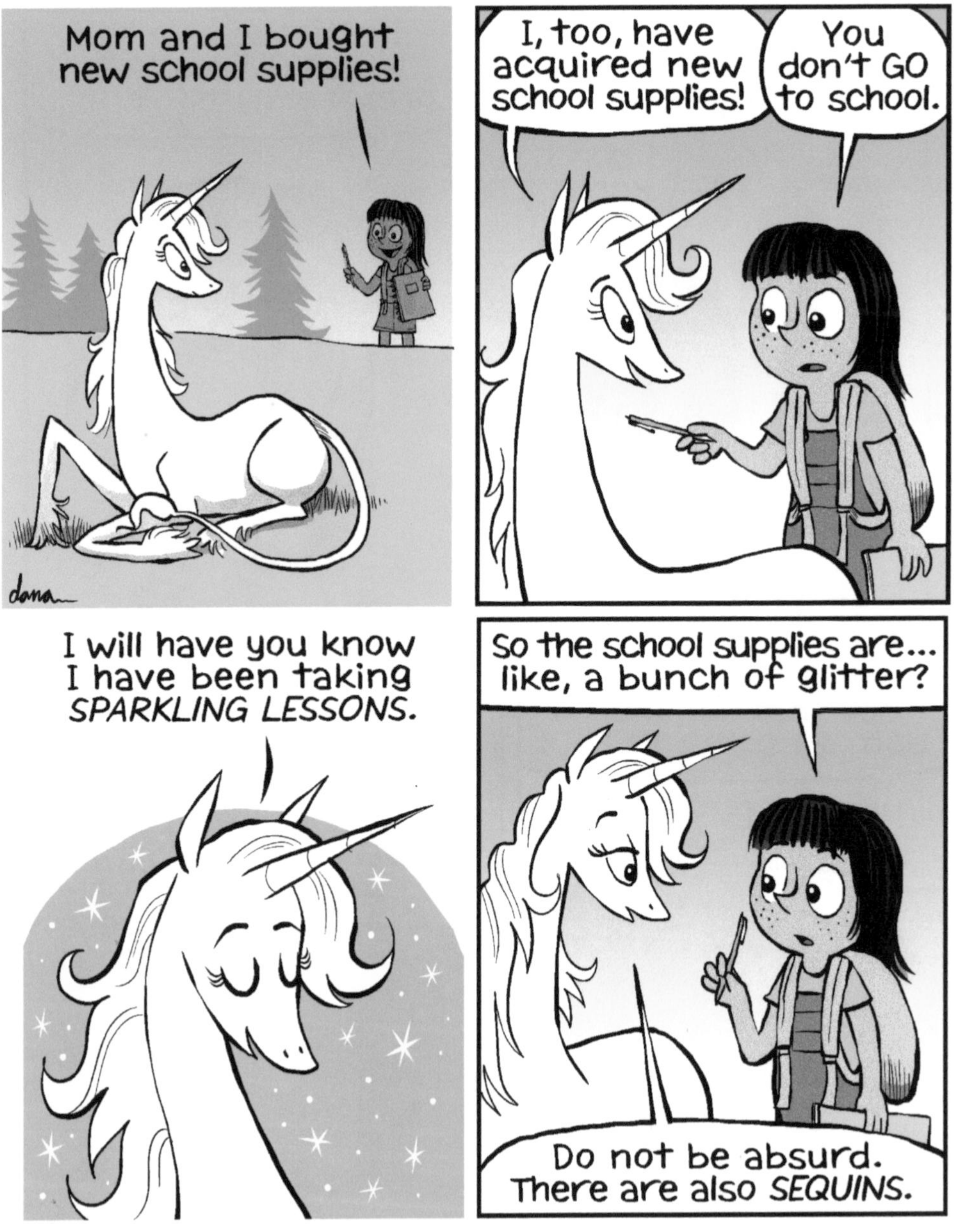
Mom and I bought new school supplies!
I, too, have acquired new school supplies!
You don't GO to school.
I will have you know I have been taking *SPARKLING LESSONS*.
So the school supplies are... like, a bunch of glitter?
Do not be absurd. There are also *SEQUINS*.

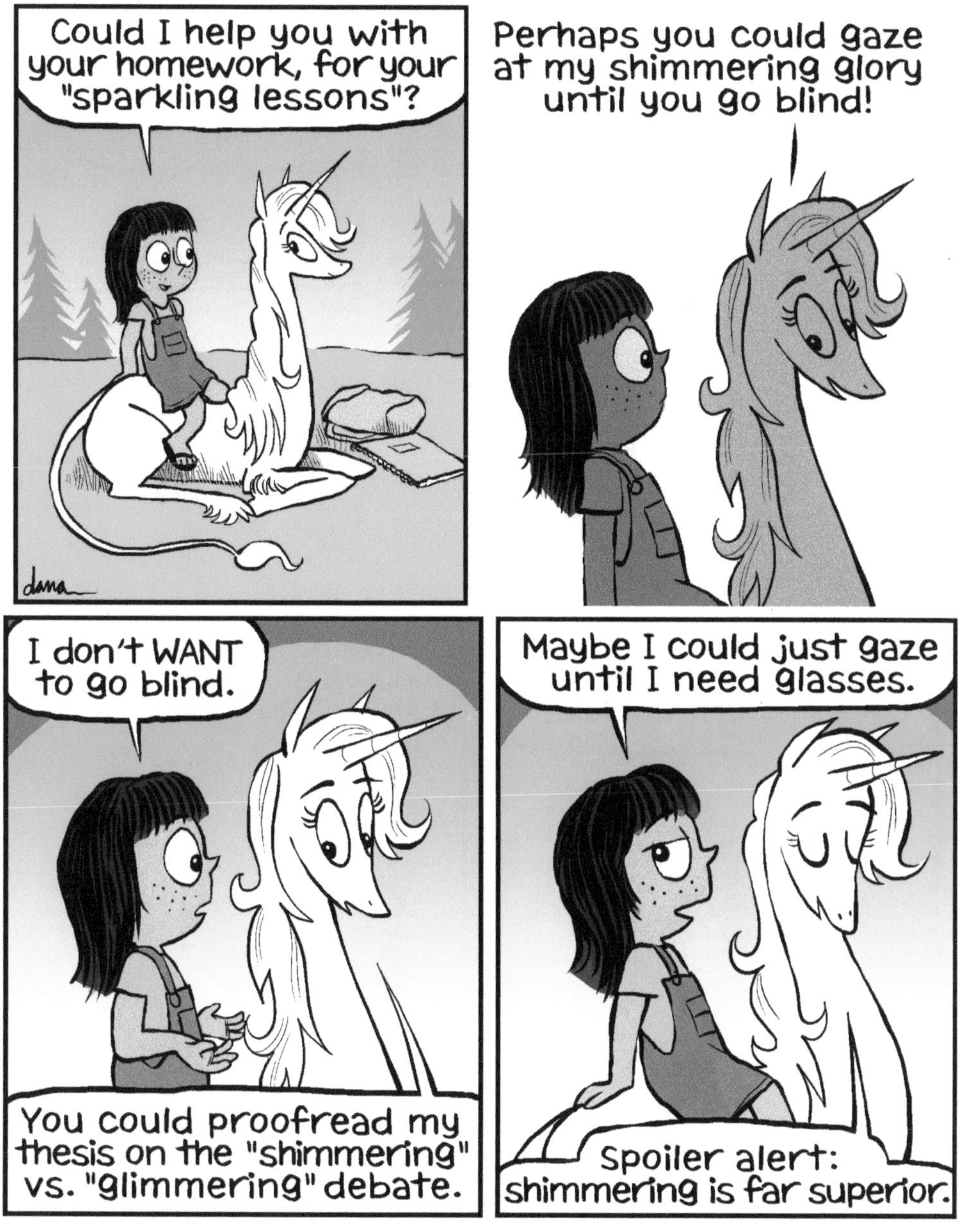

Could I help you with your homework, for your "sparkling lessons"?
Perhaps you could gaze at my shimmering glory until you go blind!
I don't WANT to go blind.
You could proofread my thesis on the "shimmering" vs. "glimmering" debate.
Maybe I could just gaze until I need glasses.
Spoiler alert: shimmering is far superior.

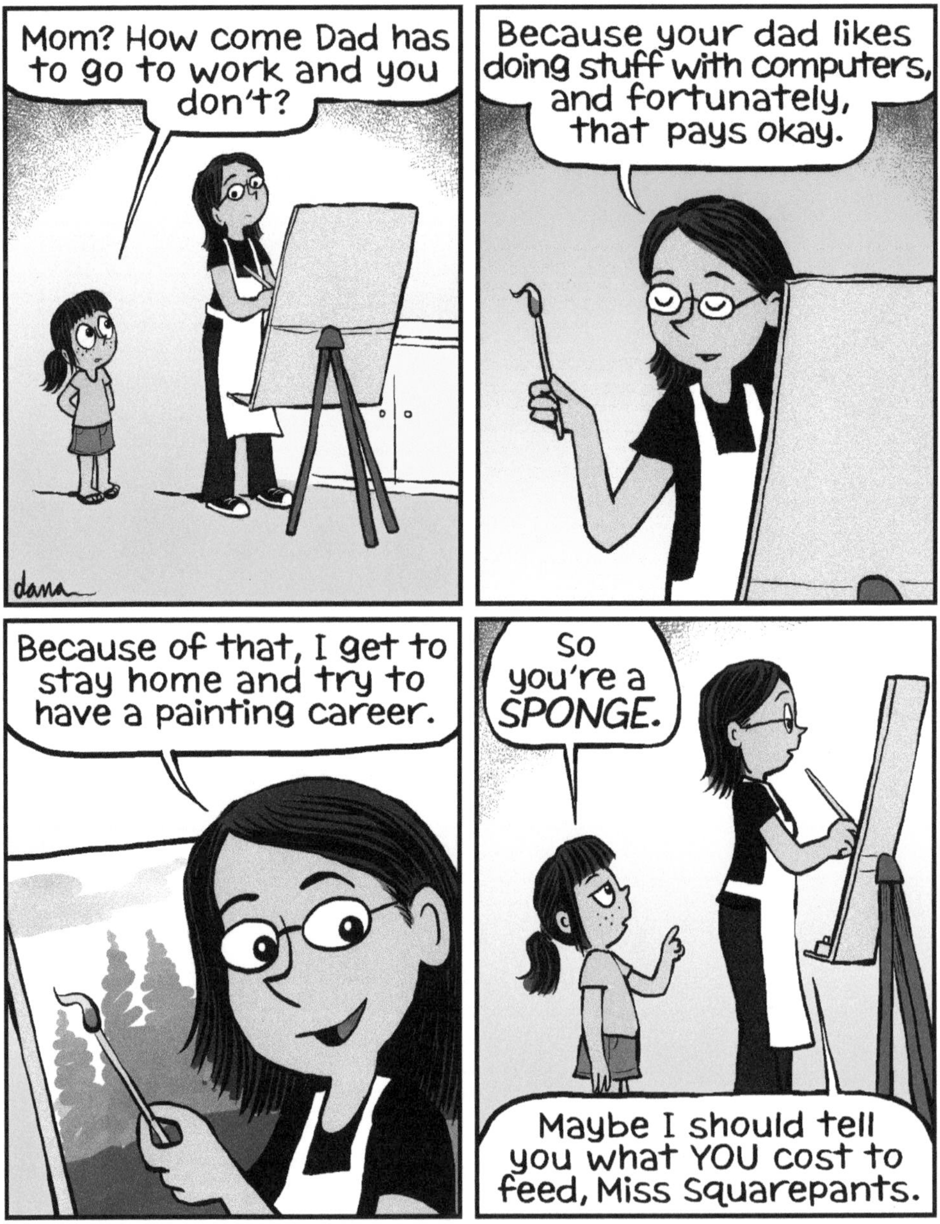
Mom? How come Dad has to go to work and you don't?
Because your dad likes doing stuff with computers, and fortunately, that pays okay.
dana
Because of that, I get to stay home and try to have a painting career.
So you're a *SPONGE.*
Maybe I should tell you what YOU cost to feed, Miss Squarepants.

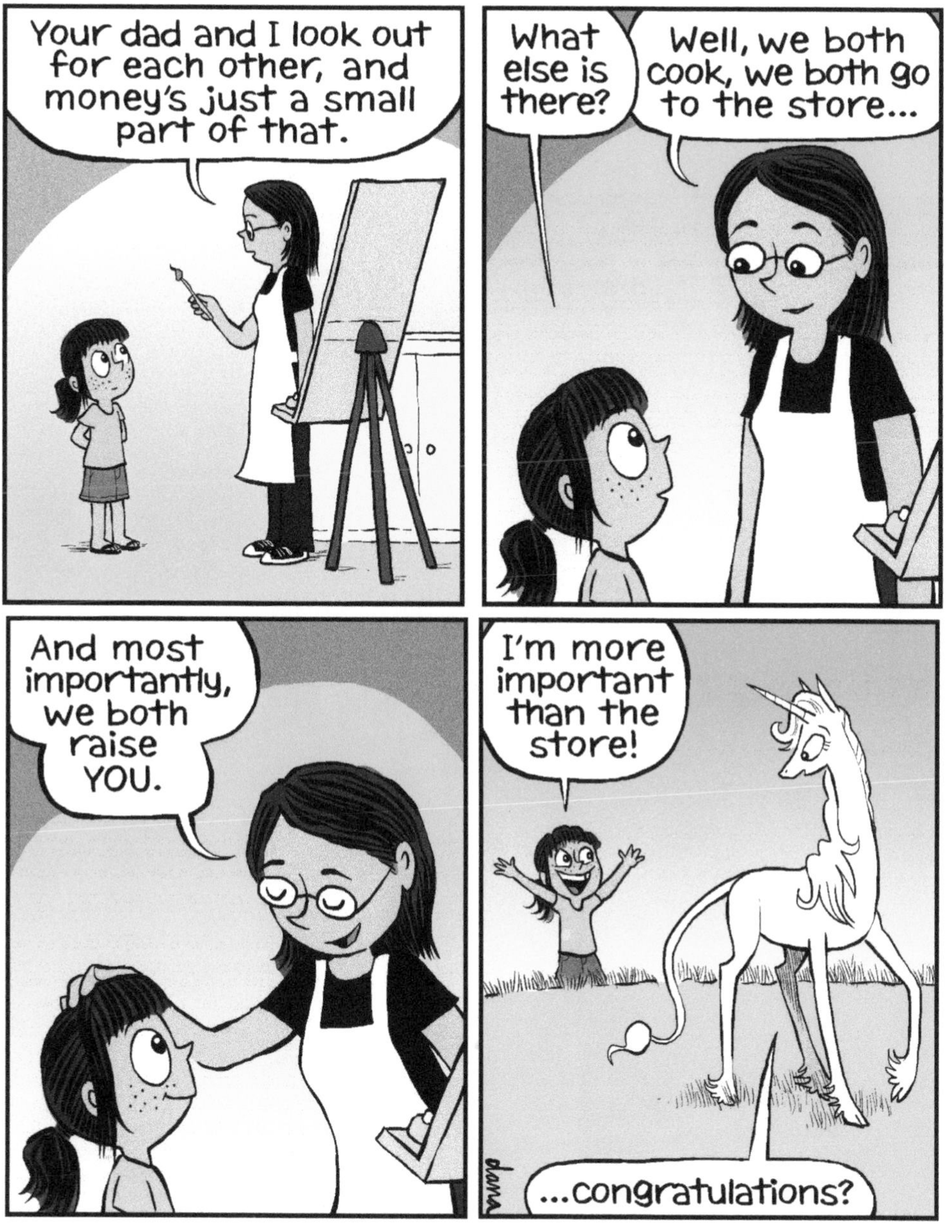
Your dad and I look out for each other, and money's just a small part of that.
What else is there?
Well, we both cook, we both go to the store...
And most importantly, we both raise YOU.
I'm more important than the store!
...congratulations?

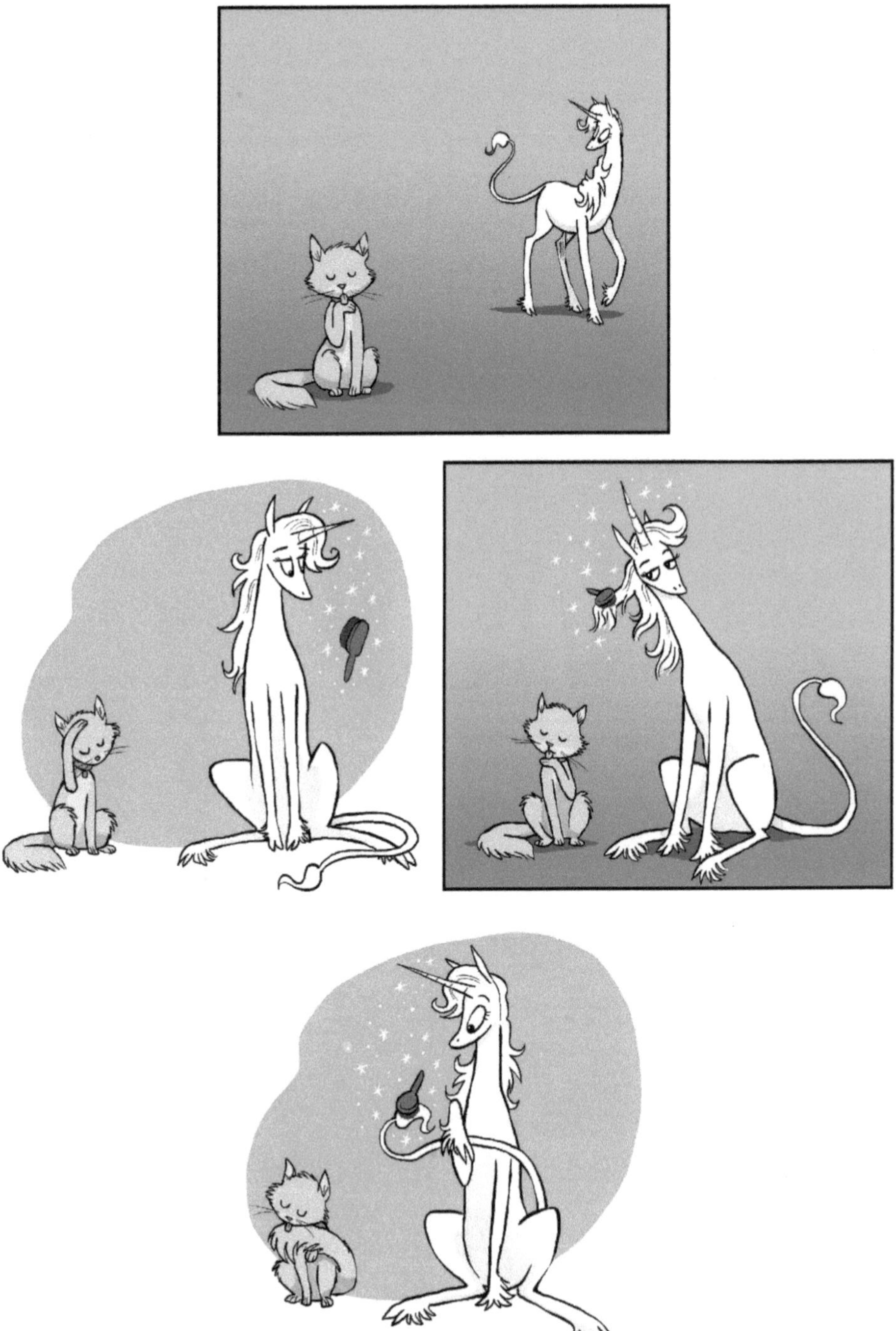

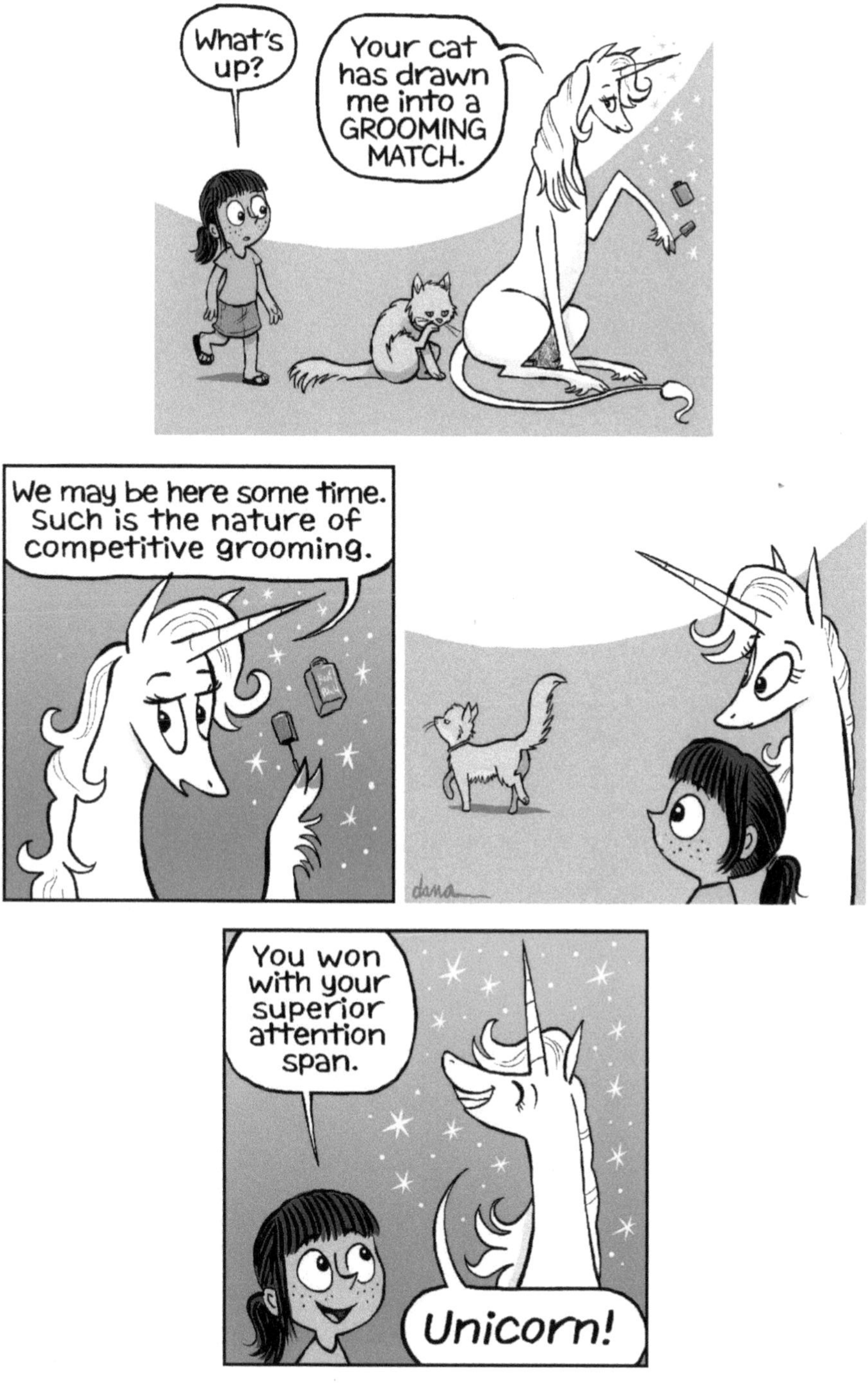
What's up?
Your cat has drawn me into a GROOMING MATCH.
We may be here some time. Such is the nature of competitive grooming.
You won with your superior attention span.
Unicorn!

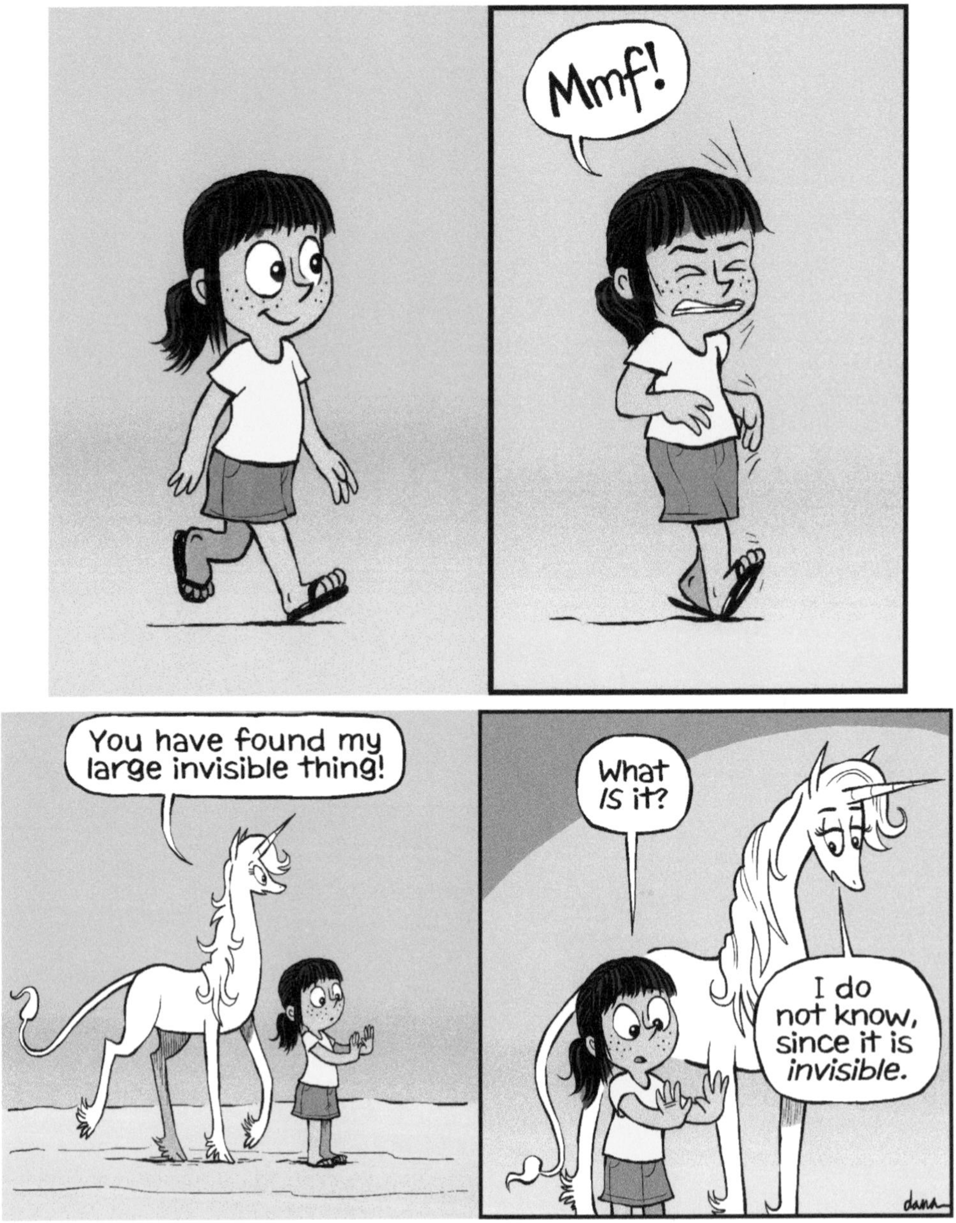
Mmf!
You have found my large invisible thing!
What *IS* it?
I do not know, since it is *invisible*.
dana

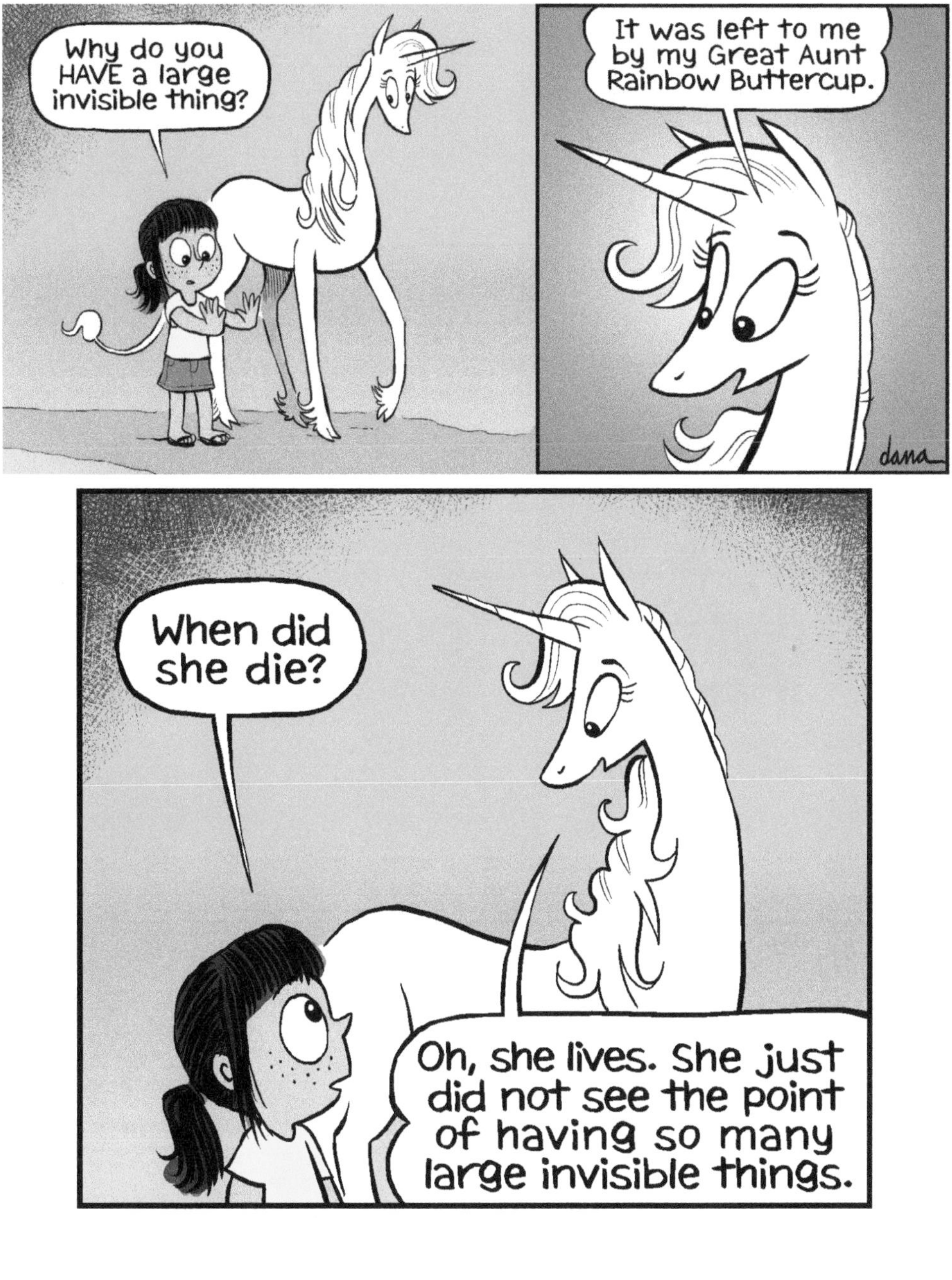
Why do you HAVE a large invisible thing?
It was left to me by my Great Aunt Rainbow Buttercup.
dana
When did she die?
Oh, she lives. She just did not see the point of having so many large invisible things.

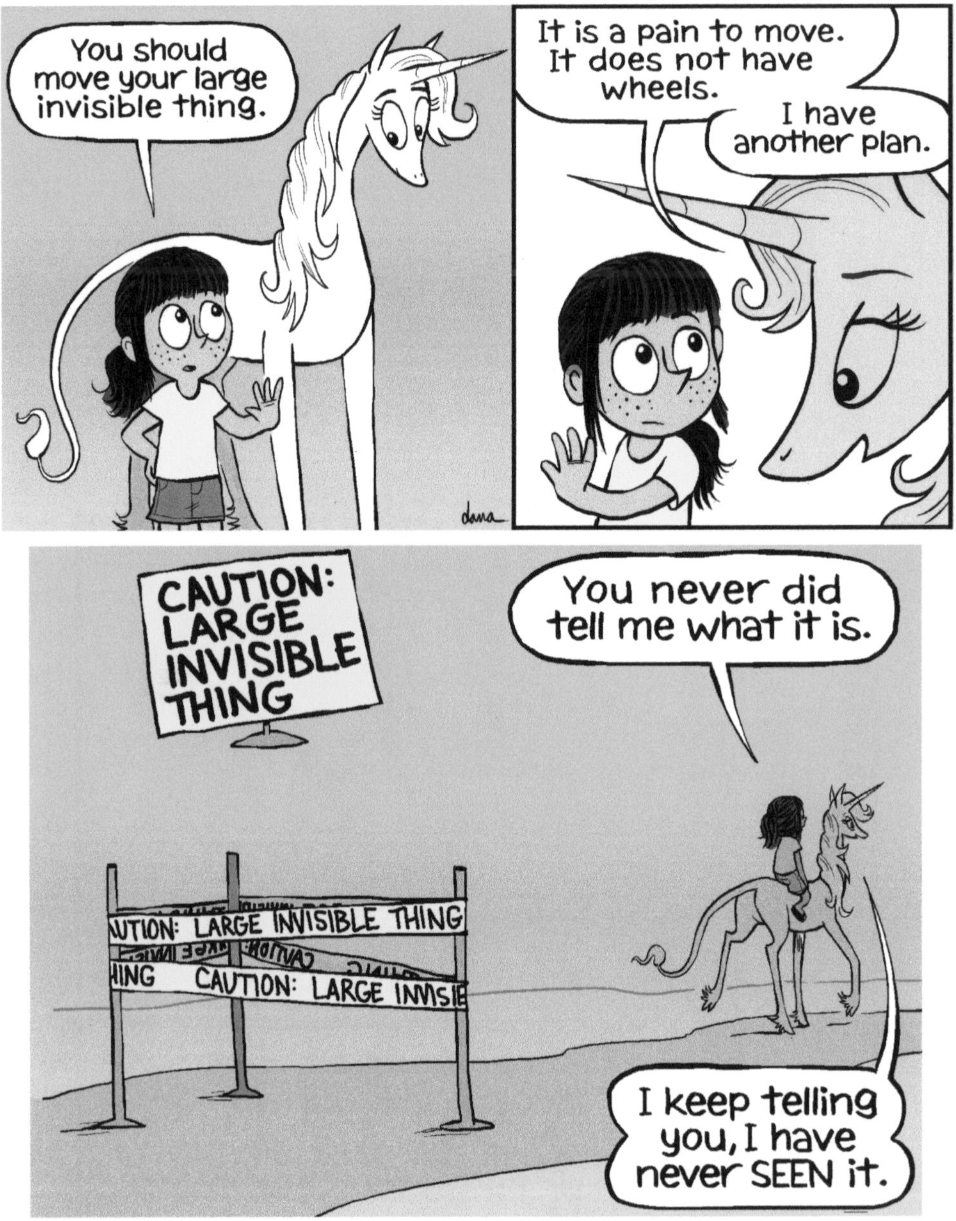
You should move your large invisible thing.
dana
It is a pain to move. It does not have wheels.
I have another plan.
CAUTION: LARGE INVISIBLE THING
You never did tell me what it is.
UTION: LARGE INVISIBLE THING
HING CAUTION: LARGE INVISI
I keep telling you, I have never SEEN it.

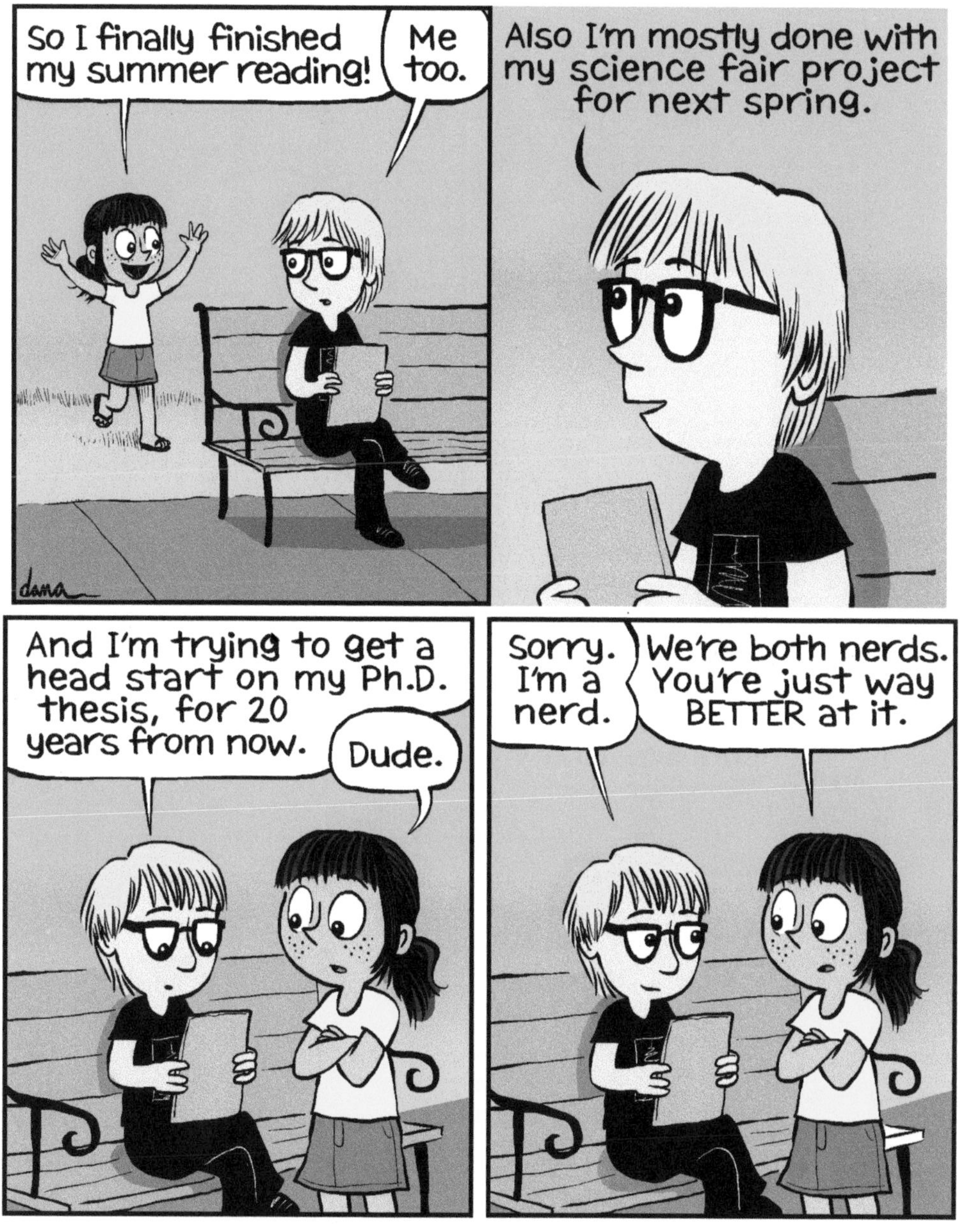
So I finally finished my summer reading!
Me too.
Also I'm mostly done with my science fair project for next spring.
And I'm trying to get a head start on my Ph.D. thesis, for 20 years from now.
Dude.
Sorry. I'm a nerd.
We're both nerds. You're just way BETTER at it.
dana

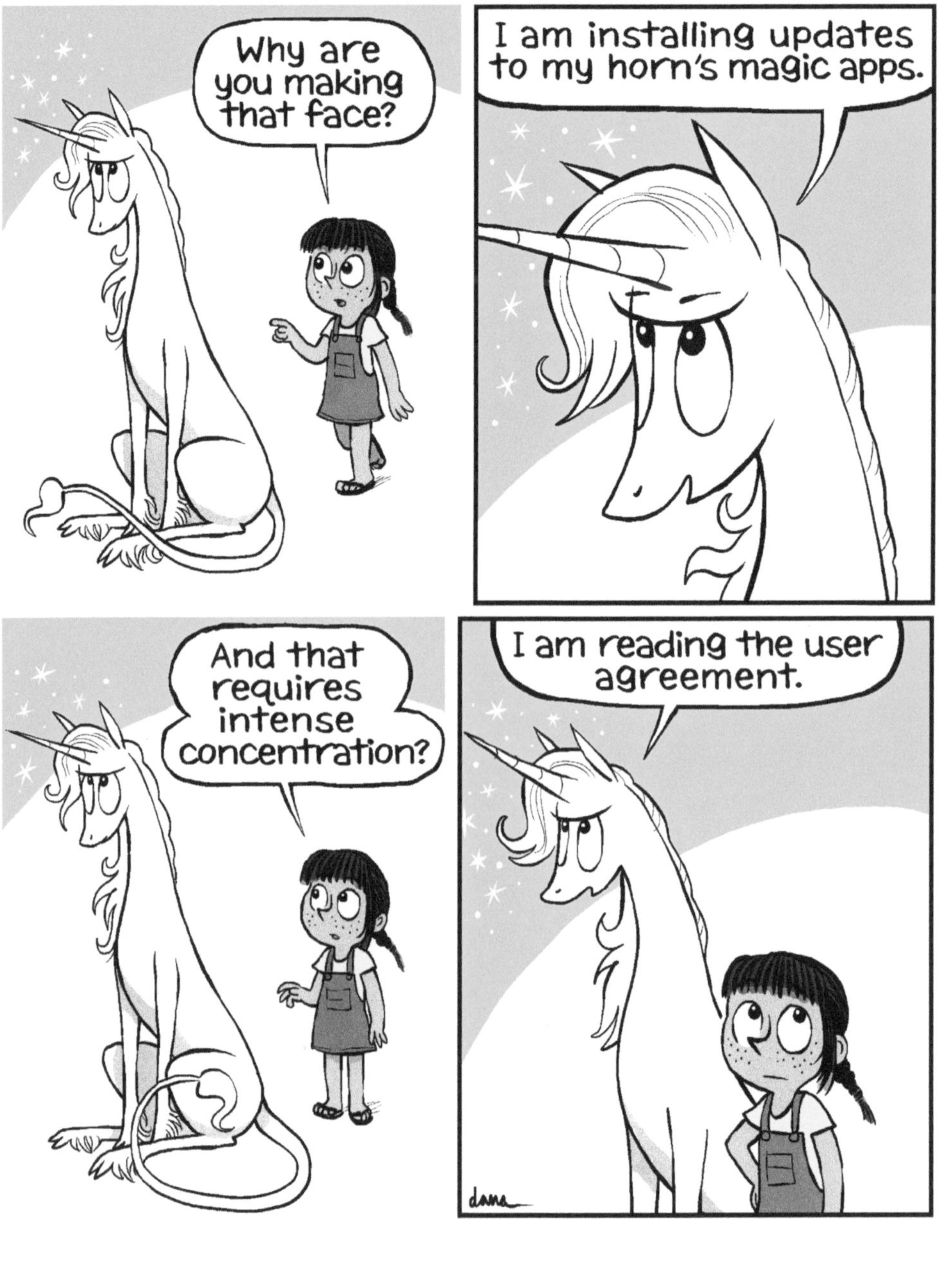
Why are you making that face?
I am installing updates to my horn's magic apps.
And that requires intense concentration?
I am reading the user agreement.
dana

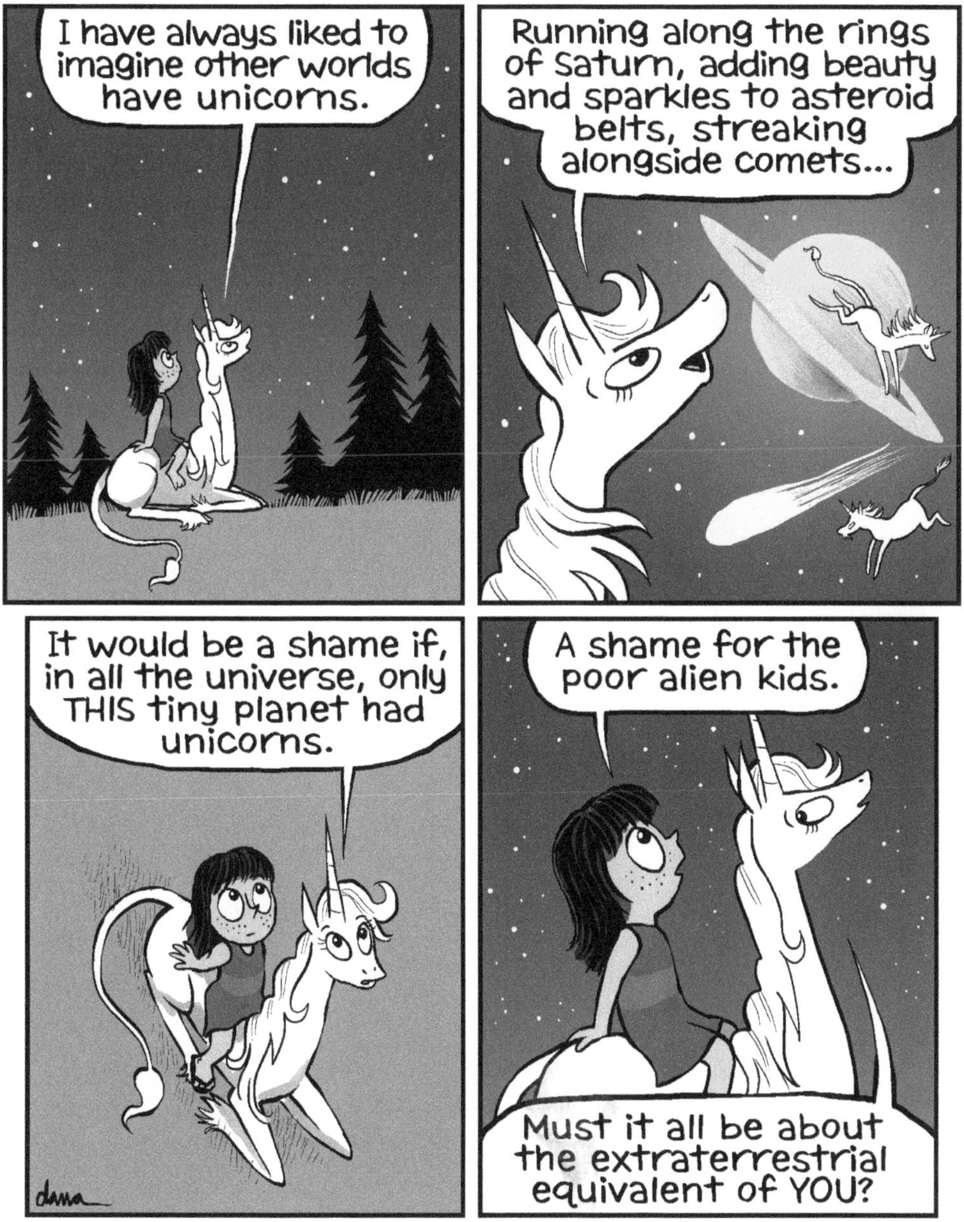
I have always liked to imagine other worlds have unicorns.
Running along the rings of Saturn, adding beauty and sparkles to asteroid belts, streaking alongside comets...
It would be a shame if, in all the universe, only THIS tiny planet had unicorns.
dana
A shame for the poor alien kids.
Must it all be about the extraterrestrial equivalent of YOU?

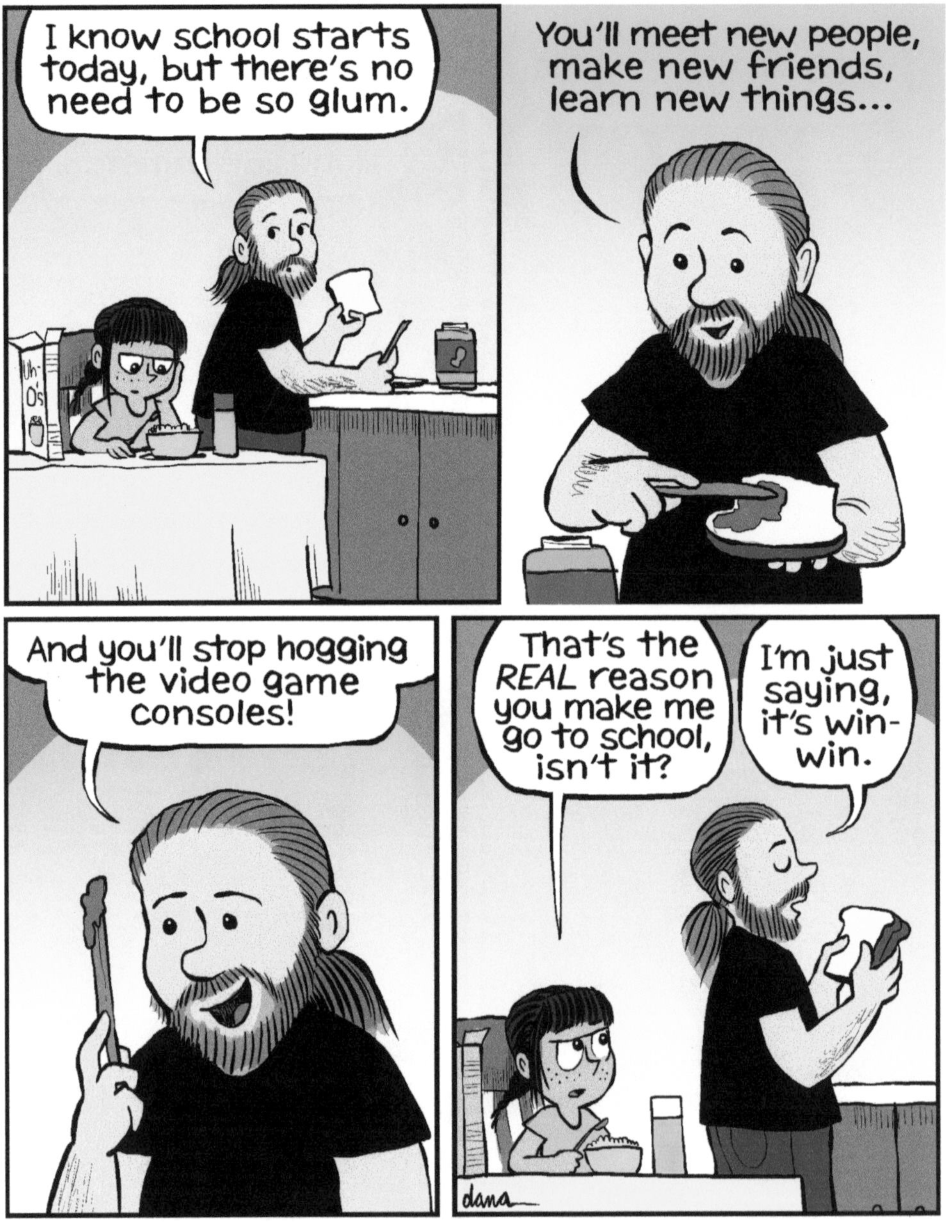
I know school starts today, but there's no need to be so glum.
Uh-O's
You'll meet new people, make new friends, learn new things...
And you'll stop hogging the video game consoles!
That's the *REAL* reason you make me go to school, isn't it?
I'm just saying, it's win-win.
dana

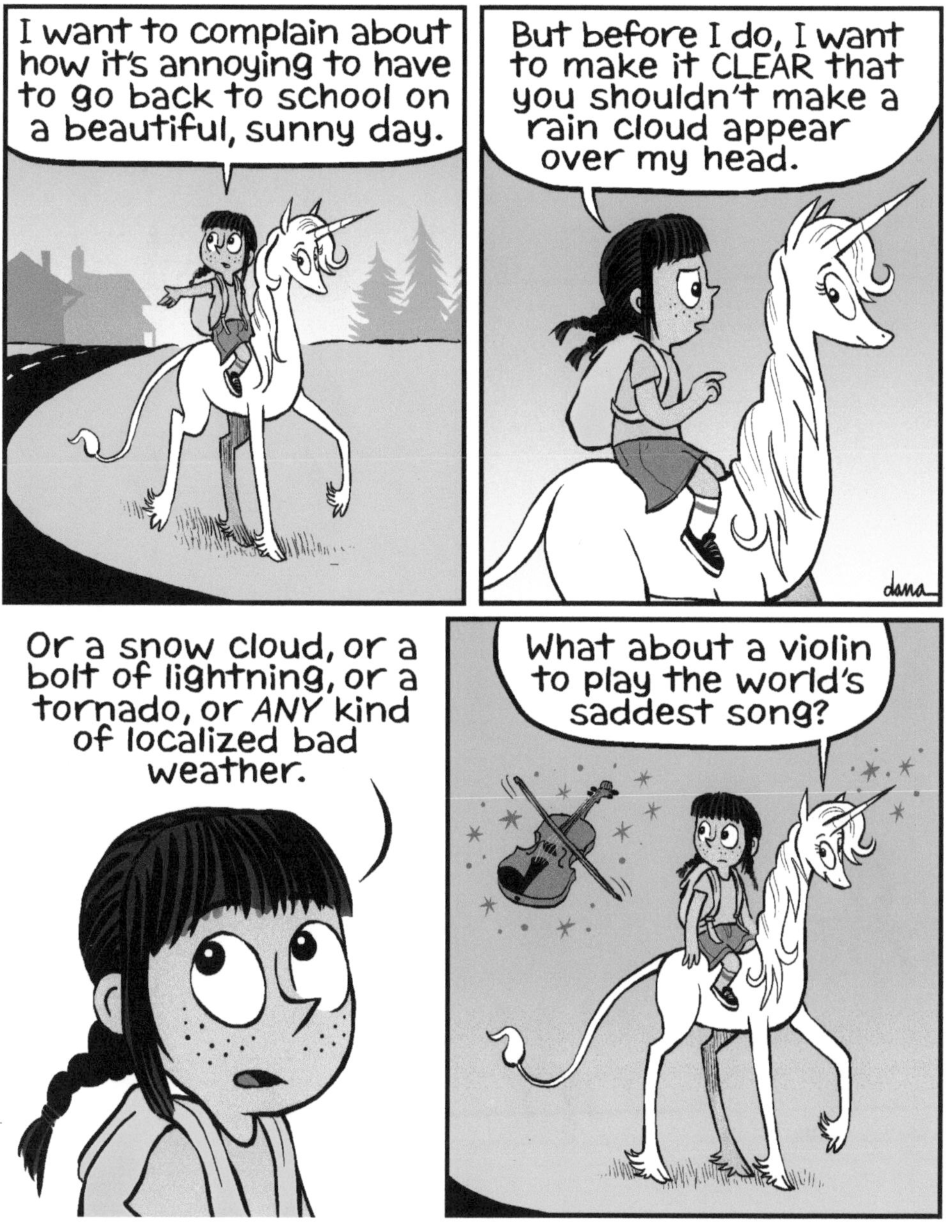
I want to complain about how it's annoying to have to go back to school on a beautiful, sunny day.
But before I do, I want to make it CLEAR that you shouldn't make a rain cloud appear over my head.
dana
Or a snow cloud, or a bolt of lightning, or a tornado, or *ANY* kind of localized bad weather.
What about a violin to play the world's saddest song?

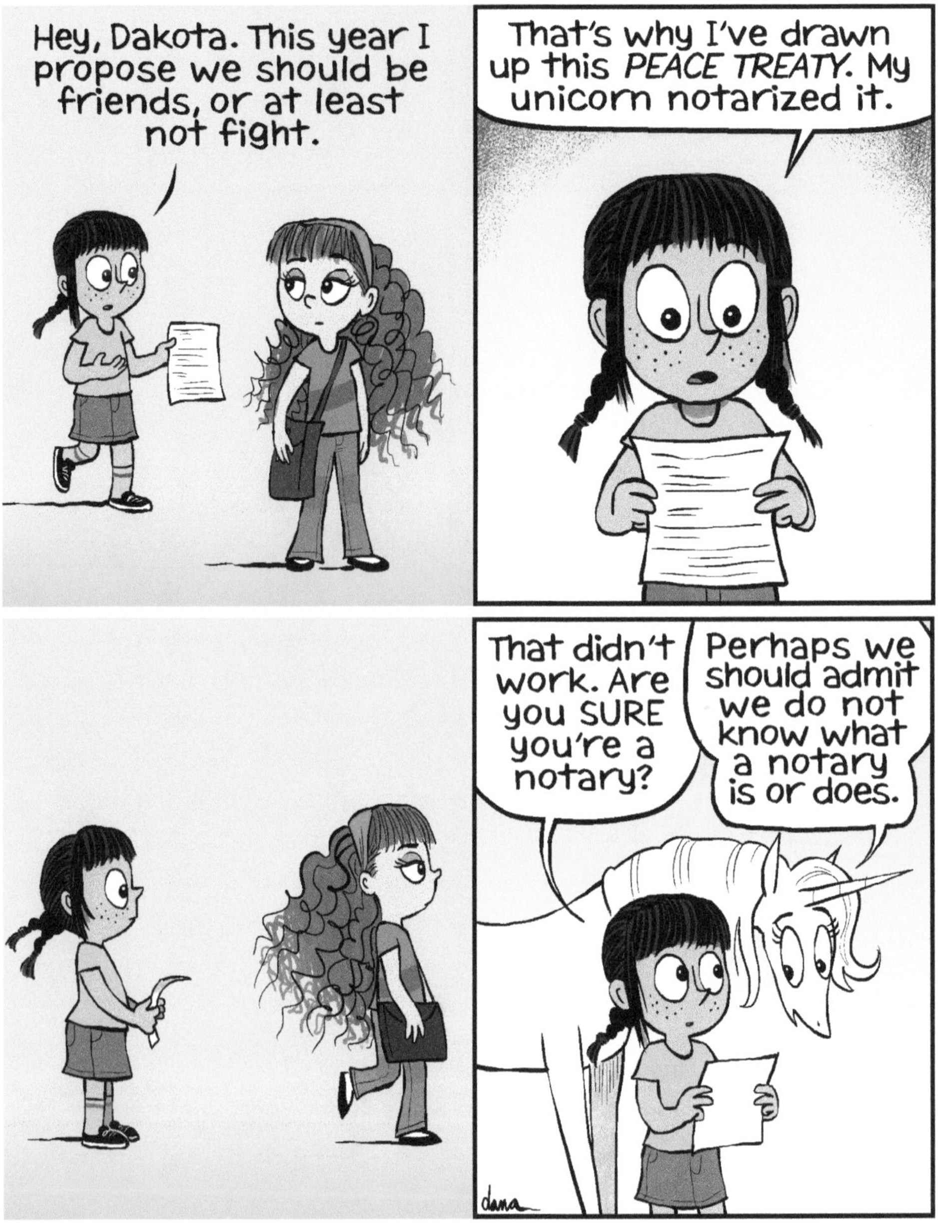
Hey, Dakota. This year I propose we should be friends, or at least not fight.
That's why I've drawn up this PEACE TREATY. My unicorn notarized it.
That didn't work. Are you SURE you're a notary?
Perhaps we should admit we do not know what a notary is or does.
dana

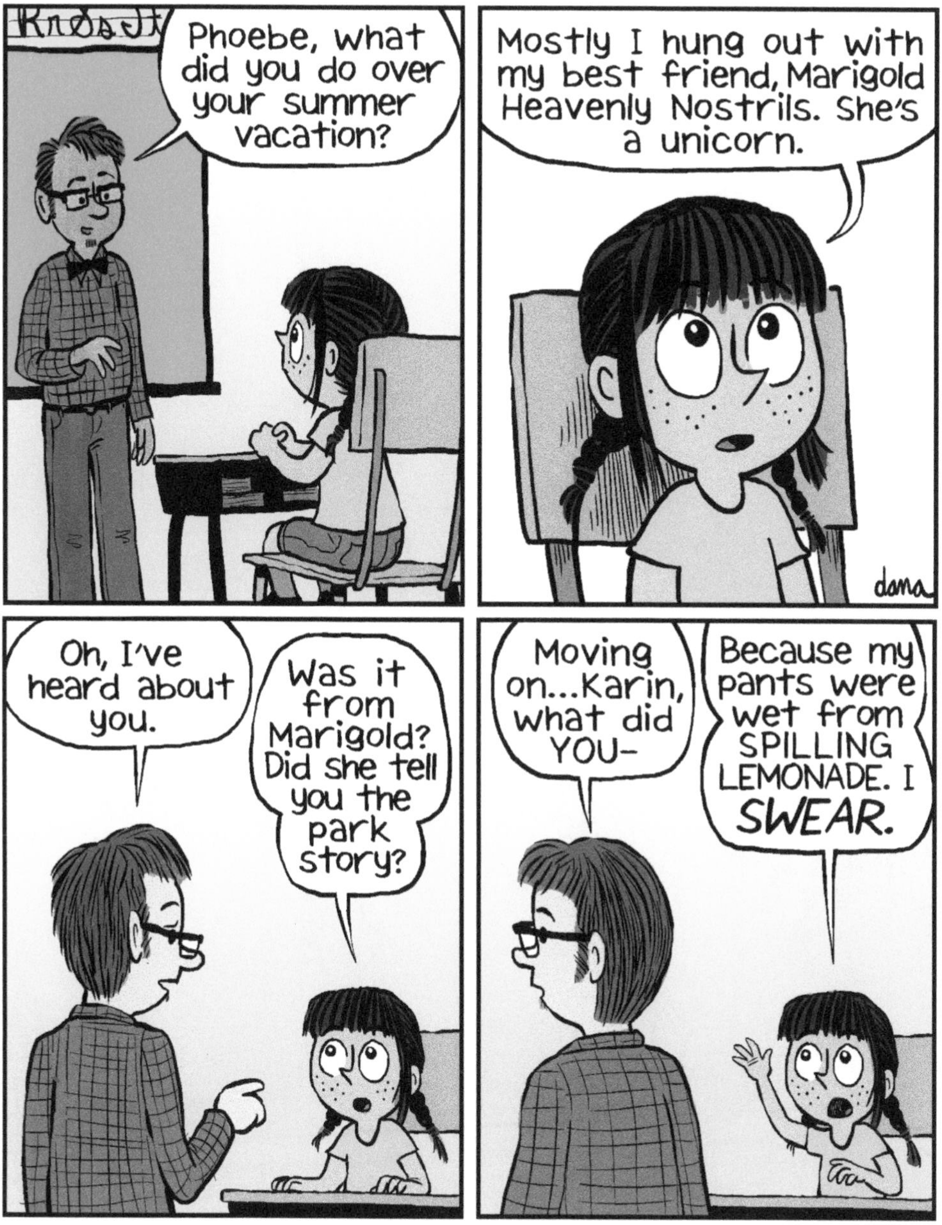
Phoebe, what did you do over your summer vacation?
Mostly I hung out with my best friend, Marigold Heavenly Nostrils. She's a unicorn.
dana
Oh, I've heard about you.
Was it from Marigold? Did she tell you the park story?
Moving on...Karin, what did YOU-
Because my pants were wet from SPILLING LEMONADE. I *SWEAR.*

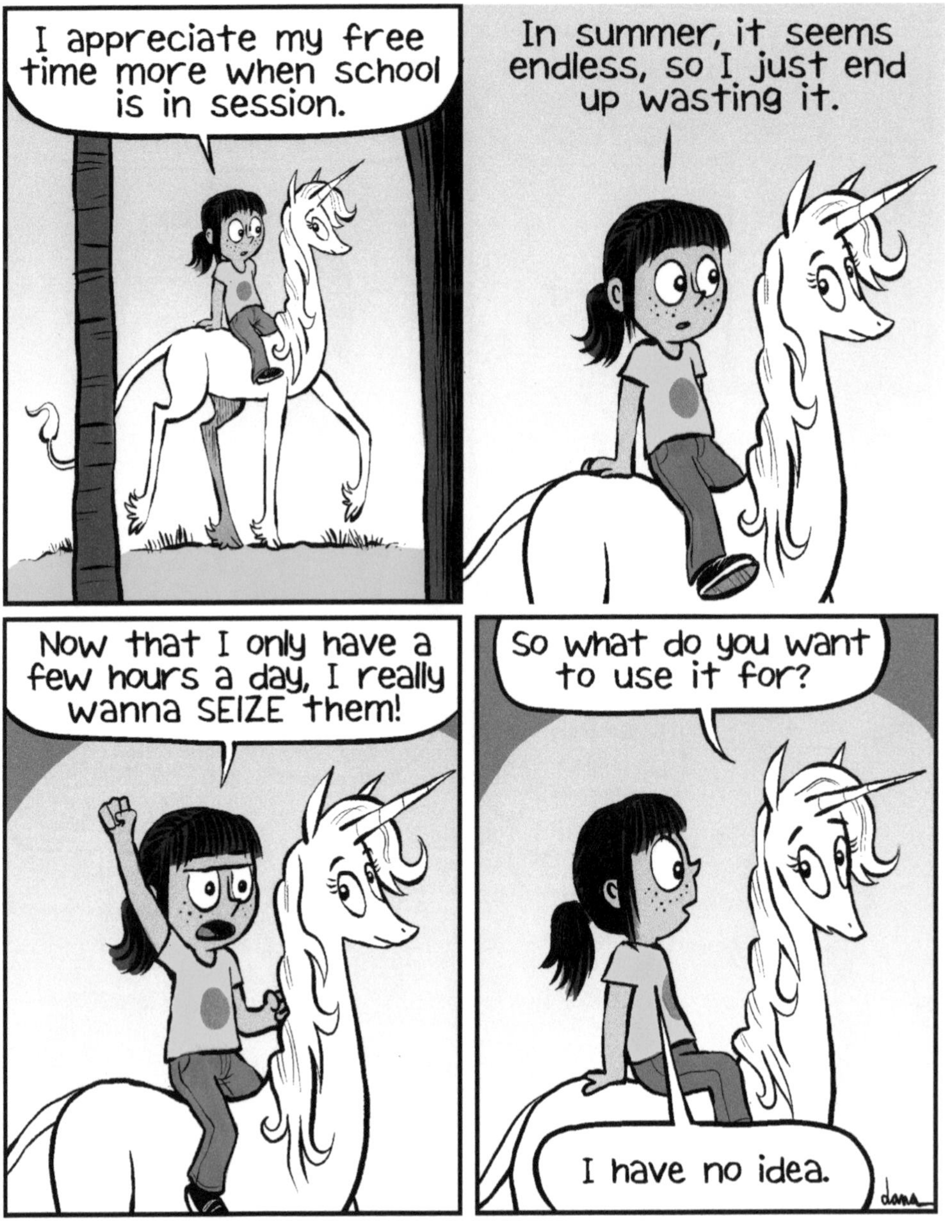
I appreciate my free time more when school is in session.
In summer, it seems endless, so I just end up wasting it.
Now that I only have a few hours a day, I really wanna SEIZE them!
So what do you want to use it for?
I have no idea.
dana

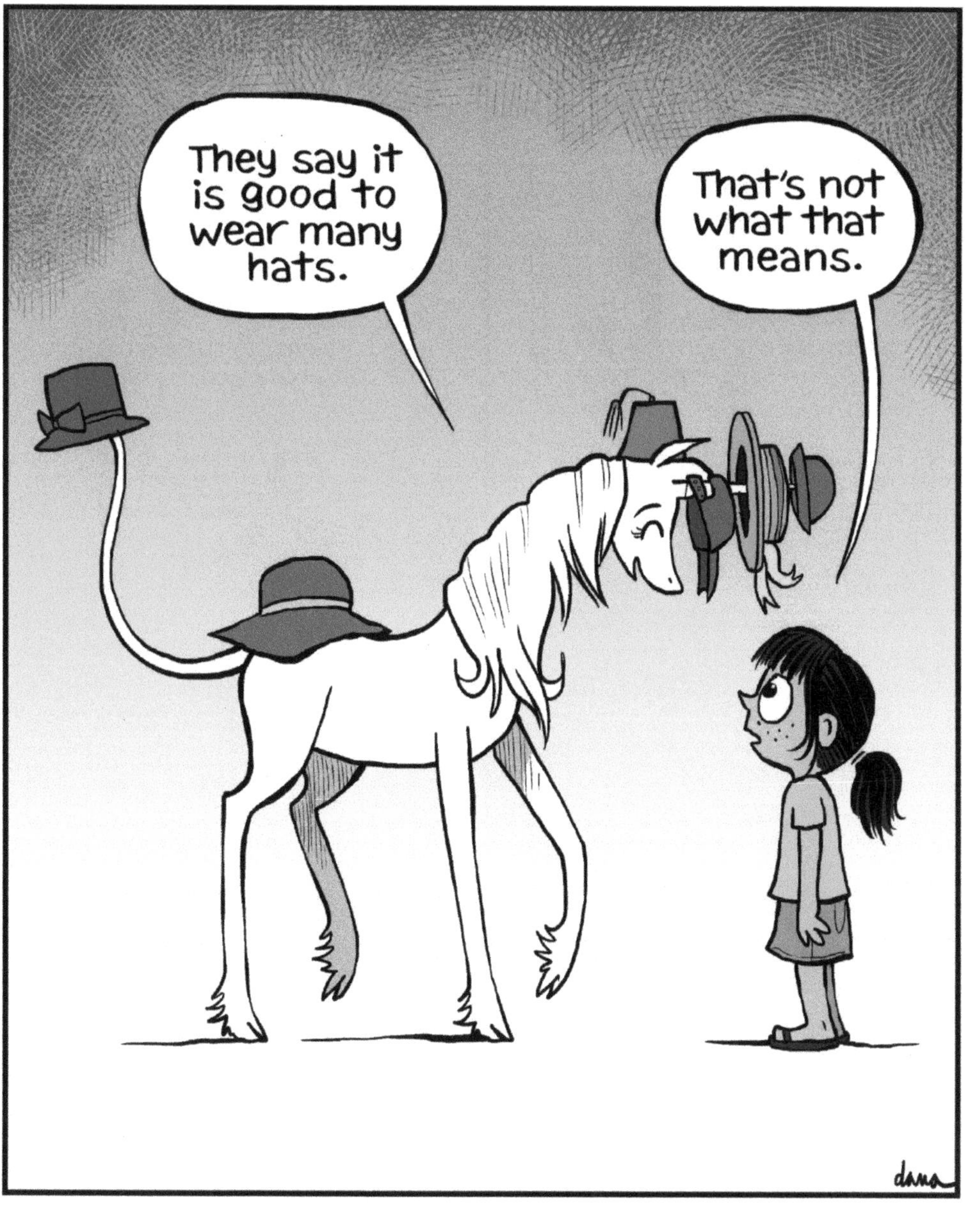
They say it is good to wear many hats.
That's not what that means.
dana

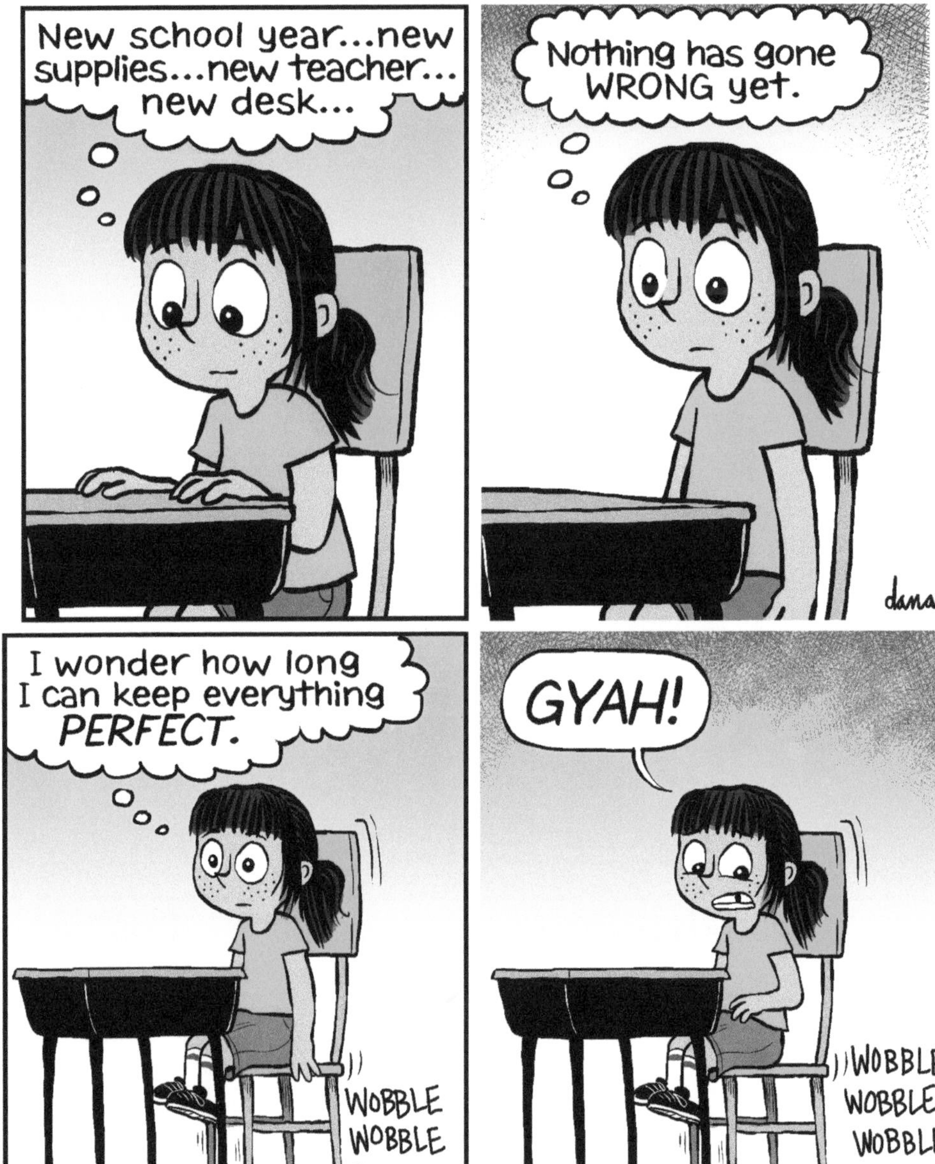
New school year...new supplies...new teacher... new desk...
Nothing has gone WRONG yet.
dana
I wonder how long I can keep everything PERFECT.
WOBBLE WOBBLE
GYAH!
WOBBLE WOBBLE WOBBLE

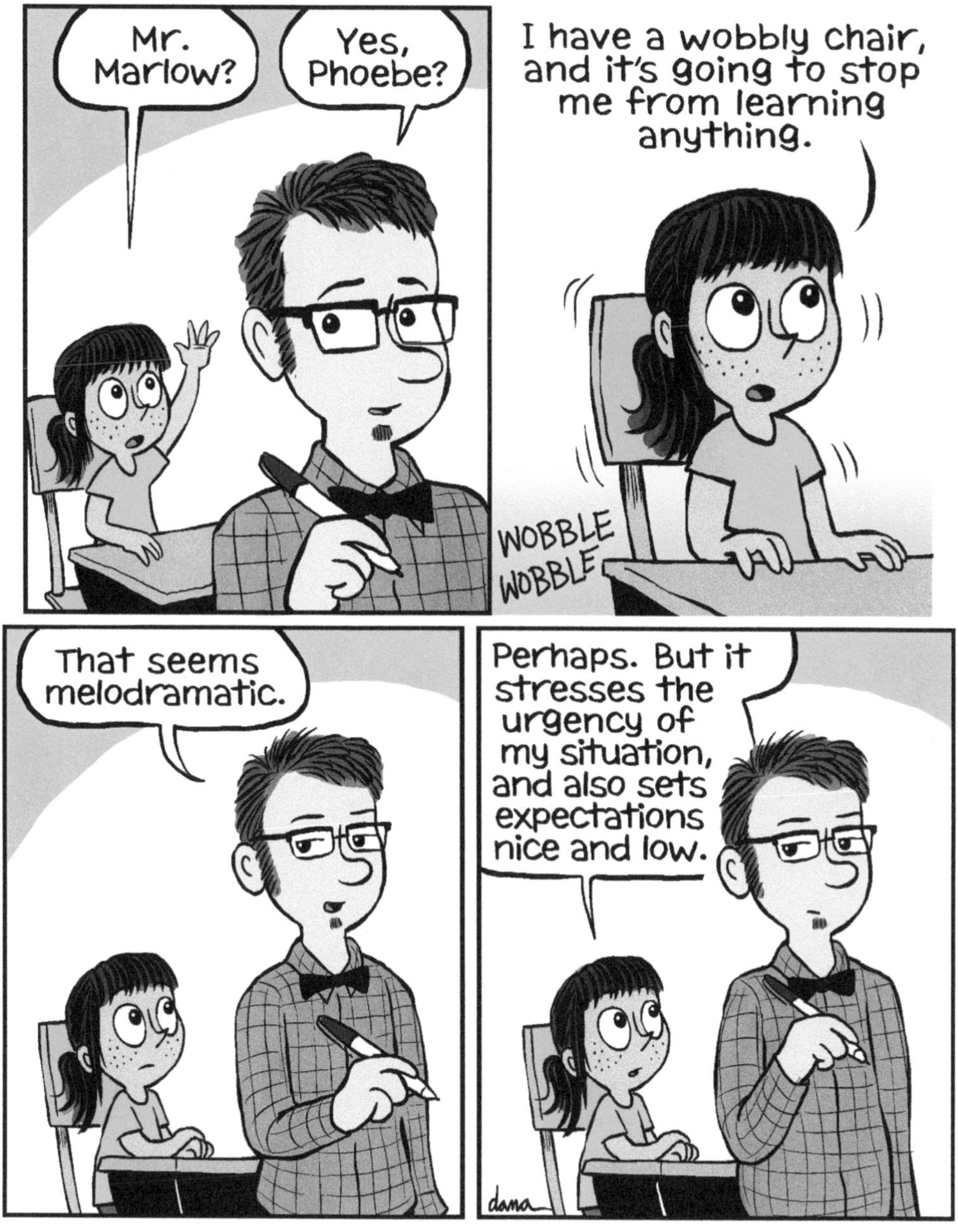
Mr. Marlow?
Yes, Phoebe?
I have a wobbly chair, and it's going to stop me from learning anything.
WOBBLE WOBBLE
That seems melodramatic.
Perhaps. But it stresses the urgency of my situation, and also sets expectations nice and low.
dana

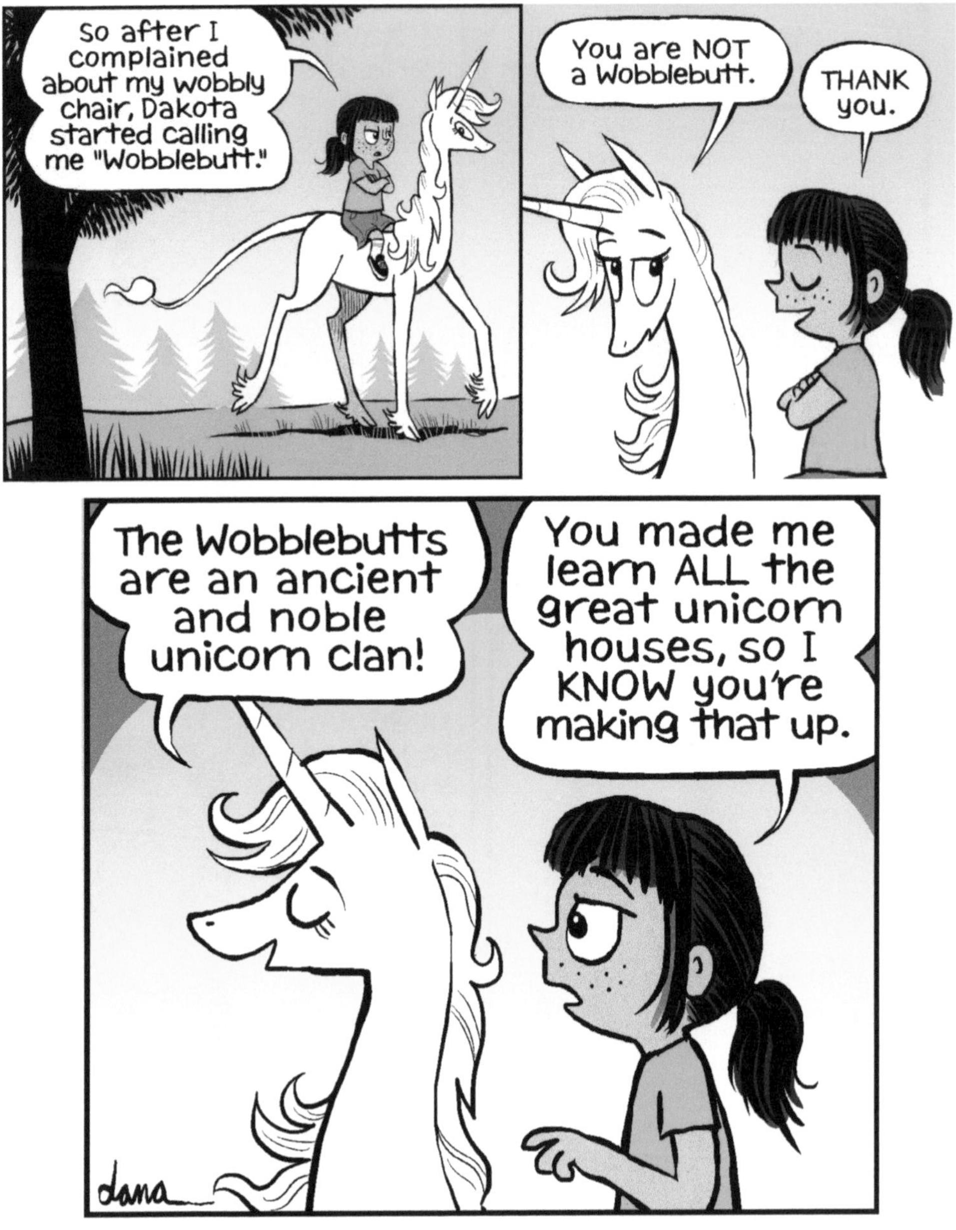
So after I complained about my wobbly chair, Dakota started calling me "Wobblebutt."
You are NOT a Wobblebutt.
THANK you.
The Wobblebutts are an ancient and noble unicorn clan!
You made me learn ALL the great unicorn houses, so I KNOW you're making that up.
dana

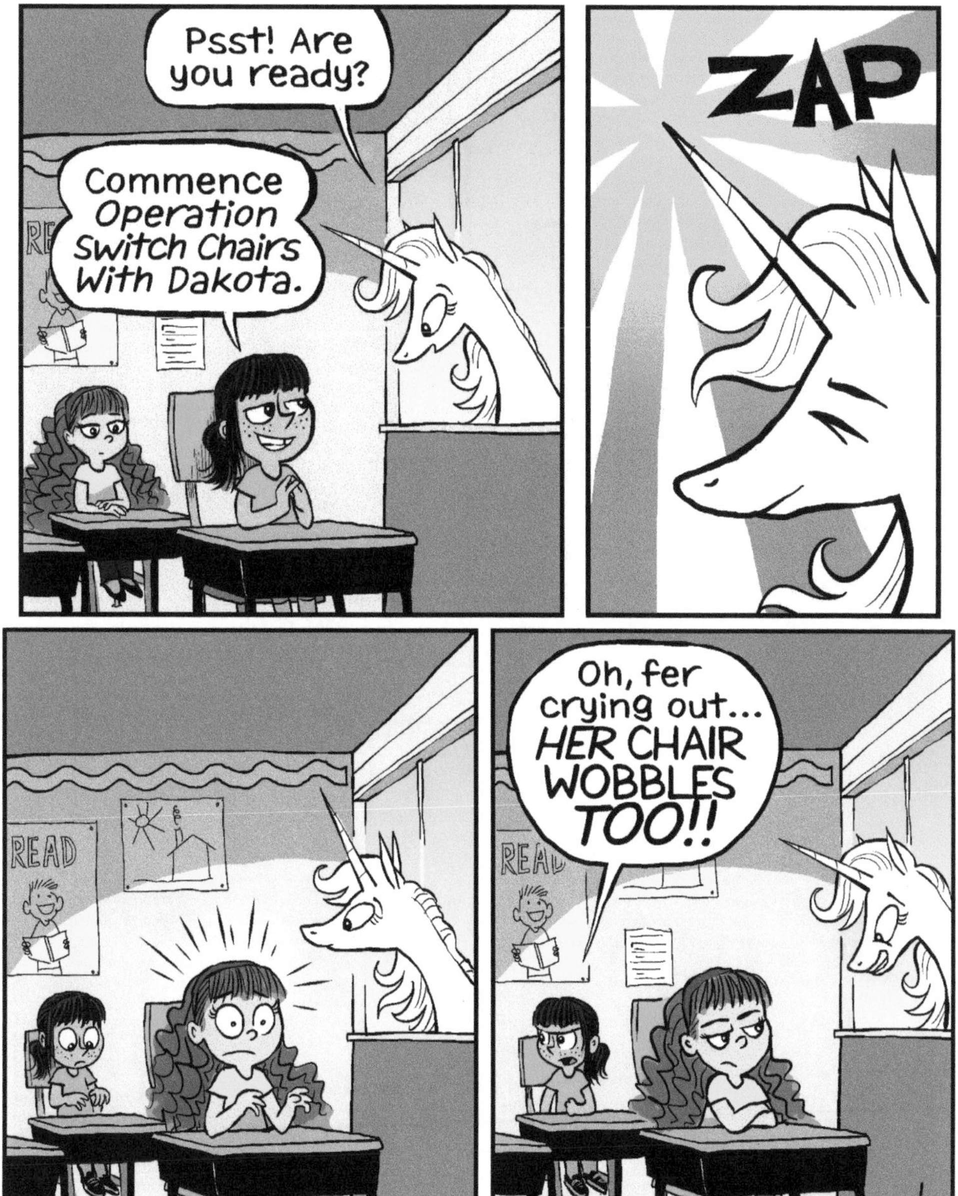
Psst! Are you ready?
Commence Operation Switch Chairs With Dakota.
READ
ZAP
READ
READ
Oh, fer crying out... HER CHAIR WOBBLES TOO!!
dana

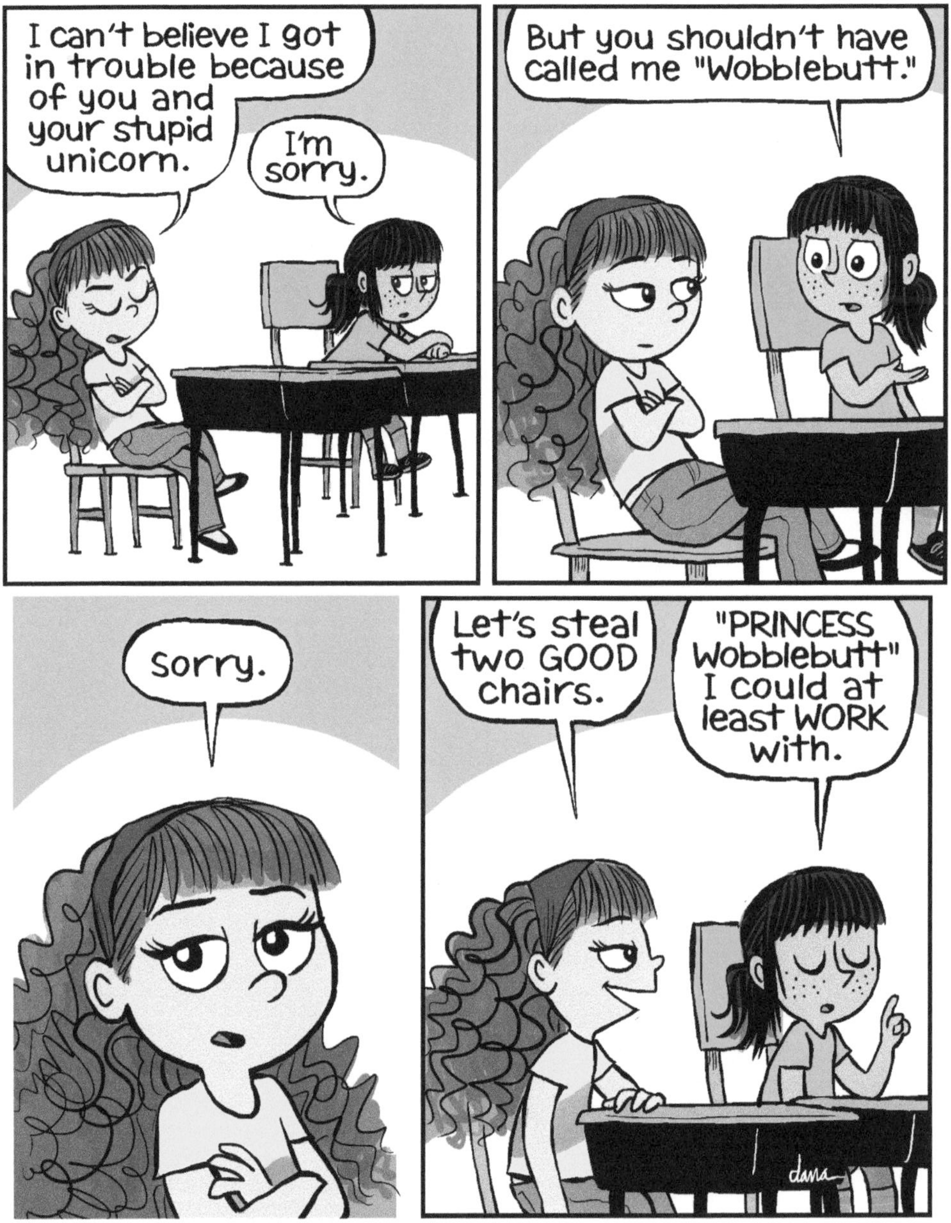

I can't believe I got in trouble because of you and your stupid unicorn.
I'm sorry.
But you shouldn't have called me "Wobblebutt."
Sorry.
Let's steal two GOOD chairs.
"PRINCESS Wobblebutt" I could at least WORK with.
dana

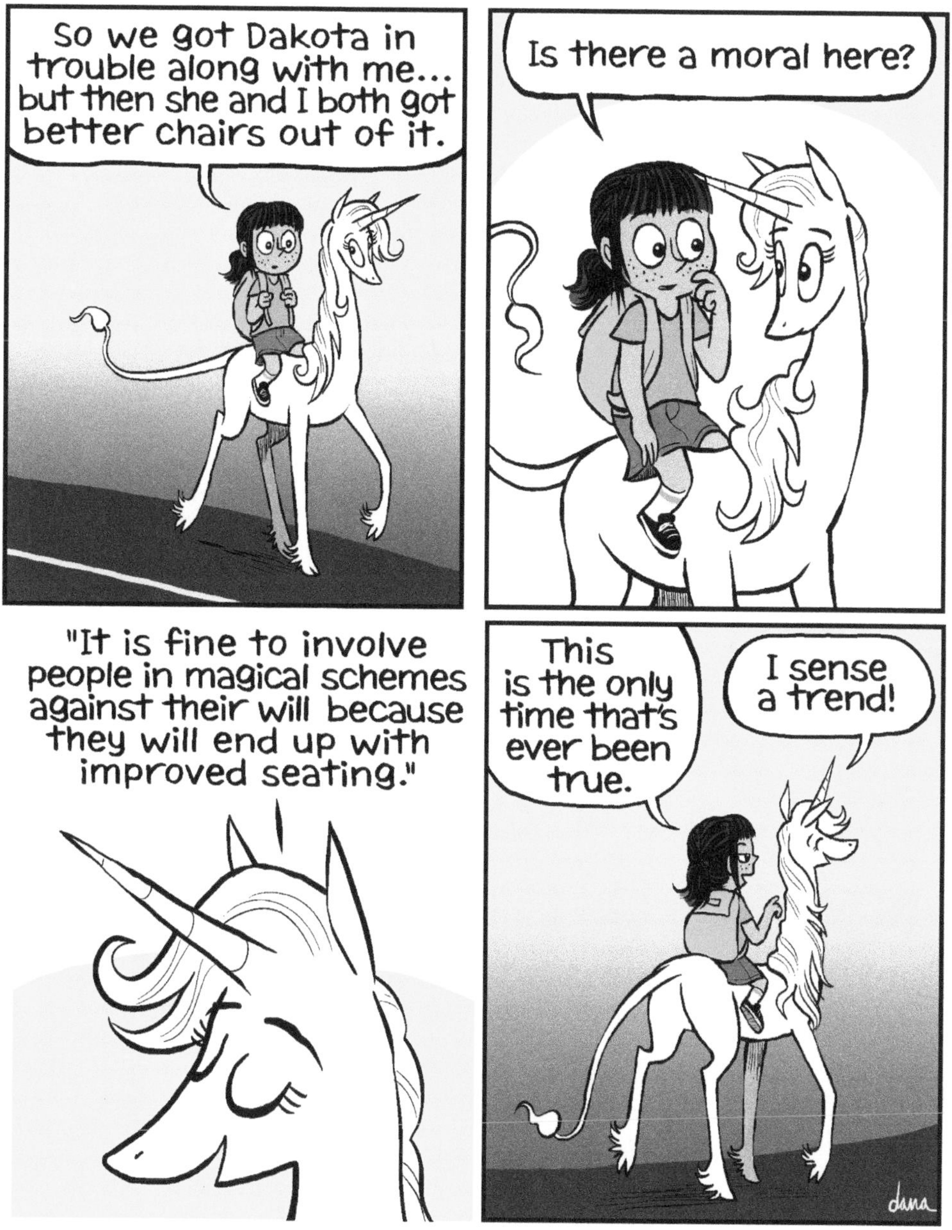
So we got Dakota in trouble along with me... but then she and I both got better chairs out of it.
Is there a moral here?
"It is fine to involve people in magical schemes against their will because they will end up with improved seating."
This is the only time that's ever been true.
I sense a trend!
dana

TVs, phones, music-playing devices...they used to be so *DIFFERENT* and *COMPLICATED*.
Now it's just *rectangles*. Rectangles everywhere. Madness!

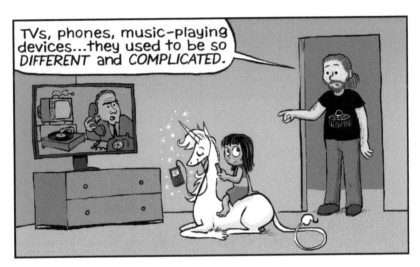

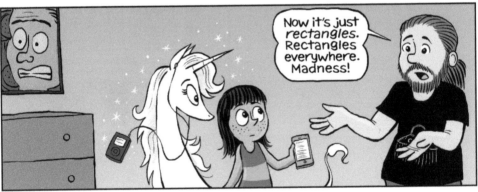

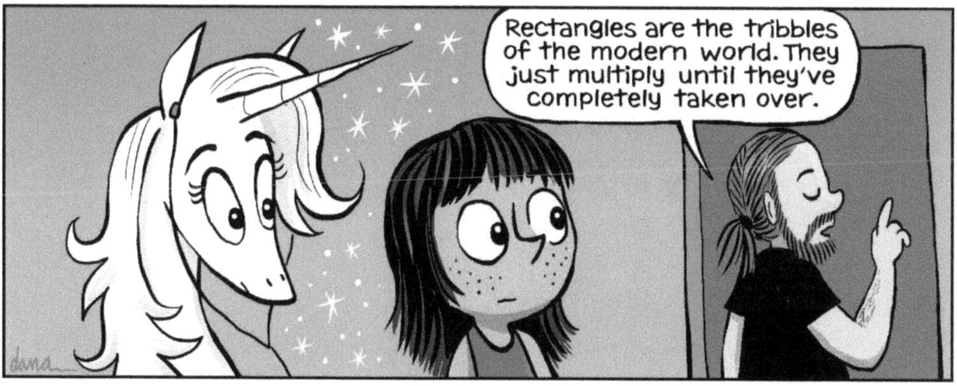
Rectangles are the tribbles of the modern world. They just multiply until they've completely taken over.
dana

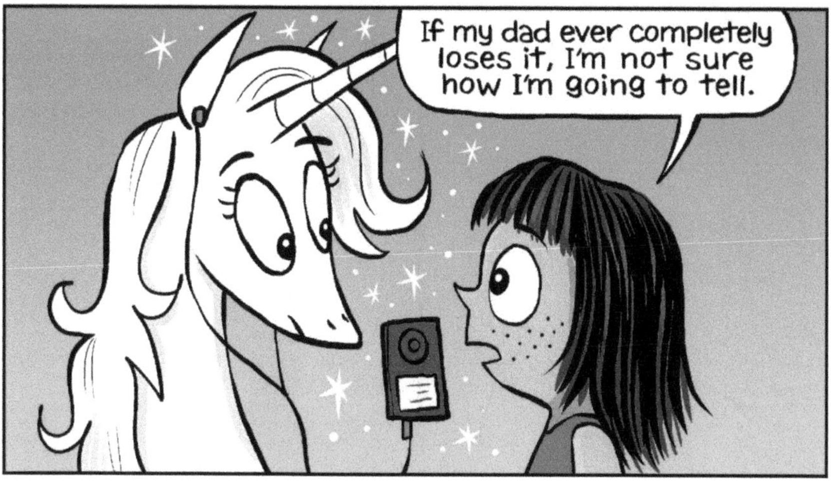
If my dad ever completely loses it, I'm not sure how I'm going to tell.

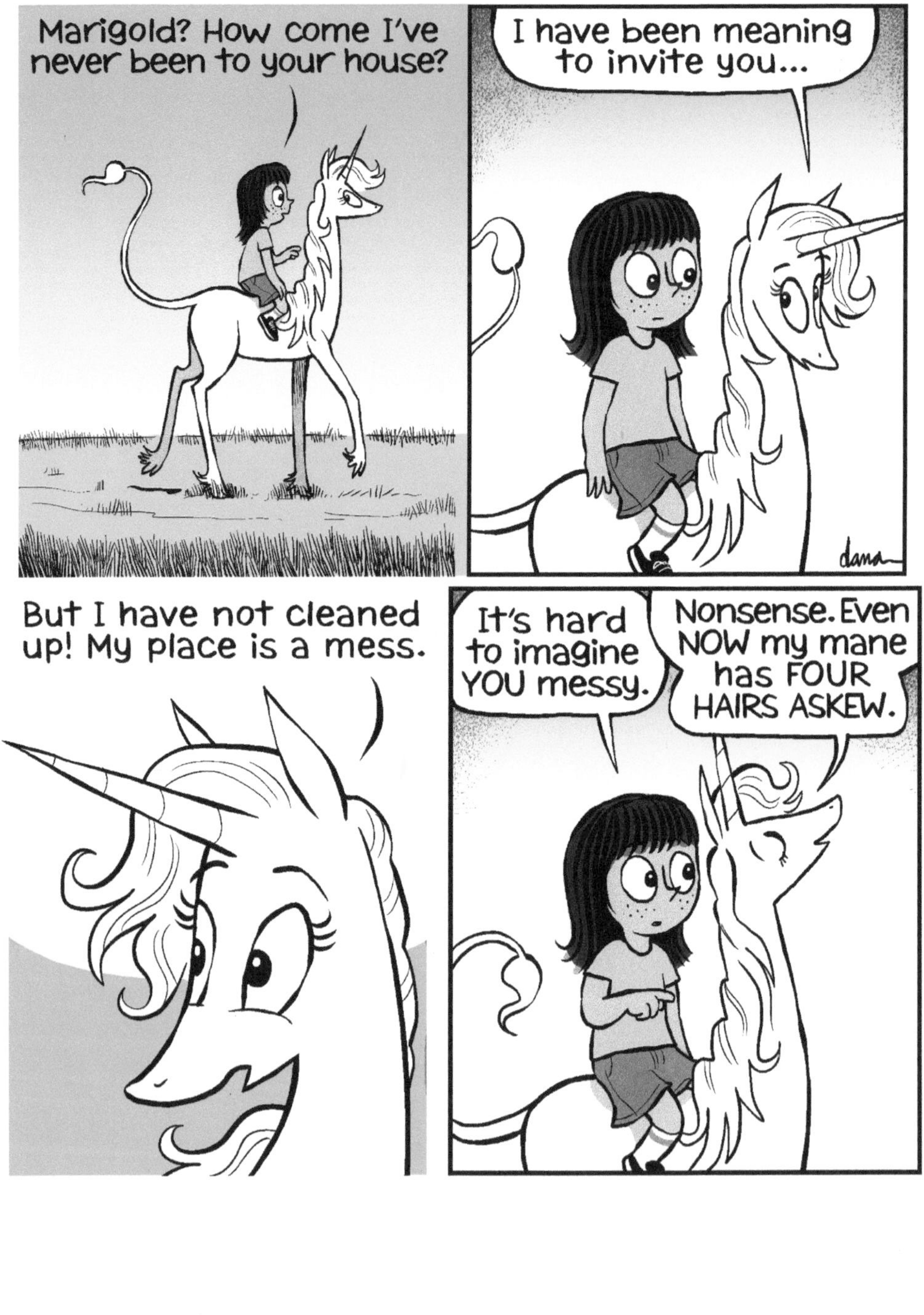
Marigold? How come I've never been to your house?
I have been meaning to invite you...
dana
But I have not cleaned up! My place is a mess.
It's hard to imagine YOU messy.
Nonsense. Even NOW my mane has FOUR HAIRS ASKEW.

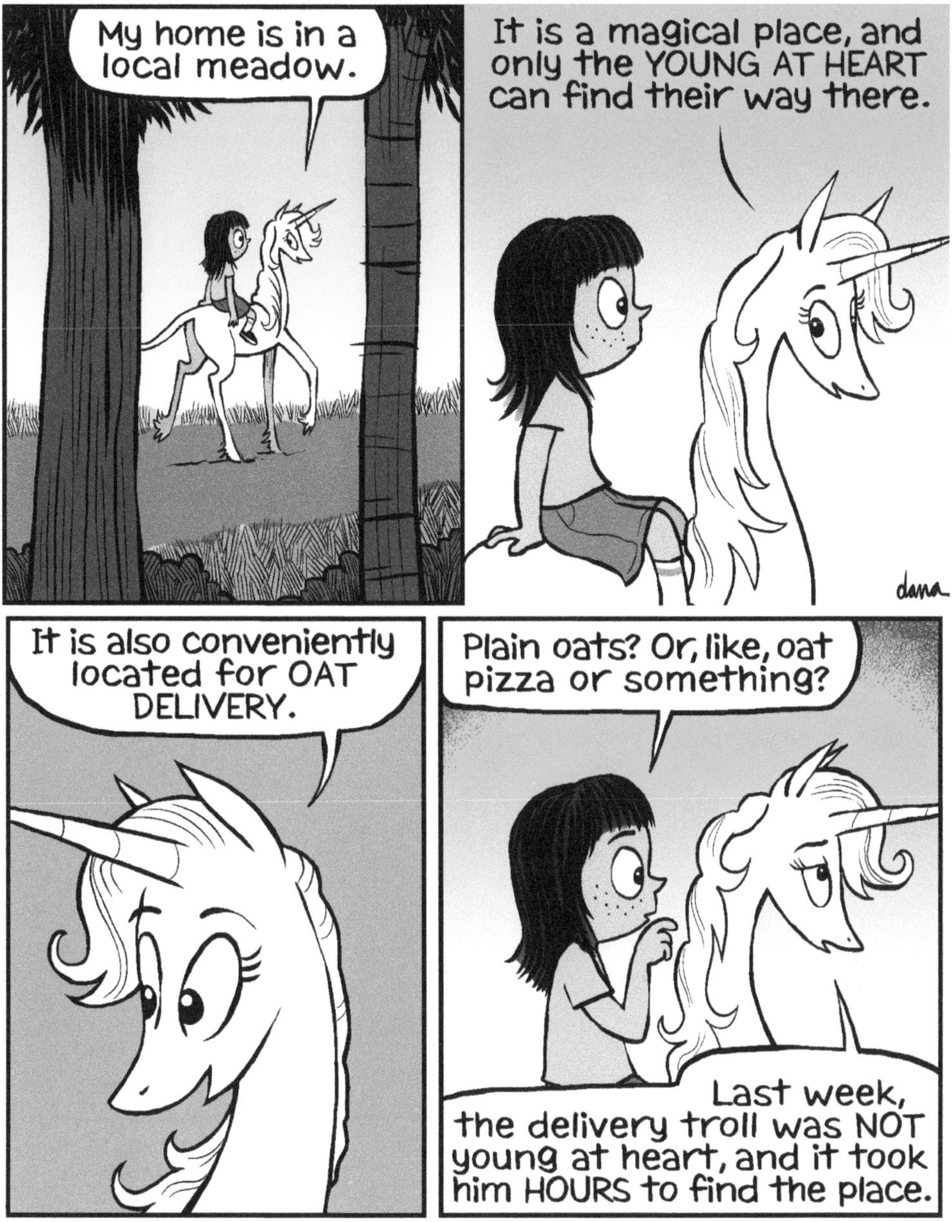
My home is in a local meadow.
It is a magical place, and only the YOUNG AT HEART can find their way there.
dana
It is also conveniently located for OAT DELIVERY.
Plain oats? Or, like, oat pizza or something?
Last week, the delivery troll was NOT young at heart, and it took him HOURS to find the place.

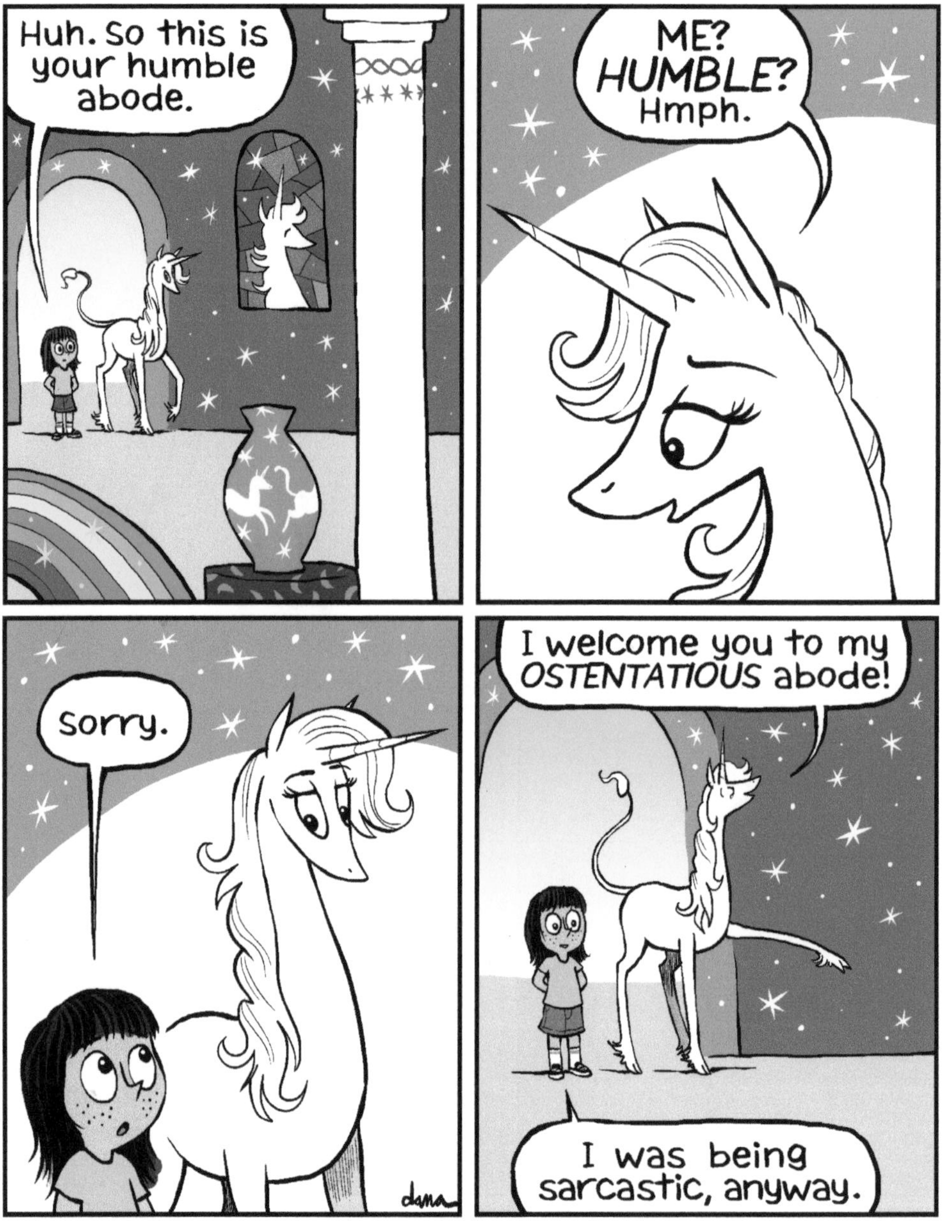
Huh. So this is your humble abode.
ME? *HUMBLE?* Hmph.
Sorry.
I welcome you to my *OSTENTATIOUS* abode!
I was being sarcastic, anyway.
dana

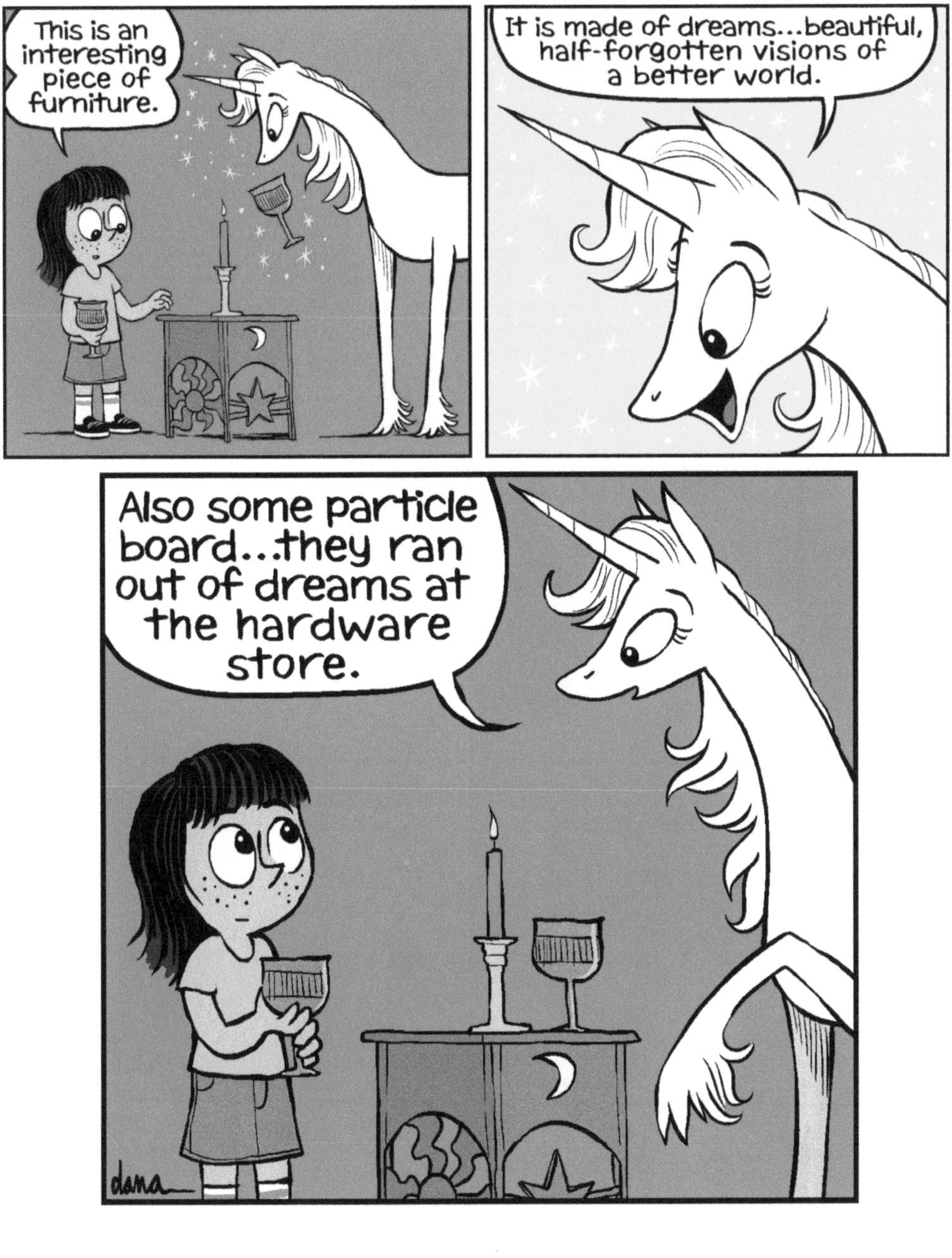
This is an interesting piece of furniture.
It is made of dreams...beautiful, half-forgotten visions of a better world.
Also some particle board...they ran out of dreams at the hardware store.
dana

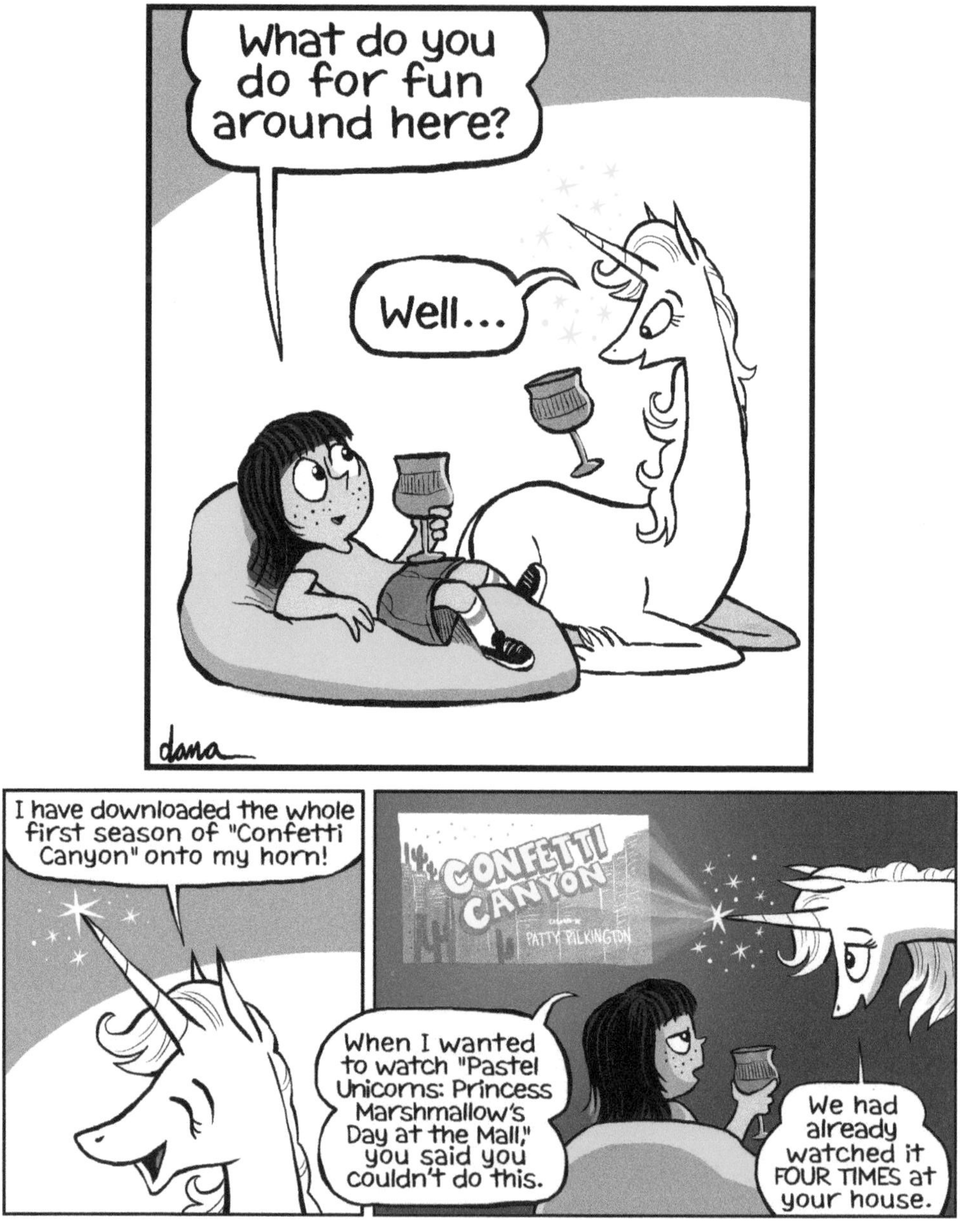

What do you do for fun around here?
Well...
dana
I have downloaded the whole first season of "Confetti Canyon" onto my horn!
CONFETTI CANYON
PATTY PILKINGTON
When I wanted to watch "Pastel Unicorns: Princess Marshmallow's Day at the Mall," you said you couldn't do this.
We had already watched it FOUR TIMES at your house.

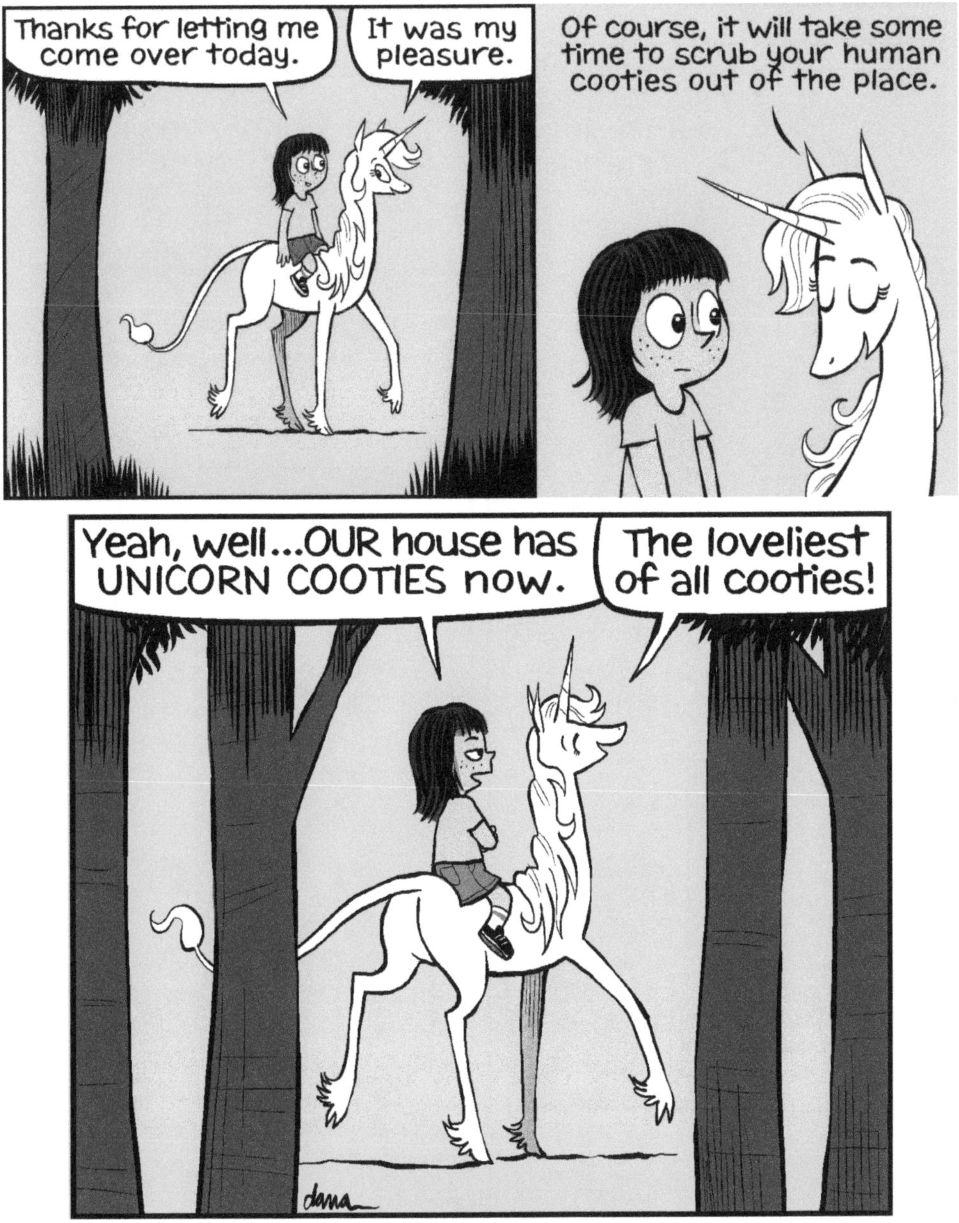
Thanks for letting me come over today.
It was my pleasure.
Of course, it will take some time to scrub your human cooties out of the place.
Yeah, well...OUR house has UNICORN COOTIES now.
The loveliest of all cooties!
dana

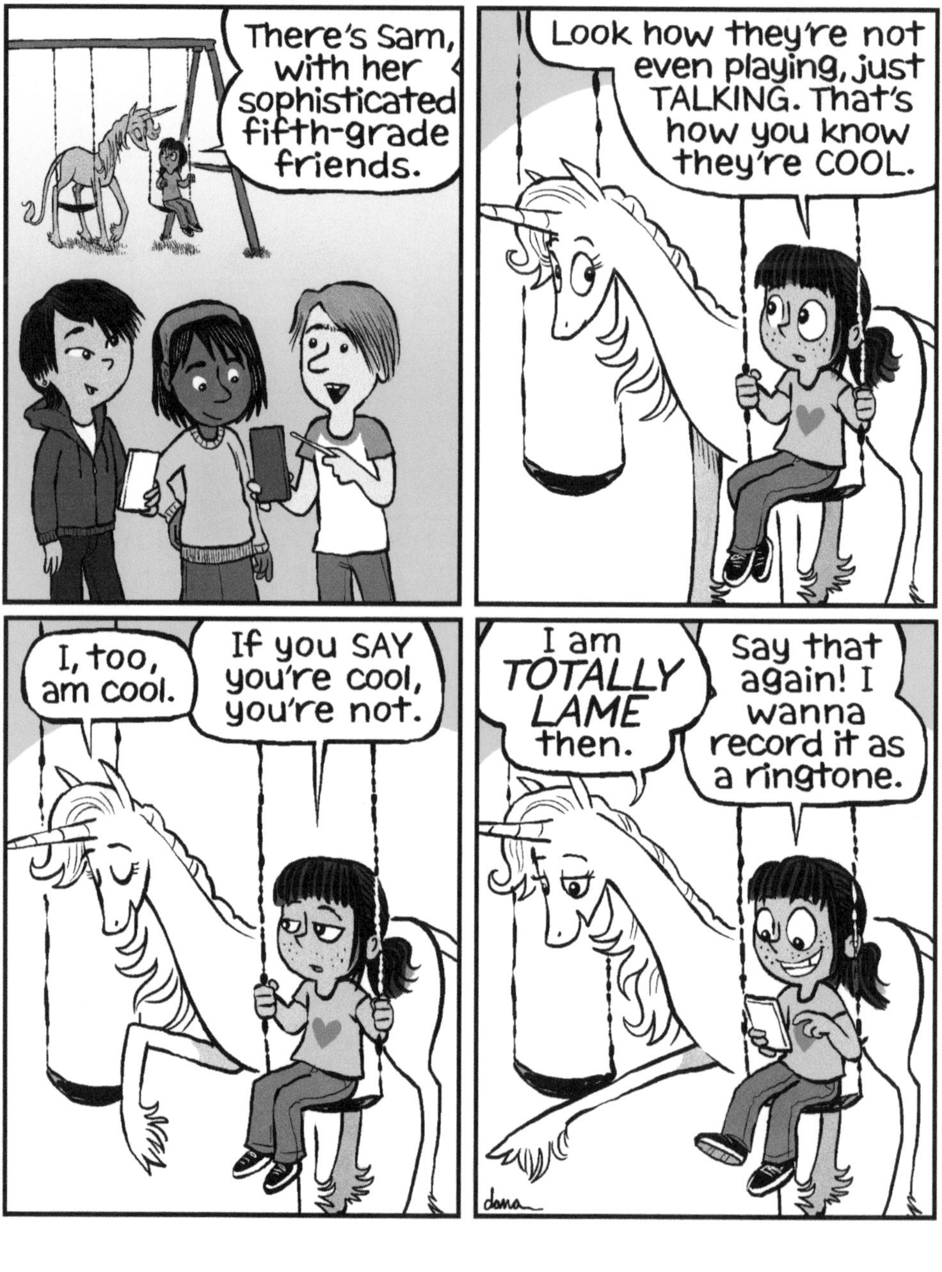
There's Sam, with her sophisticated fifth-grade friends.
Look how they're not even playing, just TALKING. That's how you know they're COOL.
I, too, am cool.
If you SAY you're cool, you're not.
I am *TOTALLY LAME* then.
Say that again! I wanna record it as a ringtone.
dana

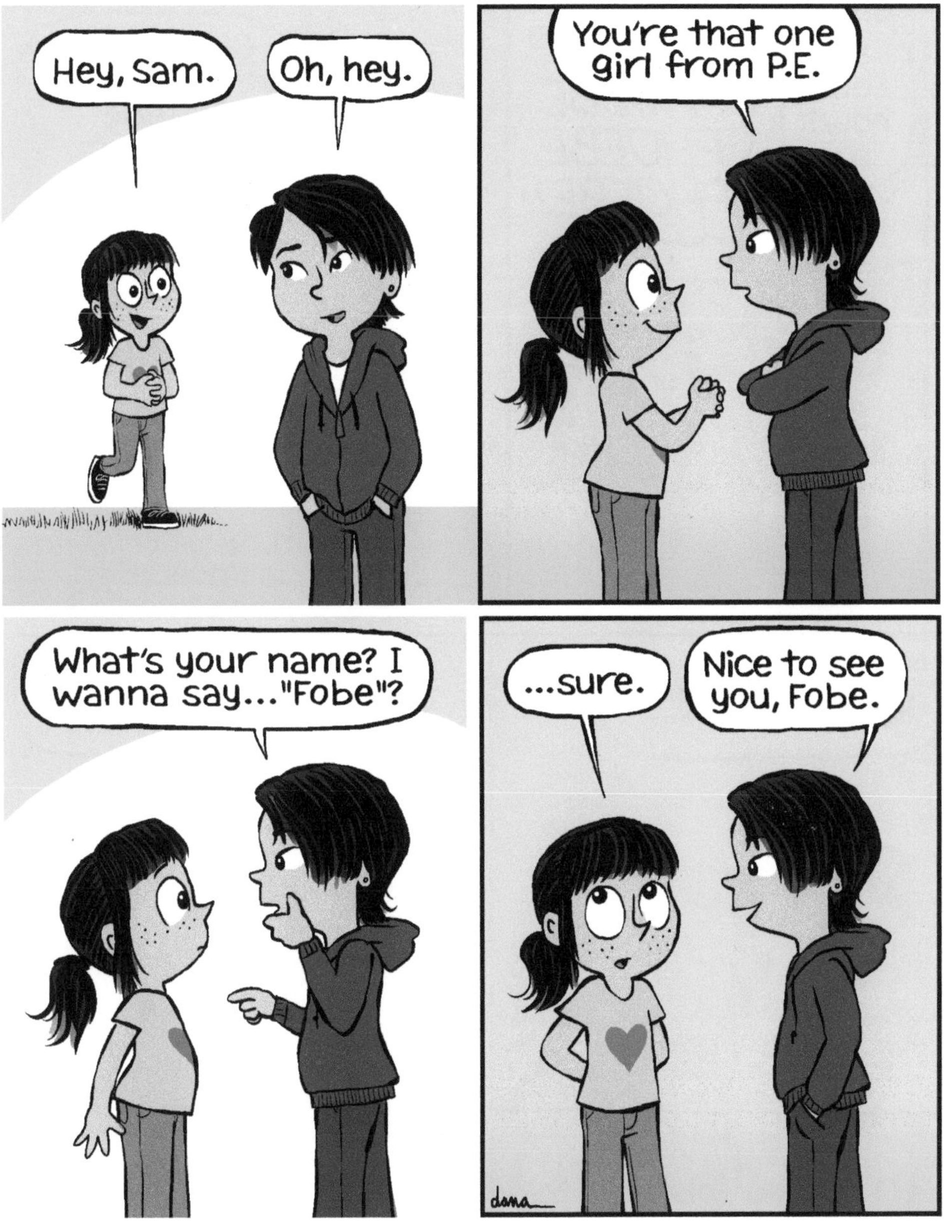
Hey, Sam.
Oh, hey.
You're that one girl from P.E.
What's your name? I wanna say..."Fobe"?
...sure.
Nice to see you, Fobe.
dana

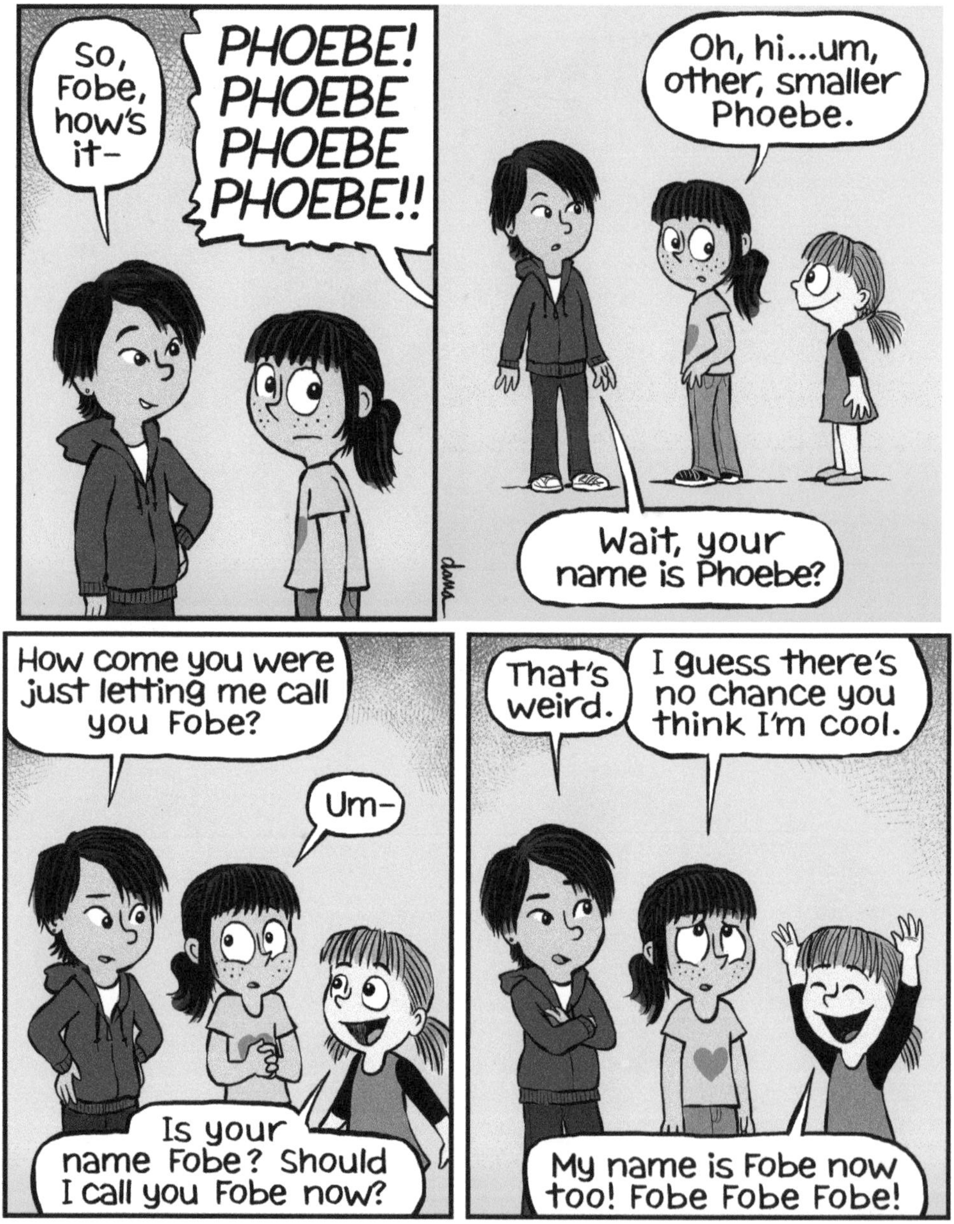
So, Fobe, how's it-
PHOEBE! PHOEBE PHOEBE PHOEBE!!
Oh, hi...um, other, smaller Phoebe.
Wait, your name is Phoebe?
How come you were just letting me call you Fobe?
Um-
Is your name Fobe? Should I call you Fobe now?
That's weird.
I guess there's no chance you think I'm cool.
My name is Fobe now too! Fobe Fobe Fobe!

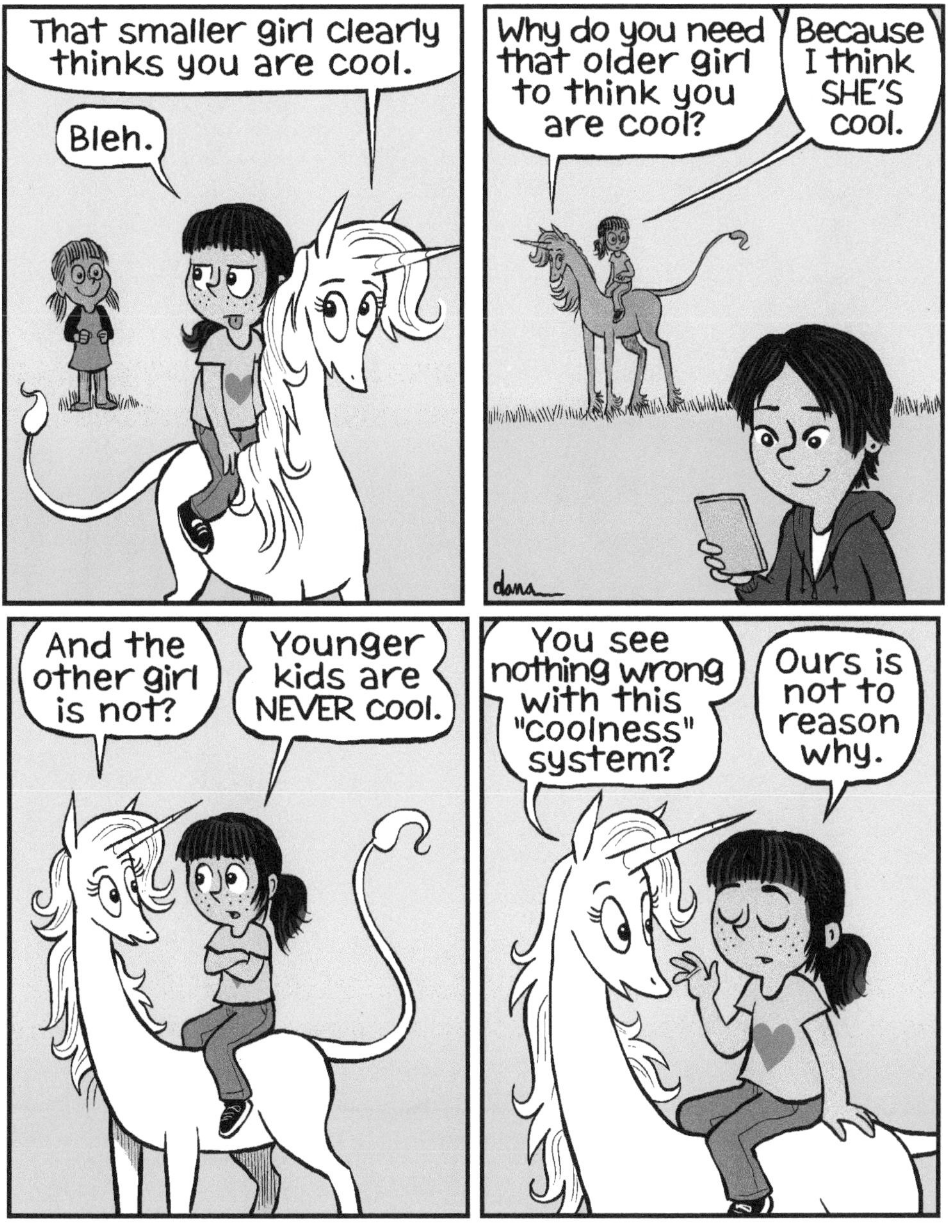
That smaller girl clearly thinks you are cool.
Bleh.
Why do you need that older girl to think you are cool?
Because I think SHE'S cool.
dana
And the other girl is not?
Younger kids are NEVER cool.
You see nothing wrong with this "coolness" system?
Ours is not to reason why.

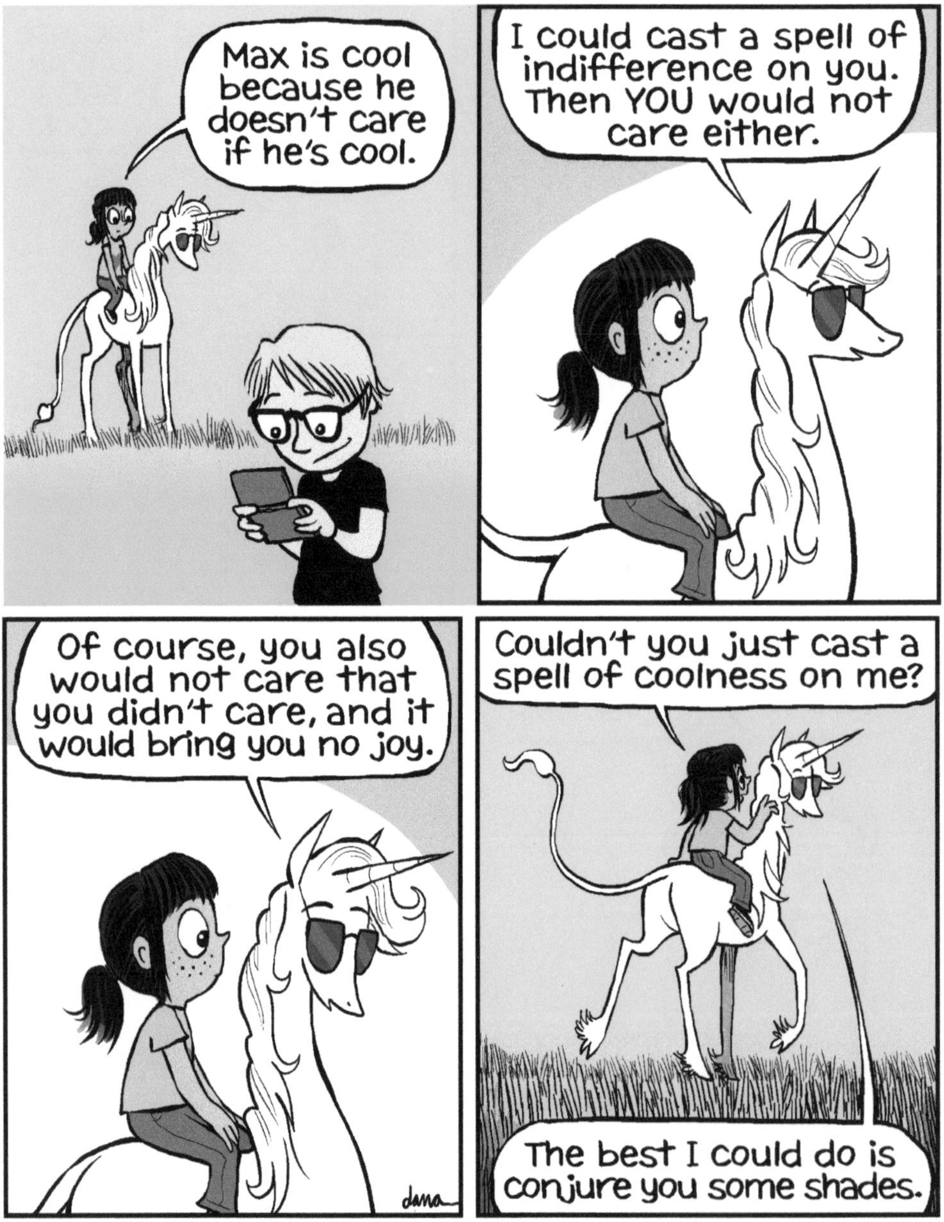
Max is cool because he doesn't care if he's cool.
I could cast a spell of indifference on you. Then YOU would not care either.
Of course, you also would not care that you didn't care, and it would bring you no joy.
dana
Couldn't you just cast a spell of coolness on me?
The best I could do is conjure you some shades.

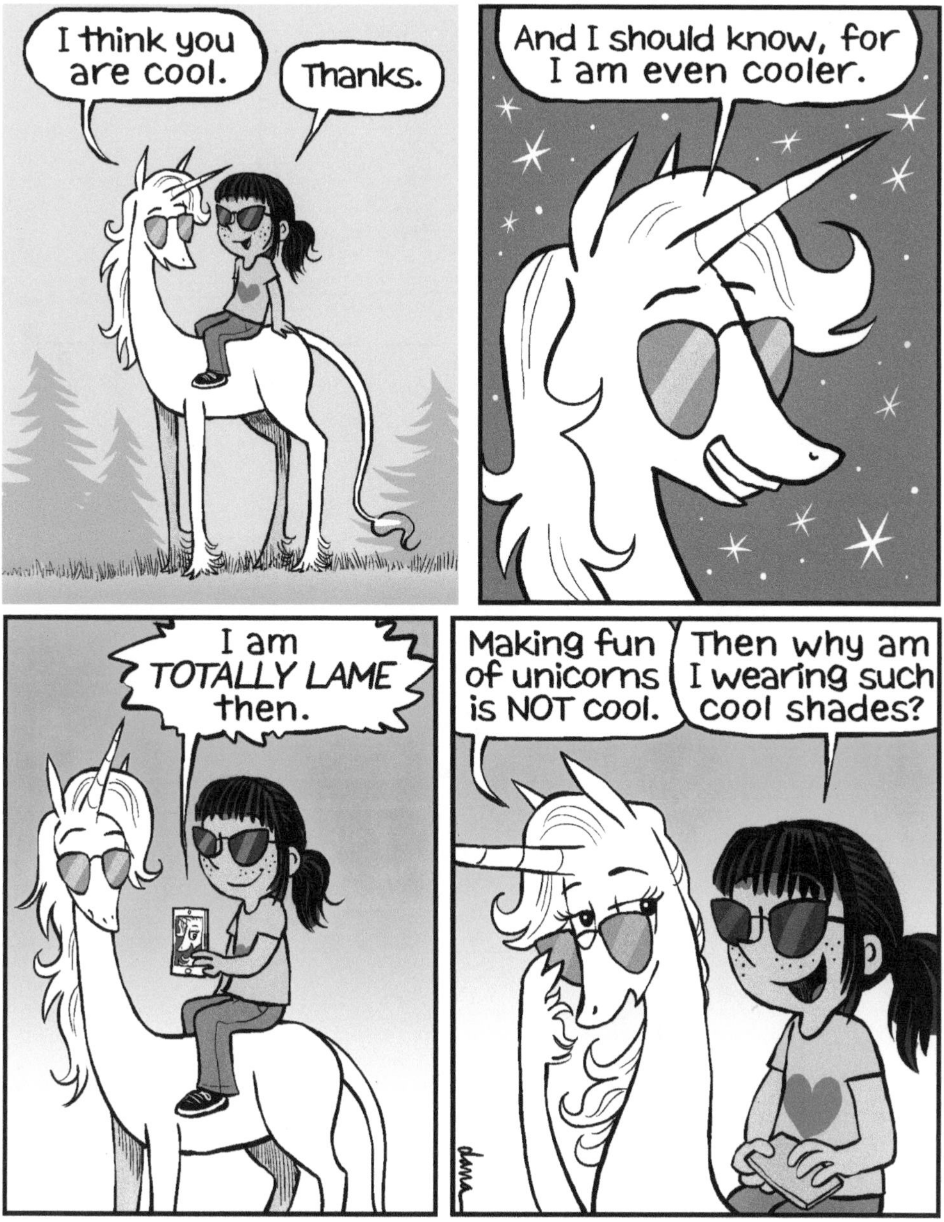

I think you are cool.
Thanks.
And I should know, for I am even cooler.
I am *TOTALLY LAME* then.
Making fun of unicorns is NOT cool.
Then why am I wearing such cool shades?

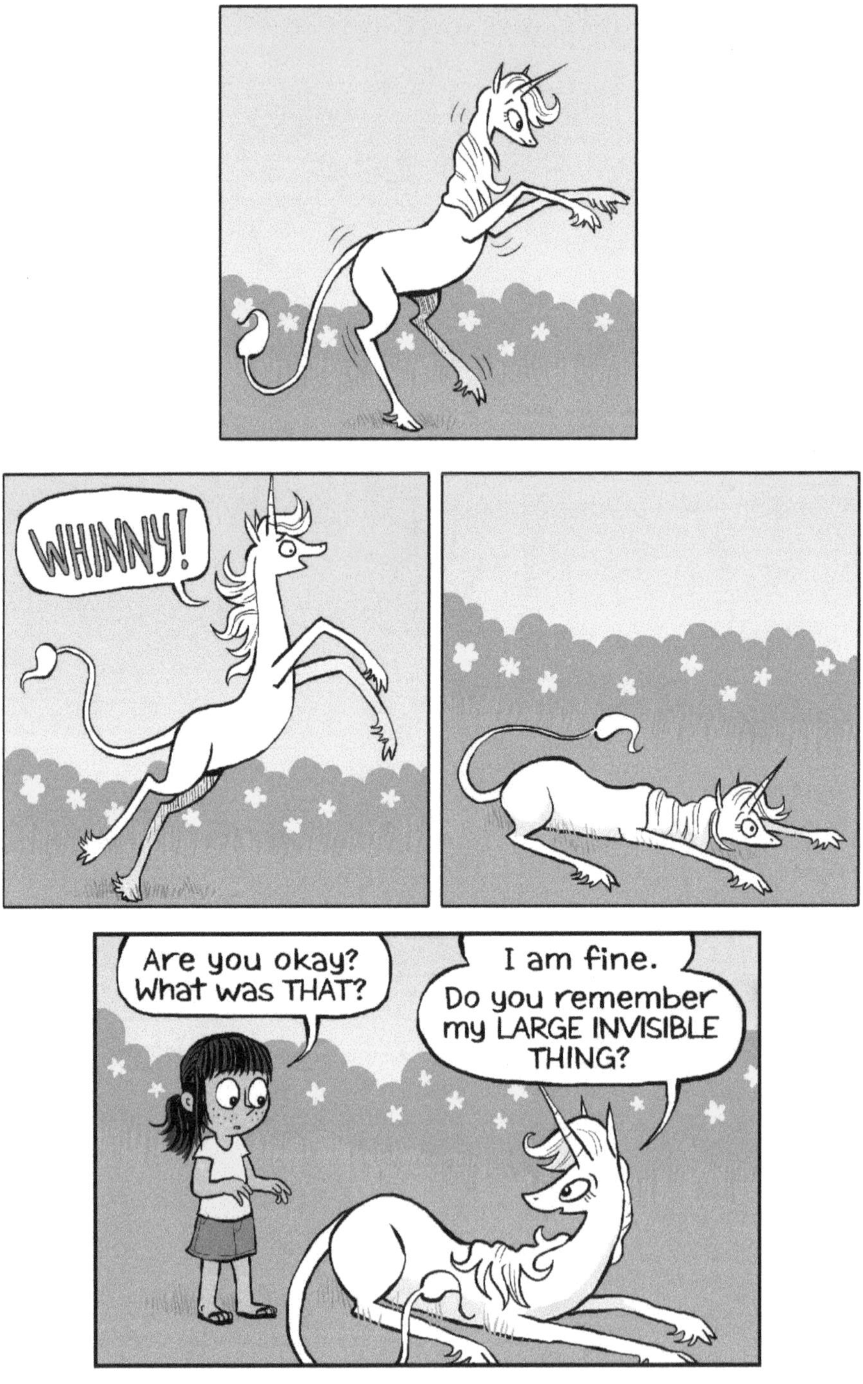
WHINNY!
Are you okay? What was THAT?
I am fine. Do you remember my LARGE INVISIBLE THING?

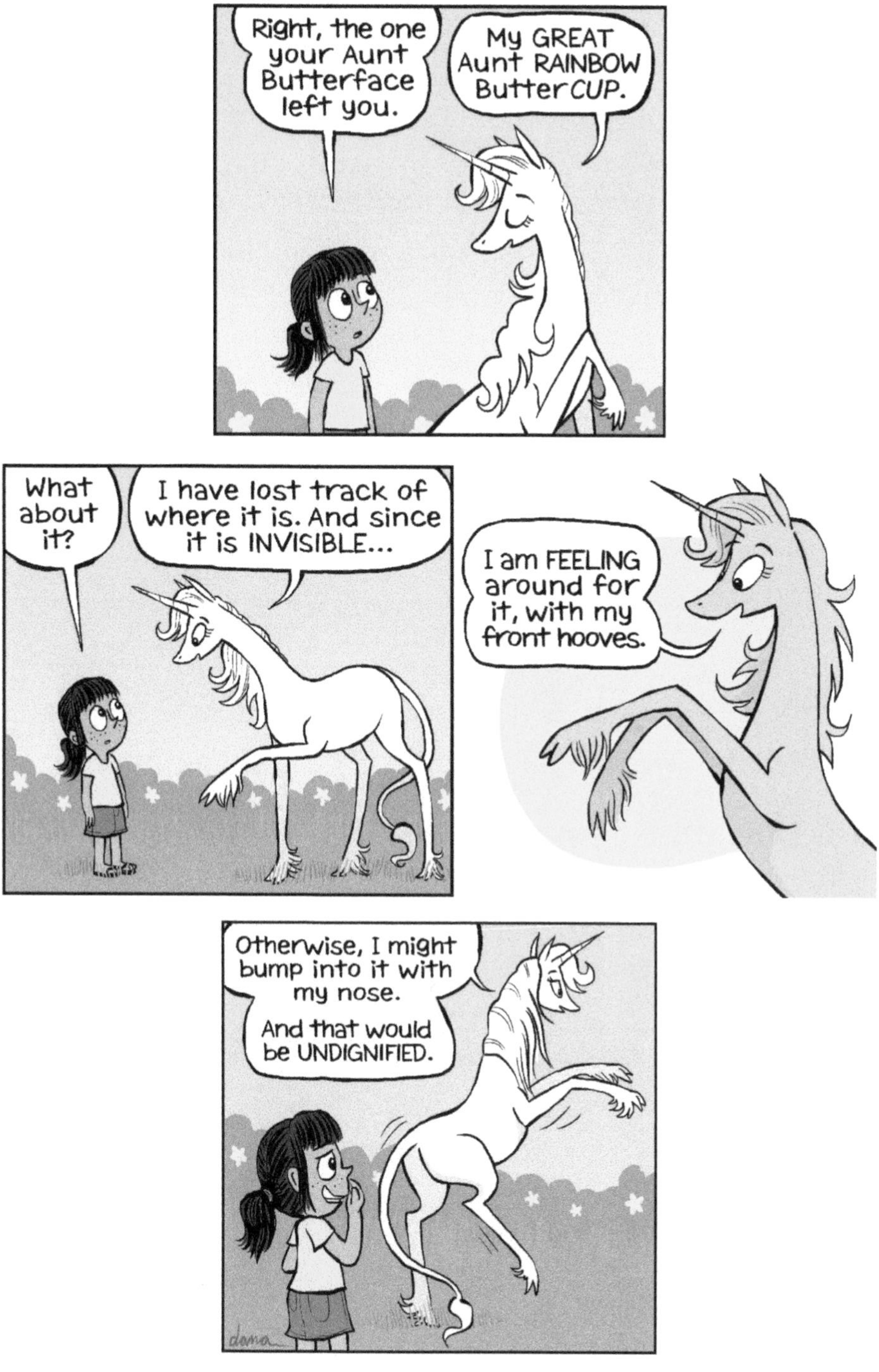
Right, the one your Aunt Butterface left you.
My GREAT Aunt RAINBOW ButterCUP.
What about it?
I have lost track of where it is. And since it is INVISIBLE...
I am FEELING around for it, with my front hooves.
Otherwise, I might bump into it with my nose.
And that would be UNDIGNIFIED.
dana

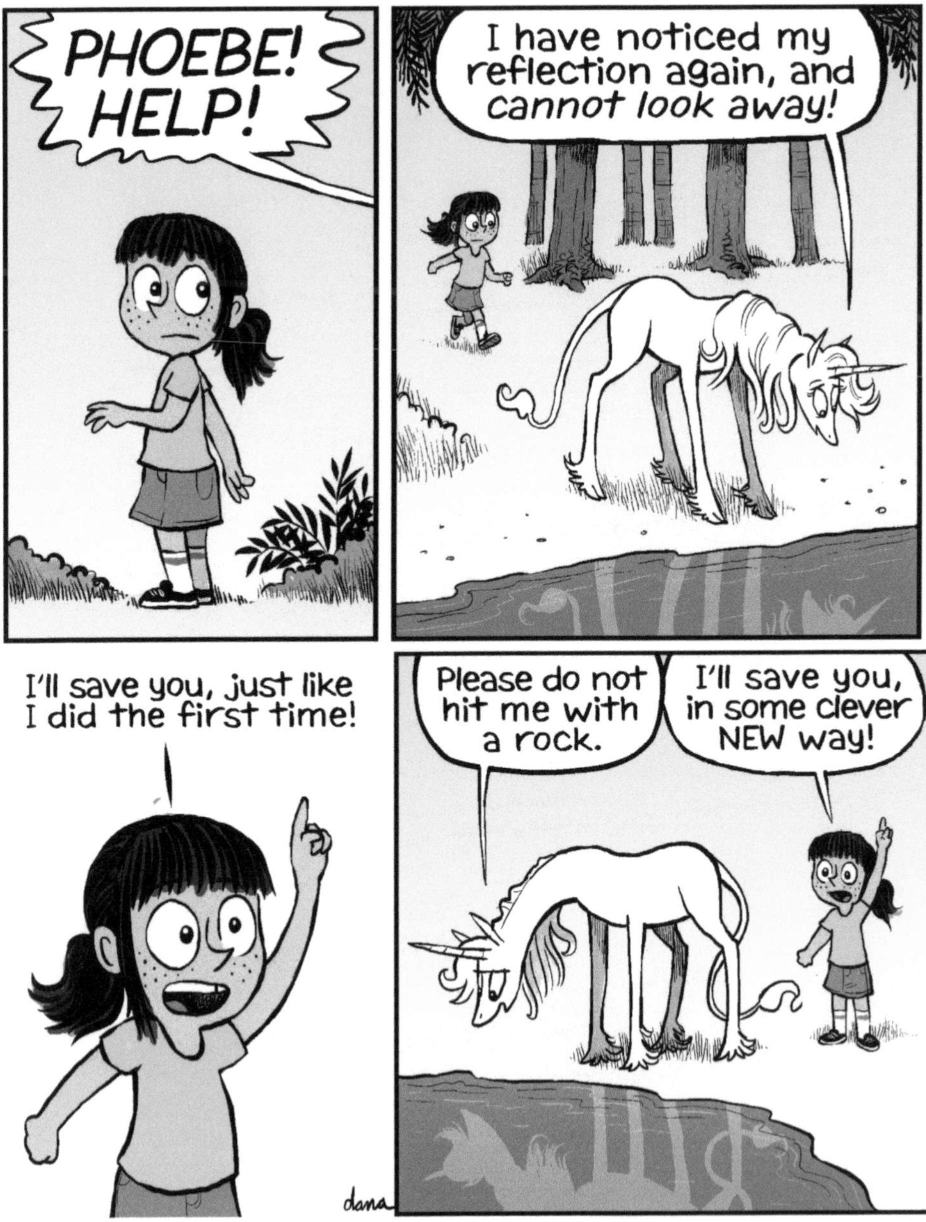
PHOEBE! HELP!
I have noticed my reflection again, and cannot look away!
I'll save you, just like I did the first time!
Please do not hit me with a rock.
I'll save you, in some clever NEW way!
dana

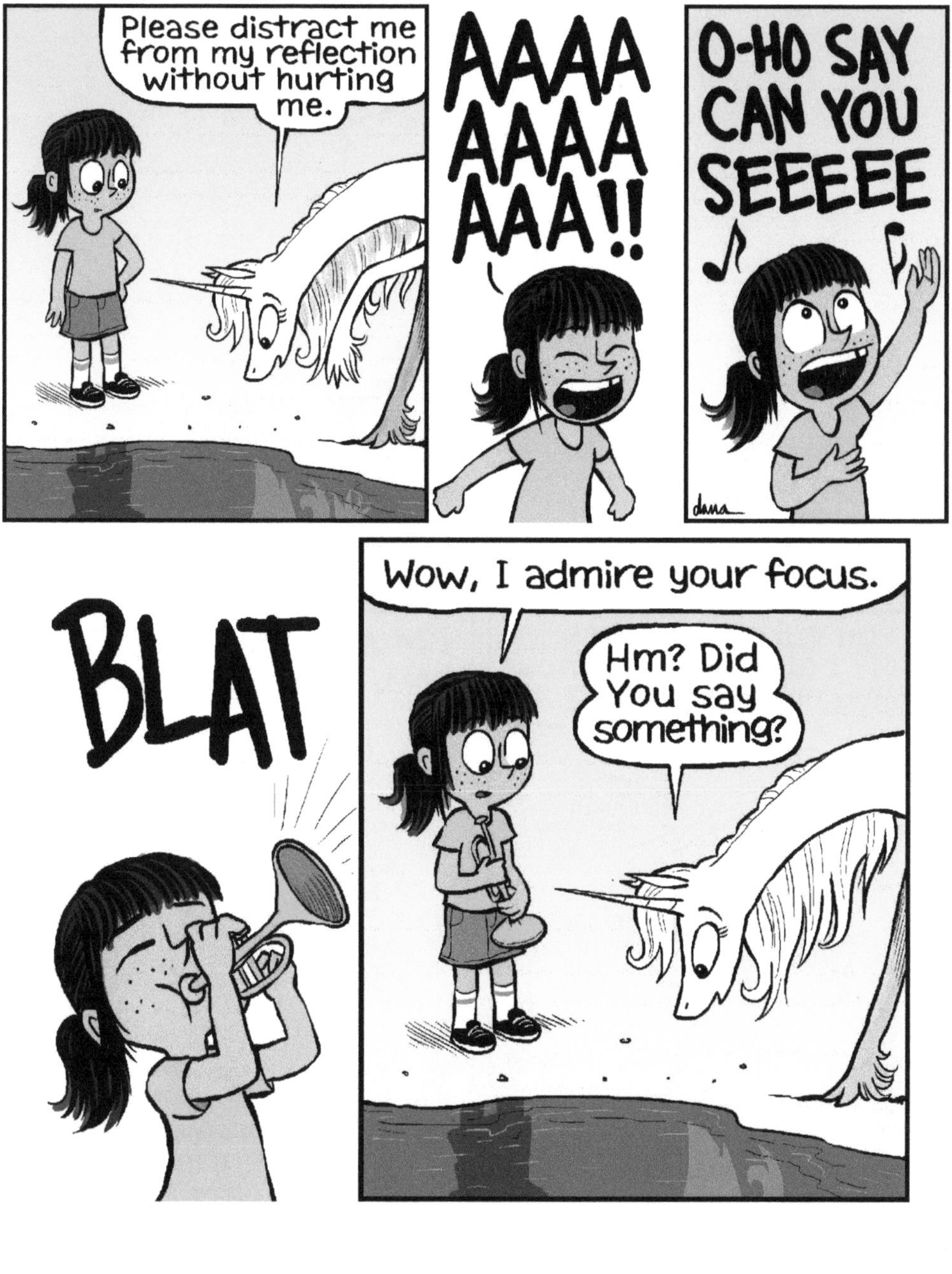
Please distract me from my reflection without hurting me.
AAAAAAAAAAA!!
O-HO SAY CAN YOU SEEEEE
dana
BLAT
Wow, I admire your focus.
Hm? Did You say something?

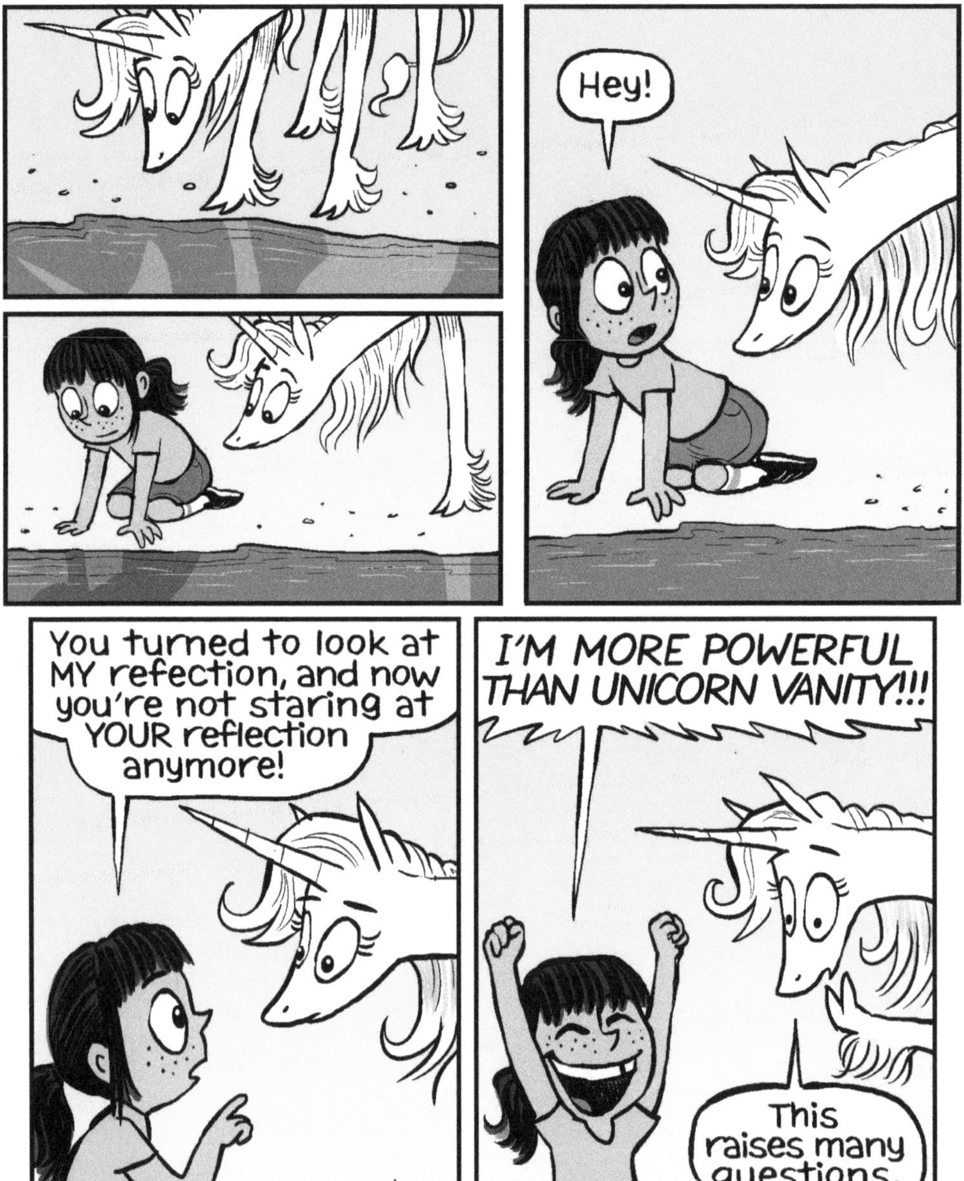
Hey!
You turned to look at MY refection, and now you're not staring at YOUR reflection anymore!
dana
I'M MORE POWERFUL THAN UNICORN VANITY!!!
This raises many questions.

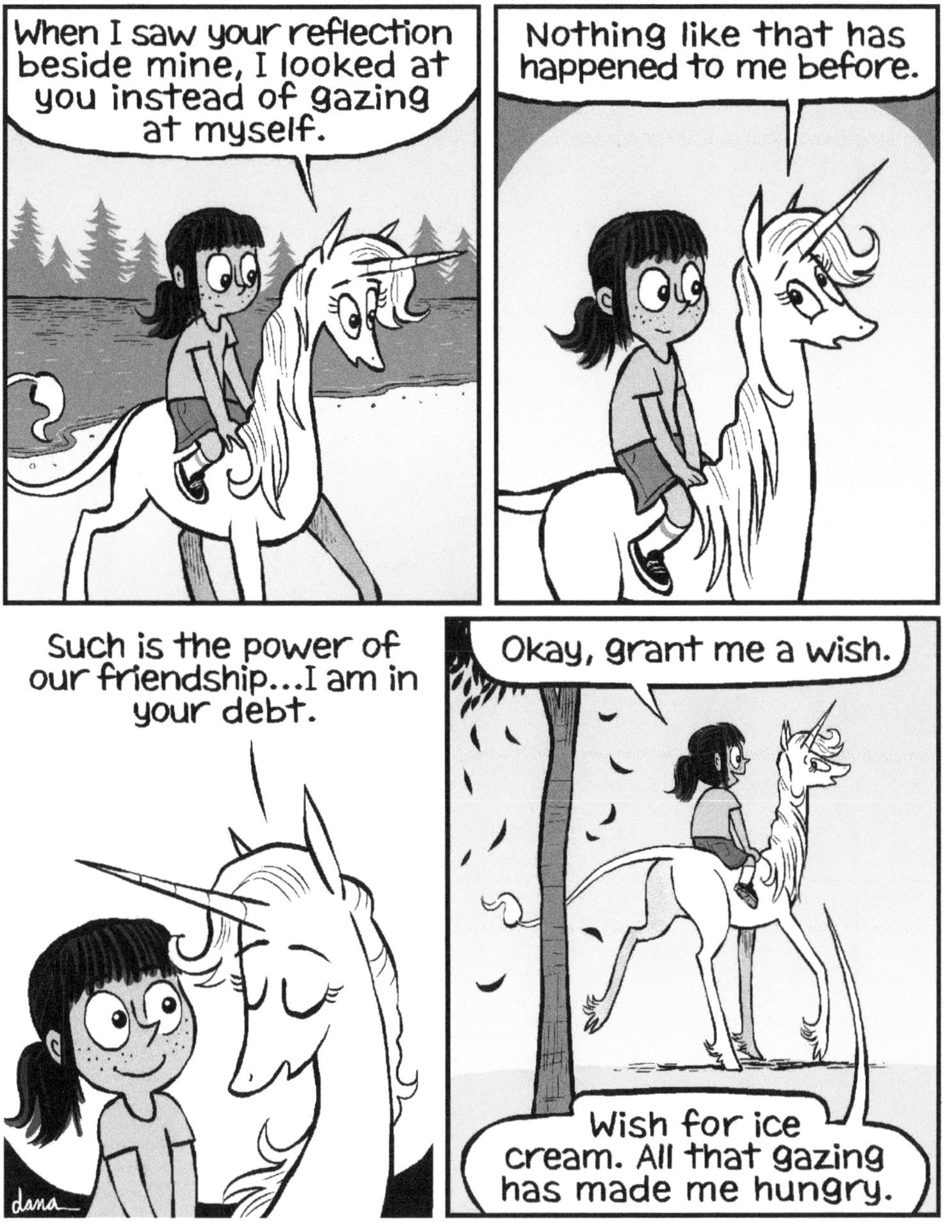
When I saw your reflection beside mine, I looked at you instead of gazing at myself.
Nothing like that has happened to me before.
Such is the power of our friendship...I am in your debt.
dana
Okay, grant me a wish.
Wish for ice cream. All that gazing has made me hungry.

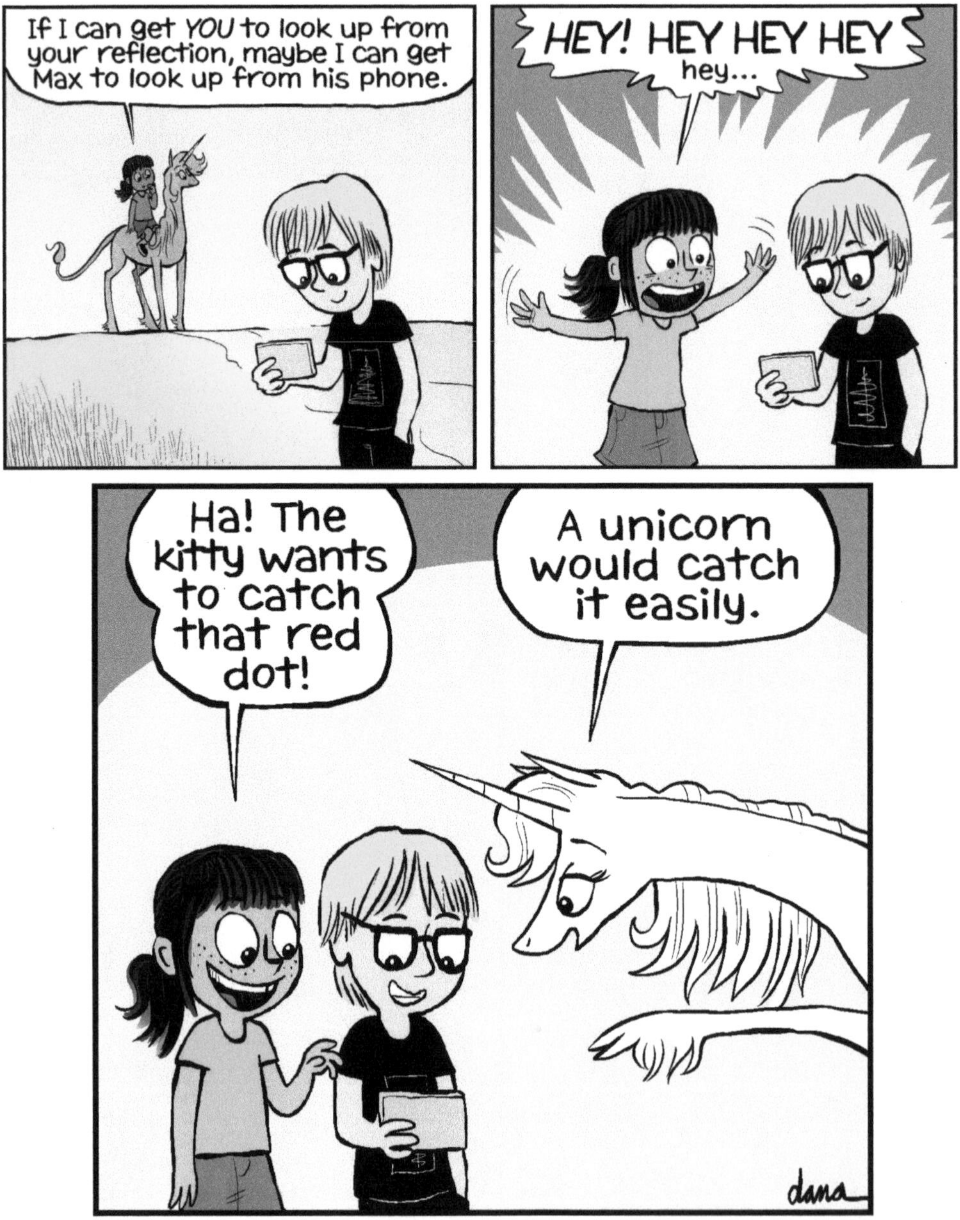

If I can get *YOU* to look up from your reflection, maybe I can get Max to look up from his phone.
*HEY!* HEY HEY HEY
hey...
Ha! The kitty wants to catch that red dot!
A unicorn would catch it easily.
dana

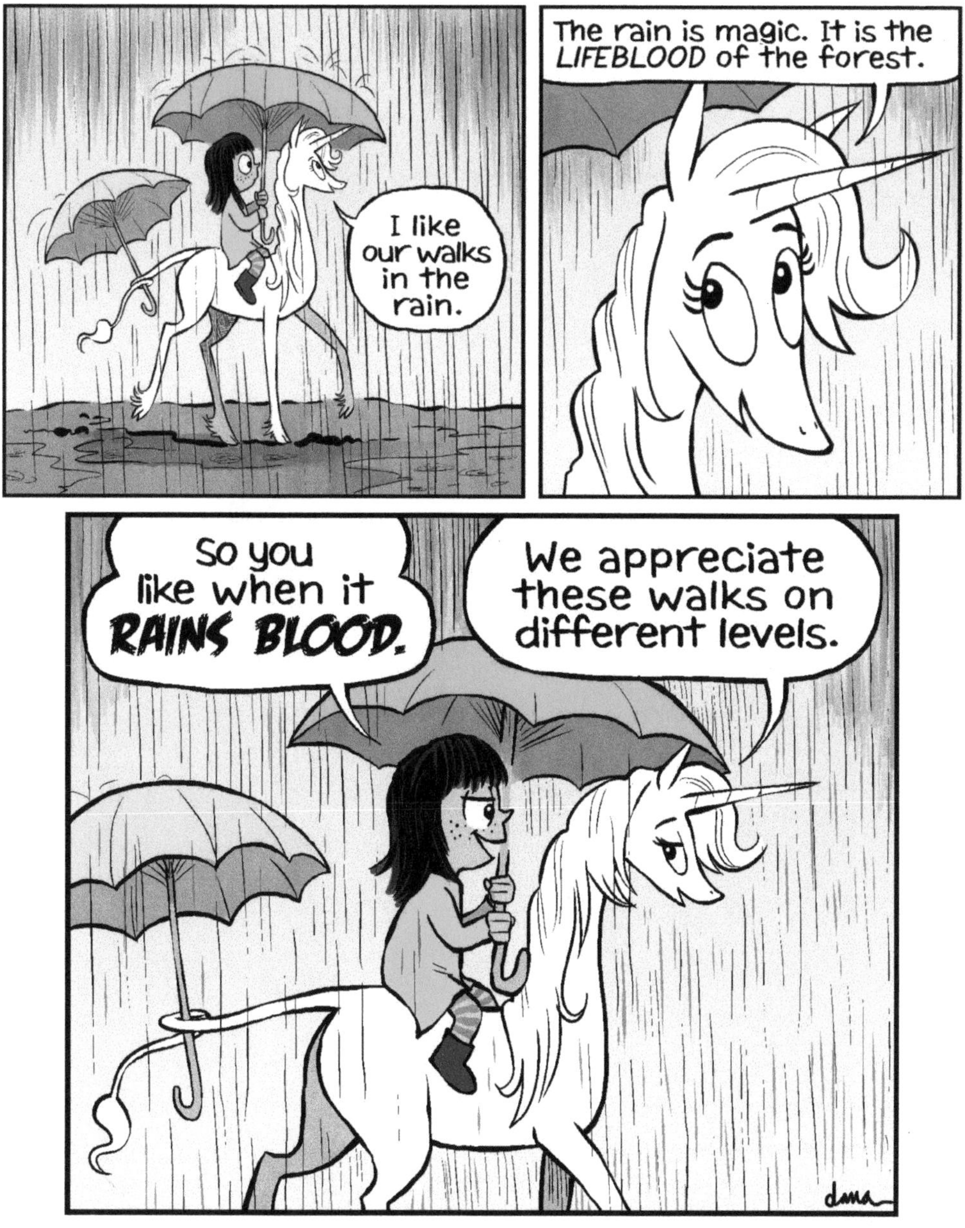
I like our walks in the rain.
The rain is magic. It is the *LIFEBLOOD* of the forest.
So you like when it **RAINS BLOOD.**
We appreciate these walks on different levels.
dana

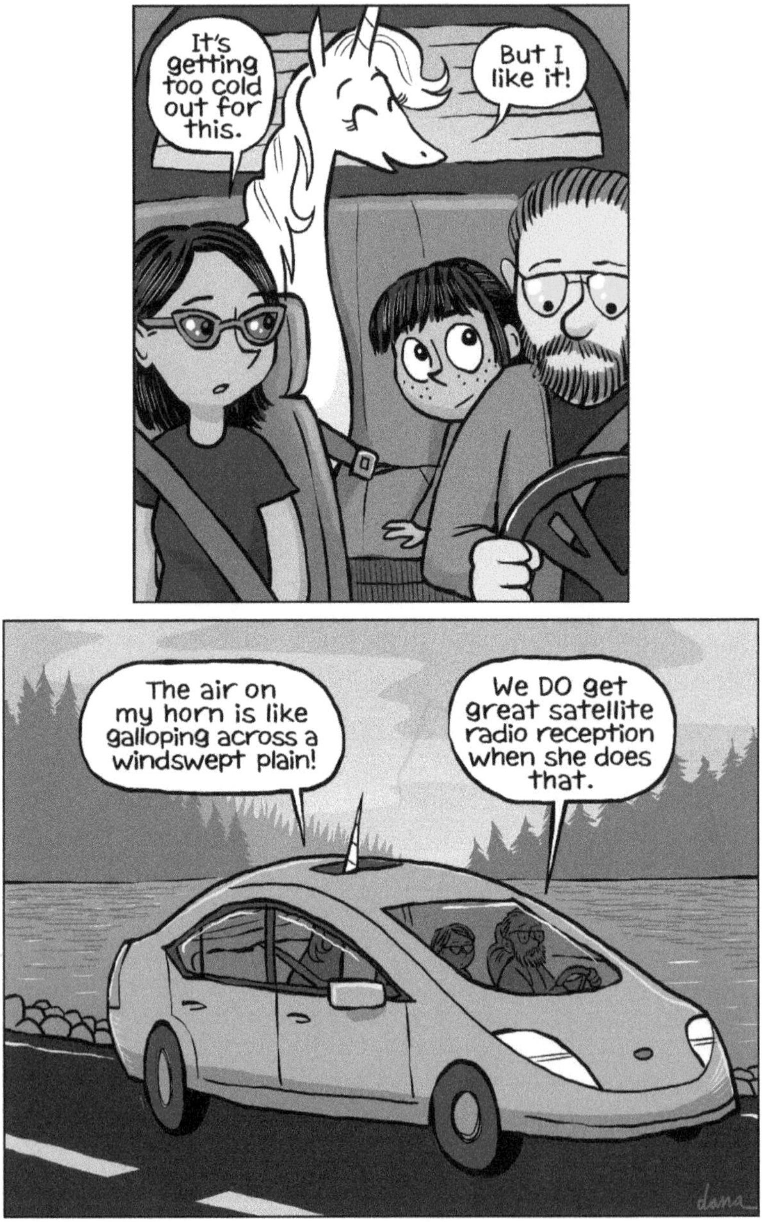
It's getting too cold out for this.
But I like it!
The air on my horn is like galloping across a windswept plain!
We DO get great satellite radio reception when she does that.
dana

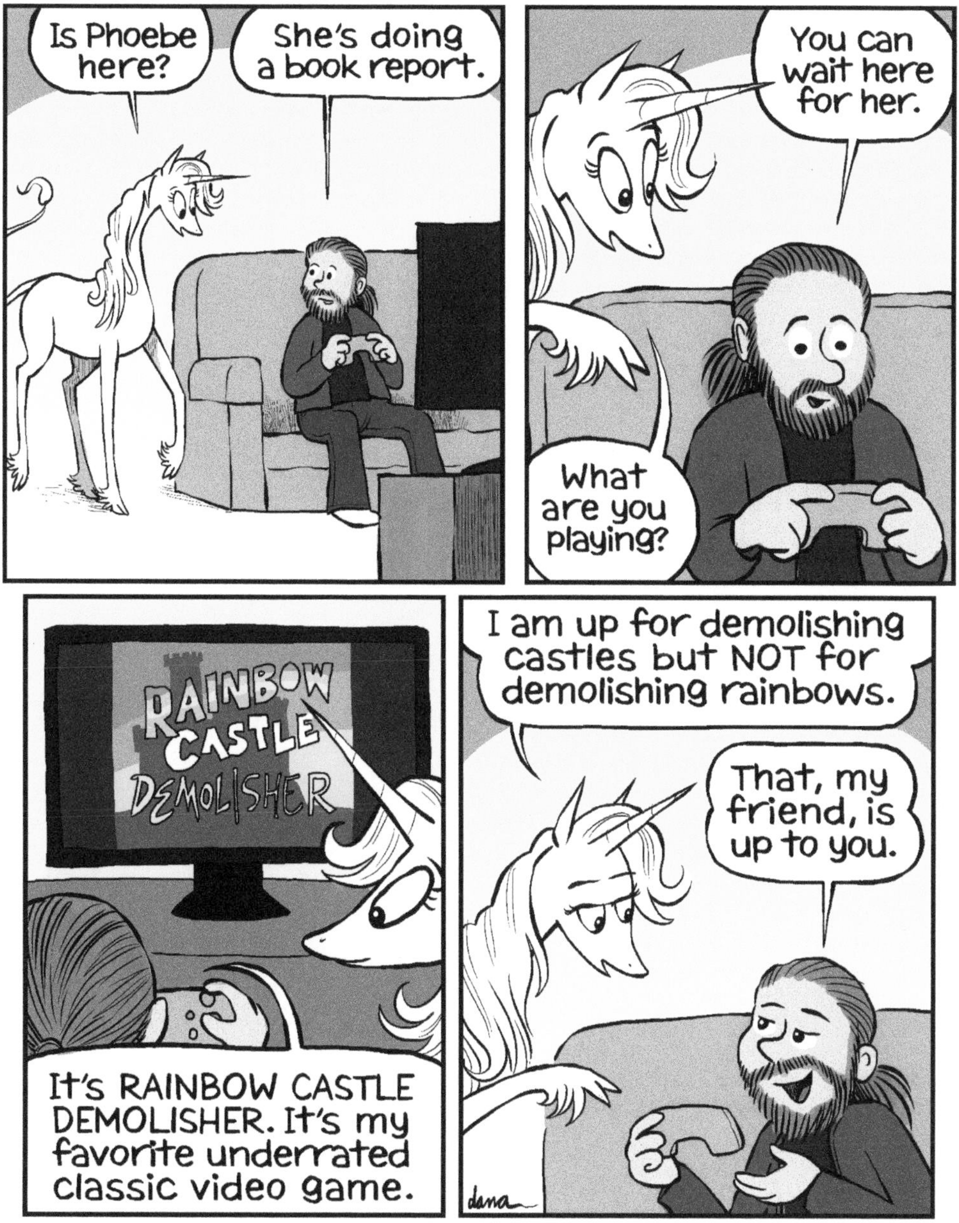
Is Phoebe here?
She's doing a book report.
You can wait here for her.
What are you playing?
RAINBOW CASTLE DEMOLISHER
It's RAINBOW CASTLE DEMOLISHER. It's my favorite underrated classic video game.
I am up for demolishing castles but NOT for demolishing rainbows.
That, my friend, is up to you.
dana

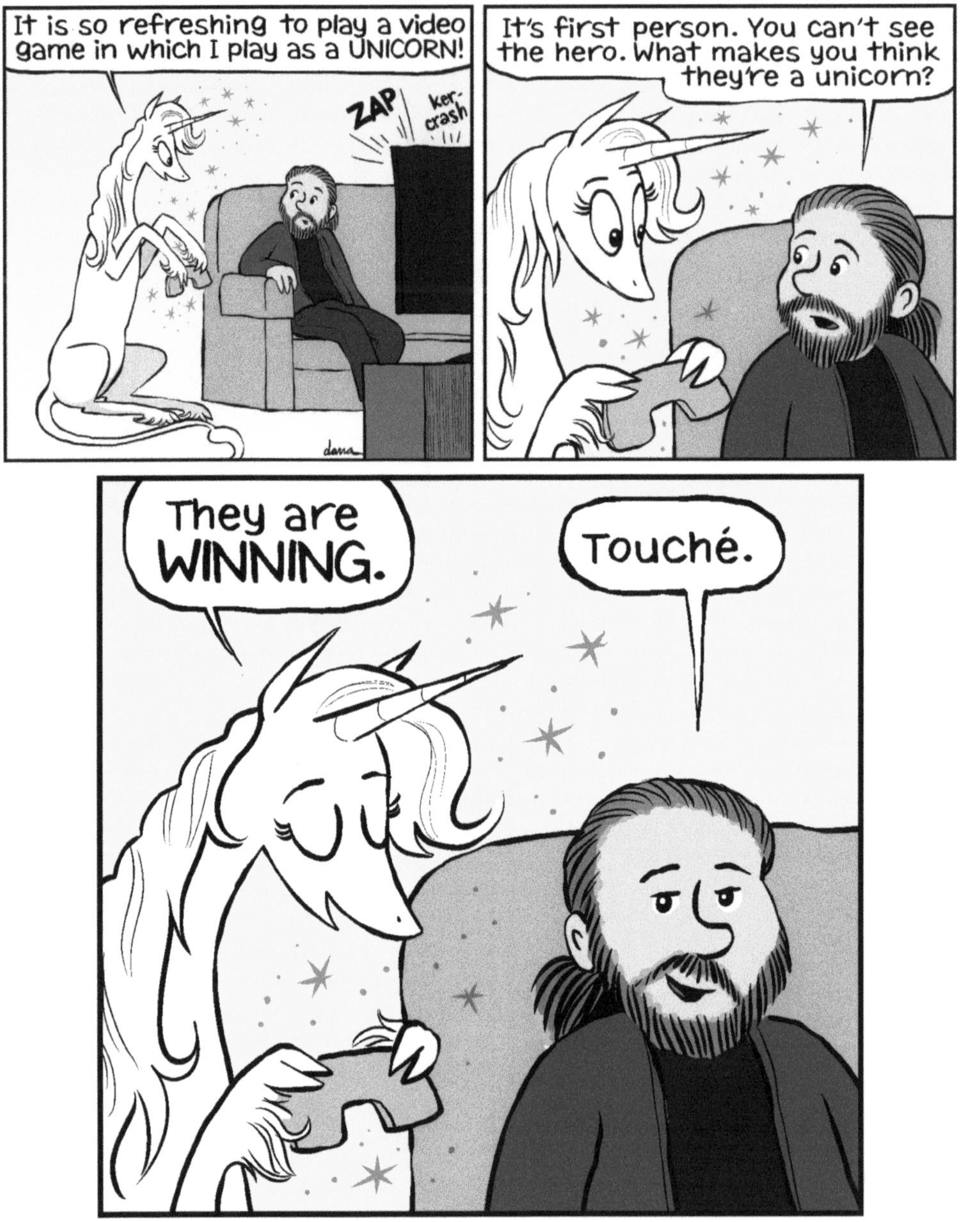
It is so refreshing to play a video game in which I play as a UNICORN!
ZAP
ker-crash
dana
It's first person. You can't see the hero. What makes you think they're a unicorn?
They are WINNING.
Touché.

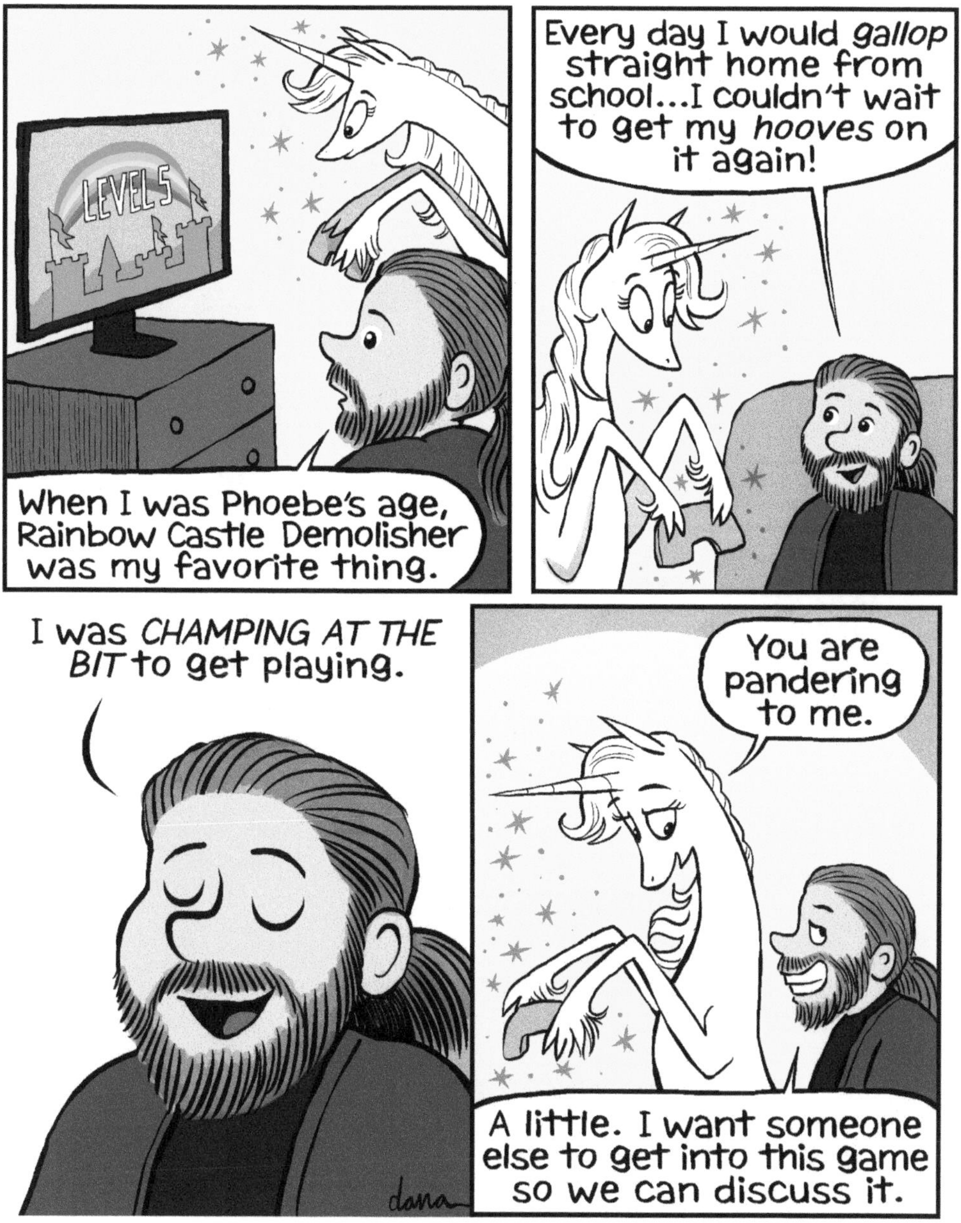
LEVEL 5
When I was Phoebe's age, Rainbow Castle Demolisher was my favorite thing.
Every day I would *gallop* straight home from school...I couldn't wait to get my *hooves* on it again!
I was *CHAMPING AT THE BIT* to get playing.
You are pandering to me.
A little. I want someone else to get into this game so we can discuss it.
dana

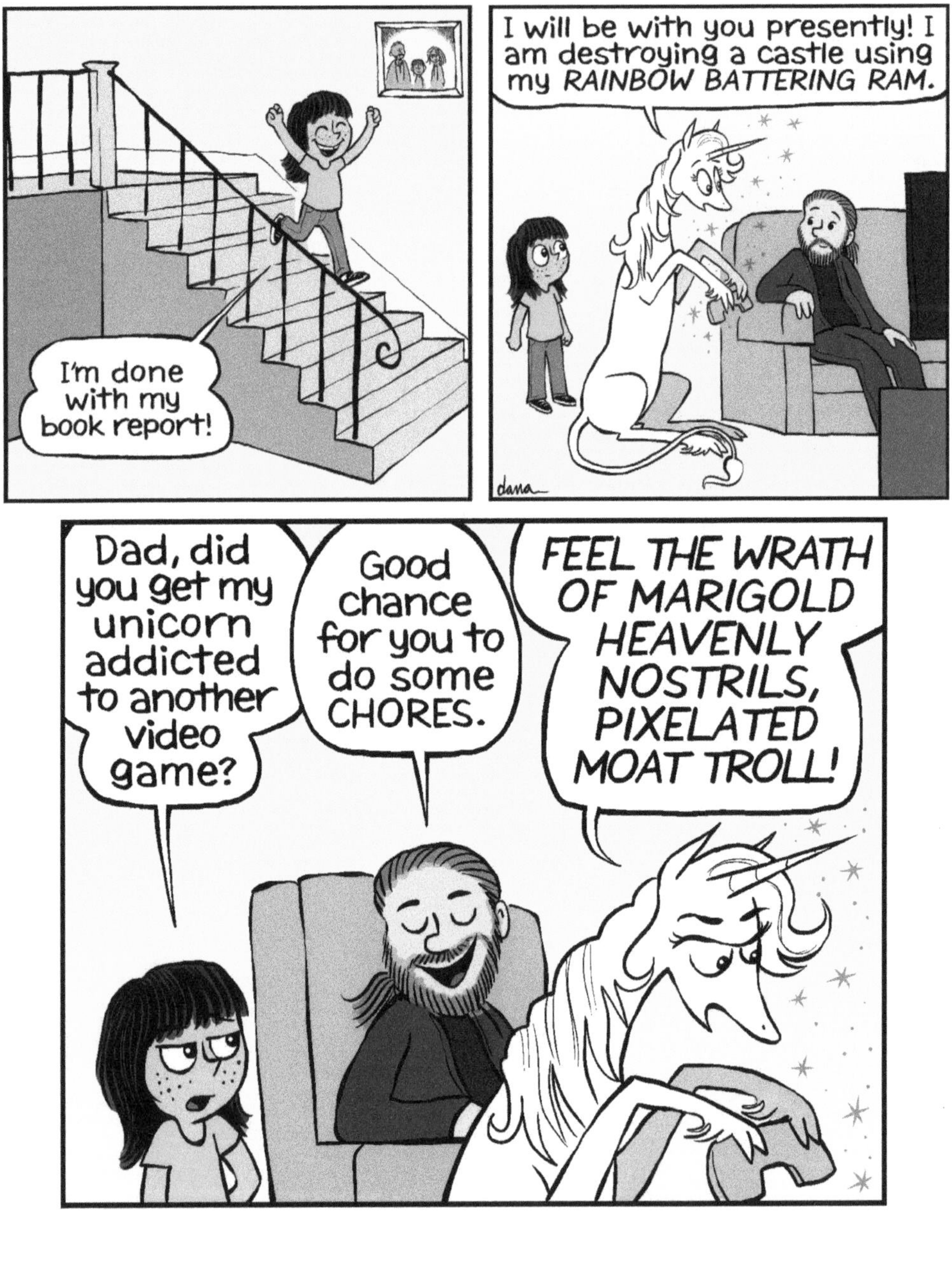
I'm done with my book report!
I will be with you presently! I am destroying a castle using my *RAINBOW BATTERING RAM.*
dana
Dad, did you get my unicorn addicted to another video game?
Good chance for you to do some CHORES.
*FEEL THE WRATH OF MARIGOLD HEAVENLY NOSTRILS, PIXELATED MOAT TROLL!*

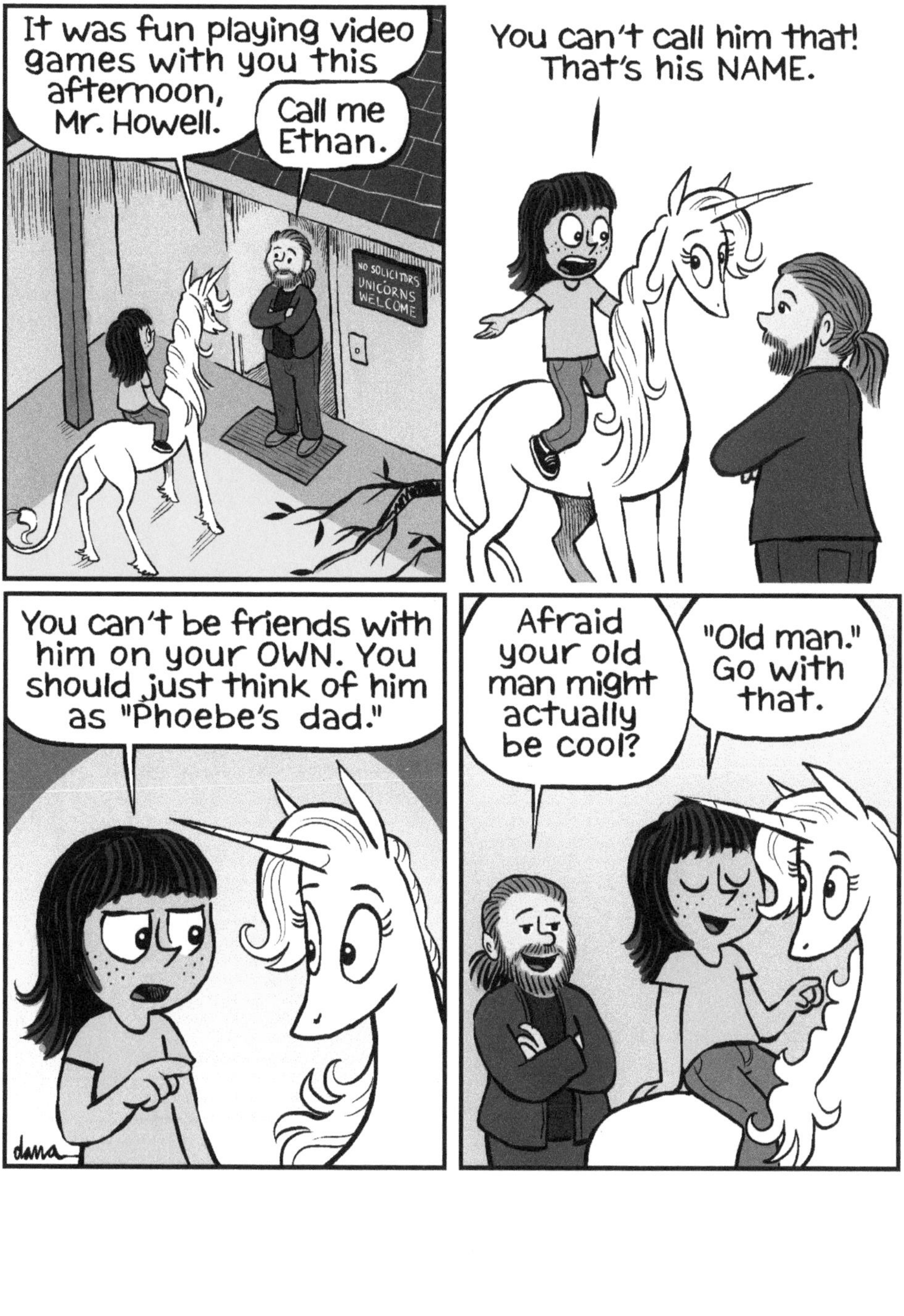
It was fun playing video games with you this afternoon, Mr. Howell.
Call me Ethan.
NO SOLICITORS
UNICORNS WELCOME
You can't call him that! That's his NAME.
You can't be friends with him on your OWN. You should just think of him as "Phoebe's dad."
dana
Afraid your old man might actually be cool?
"Old man." Go with that.

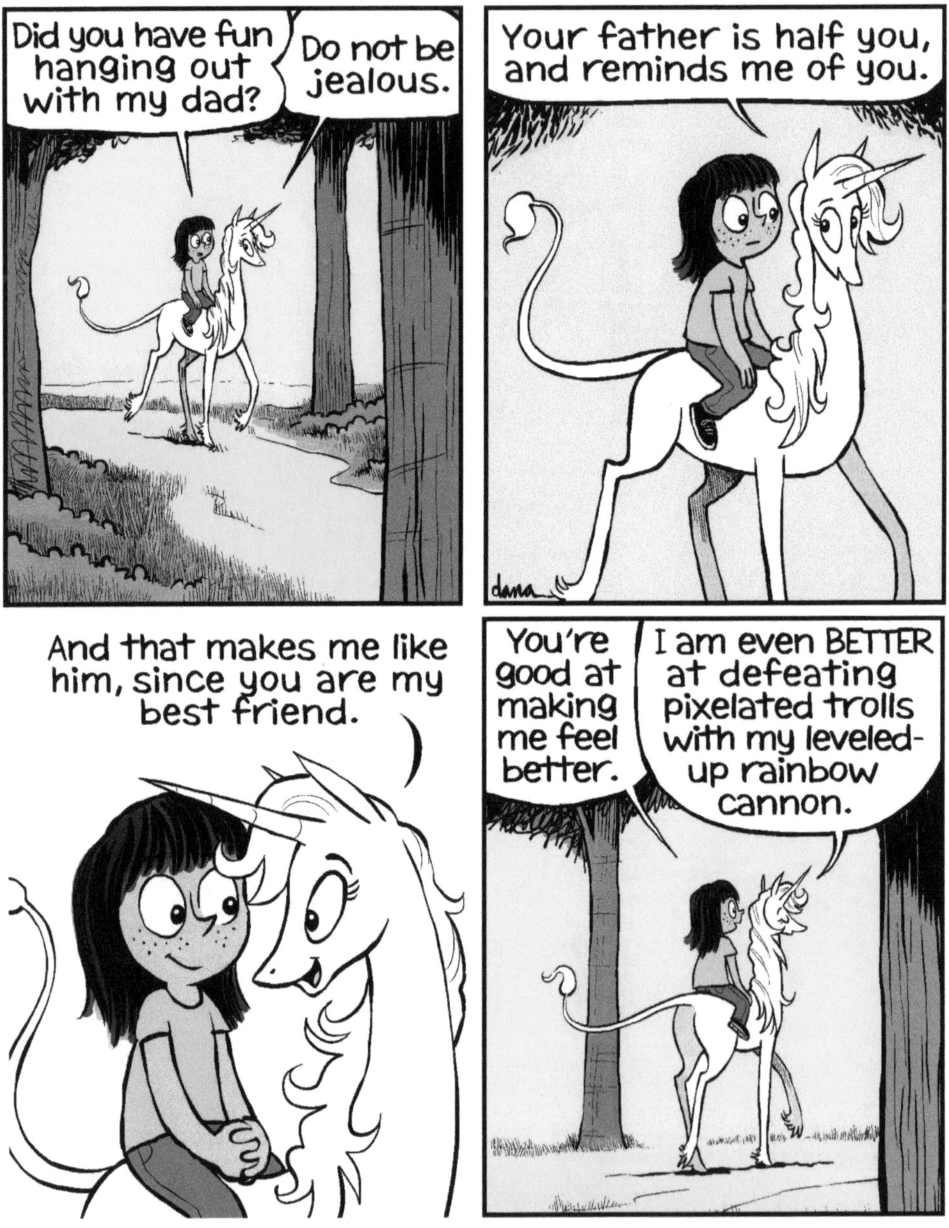
Did you have fun hanging out with my dad?
Do not be jealous.
Your father is half you, and reminds me of you.
dana
And that makes me like him, since you are my best friend.
You're good at making me feel better.
I am even BETTER at defeating pixelated trolls with my leveled-up rainbow cannon.

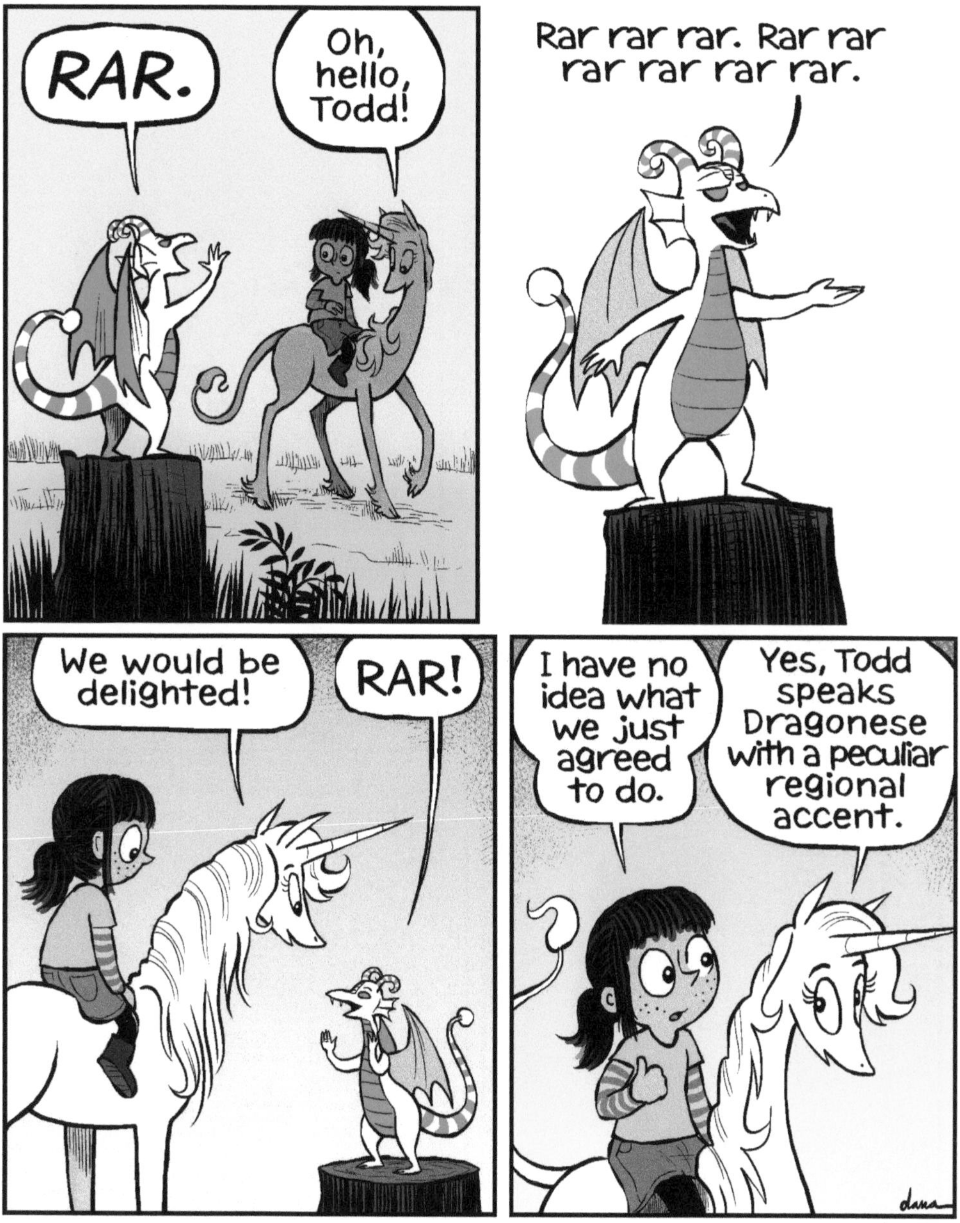
RAR.
Oh, hello, Todd!
Rar rar rar. Rar rar rar rar rar rar.
We would be delighted!
RAR!
I have no idea what we just agreed to do.
Yes, Todd speaks Dragonese with a peculiar regional accent.
dana

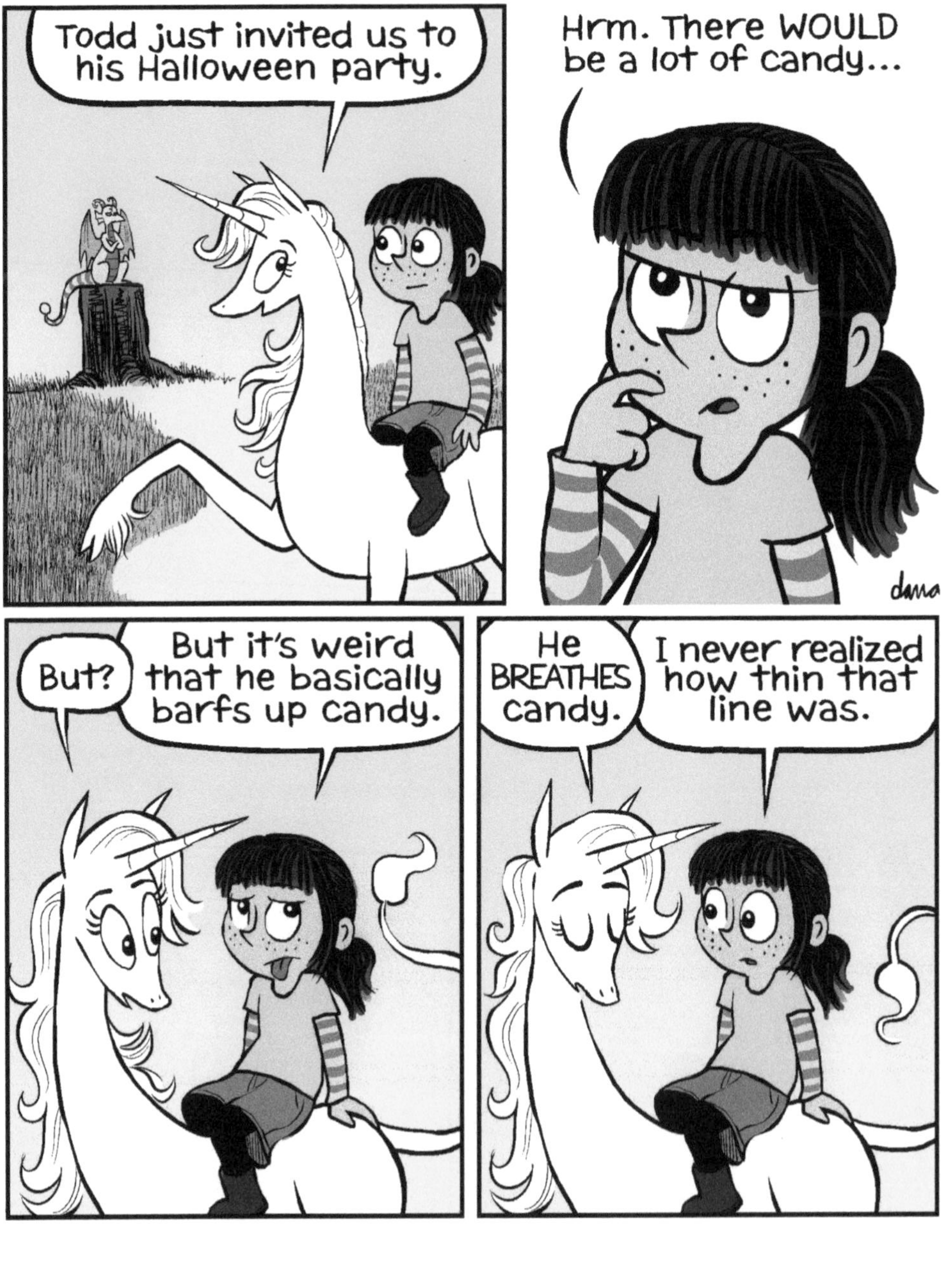
Todd just invited us to his Halloween party.
Hrm. There WOULD be a lot of candy...
dana
But?
But it's weird that he basically barfs up candy.
He BREATHES candy.
I never realized how thin that line was.

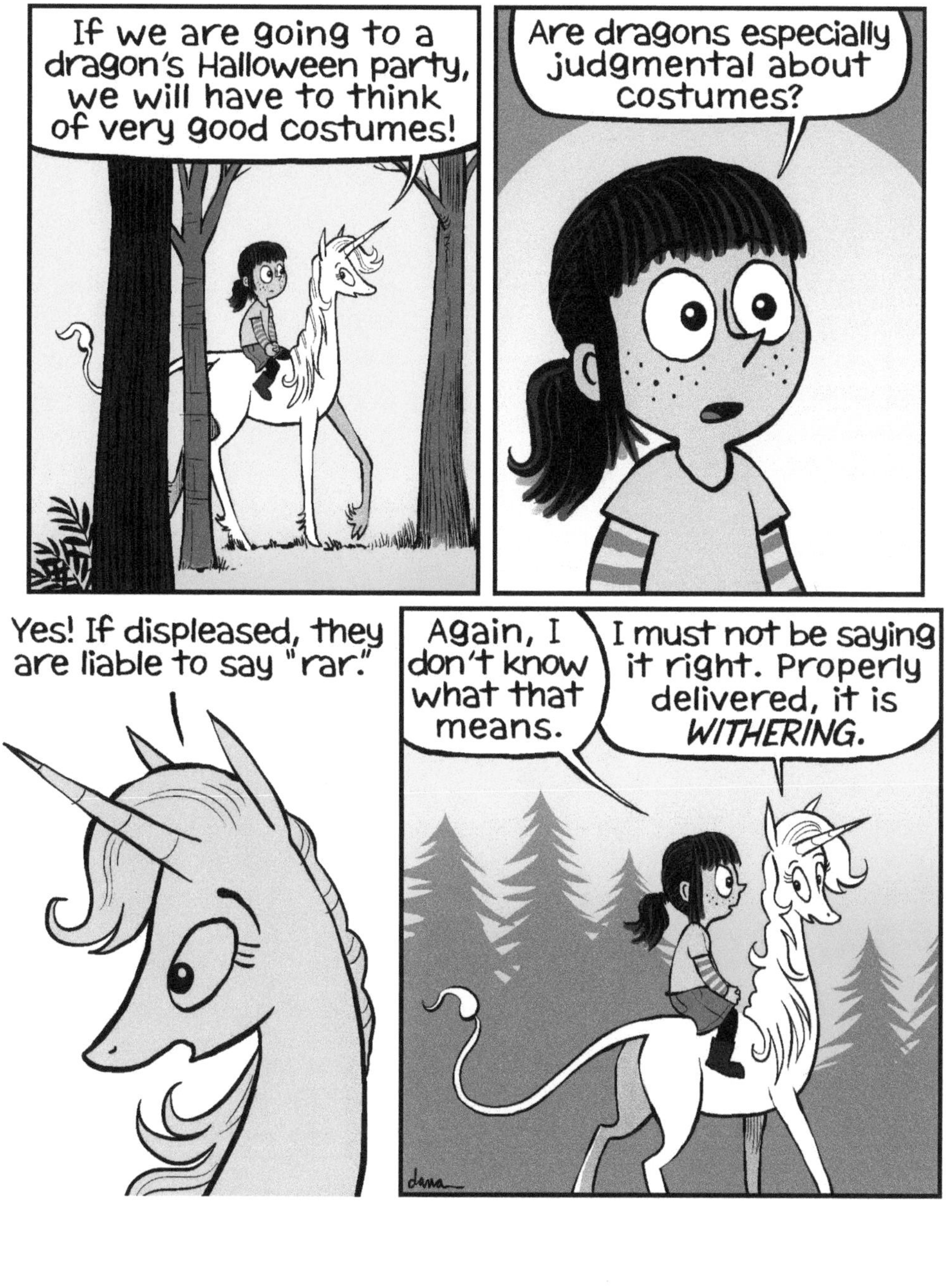
If we are going to a dragon's Halloween party, we will have to think of very good costumes!
Are dragons especially judgmental about costumes?
Yes! If displeased, they are liable to say "rar."
Again, I don't know what that means.
I must not be saying it right. Properly delivered, it is *WITHERING*.
dana

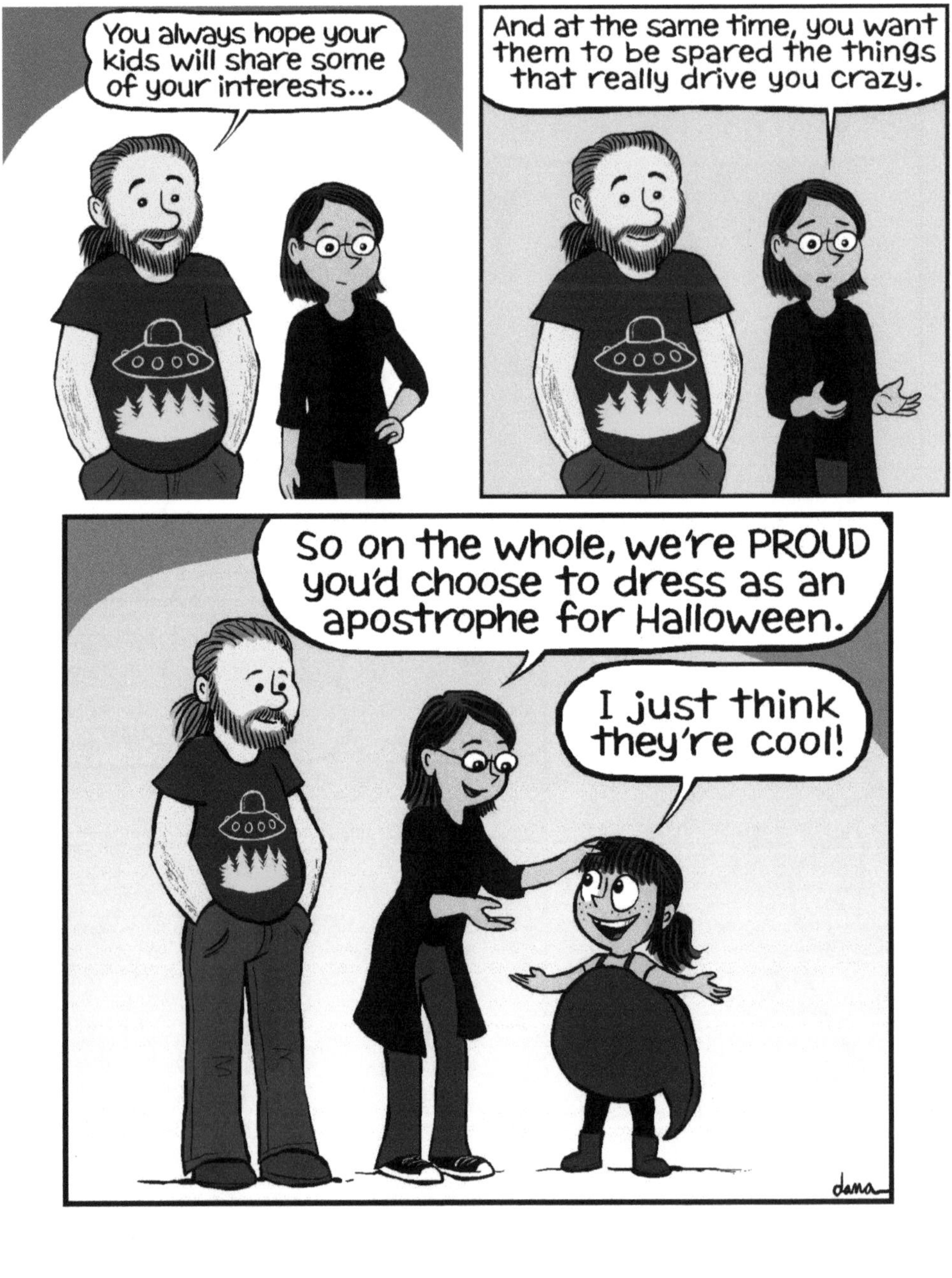
You always hope your kids will share some of your interests...
And at the same time, you want them to be spared the things that really drive you crazy.
So on the whole, we're PROUD you'd choose to dress as an apostrophe for Halloween.
I just think they're cool!
dana

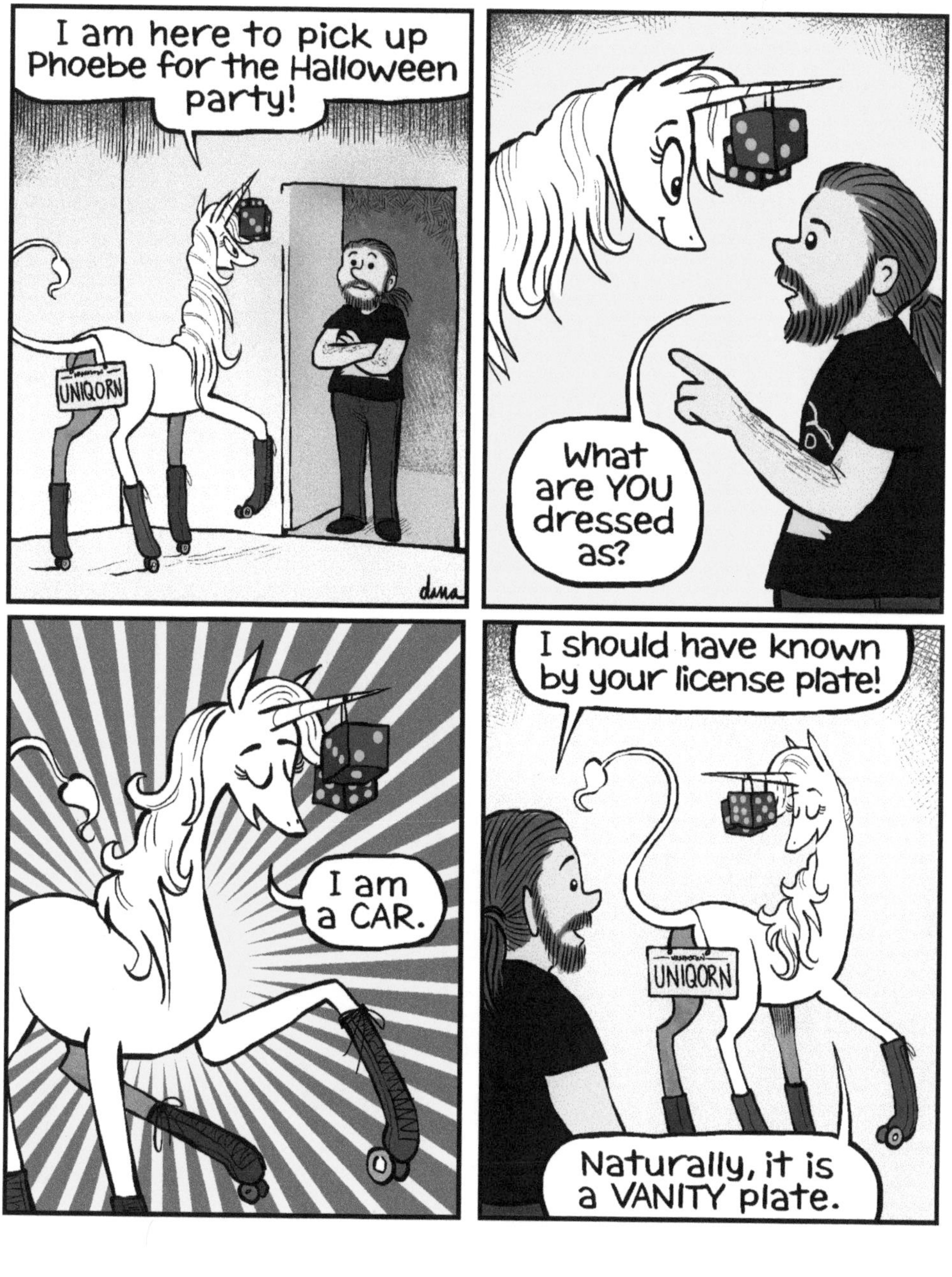
I am here to pick up Phoebe for the Halloween party!
UNIQORN
What are YOU dressed as?
I am a CAR.
I should have known by your license plate!
UNIQORN
Naturally, it is a VANITY plate.

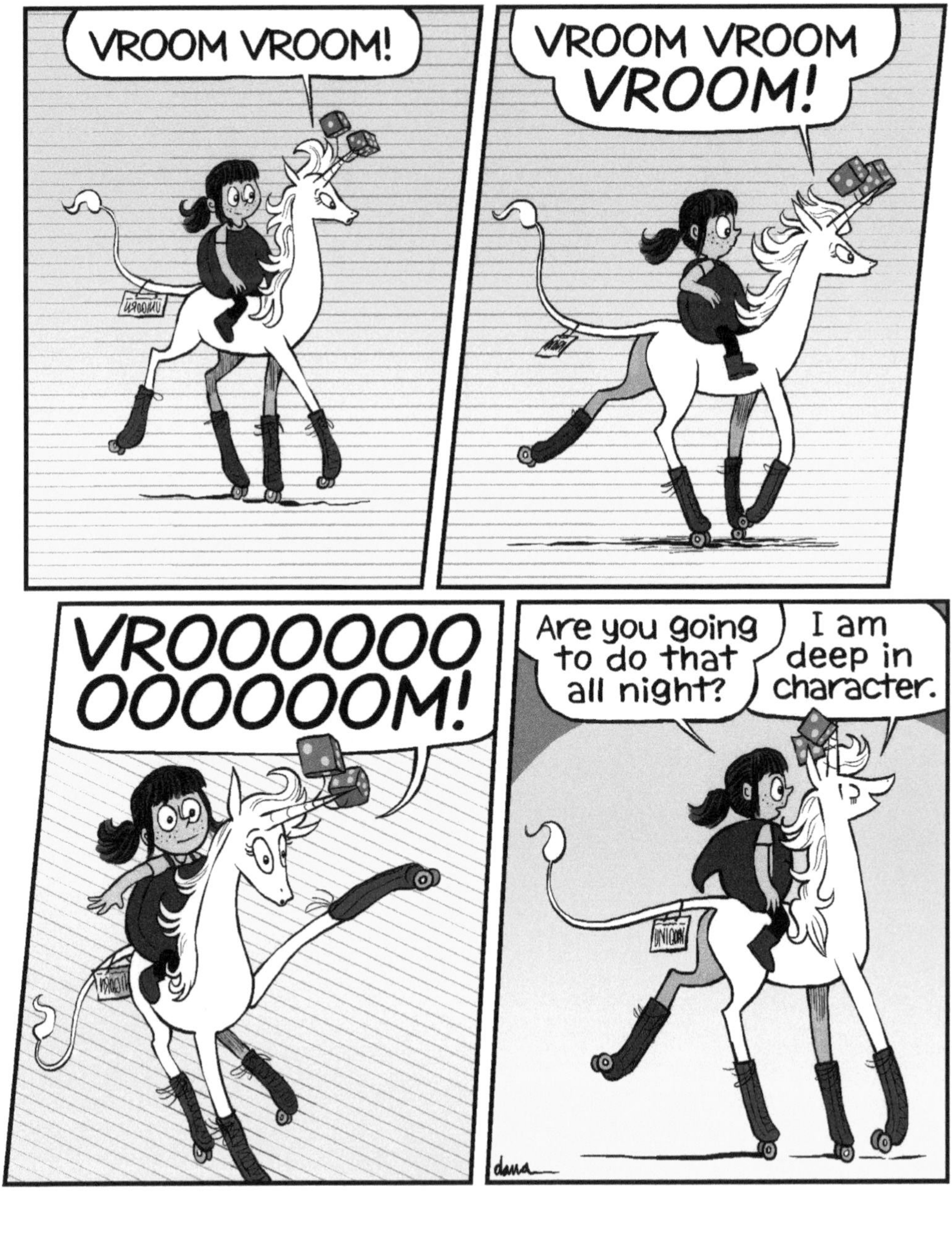
VROOM VROOM!
VROOM VROOM VROOM!
VROOOOOOO OOOOOOM!
Are you going to do that all night?
I am deep in character.
dana

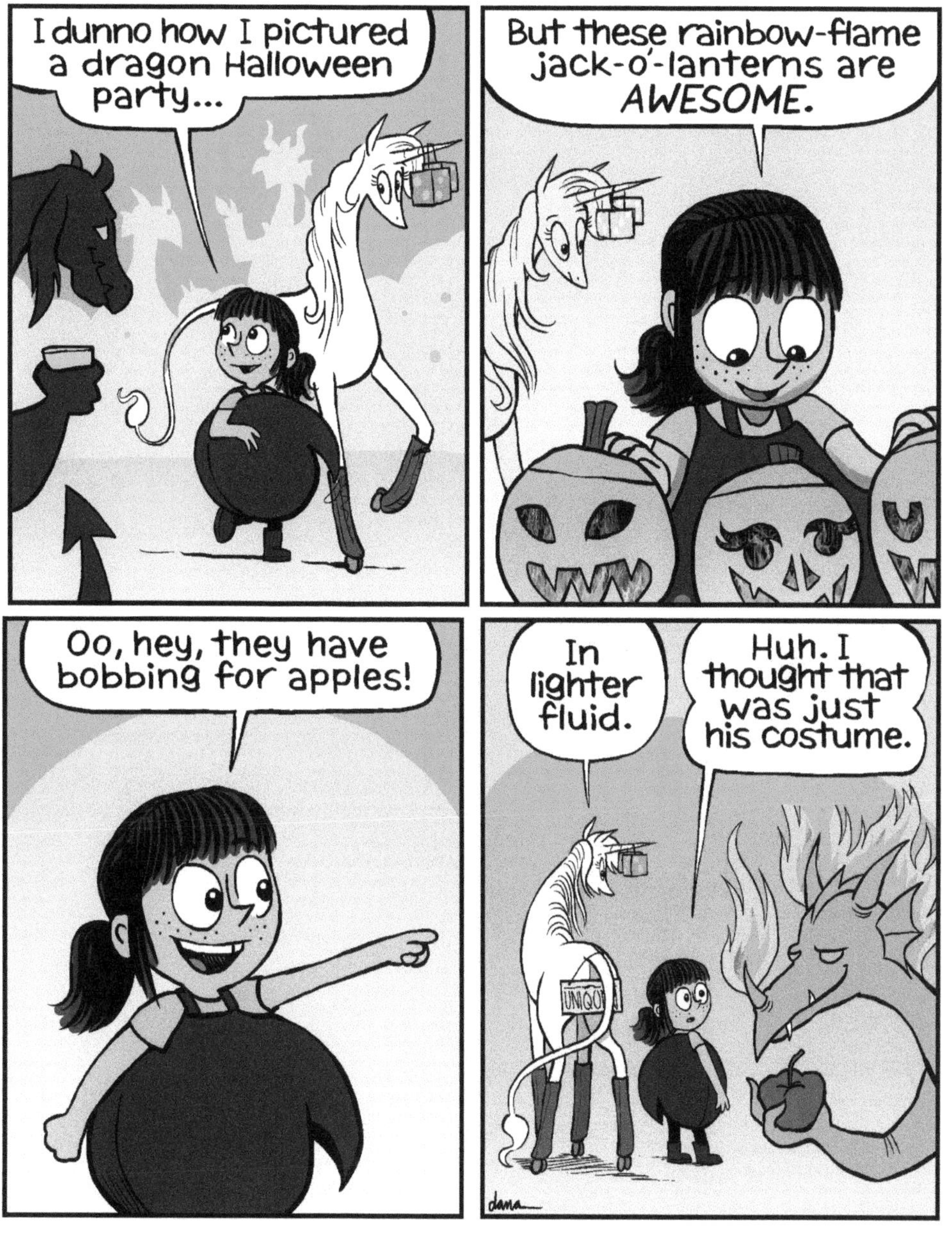
I dunno how I pictured a dragon Halloween party...
But these rainbow-flame jack-o'-lanterns are *AWESOME.*
Oo, hey, they have bobbing for apples!
In lighter fluid.
Huh. I thought that was just his costume.
UNIQO
dana

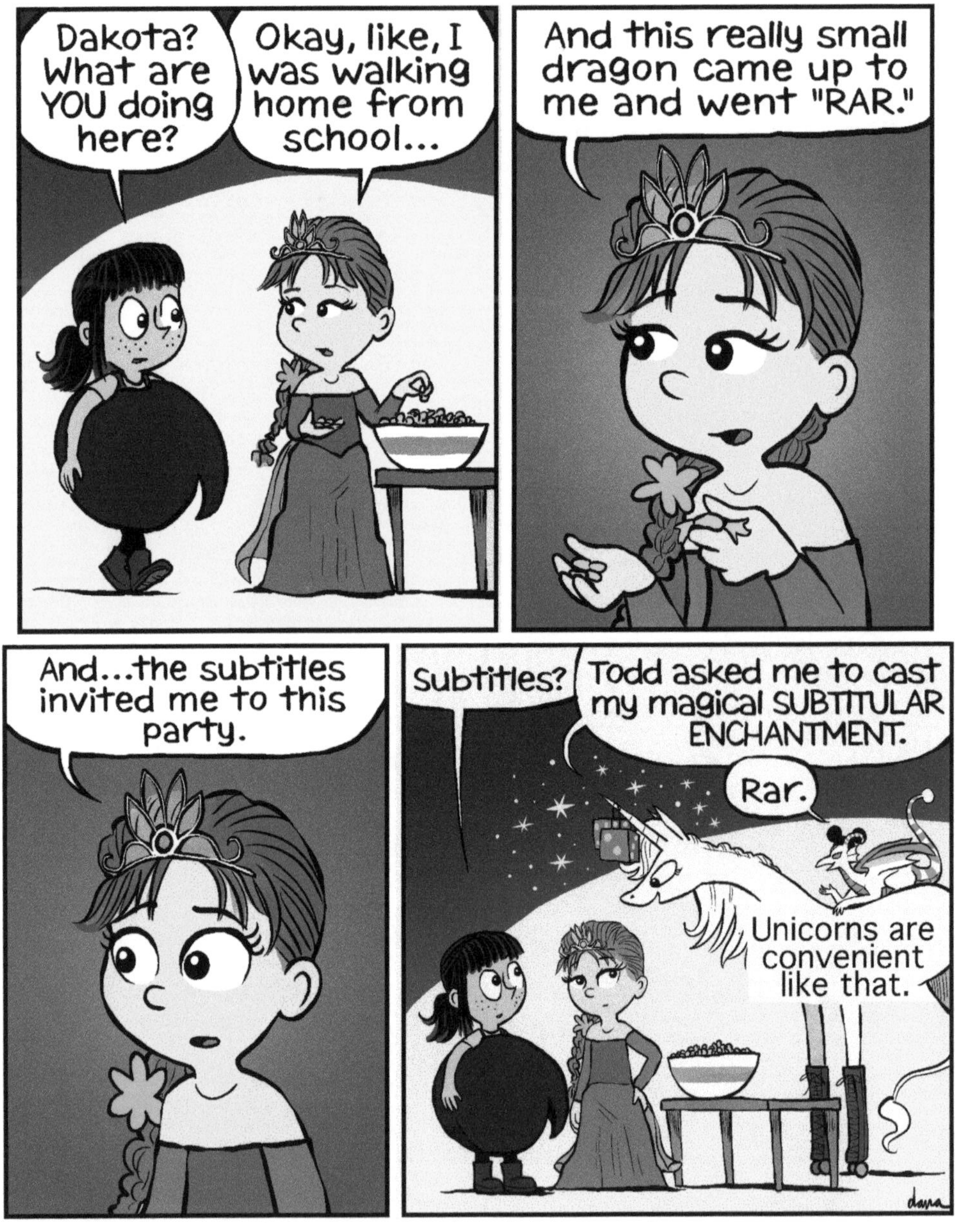
Dakota? What are YOU doing here?
Okay, like, I was walking home from school...
And this really small dragon came up to me and went "RAR."
And...the subtitles invited me to this party.
Subtitles?
Todd asked me to cast my magical SUBTITULAR ENCHANTMENT.
Rar.
Unicorns are convenient like that.
dana

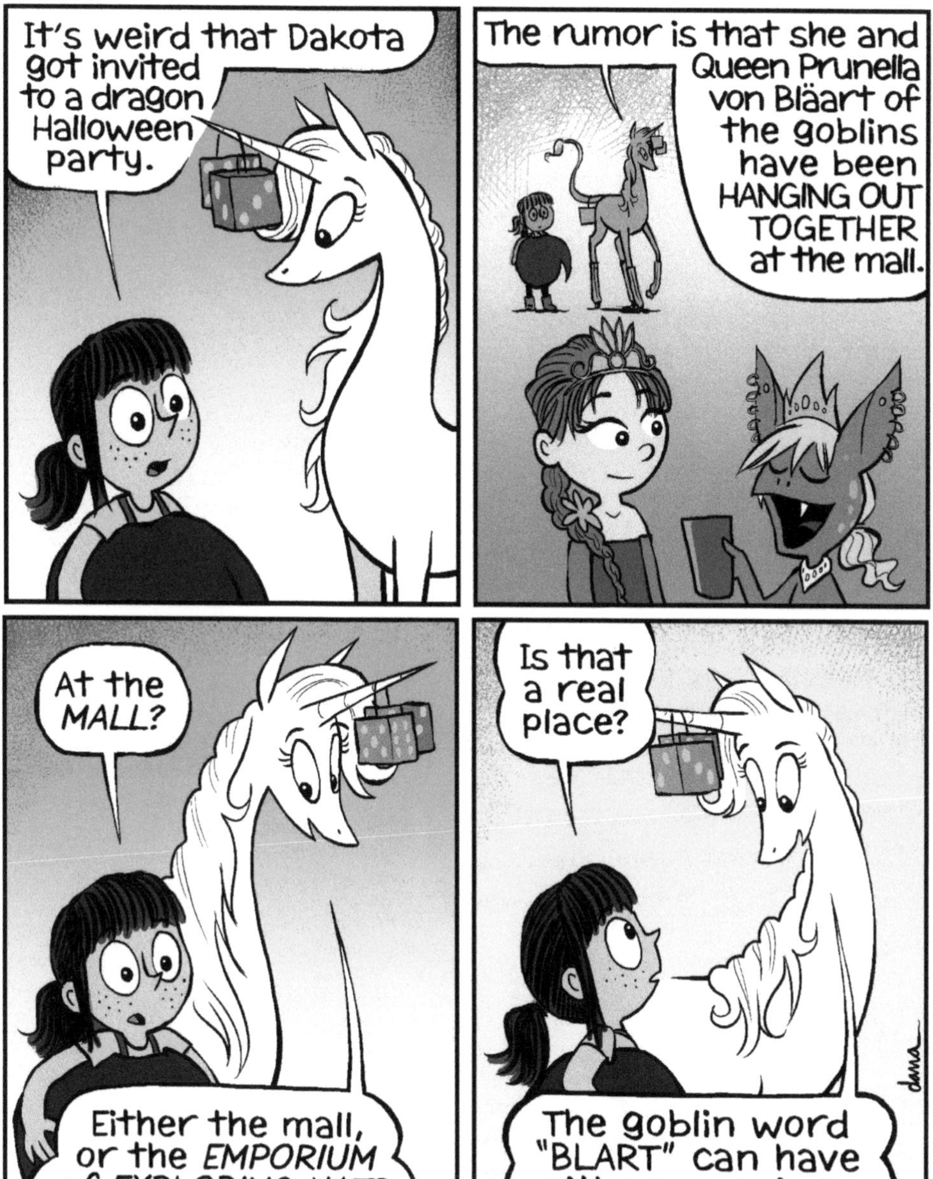
It's weird that Dakota got invited to a dragon Halloween party.
The rumor is that she and Queen Prunella von Bläart of the goblins have been HANGING OUT TOGETHER at the mall.
At the *MALL?*
Either the mall, or the *EMPORIUM of EXPLODING HATS.*
Is that a real place?
The goblin word "BLART" can have either meaning.
dana

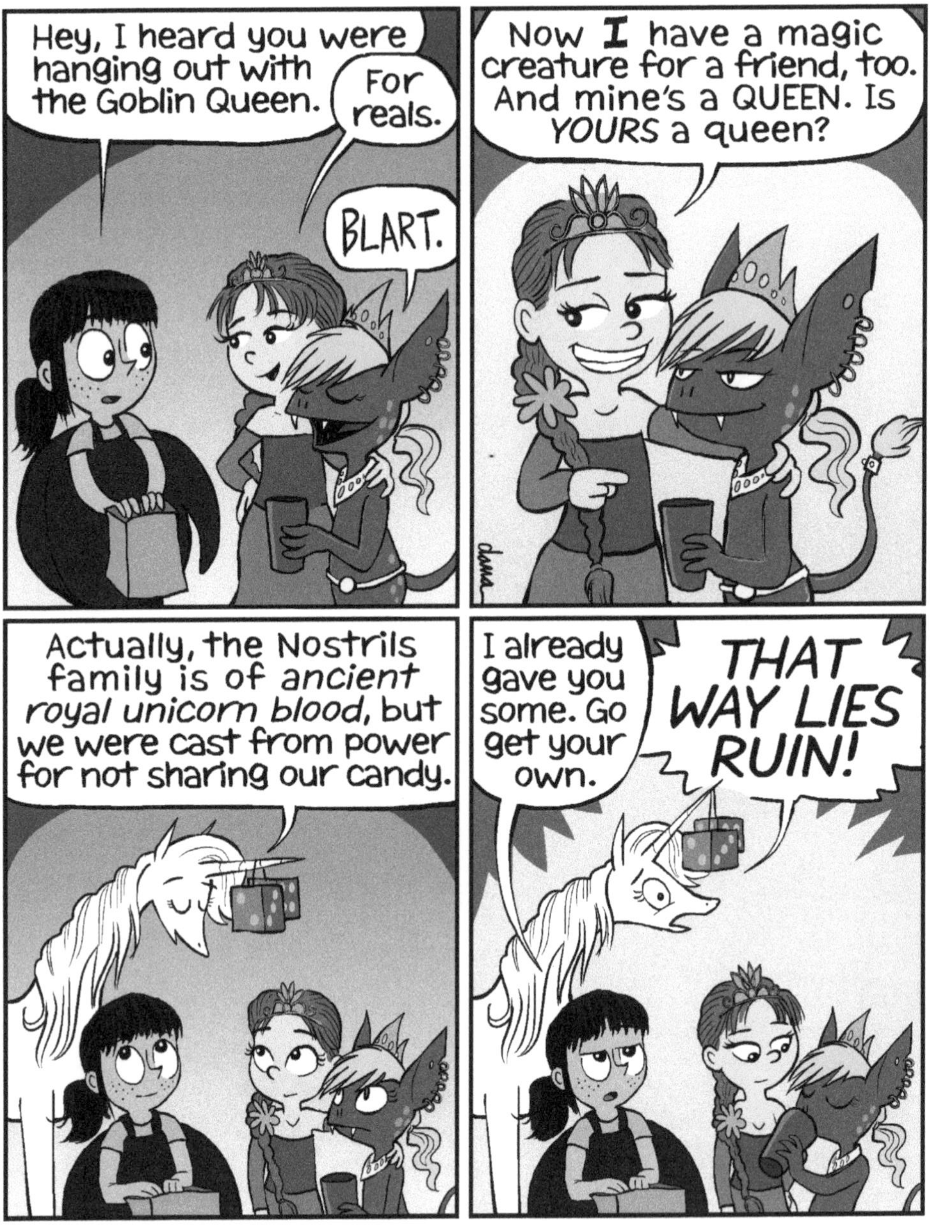
Hey, I heard you were hanging out with the Goblin Queen.
For reals.
BLART.
Now **I** have a magic creature for a friend, too. And mine's a QUEEN. Is *YOURS* a queen?
Actually, the Nostrils family is of *ancient royal unicorn blood*, but we were cast from power for not sharing our candy.
I already gave you some. Go get your own.
*THAT WAY LIES RUIN!*

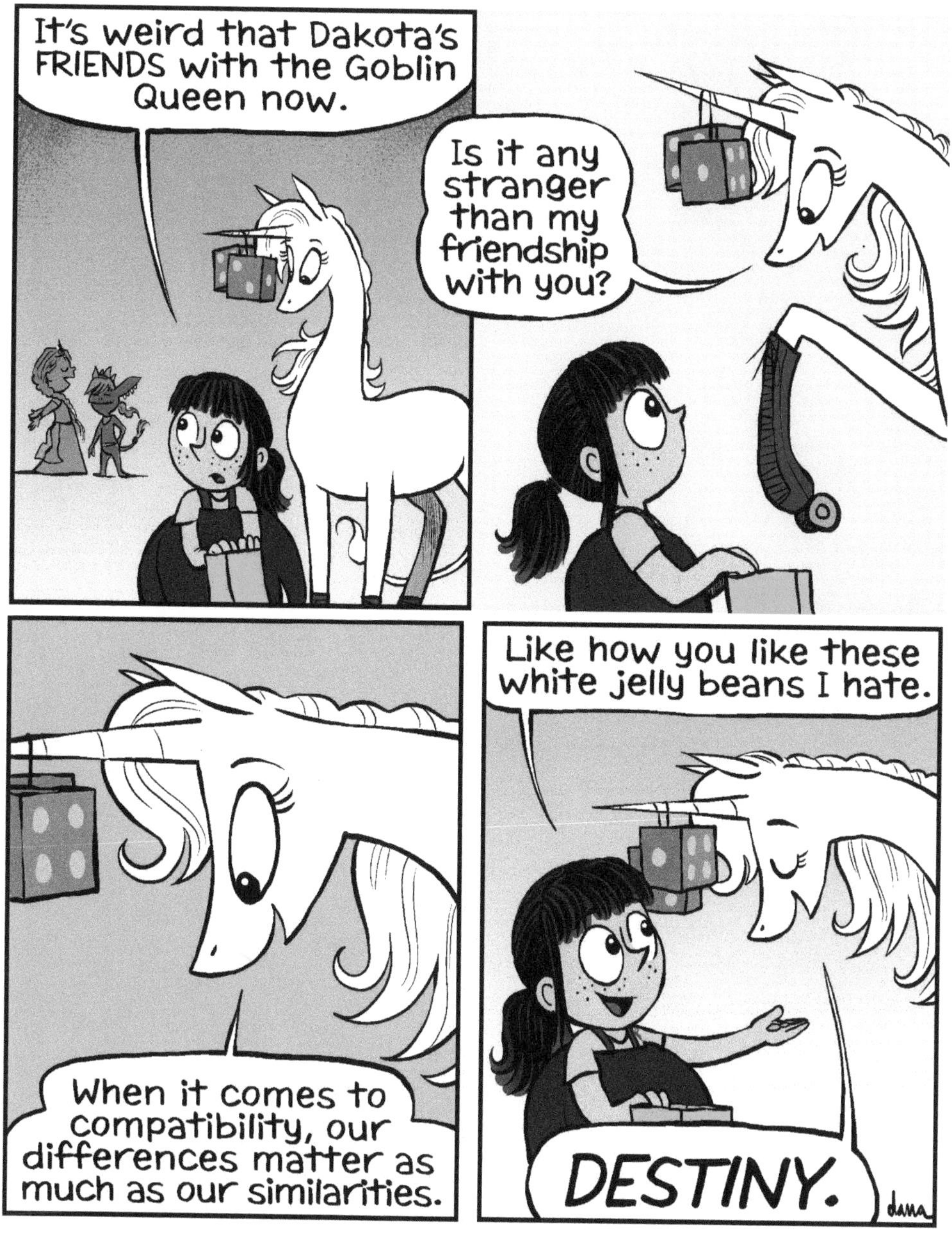
It's weird that Dakota's FRIENDS with the Goblin Queen now.
Is it any stranger than my friendship with you?
When it comes to compatibility, our differences matter as much as our similarities.
Like how you like these white jelly beans I hate.
DESTINY.
dana

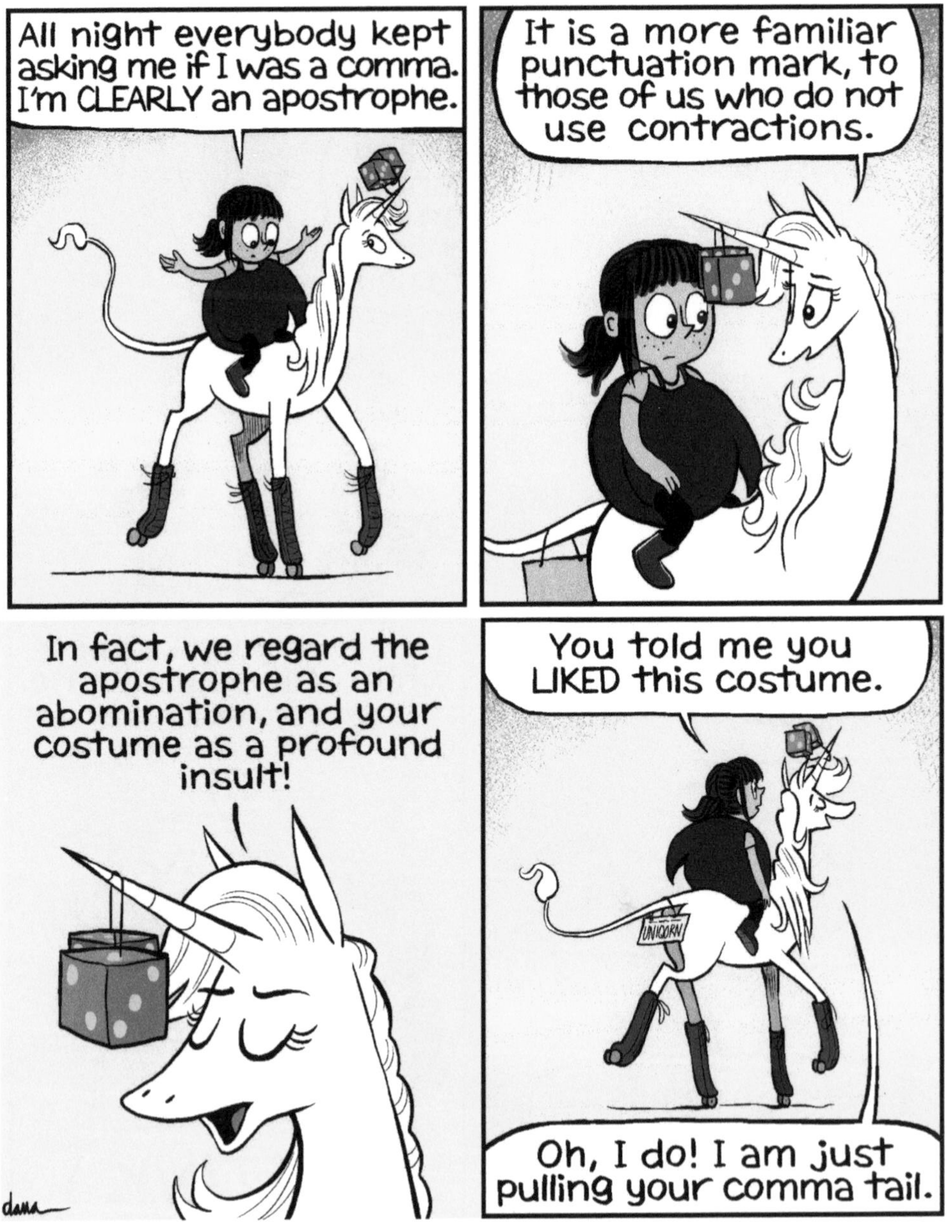
All night everybody kept asking me if I was a comma. I'm CLEARLY an apostrophe.
It is a more familiar punctuation mark, to those of us who do not use contractions.
In fact, we regard the apostrophe as an abomination, and your costume as a profound insult!
dana
You told me you LIKED this costume.
UNICORN
Oh, I do! I am just pulling your comma tail.

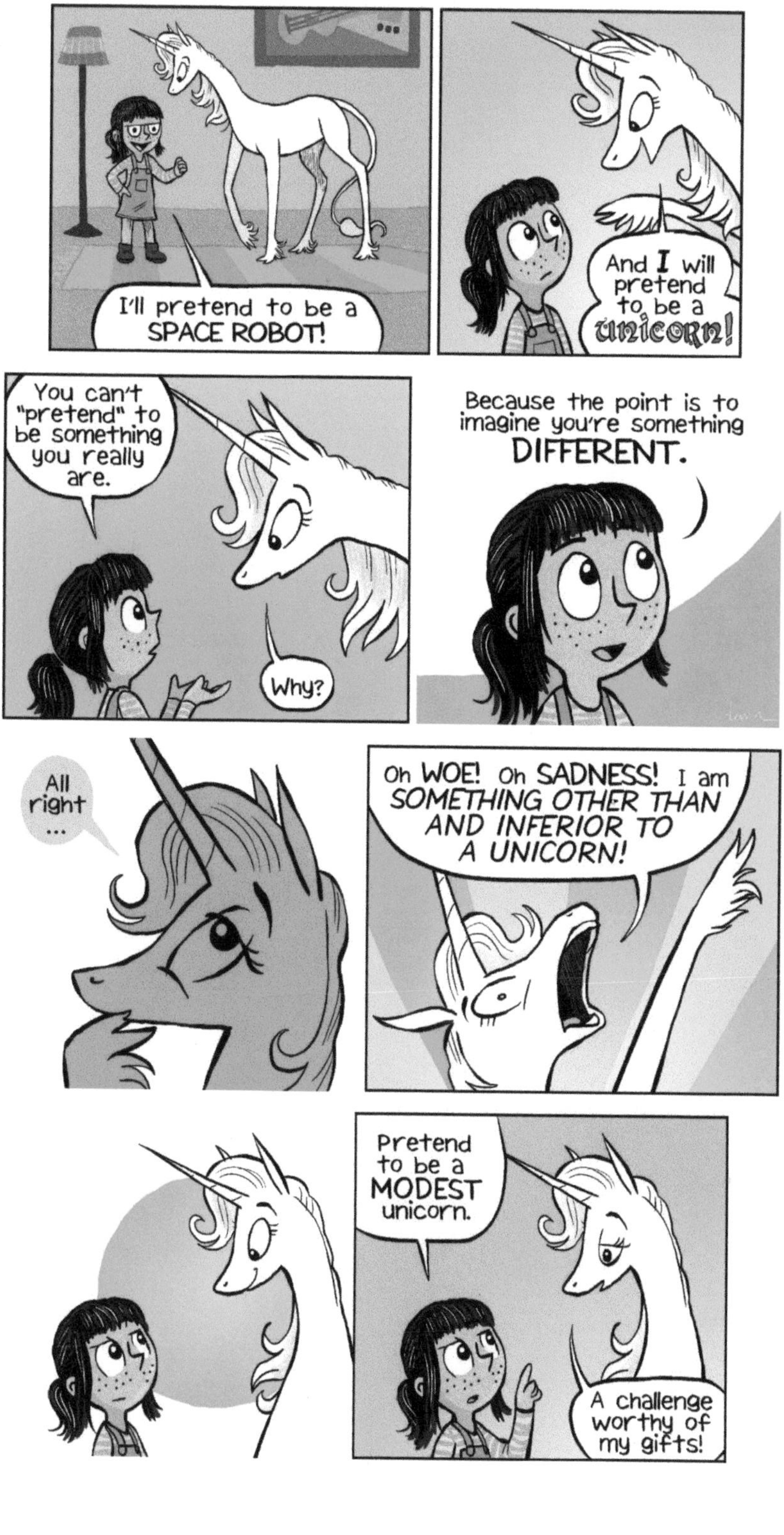
I'll pretend to be a SPACE ROBOT!
And I will pretend to be a UNICORN!
You can't "pretend" to be something you really are.
Why?
Because the point is to imagine you're something DIFFERENT.
All right ...
Oh WOE! Oh SADNESS! I am SOMETHING OTHER THAN AND INFERIOR TO A UNICORN!
Pretend to be a MODEST unicorn.
A challenge worthy of my gifts!

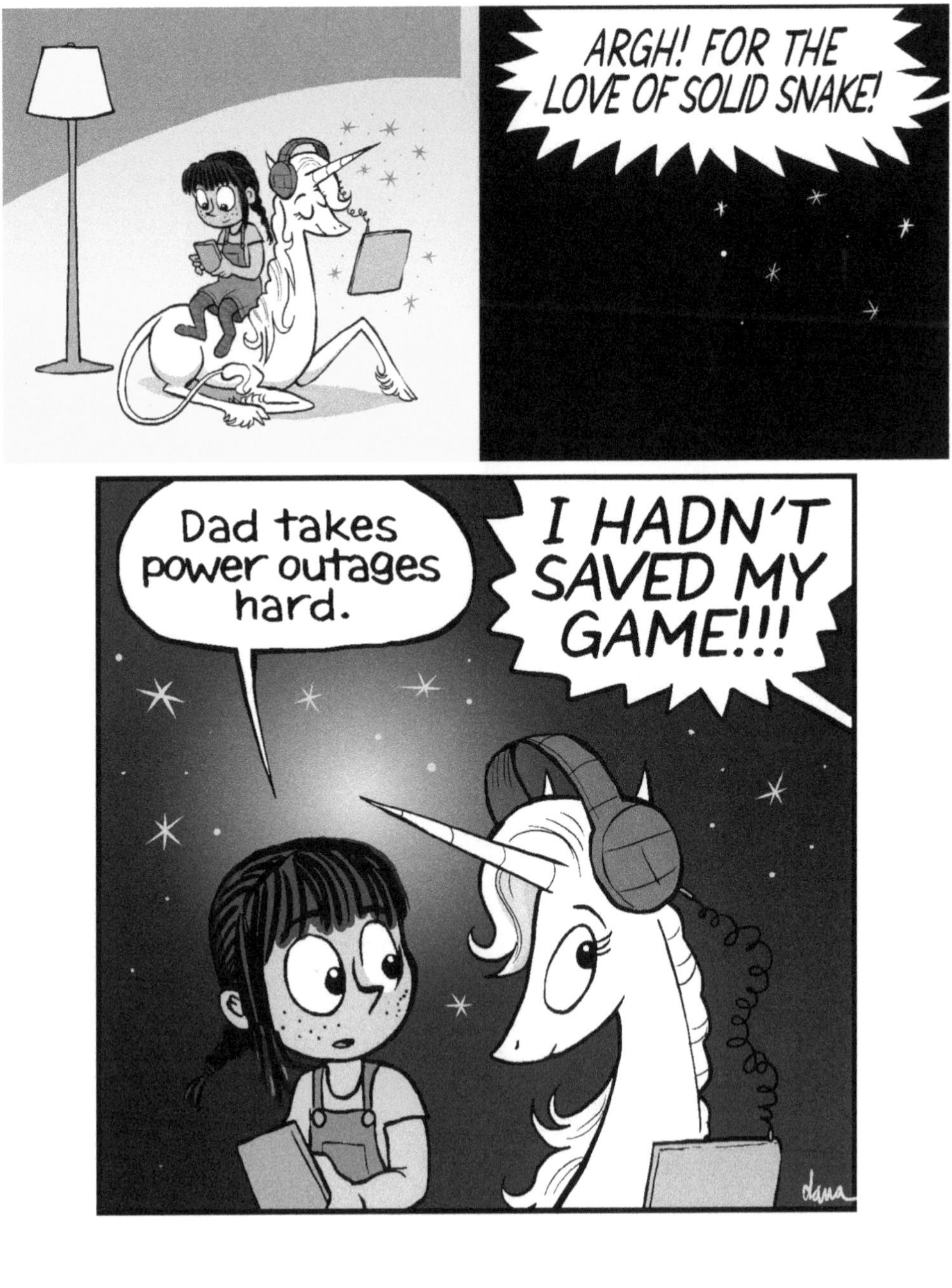
ARGH! FOR THE LOVE OF SOLID SNAKE!
Dad takes power outages hard.
I HADN'T SAVED MY GAME!!!
dana

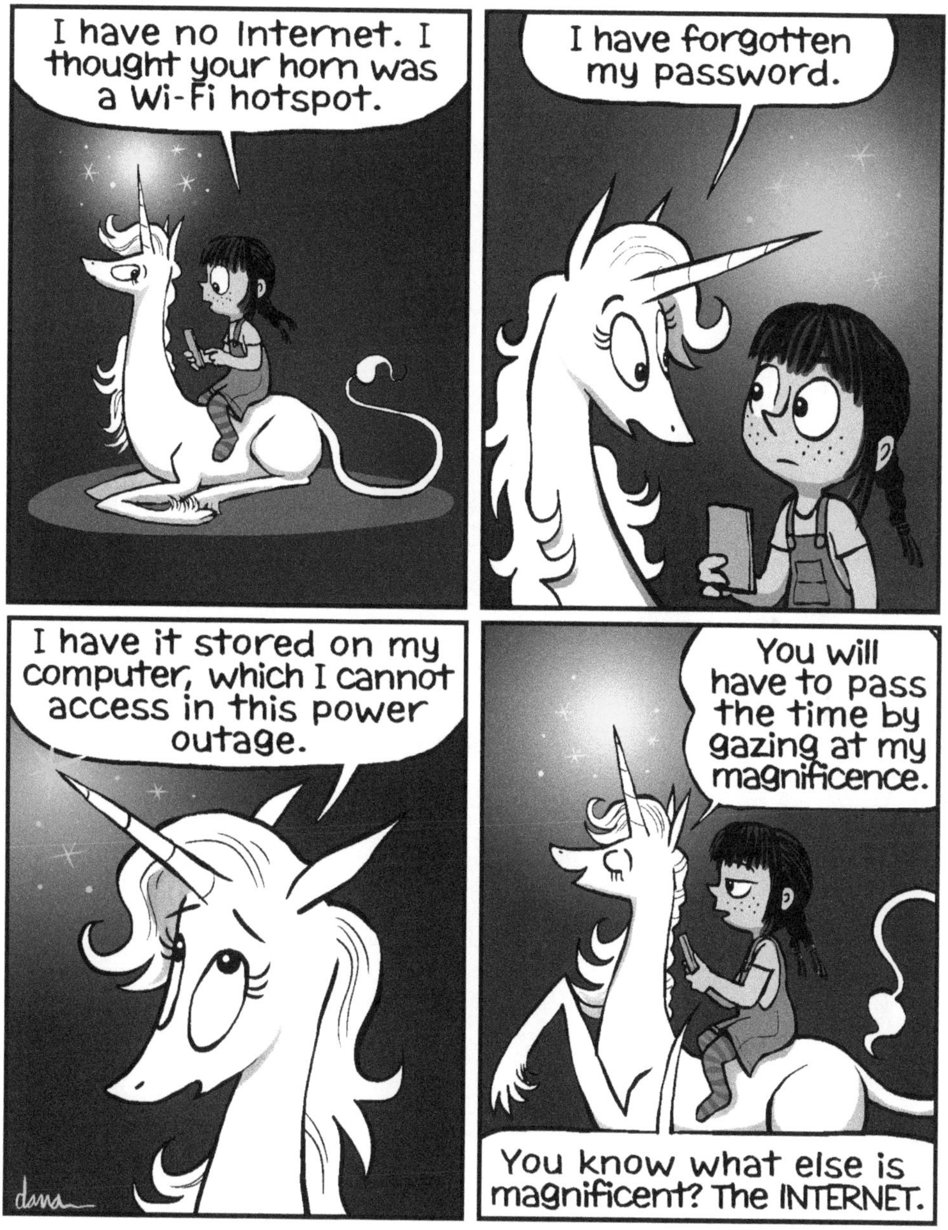
I have no Internet. I thought your horn was a Wi-Fi hotspot.
I have forgotten my password.
I have it stored on my computer, which I cannot access in this power outage.
You will have to pass the time by gazing at my magnificence.
You know what else is magnificent? The INTERNET.
dana

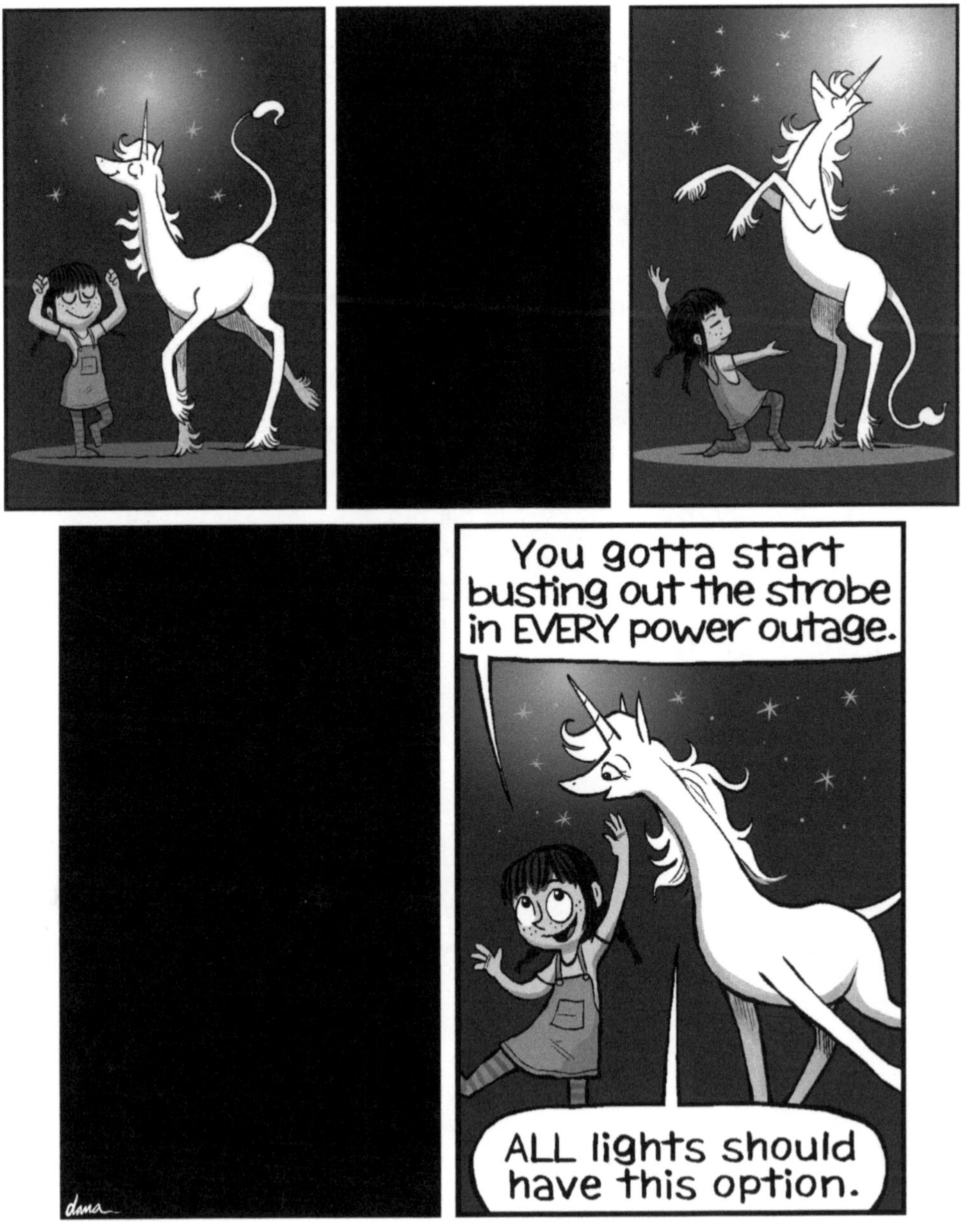
You gotta start busting out the strobe in EVERY power outage.
ALL lights should have this option.
dana

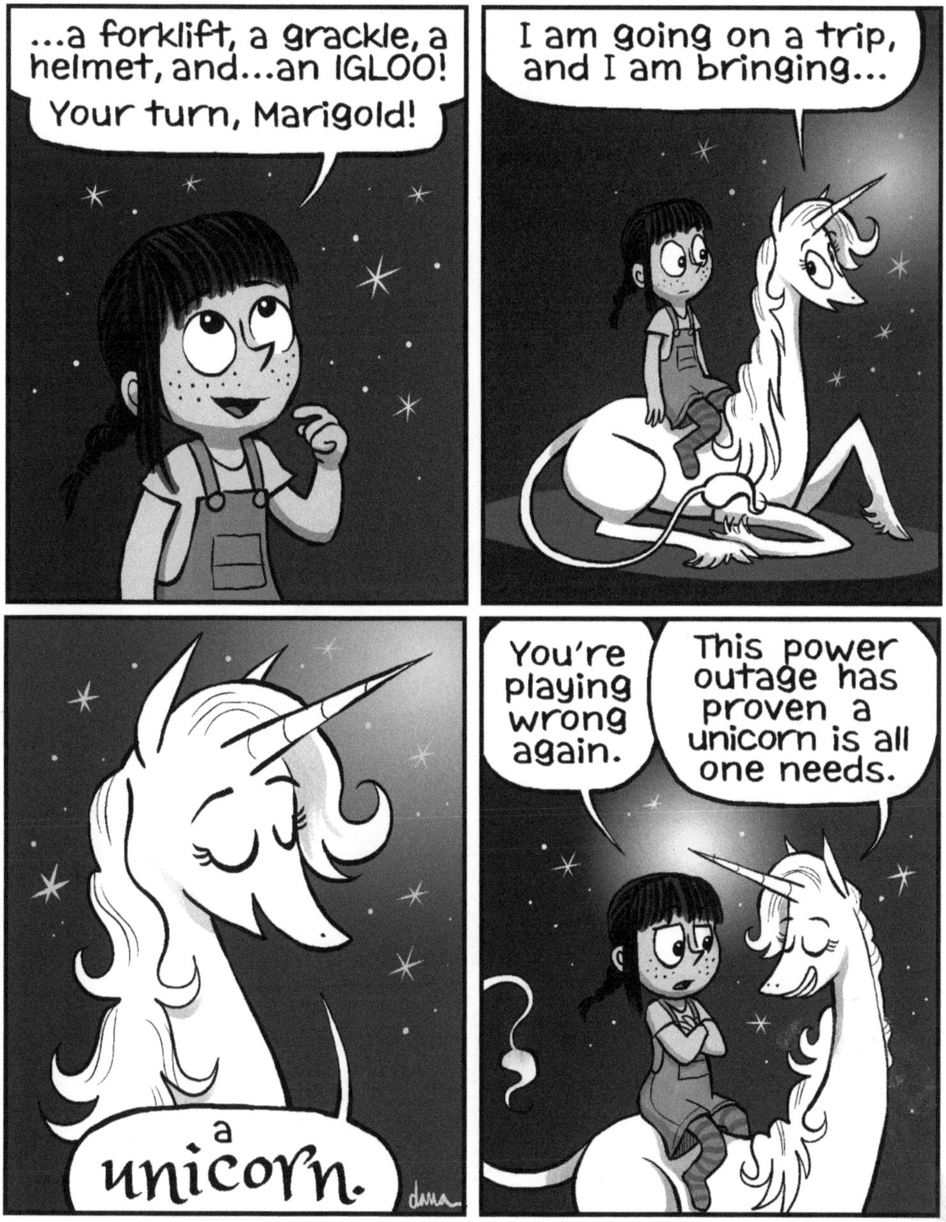
...a forklift, a grackle, a helmet, and...an IGLOO!
Your turn, Marigold!
I am going on a trip, and I am bringing...
a unicorn.
You're playing wrong again.
This power outage has proven a unicorn is all one needs.

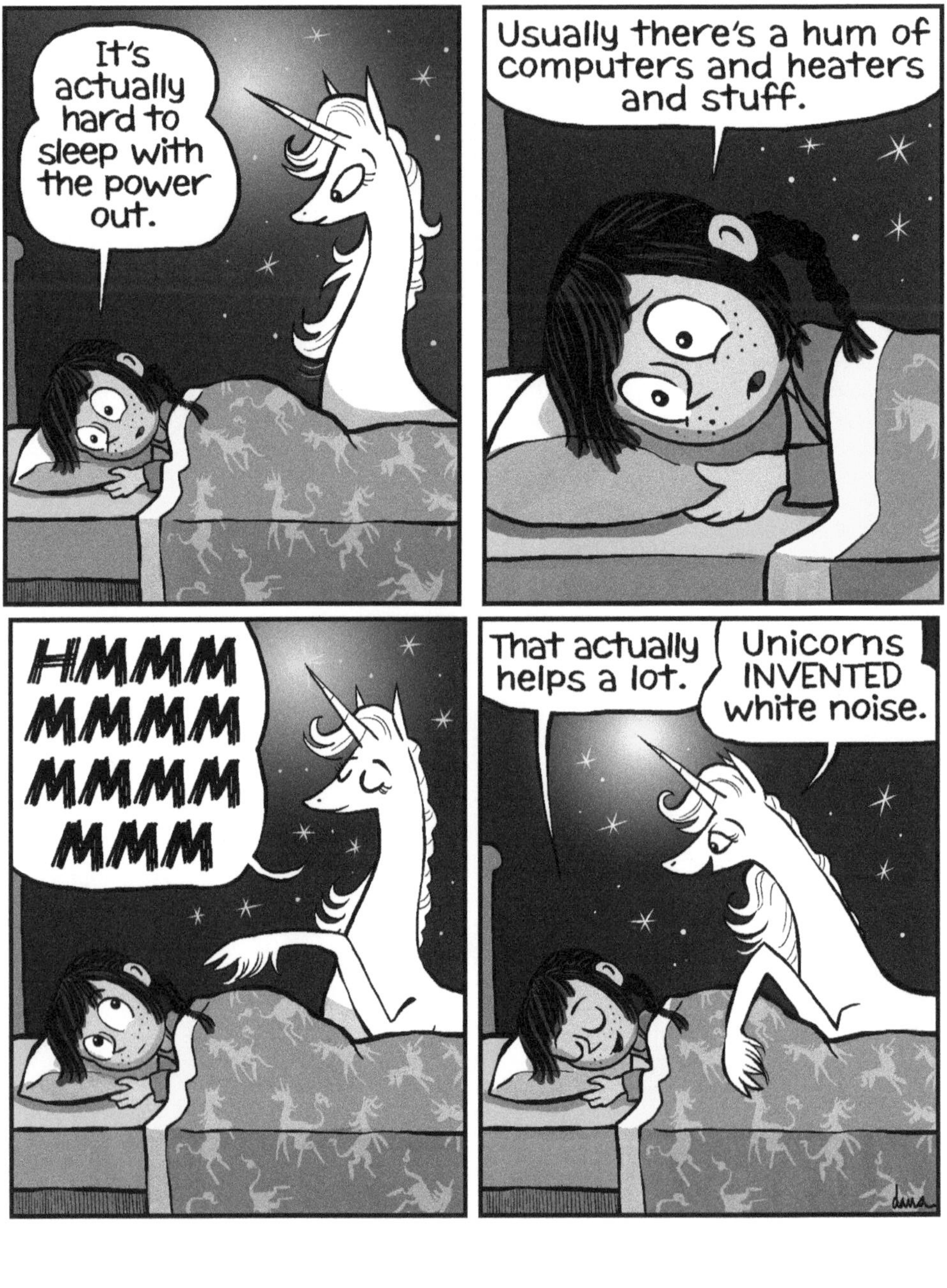
It's actually hard to sleep with the power out.
Usually there's a hum of computers and heaters and stuff.
HMMM MMMM MMMM MMM
That actually helps a lot.
Unicorns INVENTED white noise.
dana

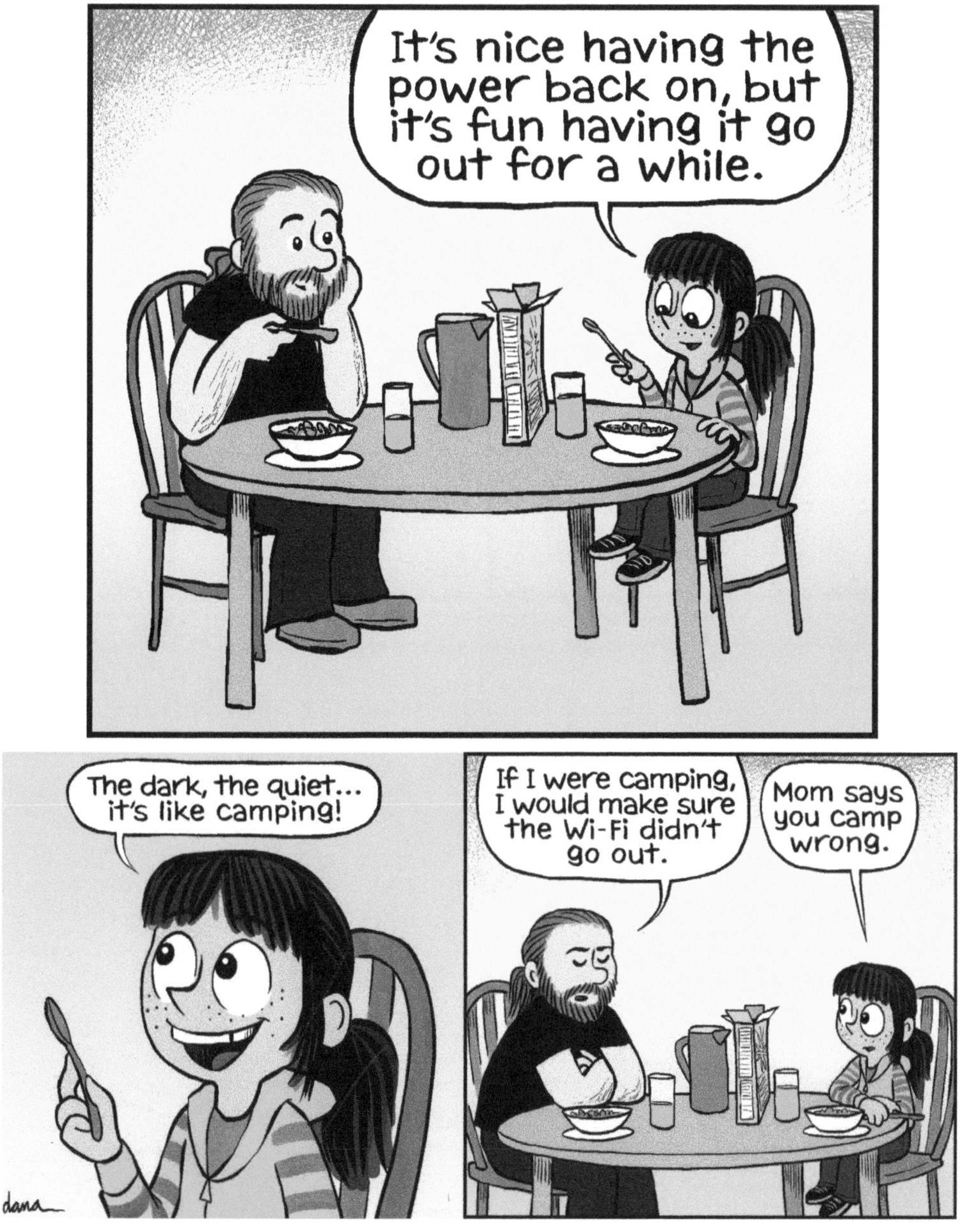
It's nice having the power back on, but it's fun having it go out for a while.
The dark, the quiet... it's like camping!
dana
If I were camping, I would make sure the Wi-Fi didn't go out.
Mom says you camp wrong.

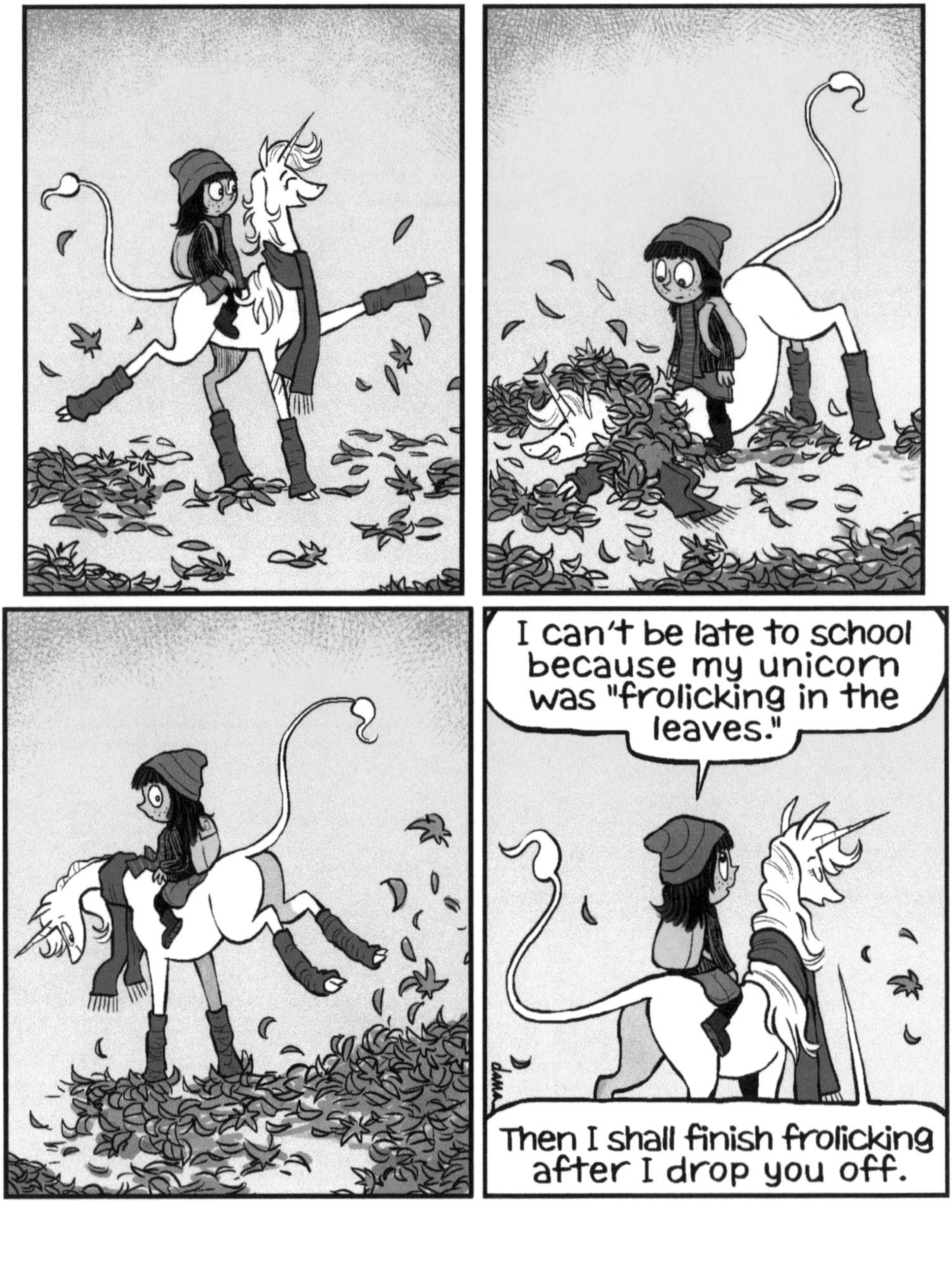
I can't be late to school because my unicorn was "frolicking in the leaves."
Then I shall finish frolicking after I drop you off.

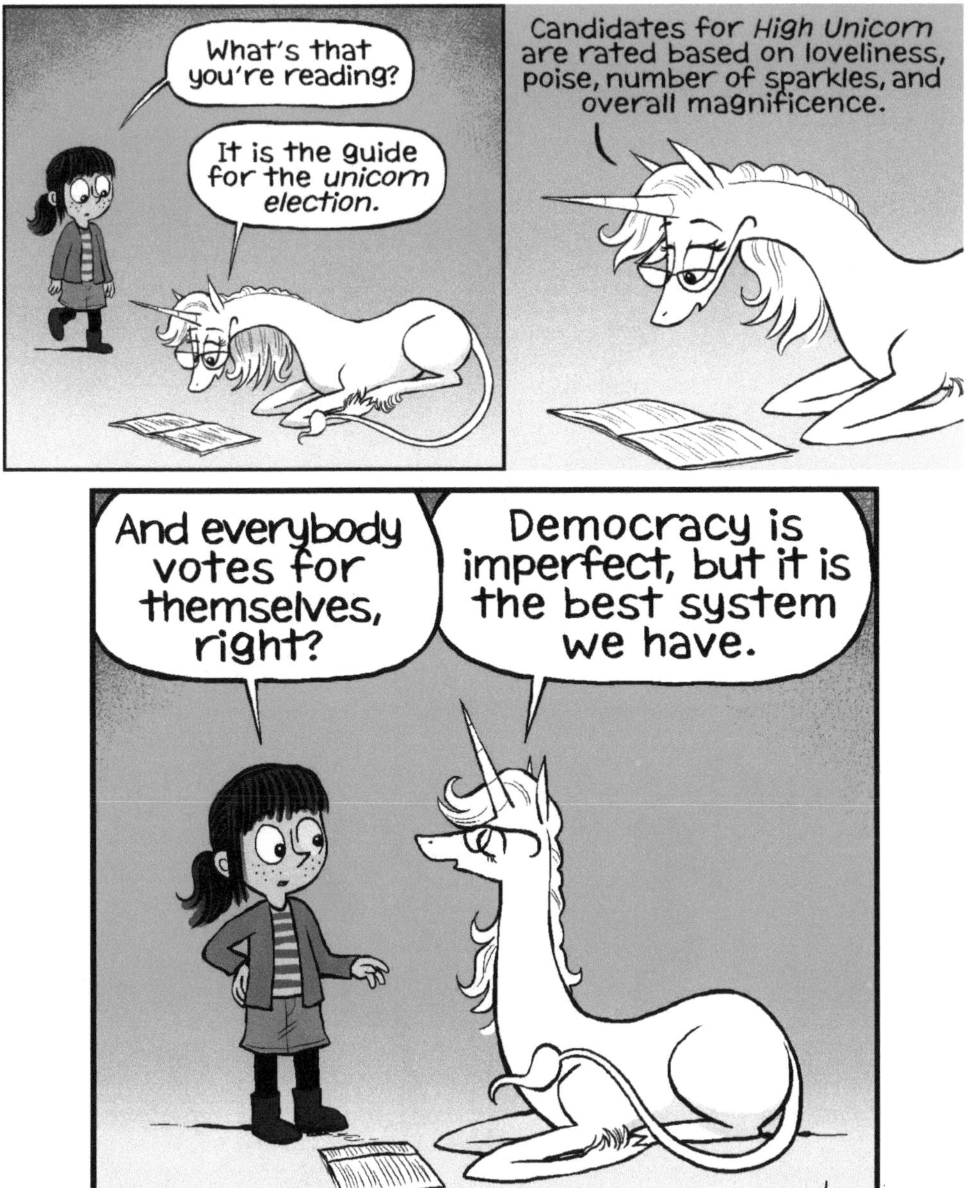
What's that you're reading?
It is the guide for the unicorn election.
Candidates for High Unicorn are rated based on loveliness, poise, number of sparkles, and overall magnificence.
And everybody votes for themselves, right?
Democracy is imperfect, but it is the best system we have.
dana

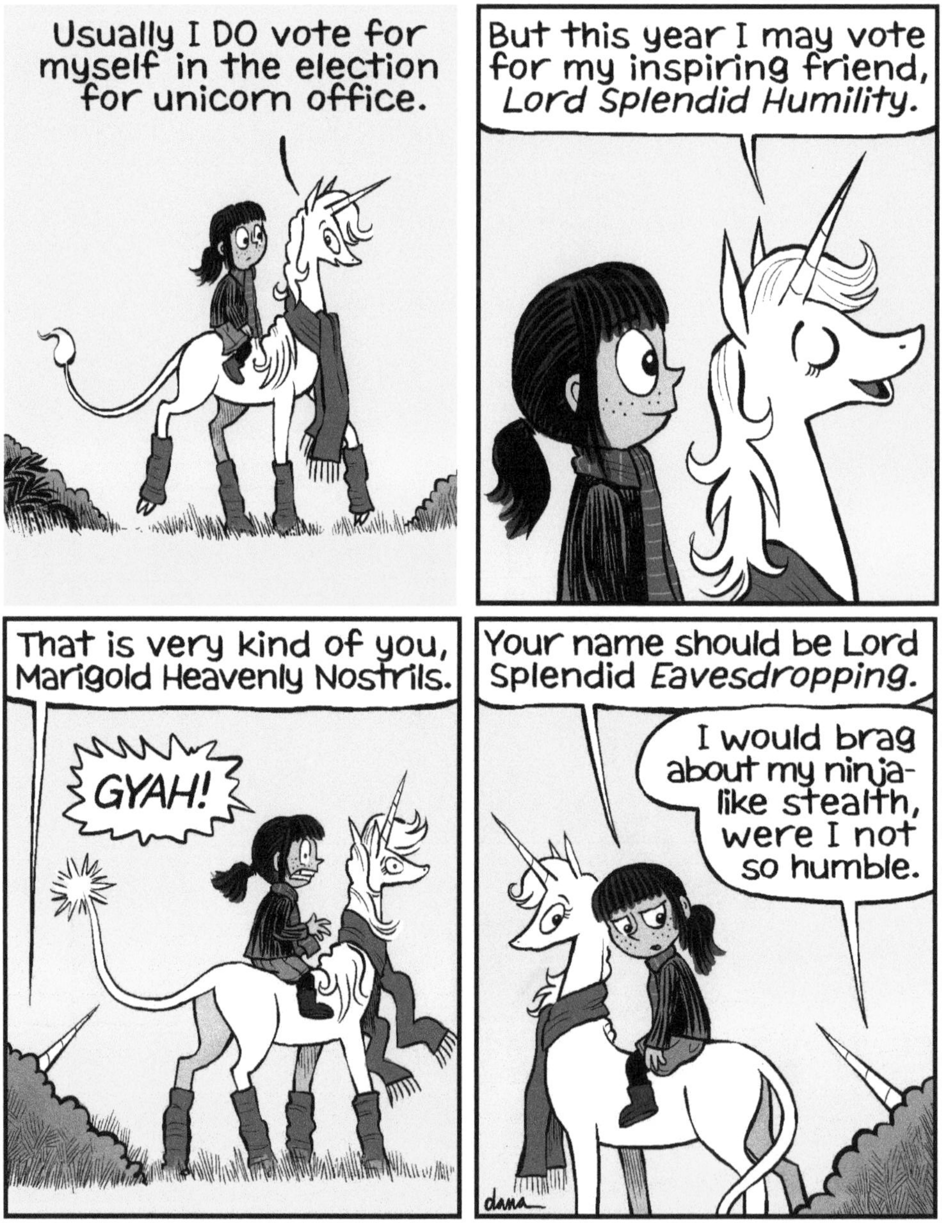
Usually I DO vote for myself in the election for unicorn office.
But this year I may vote for my inspiring friend, *Lord Splendid Humility*.
That is very kind of you, Marigold Heavenly Nostrils.
GYAH!
Your name should be Lord Splendid *Eavesdropping*.
I would brag about my ninja-like stealth, were I not so humble.
dana

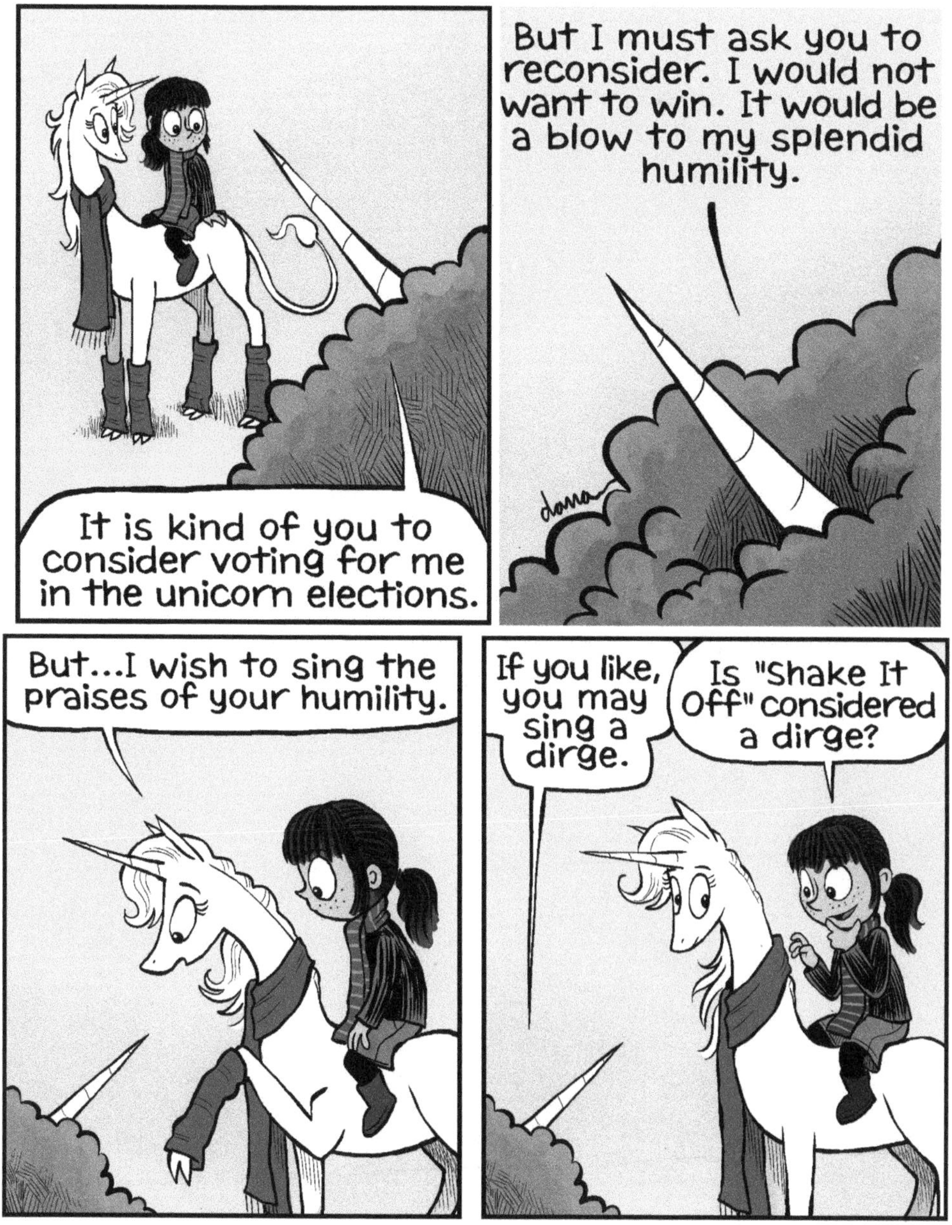
It is kind of you to consider voting for me in the unicorn elections.
But I must ask you to reconsider. I would not want to win. It would be a blow to my splendid humility.
dana
But...I wish to sing the praises of your humility.
If you like, you may sing a dirge.
Is "Shake It Off" considered a dirge?

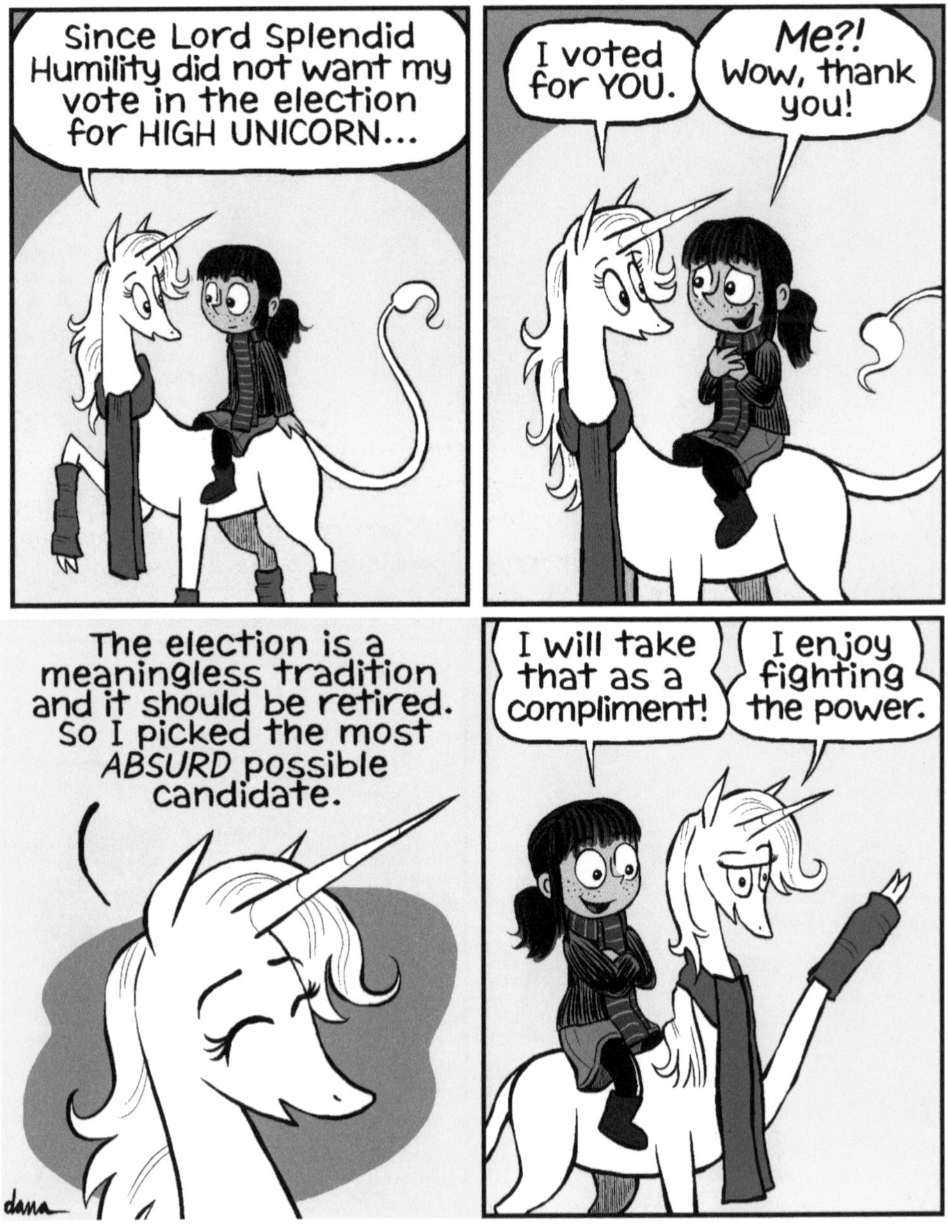
Since Lord Splendid Humility did not want my vote in the election for HIGH UNICORN...
I voted for YOU.
Me?! Wow, thank you!
The election is a meaningless tradition and it should be retired. So I picked the most *ABSURD* possible candidate.
I will take that as a compliment!
I enjoy fighting the power.
dana

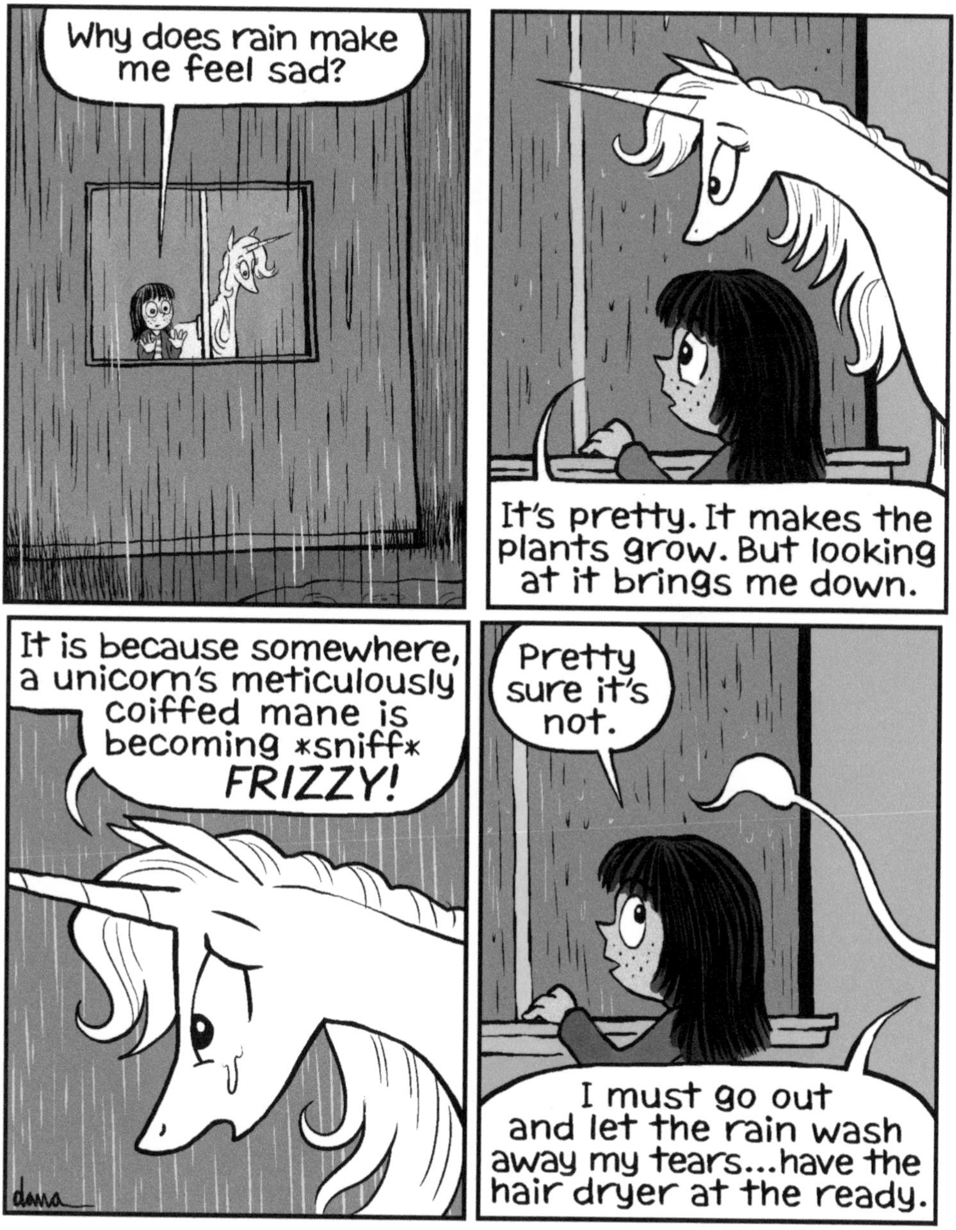
Why does rain make me feel sad?
It's pretty. It makes the plants grow. But looking at it brings me down.
It is because somewhere, a unicorn's meticulously coiffed mane is becoming *sniff* FRIZZY!
Pretty sure it's not.
I must go out and let the rain wash away my tears...have the hair dryer at the ready.
dana

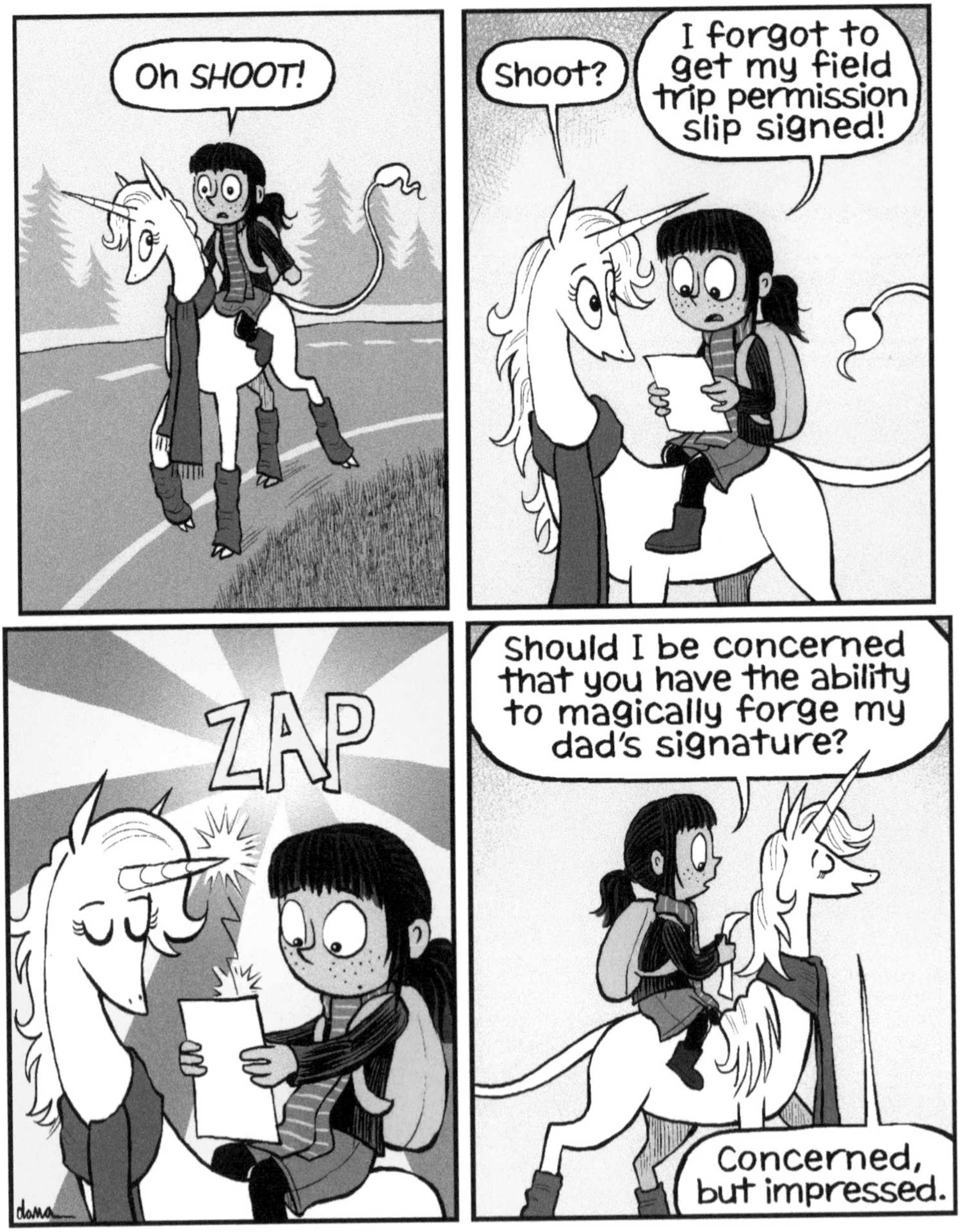
Oh SHOOT!
Shoot?
I forgot to get my field trip permission slip signed!
ZAP
Should I be concerned that you have the ability to magically forge my dad's signature?
Concerned, but impressed.
dana

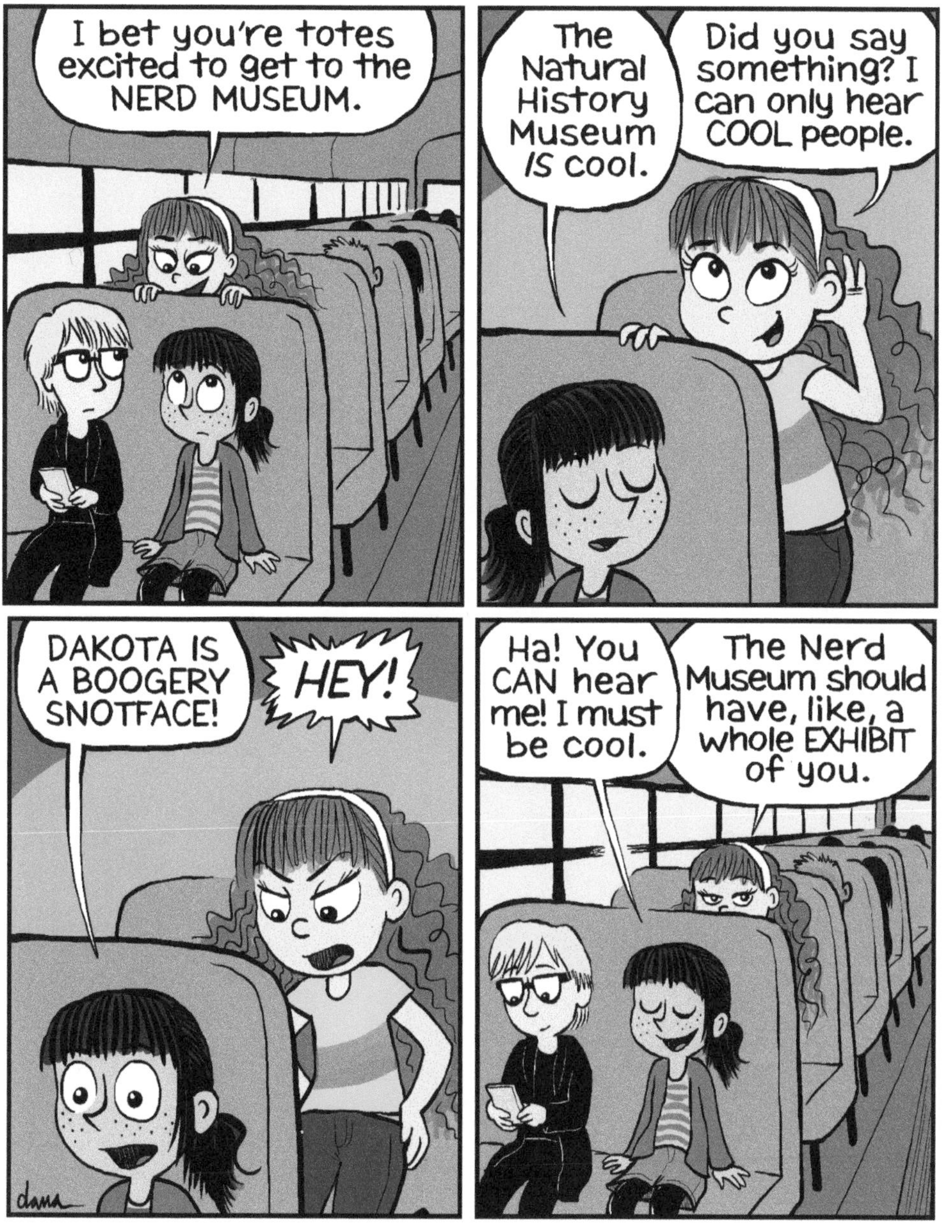
I bet you're totes excited to get to the NERD MUSEUM.
The Natural History Museum *IS* cool.
Did you say something? I can only hear COOL people.
DAKOTA IS A BOOGERY SNOTFACE!
HEY!
Ha! You CAN hear me! I must be cool.
The Nerd Museum should have, like, a whole EXHIBIT of you.
dana

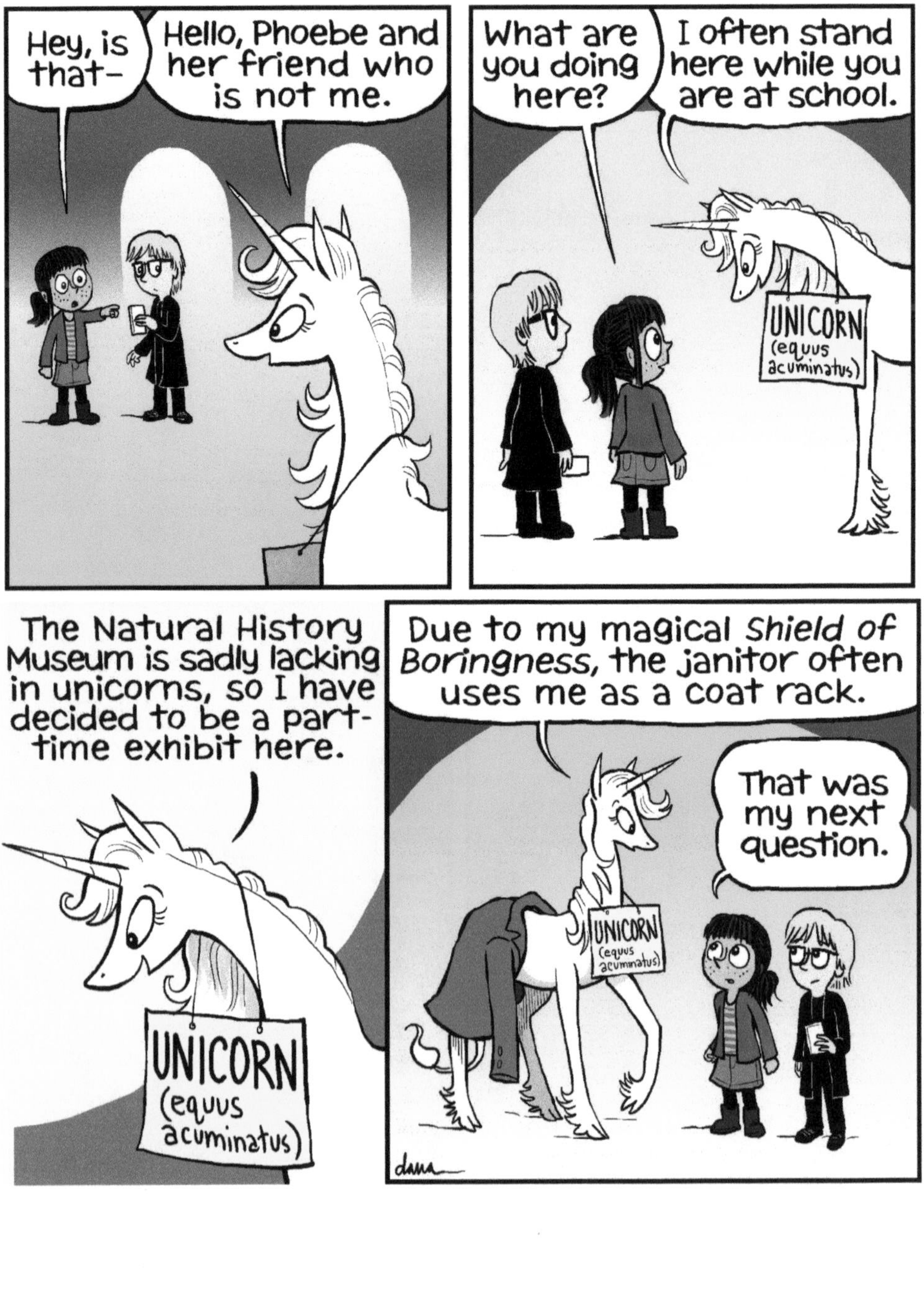

Hey, is that-
Hello, Phoebe and her friend who is not me.
What are you doing here?
I often stand here while you are at school.
UNICORN (equus acuminatus)
The Natural History Museum is sadly lacking in unicorns, so I have decided to be a part-time exhibit here.
UNICORN (equus acuminatus)
Due to my magical *Shield of Boringness,* the janitor often uses me as a coat rack.
That was my next question.
UNICORN (equus acuminatus)
dana

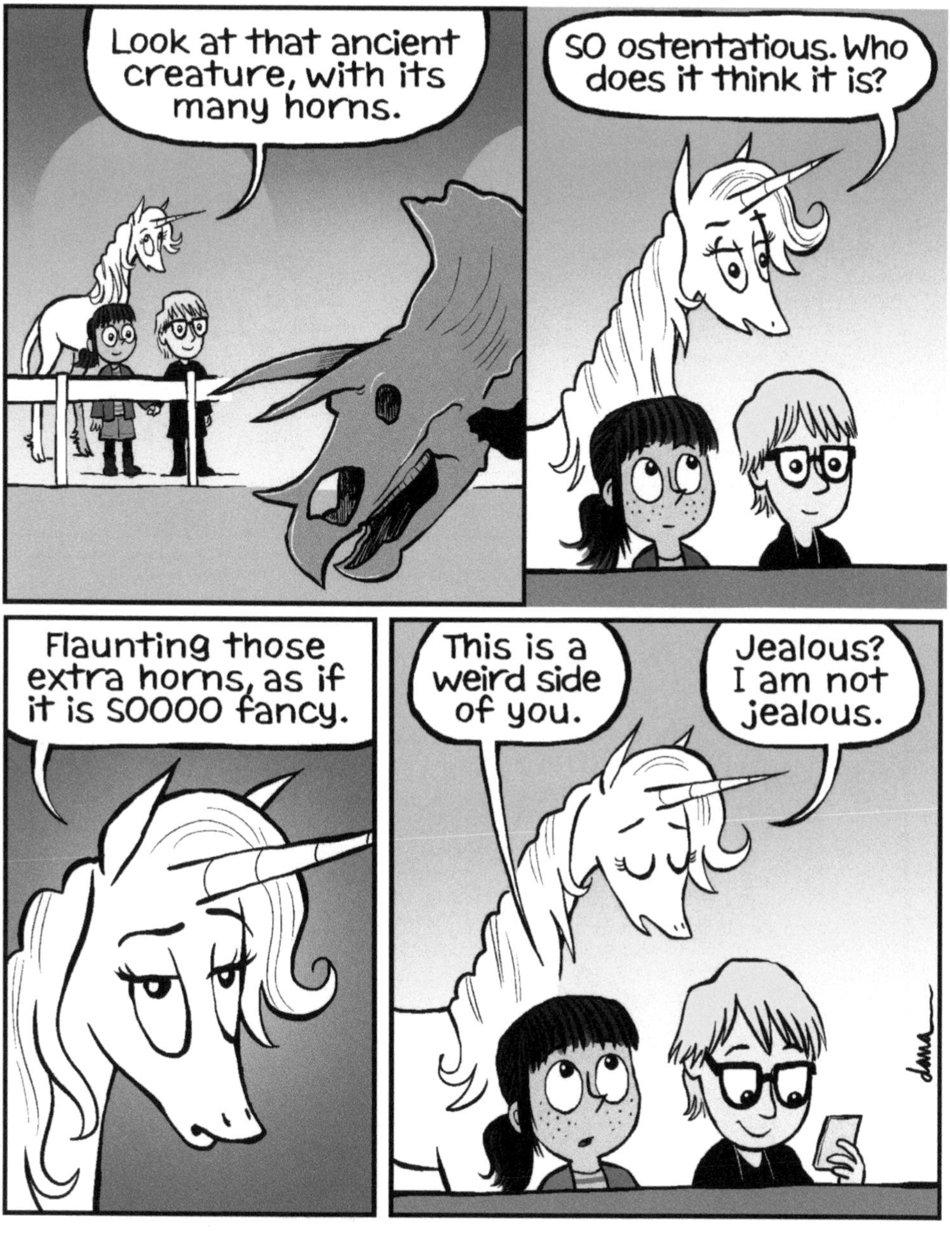
Look at that ancient creature, with its many horns.
SO ostentatious. Who does it think it is?
Flaunting those extra horns, as if it is SOOOO fancy.
This is a weird side of you.
Jealous? I am not jealous.
dana

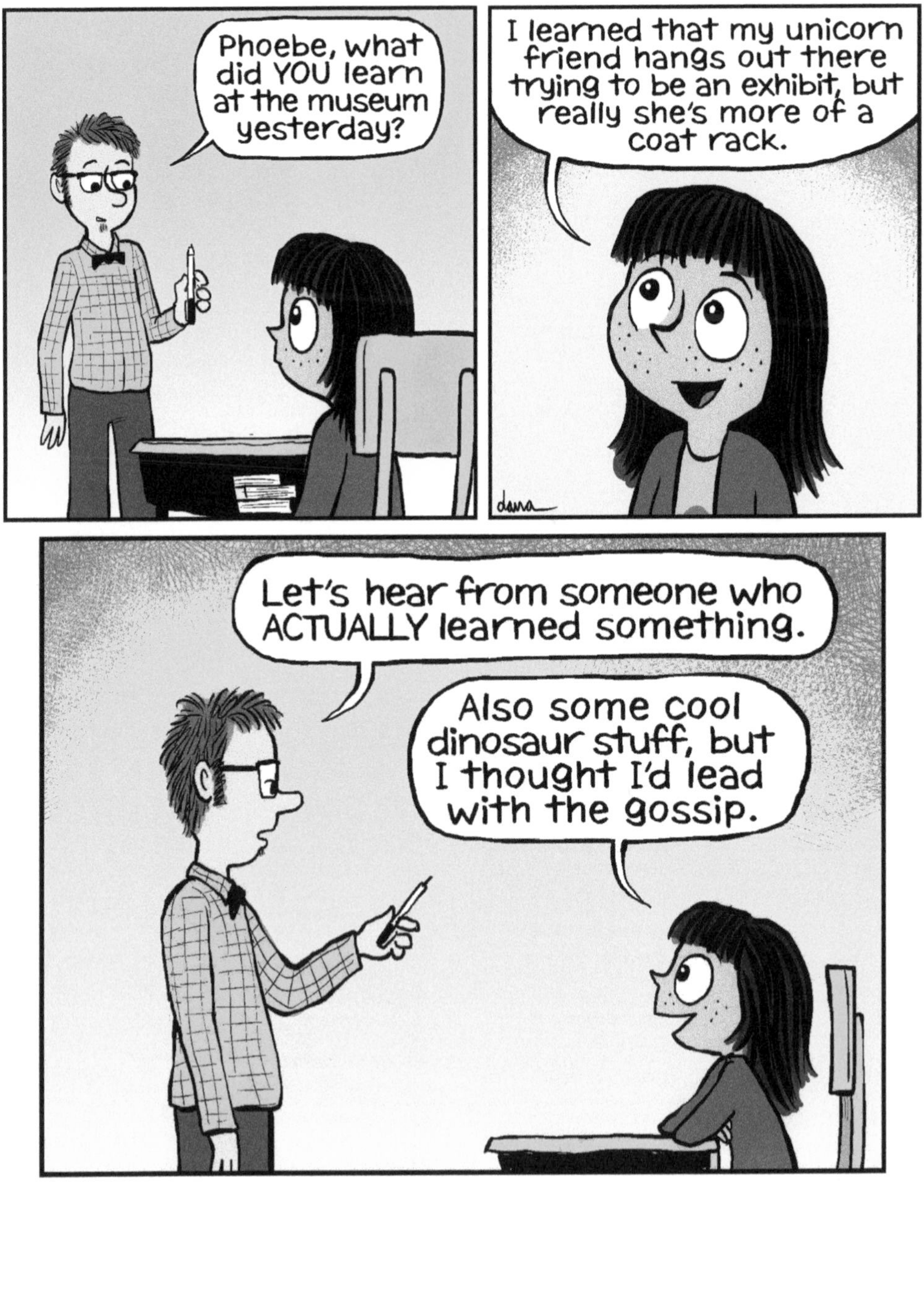
Phoebe, what did YOU learn at the museum yesterday?
I learned that my unicorn friend hangs out there trying to be an exhibit, but really she's more of a coat rack.
dana
Let's hear from someone who ACTUALLY learned something.
Also some cool dinosaur stuff, but I thought I'd lead with the gossip.

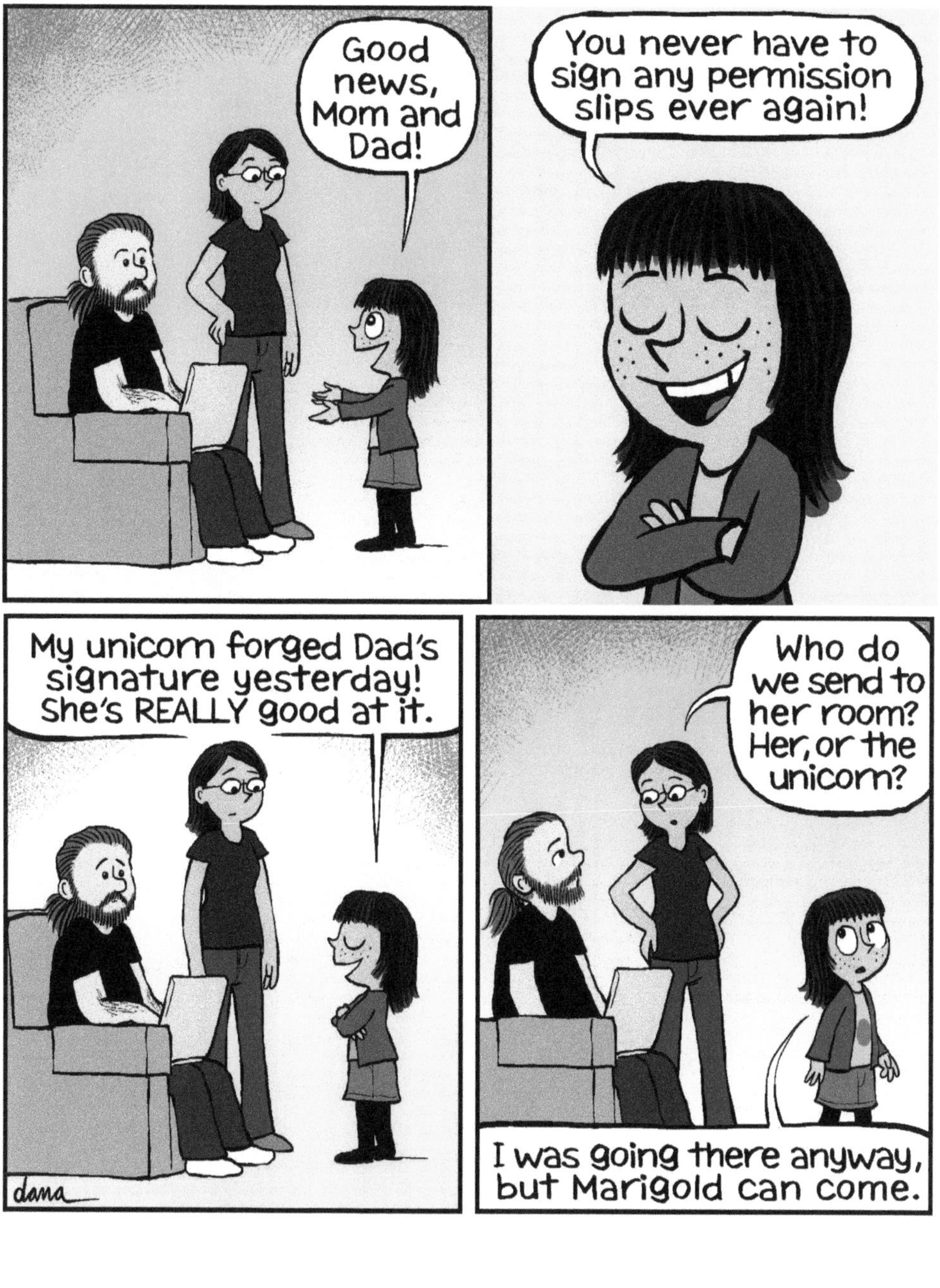
Good news, Mom and Dad!
You never have to sign any permission slips ever again!
My unicorn forged Dad's signature yesterday! She's REALLY good at it.
dana
Who do we send to her room? Her, or the unicorn?
I was going there anyway, but Marigold can come.

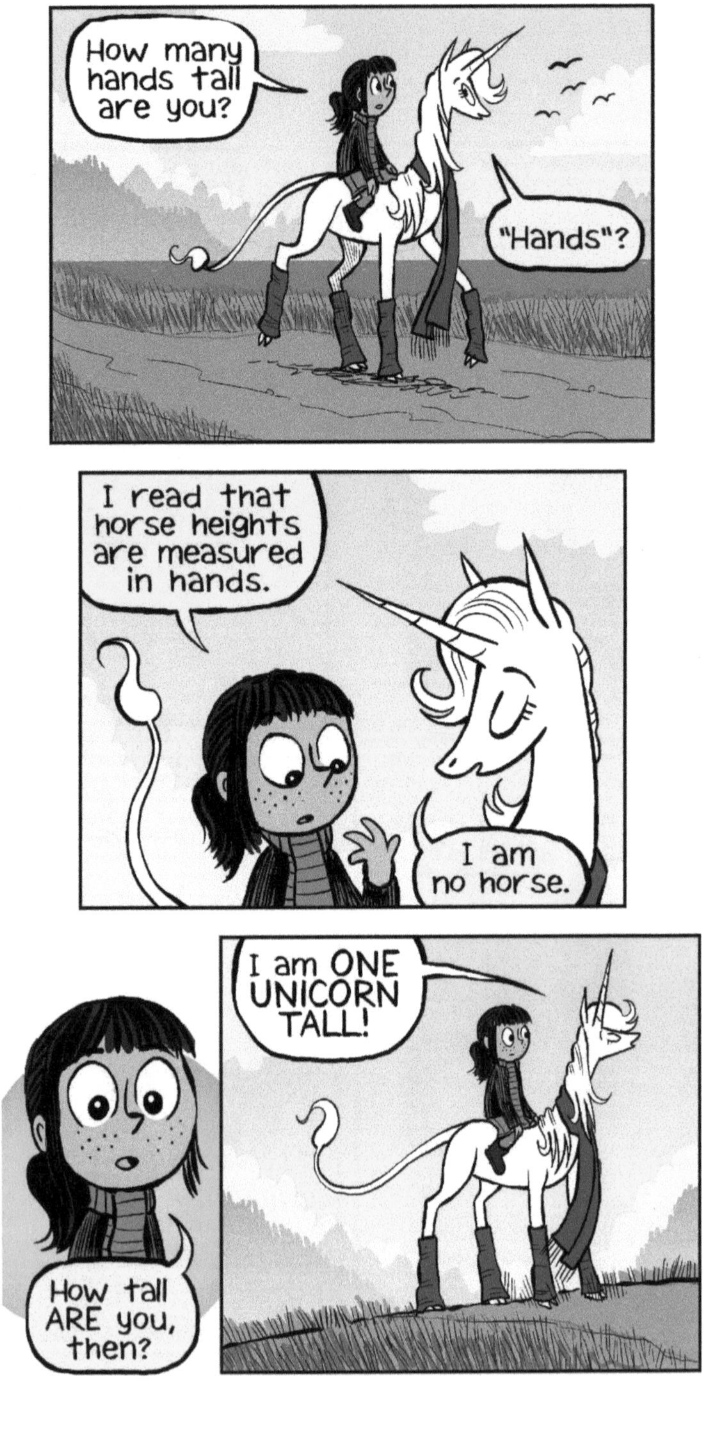
How many hands tall are you?
"Hands"?
I read that horse heights are measured in hands.
I am no horse.
How tall ARE you, then?
I am ONE UNICORN TALL!

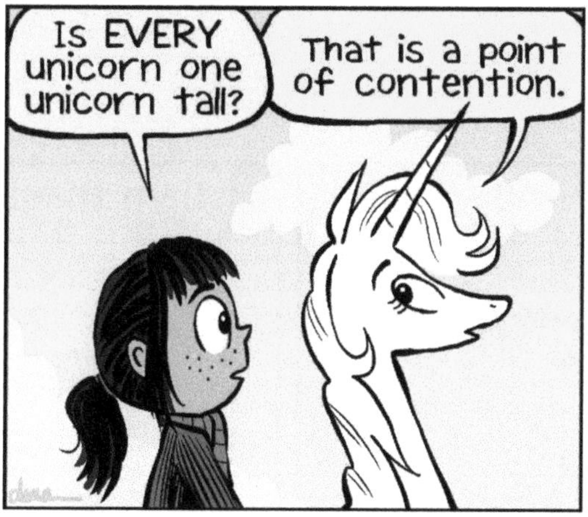
Is EVERY unicorn one unicorn tall?
That is a point of contention.

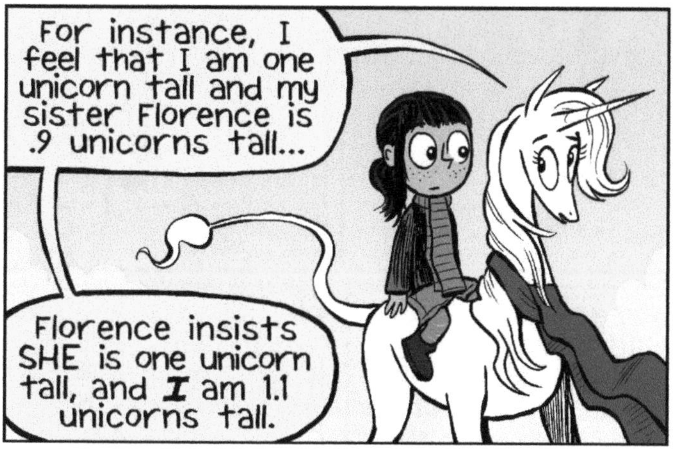
For instance, I feel that I am one unicorn tall and my sister Florence is .9 unicorns tall...
Florence insists SHE is one unicorn tall, and I am 1.1 unicorns tall.

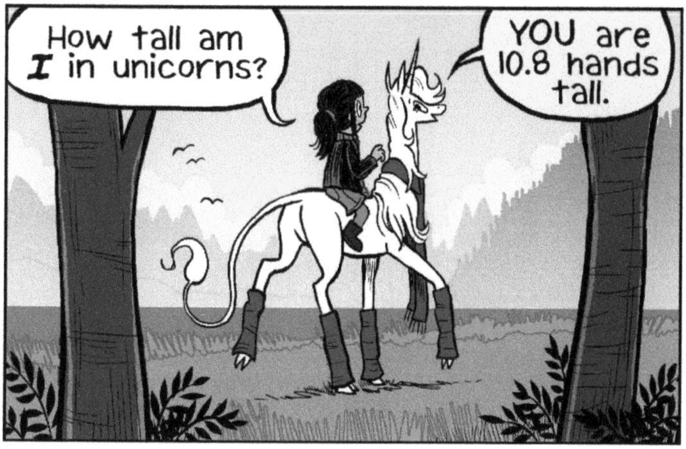
How tall am I in unicorns?
YOU are 10.8 hands tall.

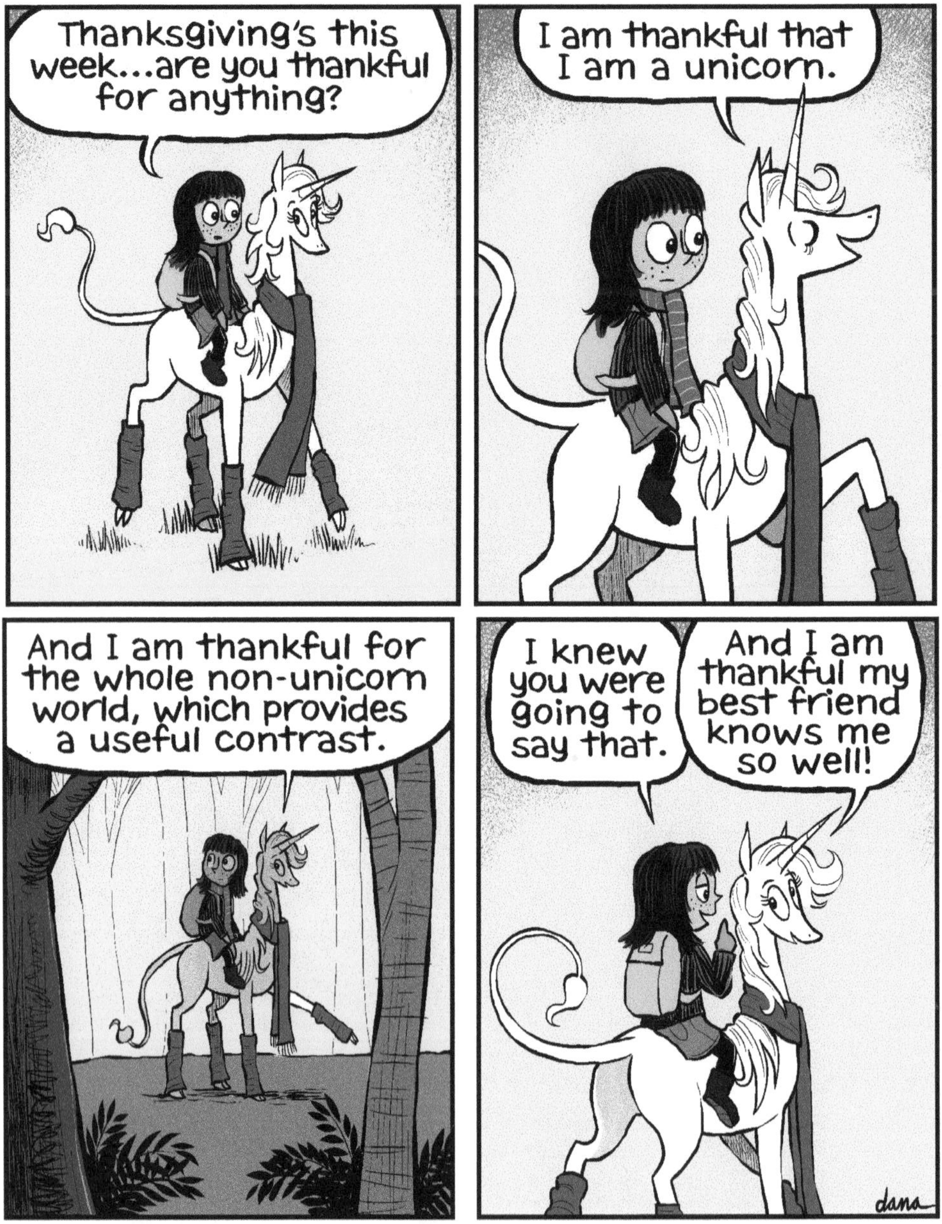
Thanksgiving's this week...are you thankful for anything?
I am thankful that I am a unicorn.
And I am thankful for the whole non-unicorn world, which provides a useful contrast.
I knew you were going to say that.
And I am thankful my best friend knows me so well!
dana

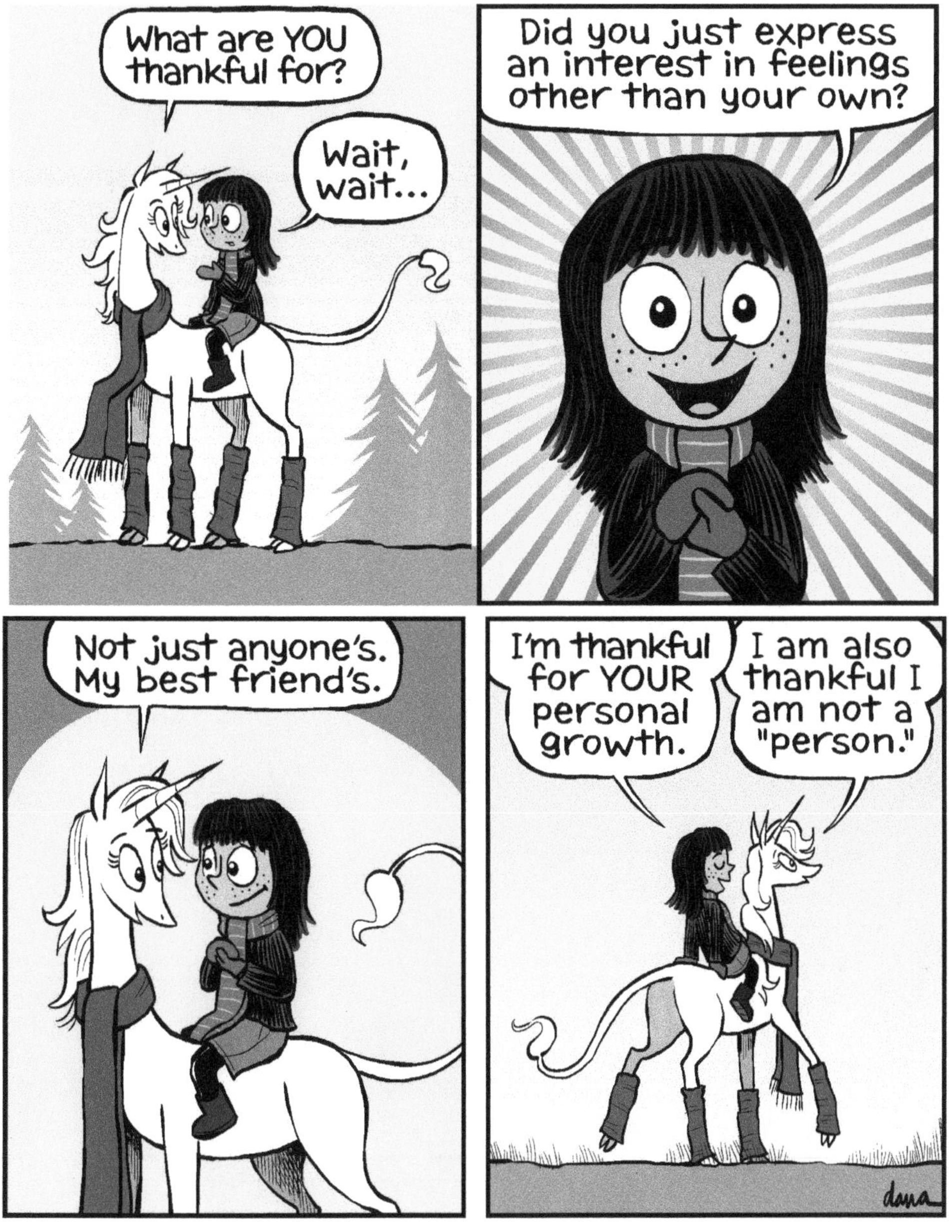

What are YOU thankful for?
Wait, wait...
Did you just express an interest in feelings other than your own?
Not just anyone's. My best friend's.
I'm thankful for YOUR personal growth.
I am also thankful I am not a "person."
dana

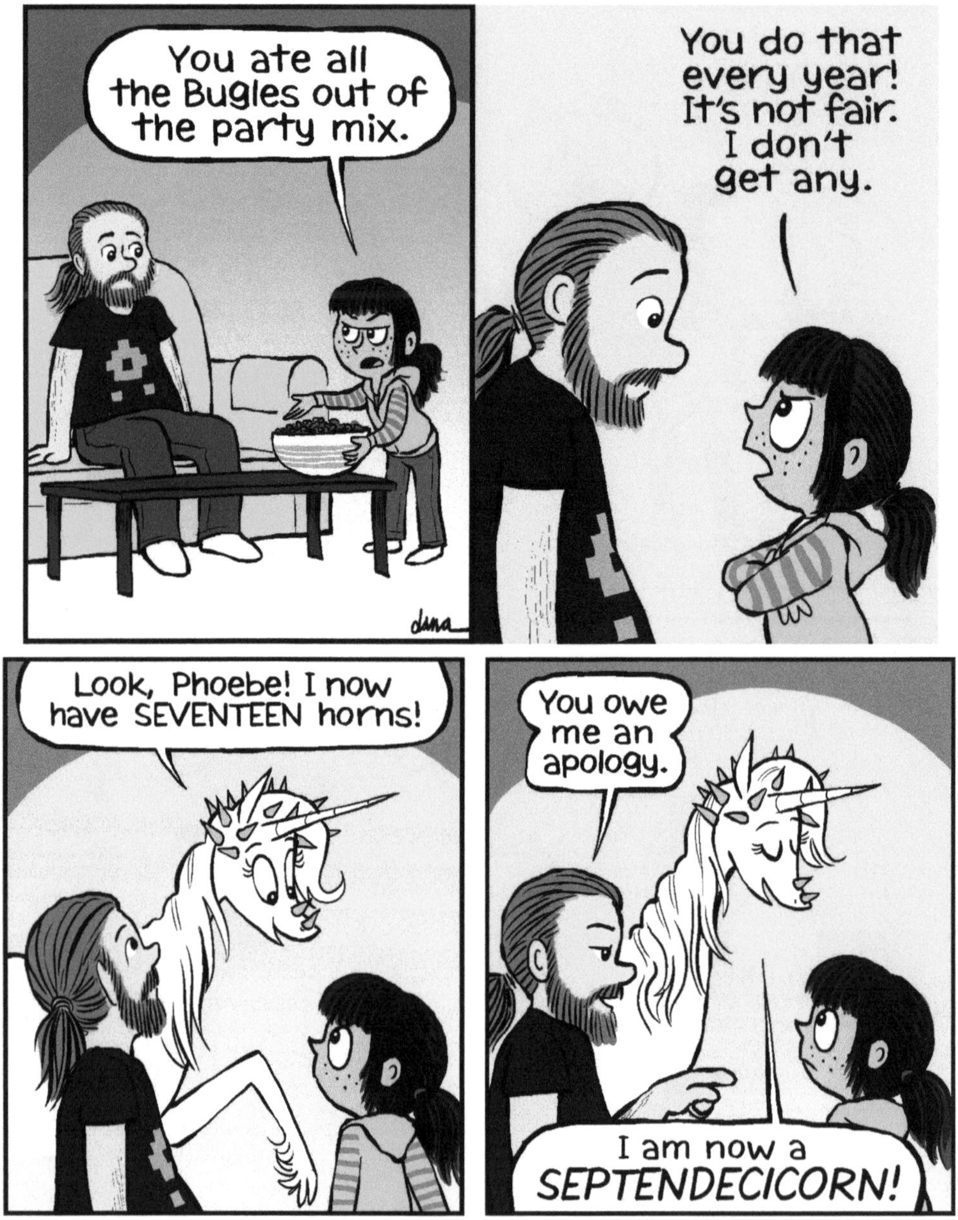
You ate all the Bugles out of the party mix.
You do that every year! It's not fair. I don't get any.
Look, Phoebe! I now have SEVENTEEN horns!
You owe me an apology.
I am now a *SEPTENDECICORN!*

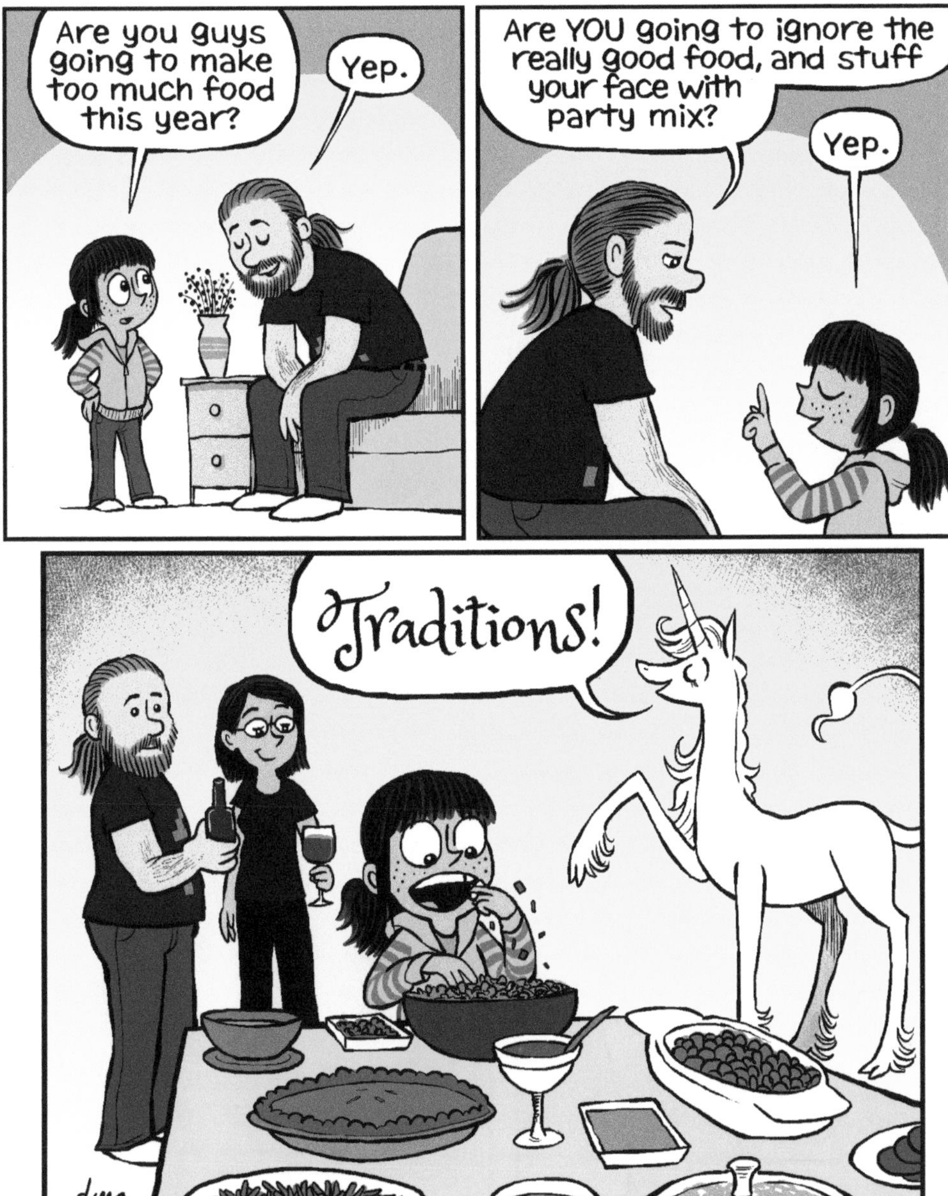
Are you guys going to make too much food this year?
Yep.
Are YOU going to ignore the really good food, and stuff your face with party mix?
Yep.
Traditions!
dana

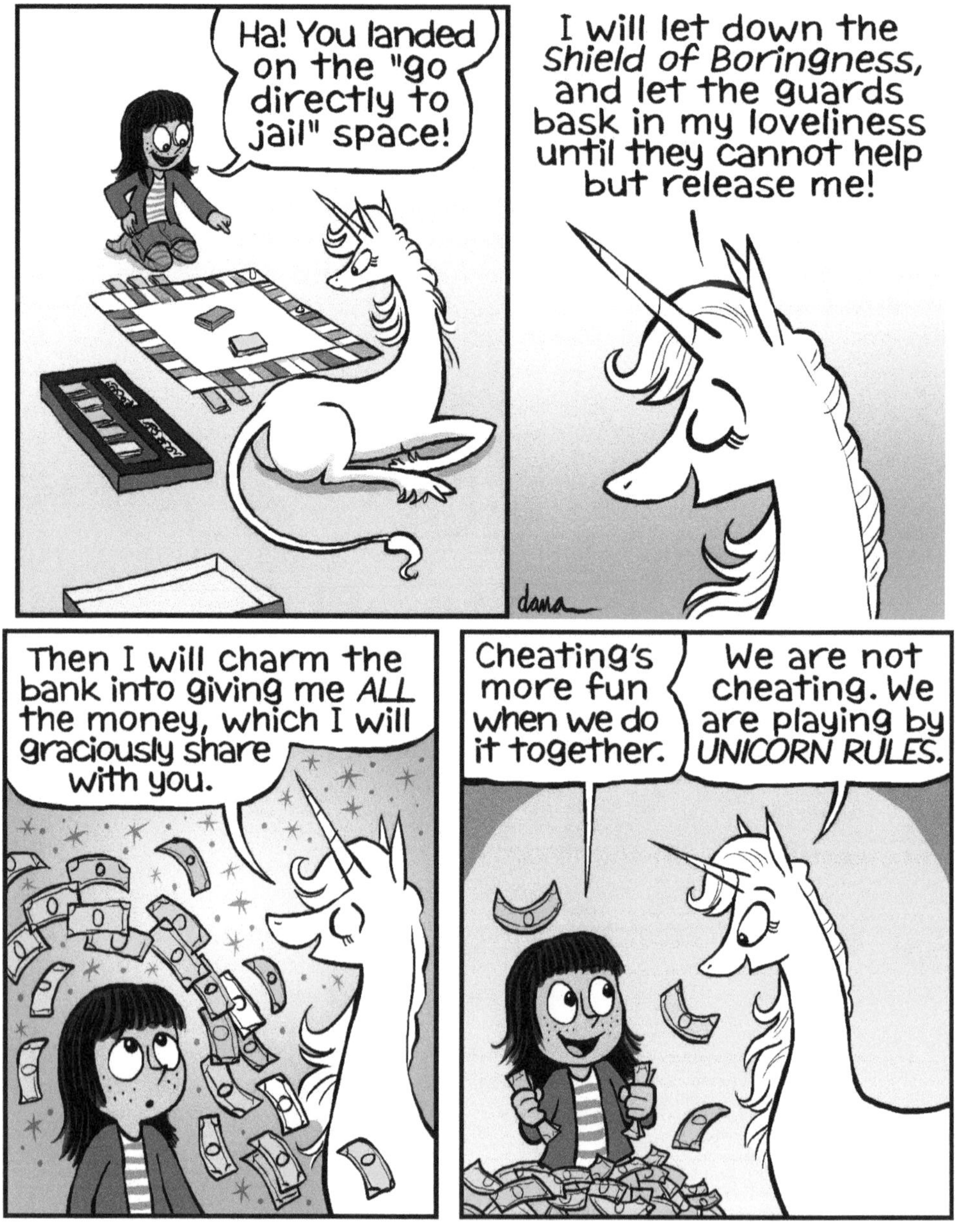
Ha! You landed on the "go directly to jail" space!
I will let down the *Shield of Boringness,* and let the guards bask in my loveliness until they cannot help but release me!
dana
Then I will charm the bank into giving me *ALL* the money, which I will graciously share with you.
Cheating's more fun when we do it together.
We are not cheating. We are playing by *UNICORN RULES.*

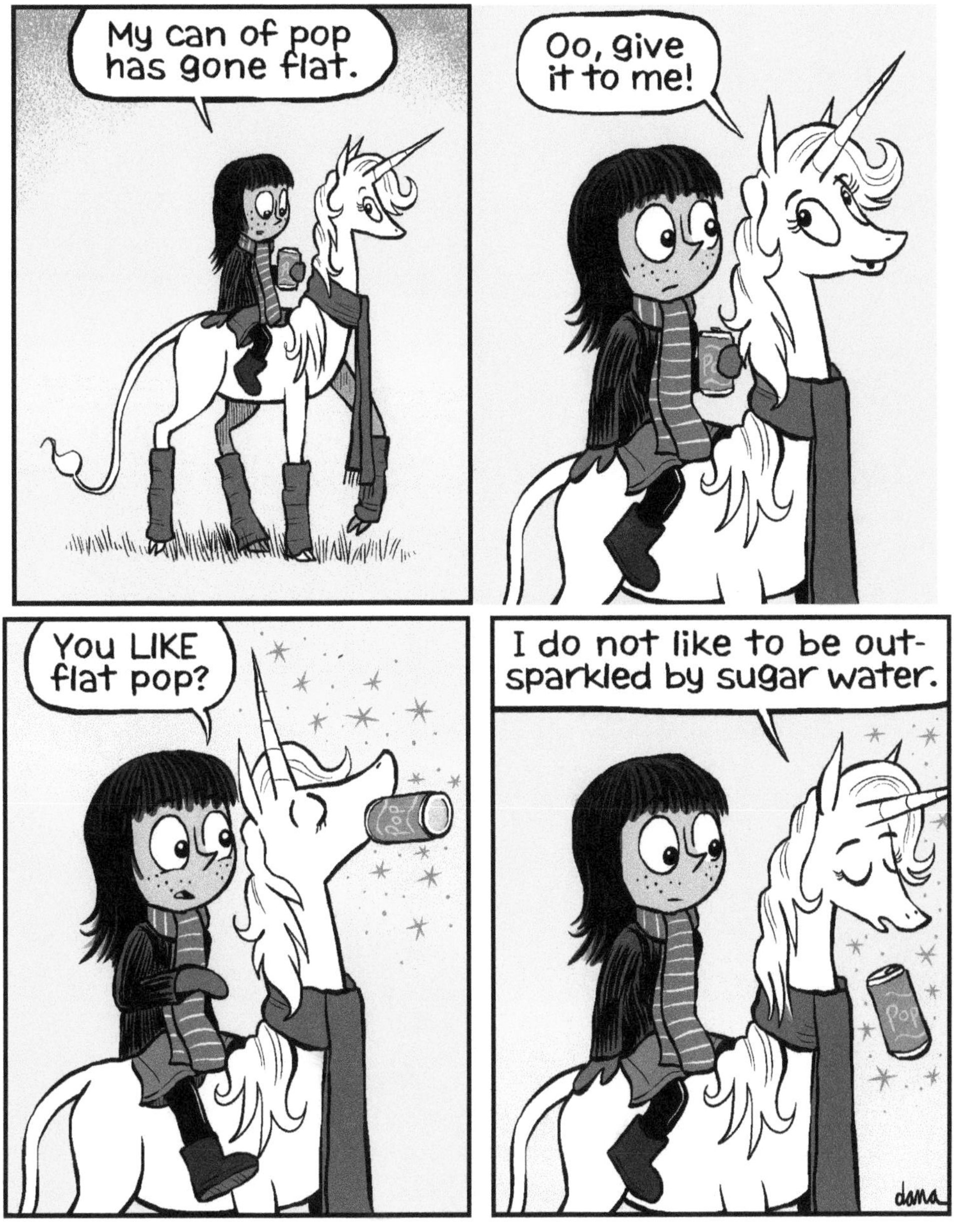
My can of pop has gone flat.
Oo, give it to me!
You LIKE flat pop?
I do not like to be out-sparkled by sugar water.
dana

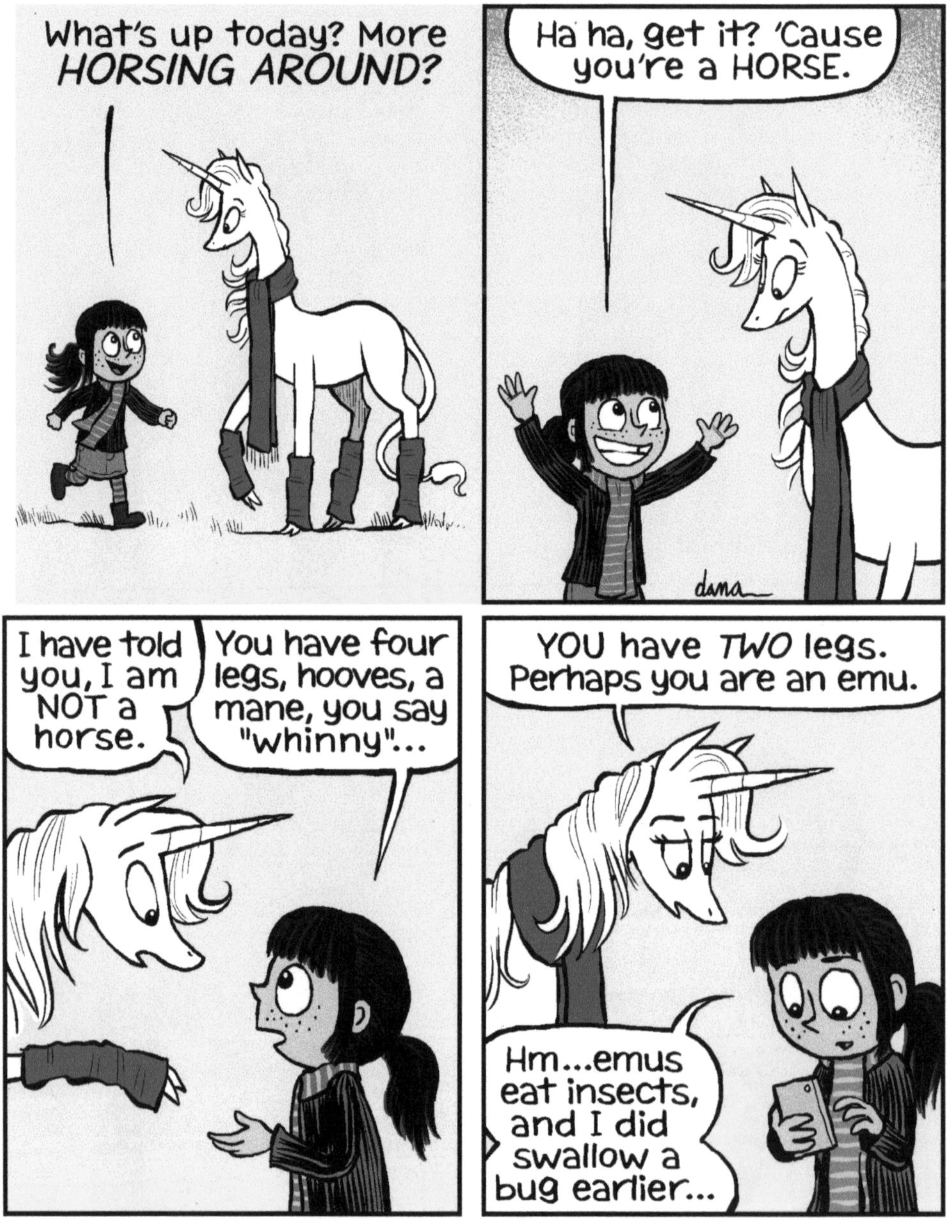
What's up today? More HORSING AROUND?
Ha ha, get it? 'Cause you're a HORSE.
dana
I have told you, I am NOT a horse.
You have four legs, hooves, a mane, you say "whinny"...
YOU have TWO legs. Perhaps you are an emu.
Hm...emus eat insects, and I did swallow a bug earlier...

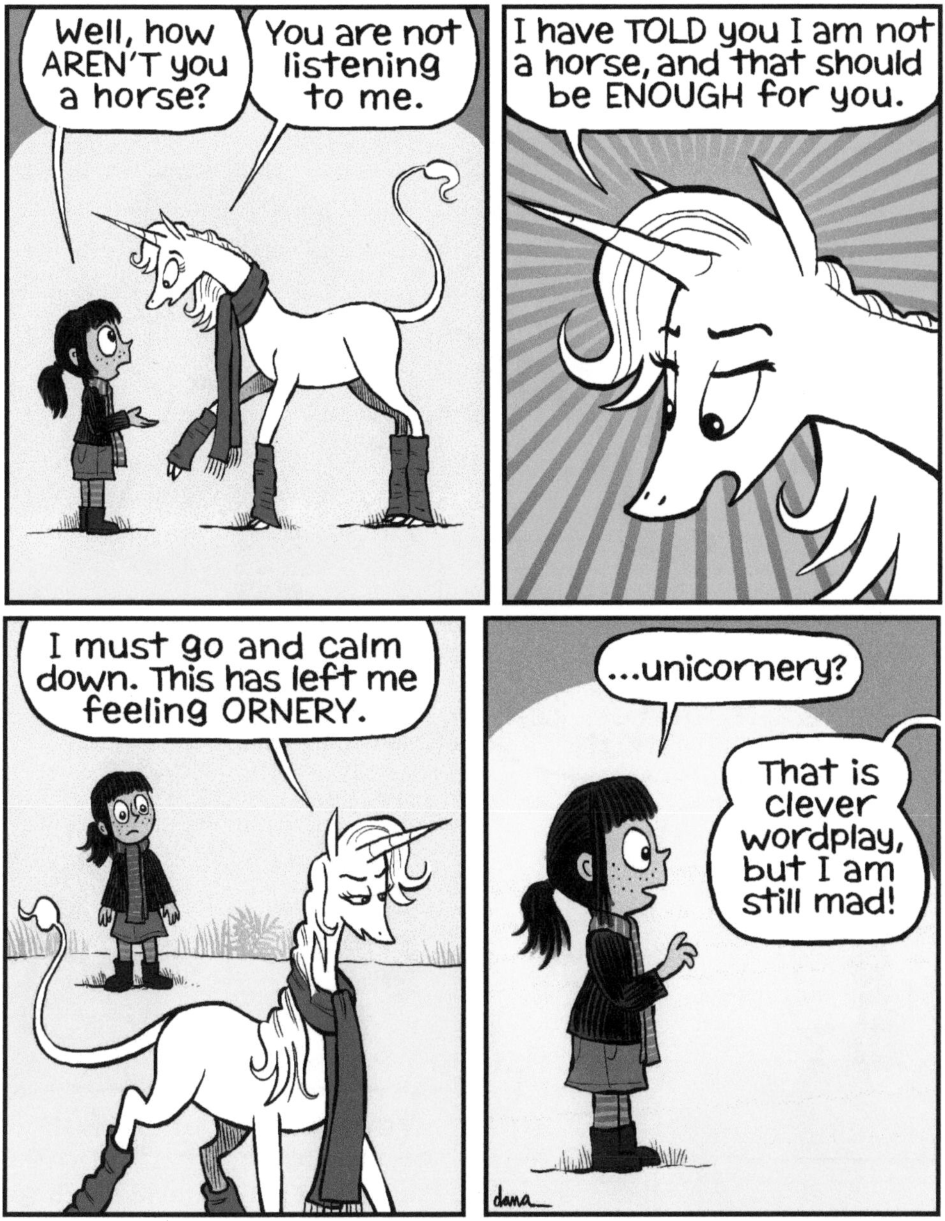
Well, how AREN'T you a horse?
You are not listening to me.
I have TOLD you I am not a horse, and that should be ENOUGH for you.
I must go and calm down. This has left me feeling ORNERY.
...unicornery?
That is clever wordplay, but I am still mad!
dana

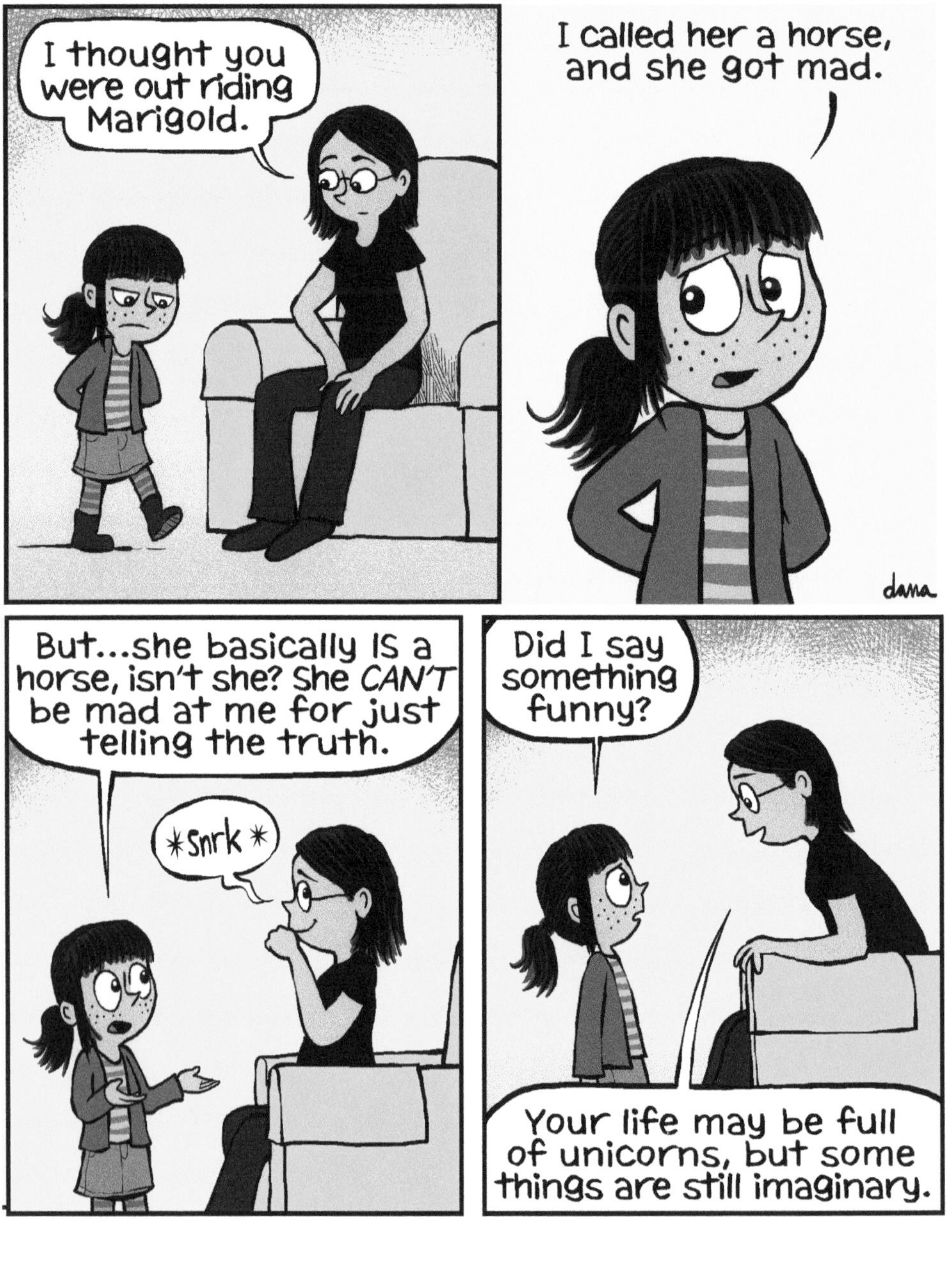
I thought you were out riding Marigold.
I called her a horse, and she got mad.
dana
But...she basically IS a horse, isn't she? She *CAN'T* be mad at me for just telling the truth.
*snrk*
Did I say something funny?
Your life may be full of unicorns, but some things are still imaginary.

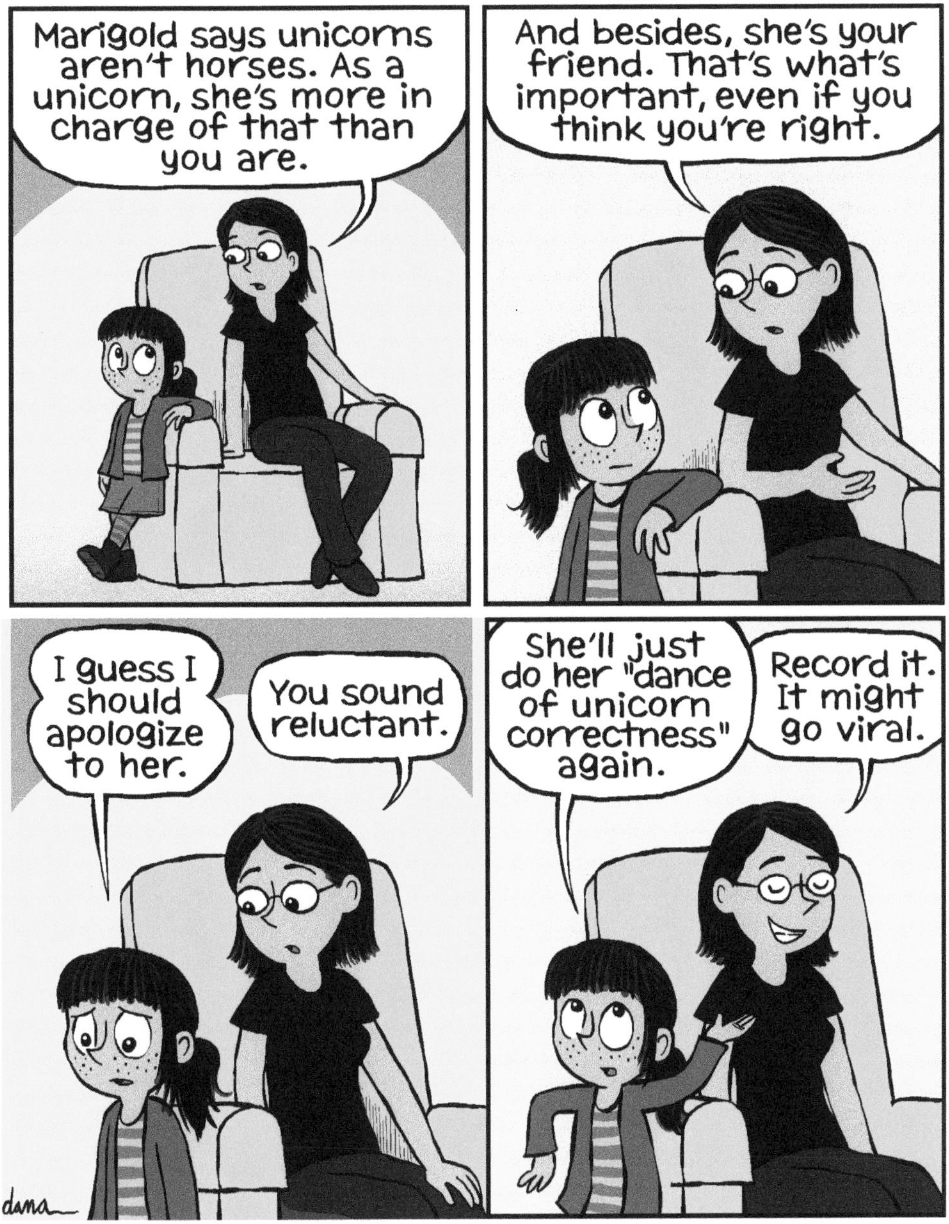
Marigold says unicorns aren't horses. As a unicorn, she's more in charge of that than you are.
And besides, she's your friend. That's what's important, even if you think you're right.
I guess I should apologize to her.
You sound reluctant.
She'll just do her "dance of unicorn correctness" again.
Record it. It might go viral.
dana

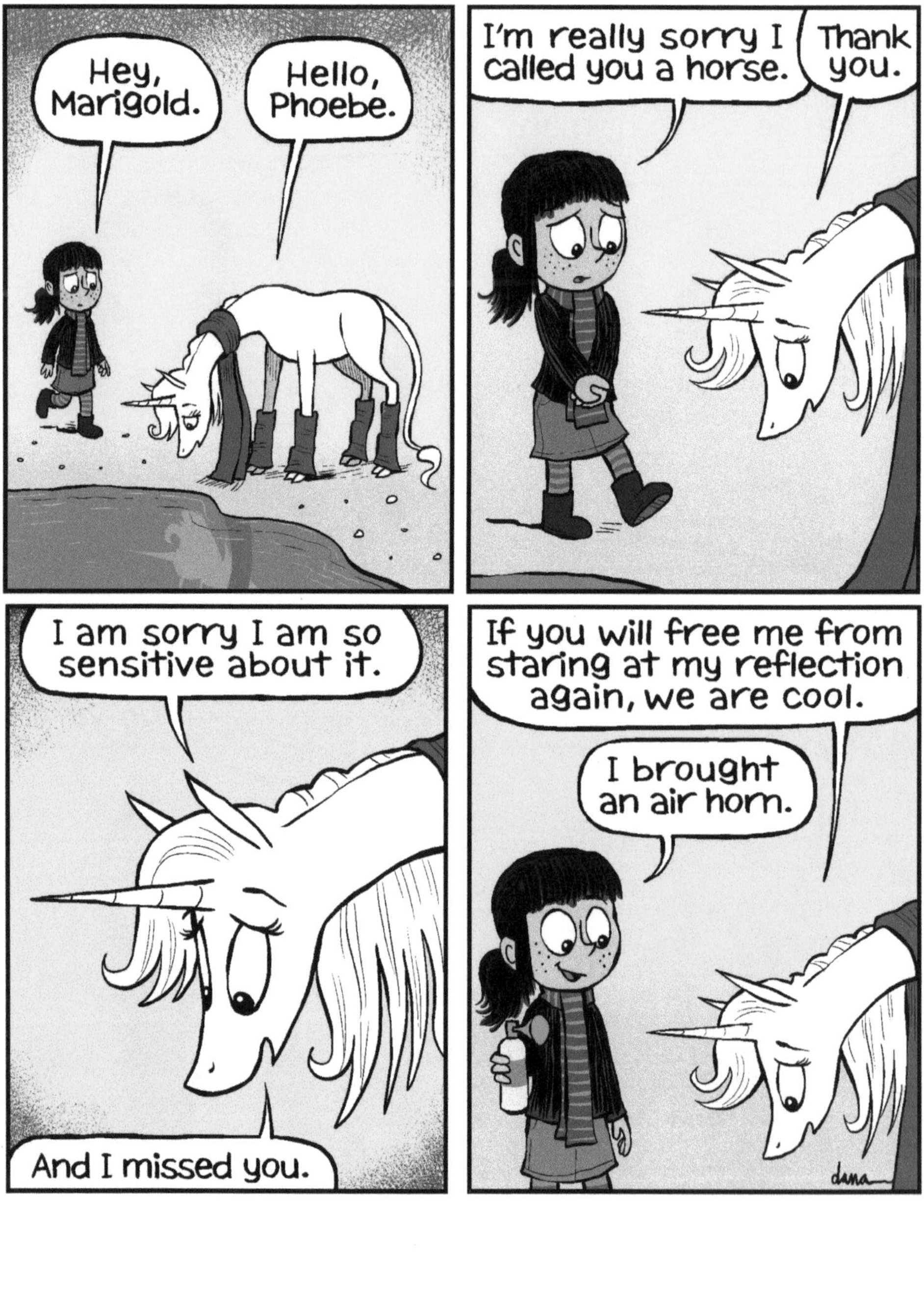
Hey, Marigold.
Hello, Phoebe.
I'm really sorry I called you a horse.
Thank you.
I am sorry I am so sensitive about it.
And I missed you.
If you will free me from staring at my reflection again, we are cool.
I brought an air horn.
dana

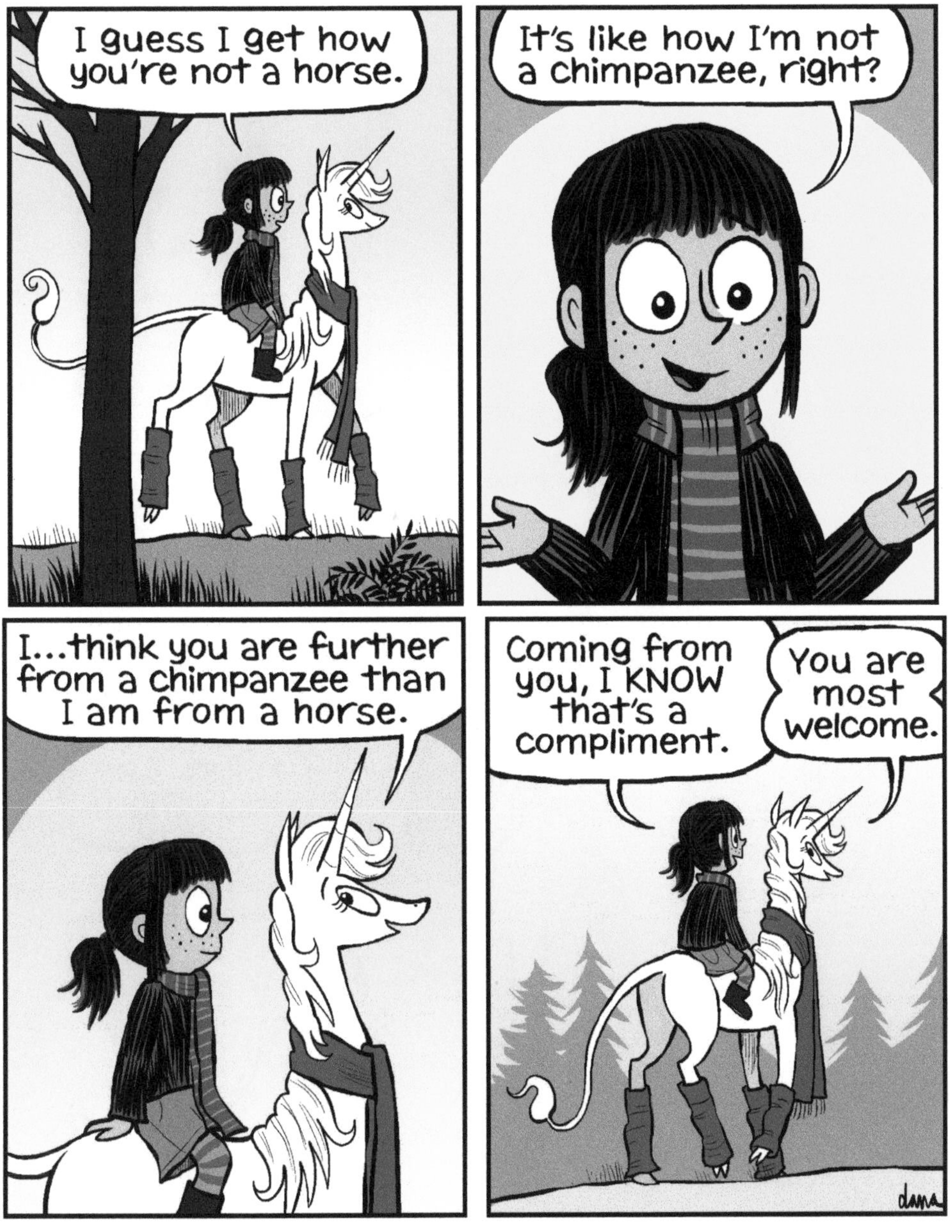
I guess I get how you're not a horse.
It's like how I'm not a chimpanzee, right?
I...think you are further from a chimpanzee than I am from a horse.
Coming from you, I KNOW that's a compliment.
You are most welcome.
dana

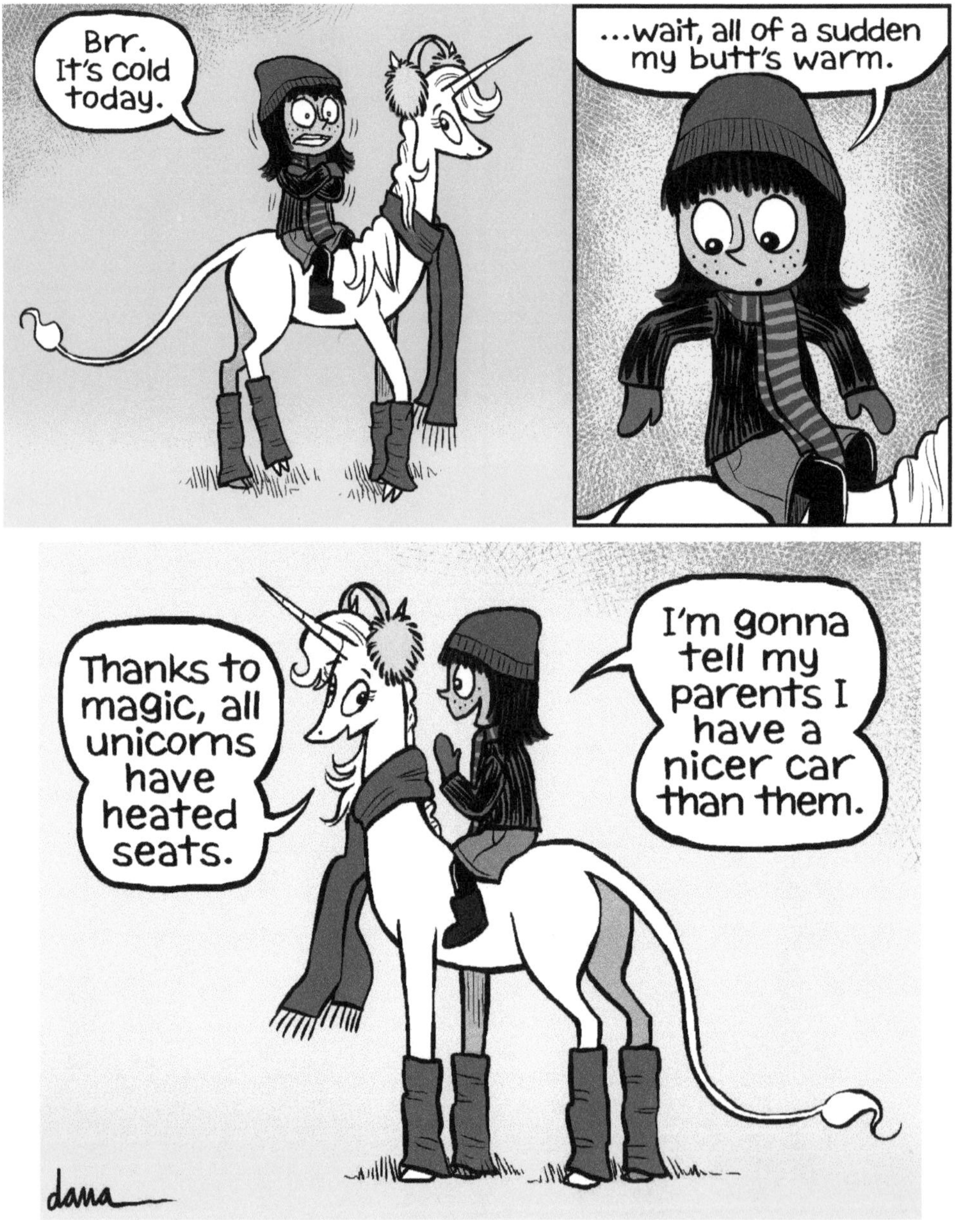
Brr. It's cold today.
...wait, all of a sudden my butt's warm.
Thanks to magic, all unicorns have heated seats.
I'm gonna tell my parents I have a nicer car than them.
dana

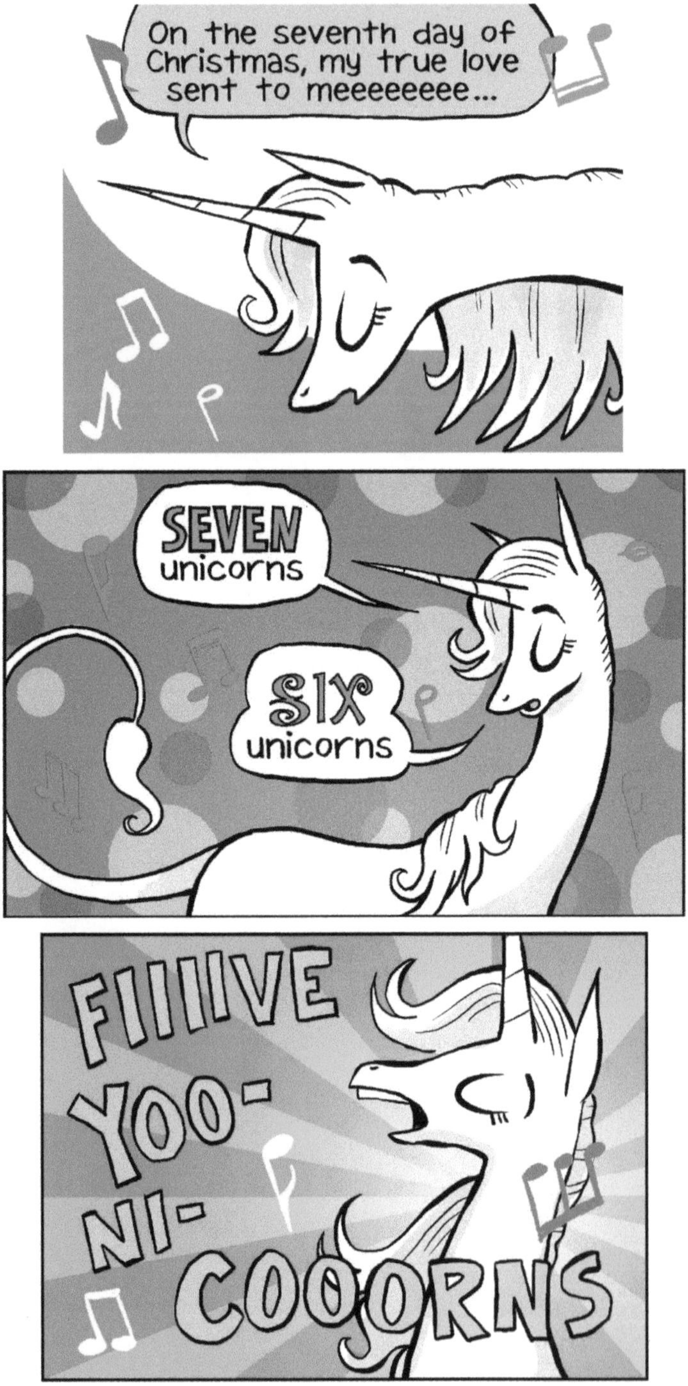

On the seventh day of Christmas, my true love sent to meeeeeeee...
SEVEN unicorns
SIX unicorns
FIIIVE YOO-NI-COOORNS

FOUR unicorns
THREE unicorns
TWO-OO unicorns
And a YOO-OO-OO OO-NI-COOORN!
Now you have a UNICORNAMENT!
dana

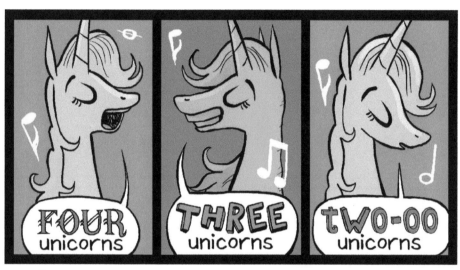

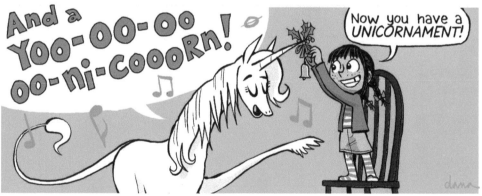

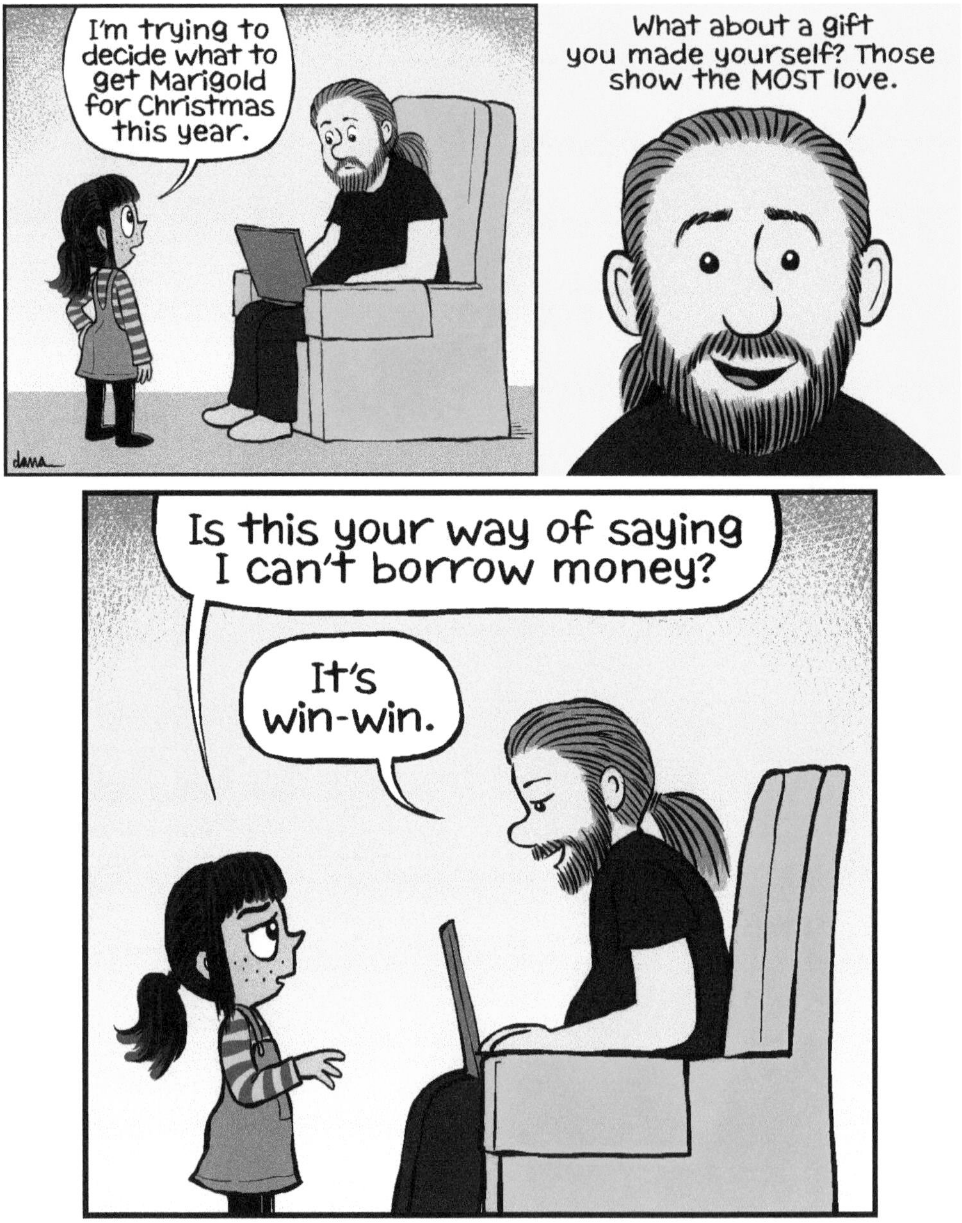
I'm trying to decide what to get Marigold for Christmas this year.
What about a gift you made yourself? Those show the MOST love.
Is this your way of saying I can't borrow money?
It's win-win.

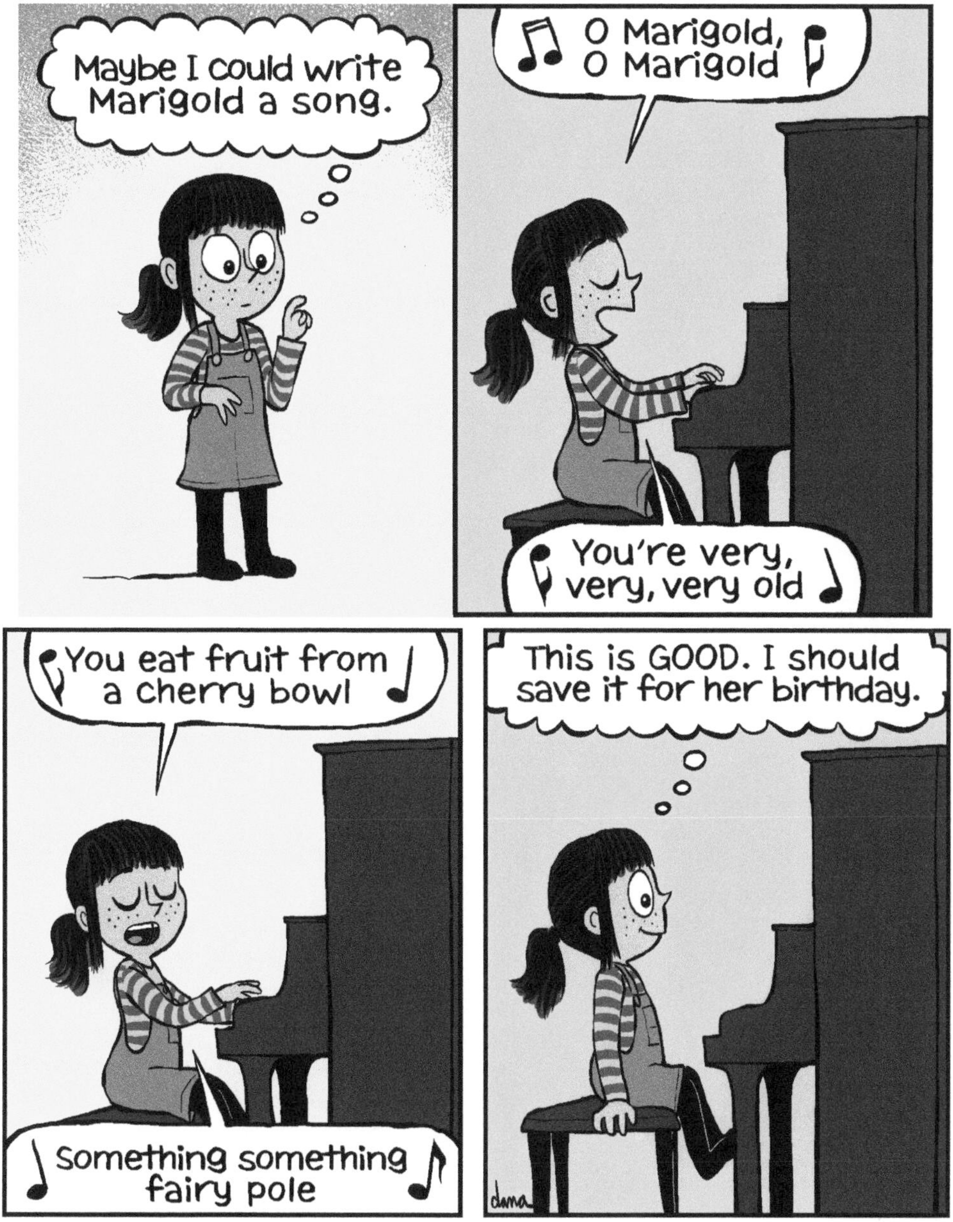
Maybe I could write Marigold a song.
O Marigold, O Marigold
You're very, very, very old
You eat fruit from a cherry bowl
Something something fairy pole
This is GOOD. I should save it for her birthday.

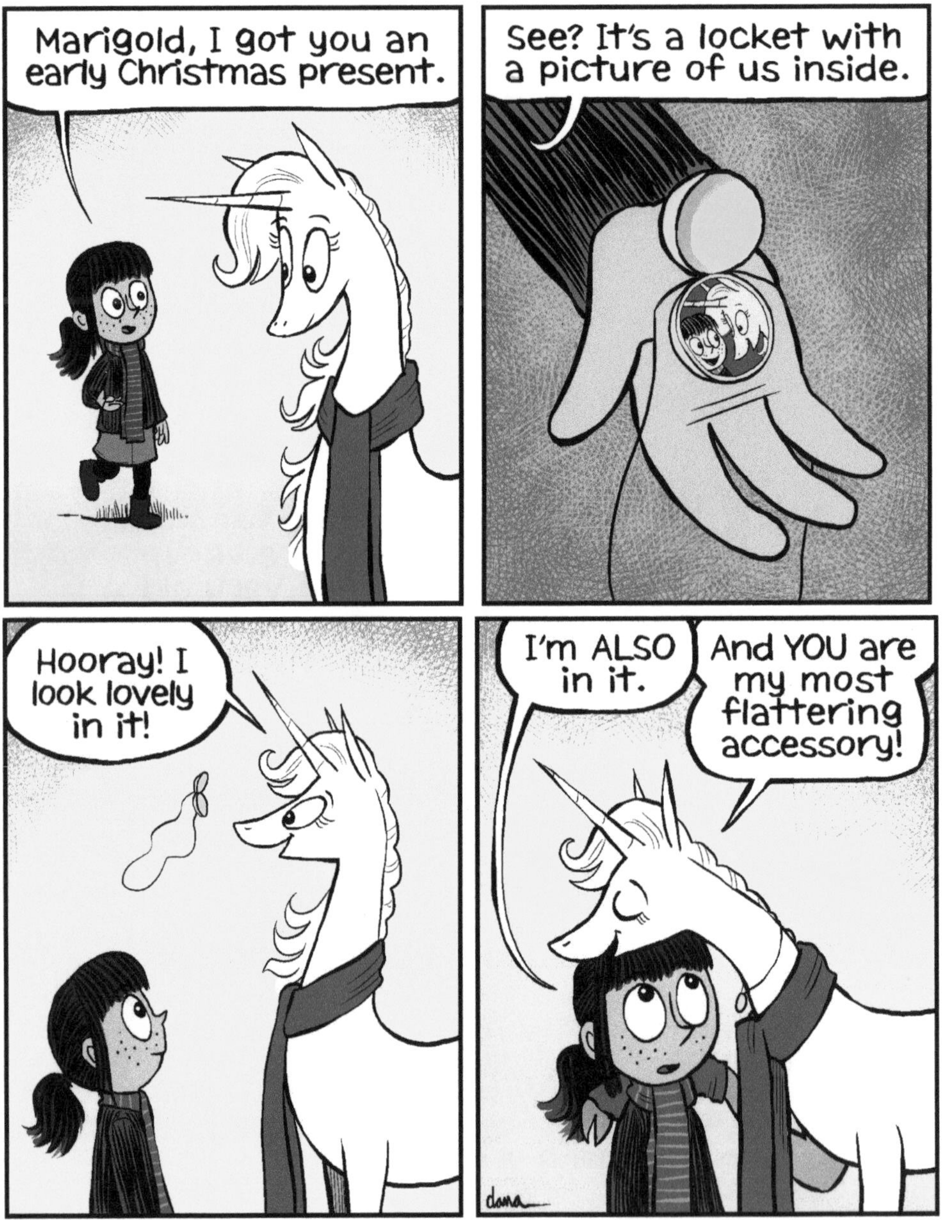
Marigold, I got you an early Christmas present.
See? It's a locket with a picture of us inside.
Hooray! I look lovely in it!
I'm ALSO in it.
And YOU are my most flattering accessory!
dana

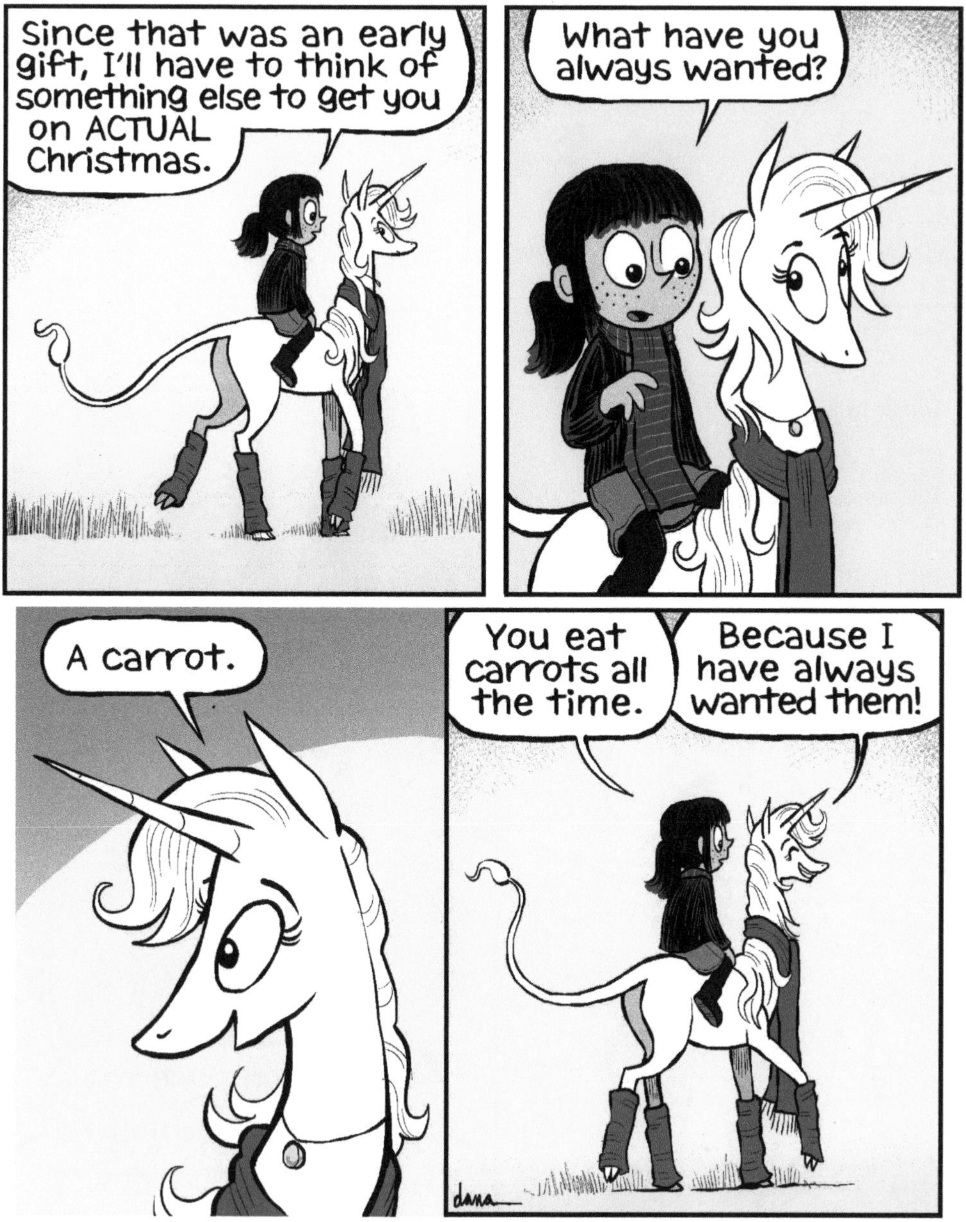
Since that was an early gift, I'll have to think of something else to get you on ACTUAL Christmas.
What have you always wanted?
A carrot.
You eat carrots all the time.
Because I have always wanted them!
dana

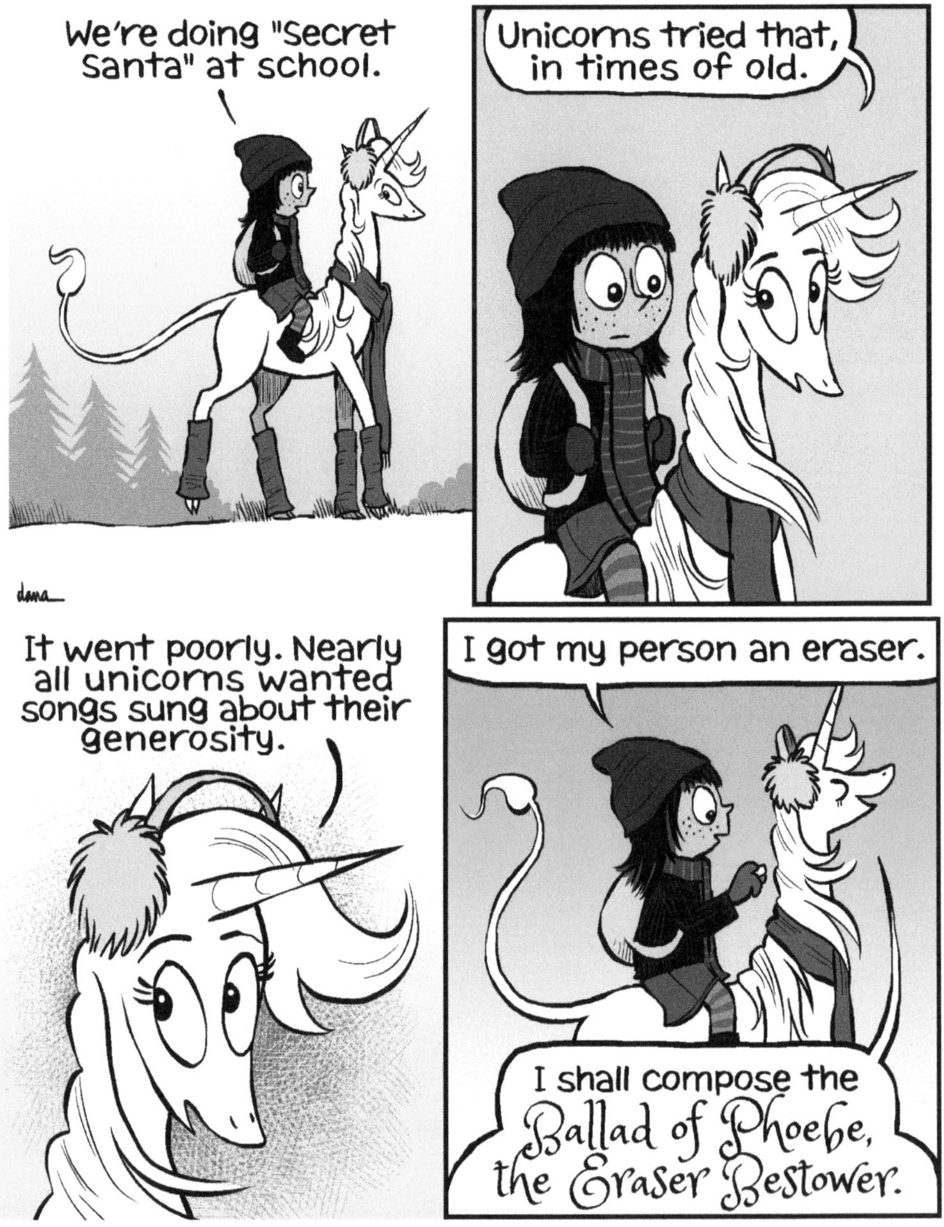
We're doing "Secret Santa" at school.
Unicorns tried that, in times of old.
dana
It went poorly. Nearly all unicorns wanted songs sung about their generosity.
I got my person an eraser.
I shall compose the Ballad of Phoebe, the Eraser Bestower.

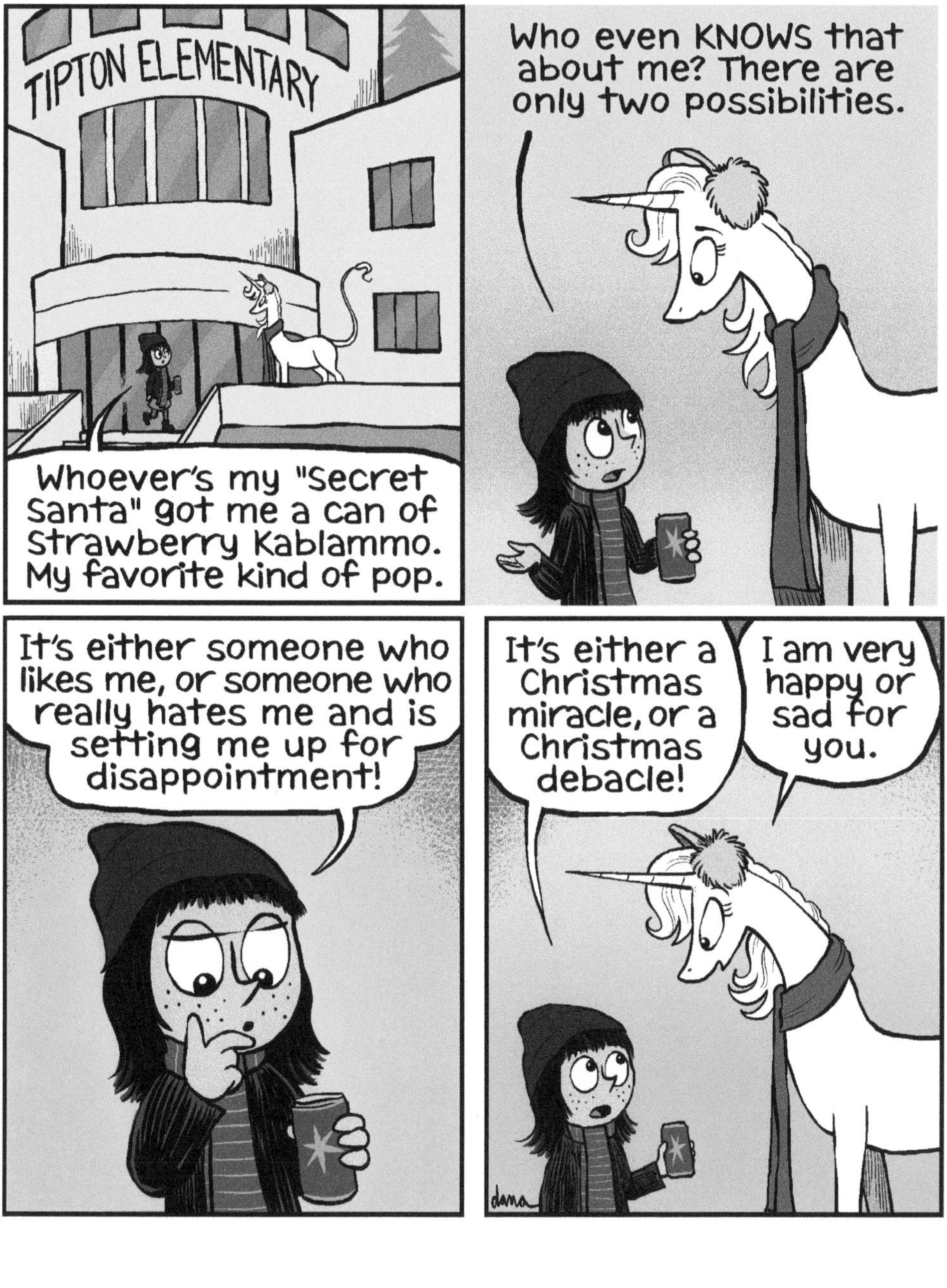
TIPTON ELEMENTARY
Whoever's my "Secret Santa" got me a can of Strawberry Kablammo. My favorite kind of pop.
Who even KNOWS that about me? There are only two possibilities.
It's either someone who likes me, or someone who really hates me and is setting me up for disappointment!
It's either a Christmas miracle, or a Christmas debacle!
I am very happy or sad for you.
dana

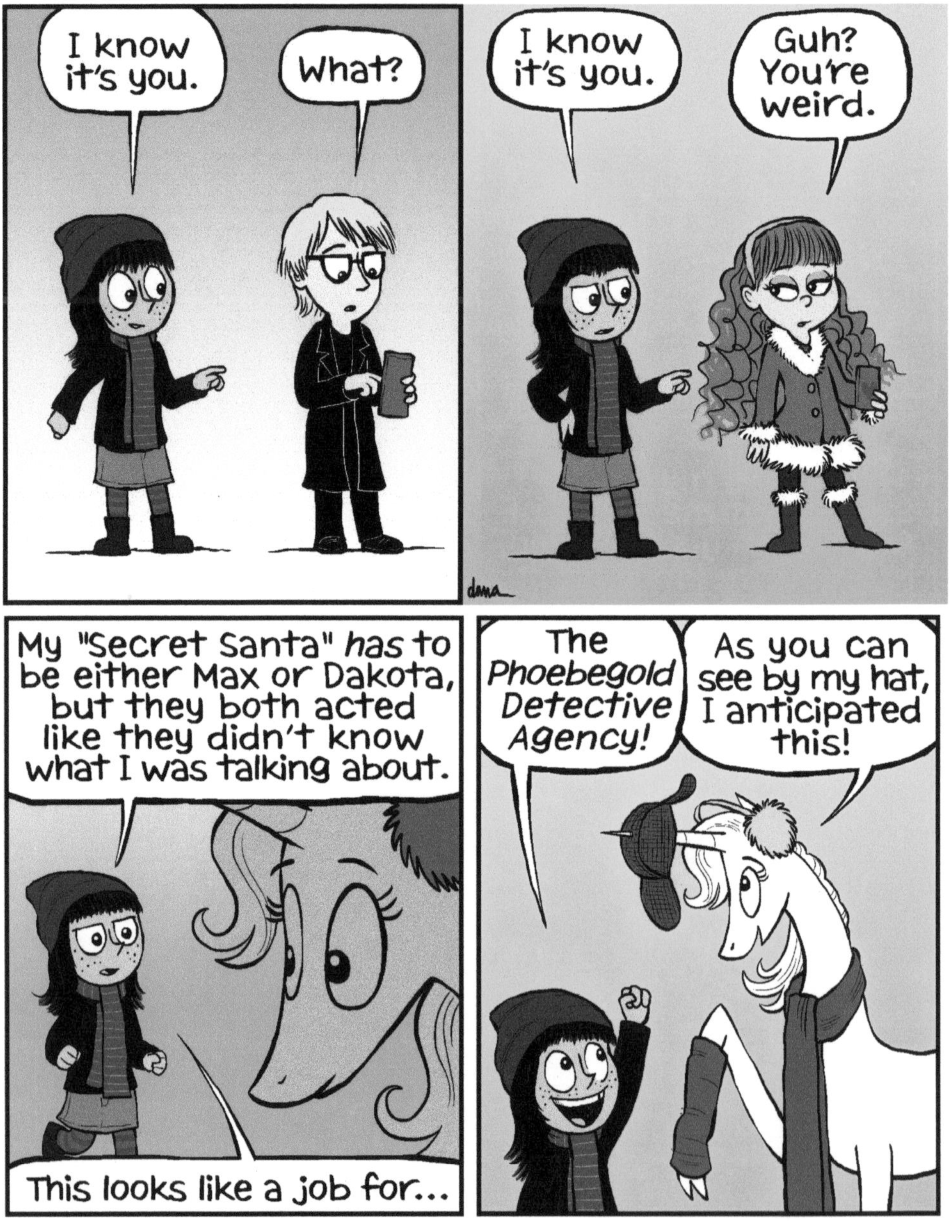
I know it's you.
What?
I know it's you.
Guh? You're weird.
My "Secret Santa" *has* to be either Max or Dakota, but they both acted like they didn't know what I was talking about.
This looks like a job for...
The *Phoebegold Detective Agency!*
As you can see by my hat, I anticipated this!

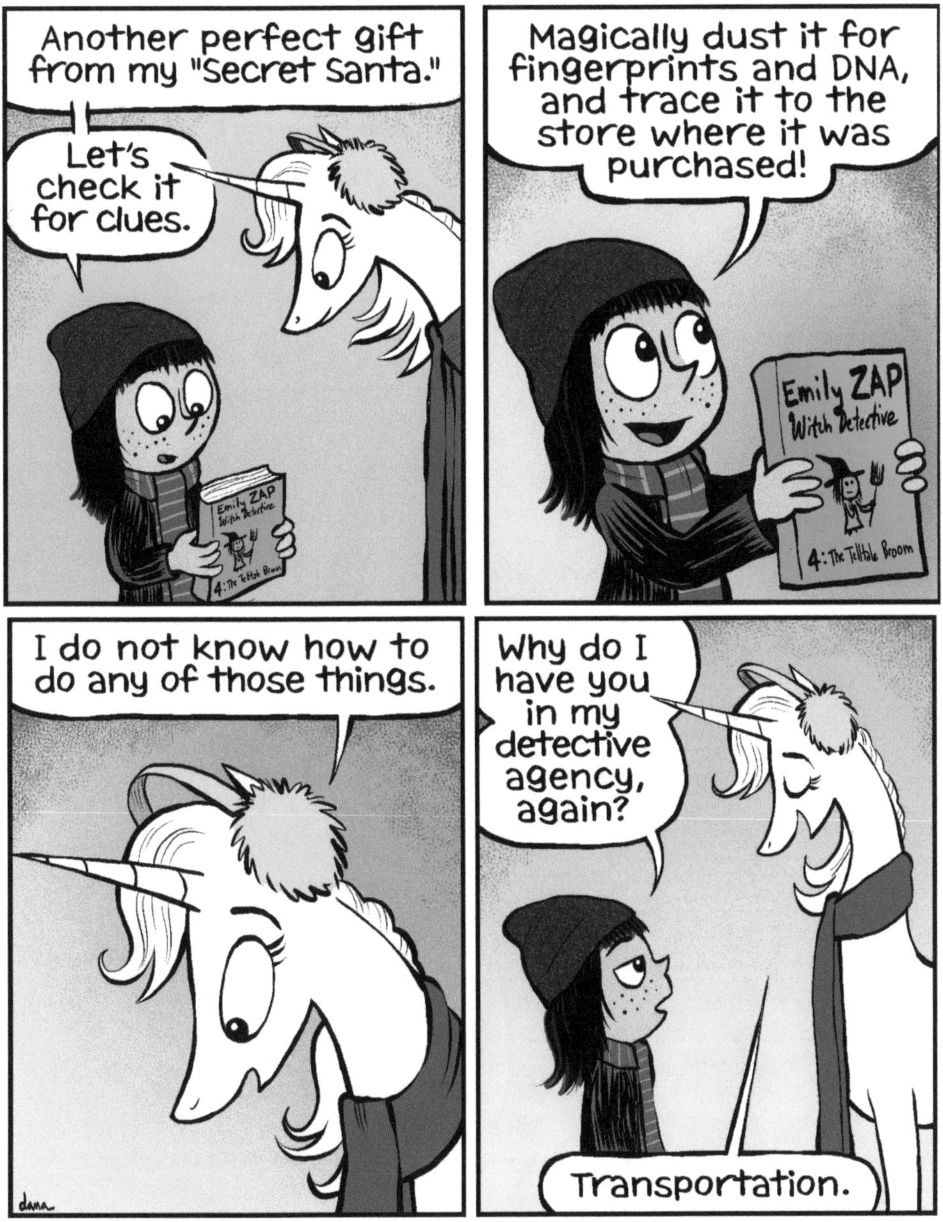
Another perfect gift from my "Secret Santa."
Let's check it for clues.
Emily ZAP Witch Detective 4: The Telltale Broom
Magically dust it for fingerprints and DNA, and trace it to the store where it was purchased!
Emily ZAP Witch Detective 4: The Telltale Broom
I do not know how to do any of those things.
Why do I have you in my detective agency, again?
Transportation.
dana

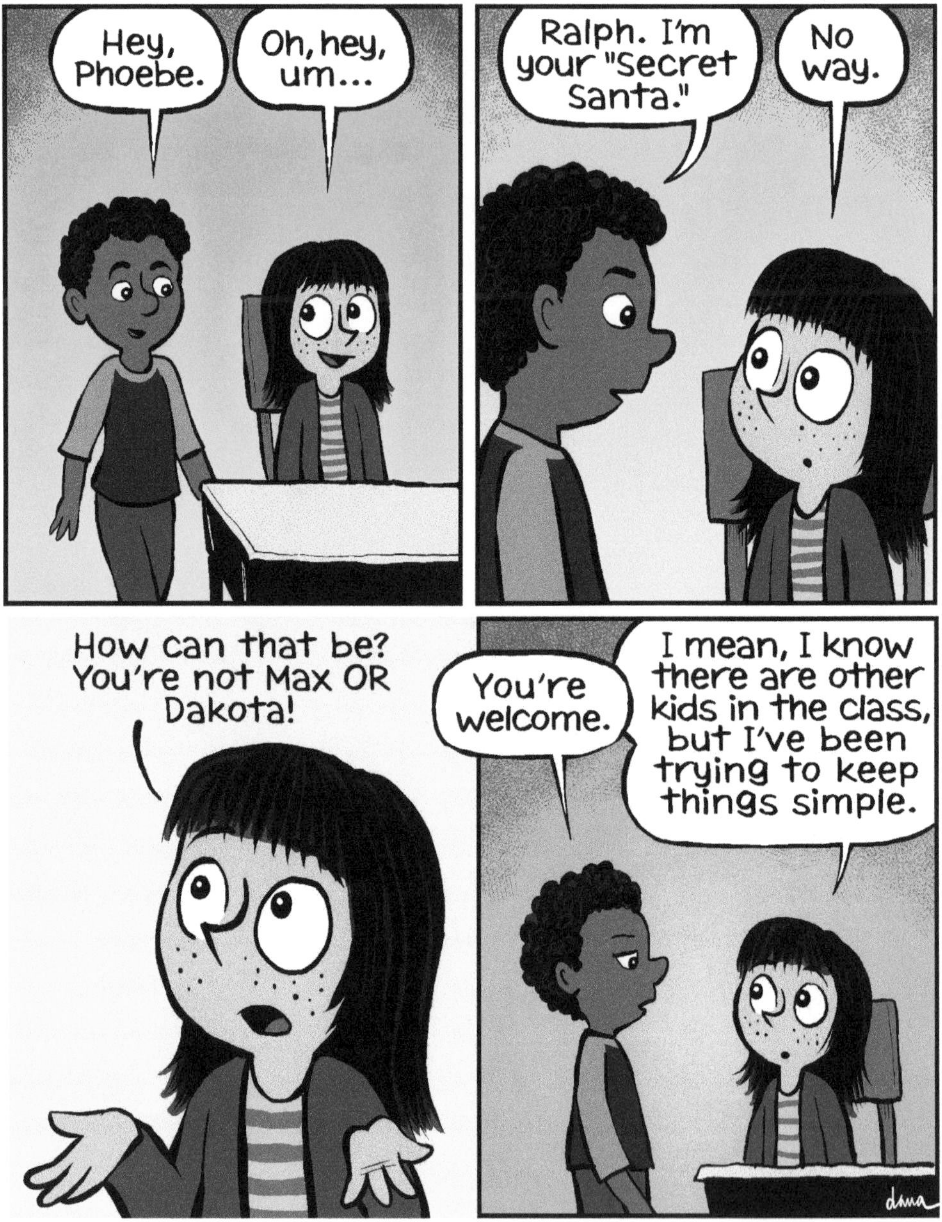
Hey, Phoebe.
Oh, hey, um...
Ralph. I'm your "Secret Santa."
No way.
How can that be? You're not Max OR Dakota!
You're welcome.
I mean, I know there are other kids in the class, but I've been trying to keep things simple.
dana

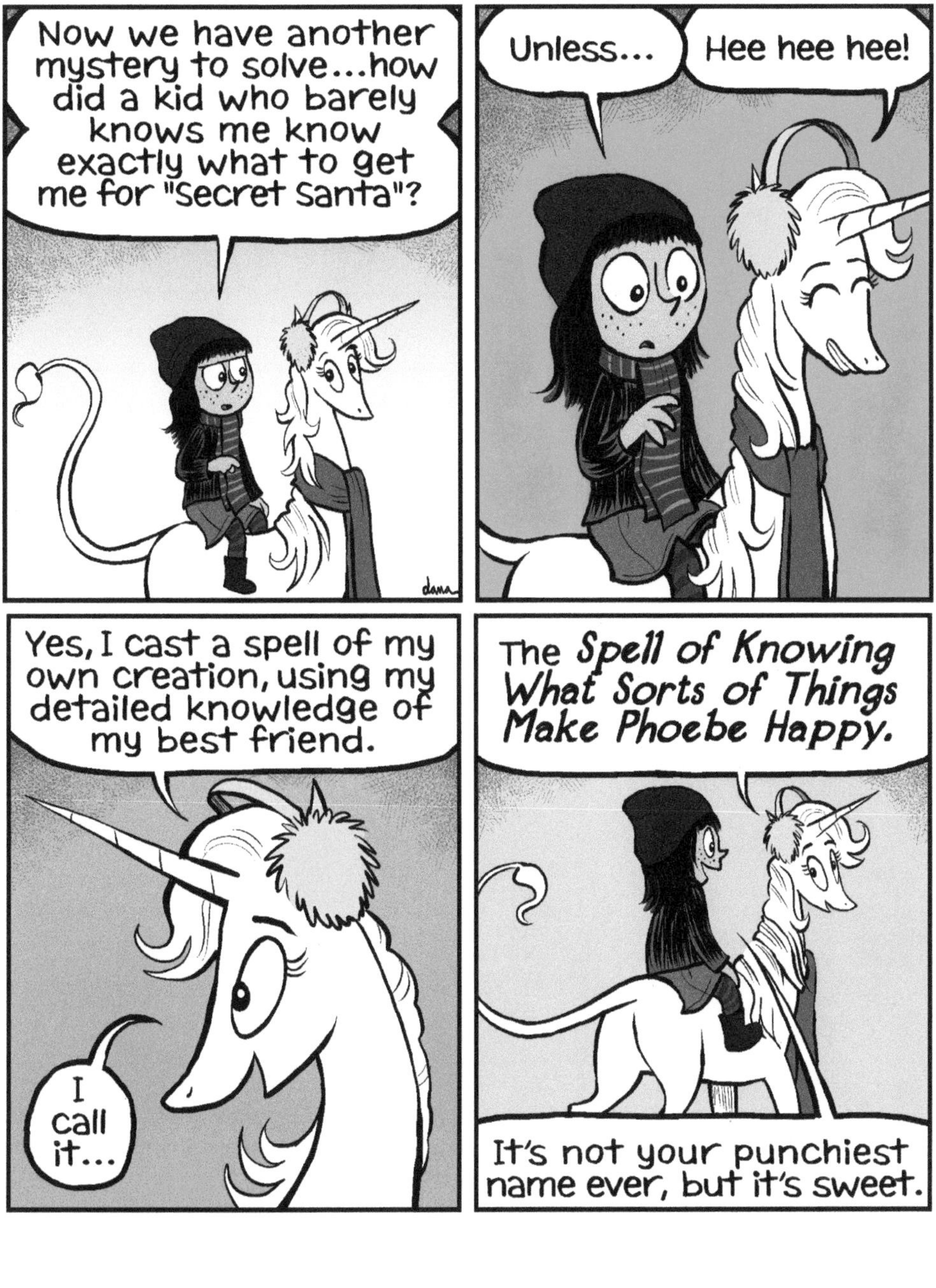

Now we have another mystery to solve...how did a kid who barely knows me know exactly what to get me for "Secret Santa"?
Unless...
Hee hee hee!
Yes, I cast a spell of my own creation, using my detailed knowledge of my best friend.
I call it...
The *Spell of Knowing What Sorts of Things Make Phoebe Happy.*
It's not your punchiest name ever, but it's sweet.

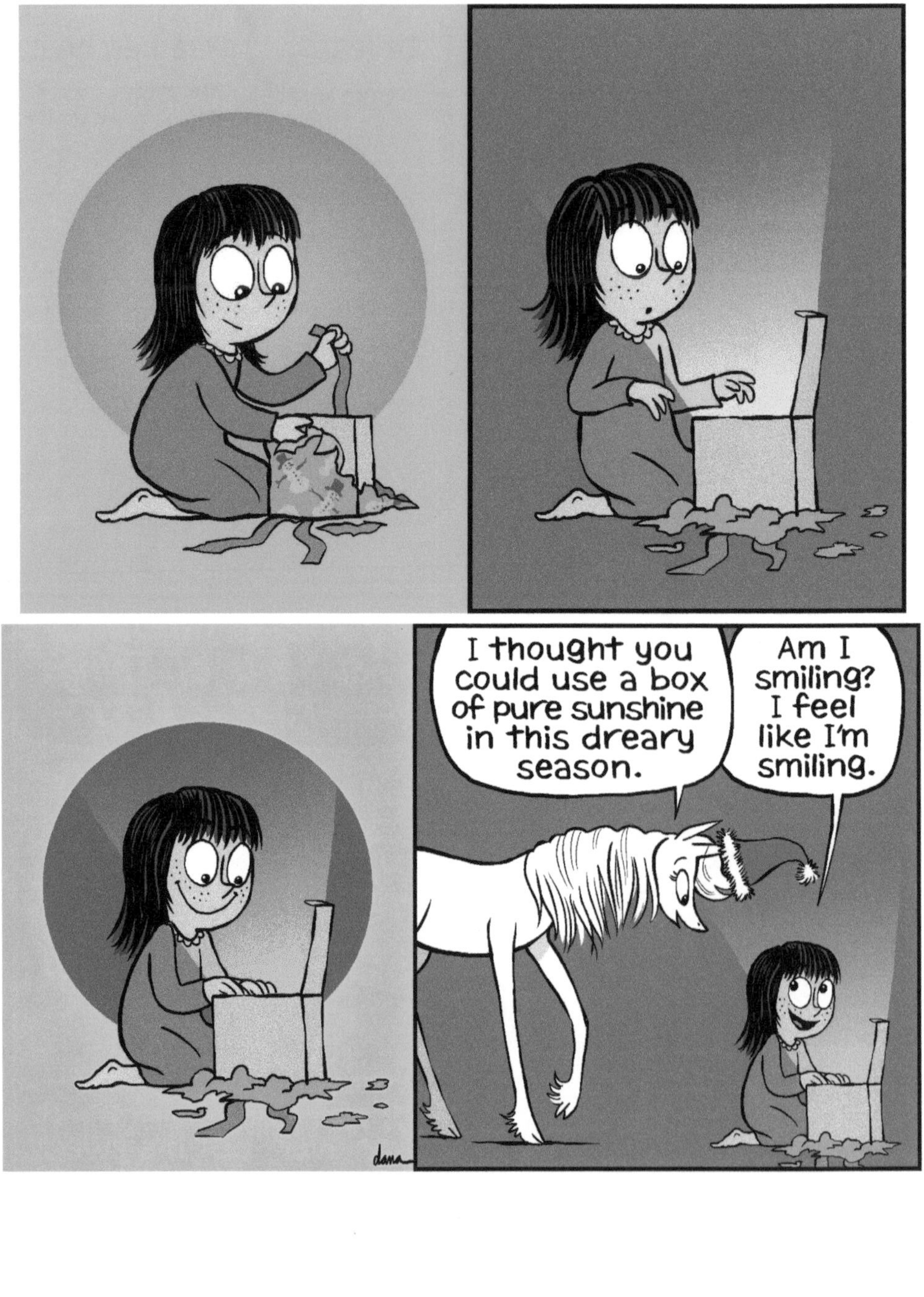
I thought you could use a box of pure sunshine in this dreary season.
Am I smiling? I feel like I'm smiling.
dana

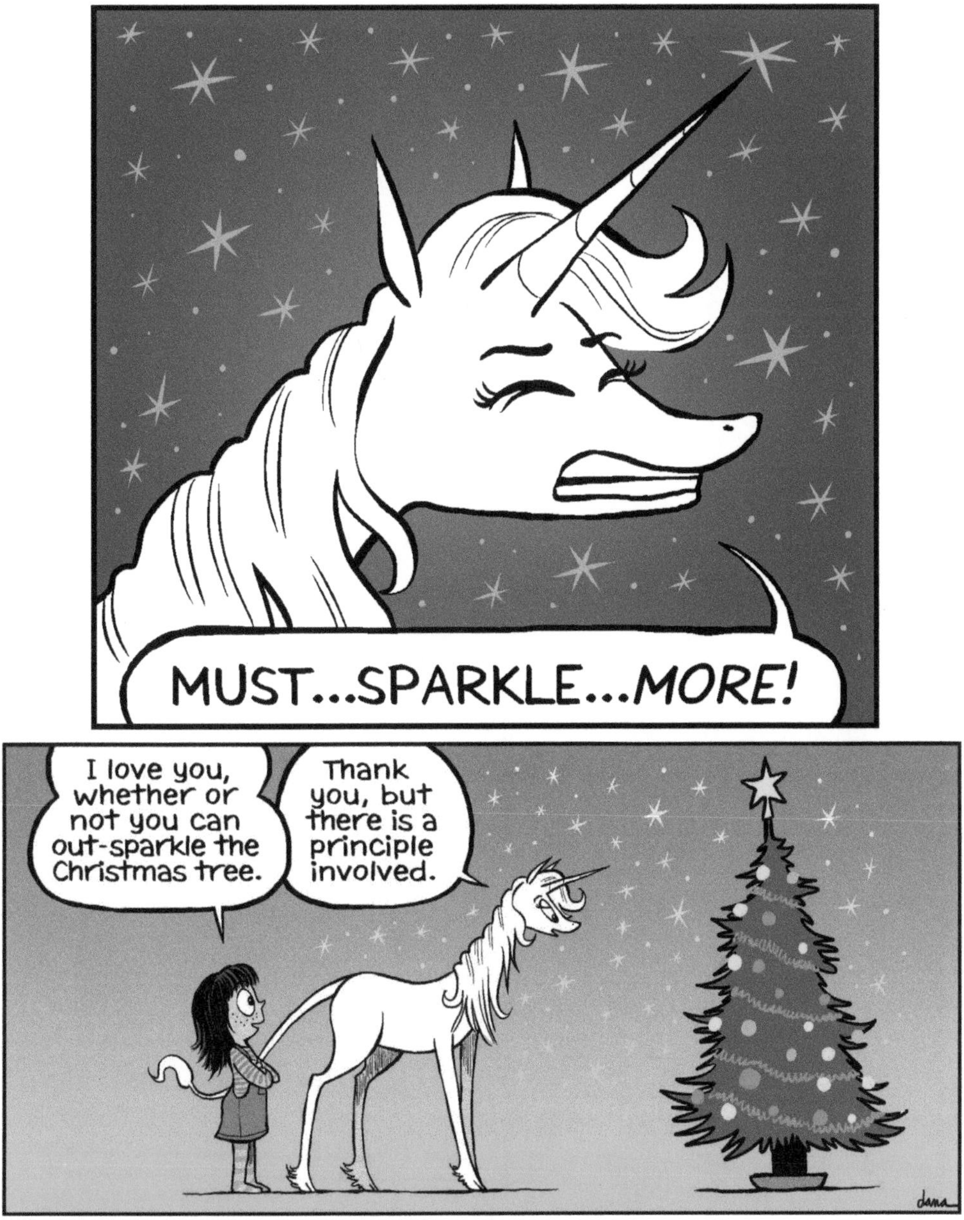
MUST...SPARKLE...MORE!
I love you, whether or not you can out-sparkle the Christmas tree.
Thank you, but there is a principle involved.
dana

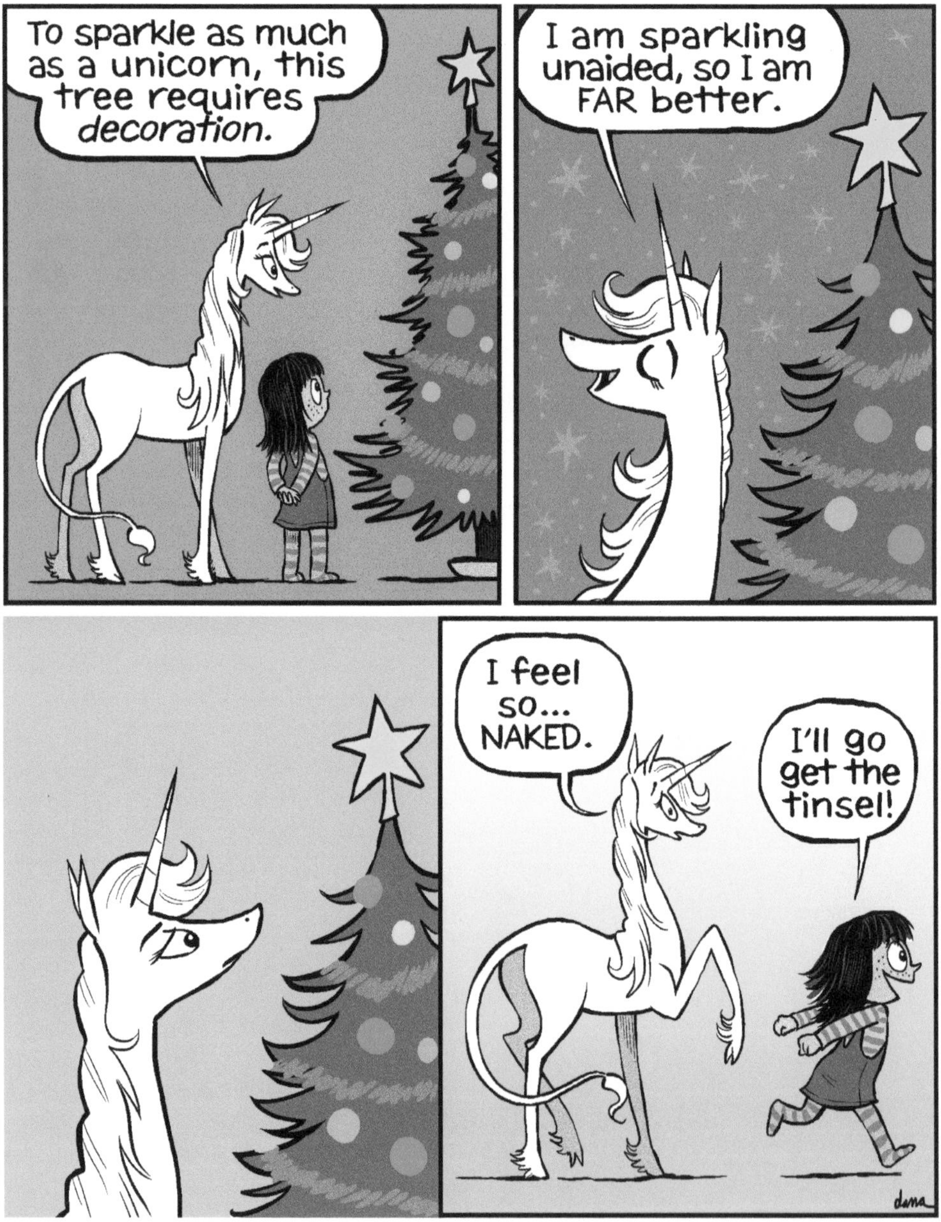
To sparkle as much as a unicorn, this tree requires *decoration*.
I am sparkling unaided, so I am FAR better.
I feel so... NAKED.
I'll go get the tinsel!
dana

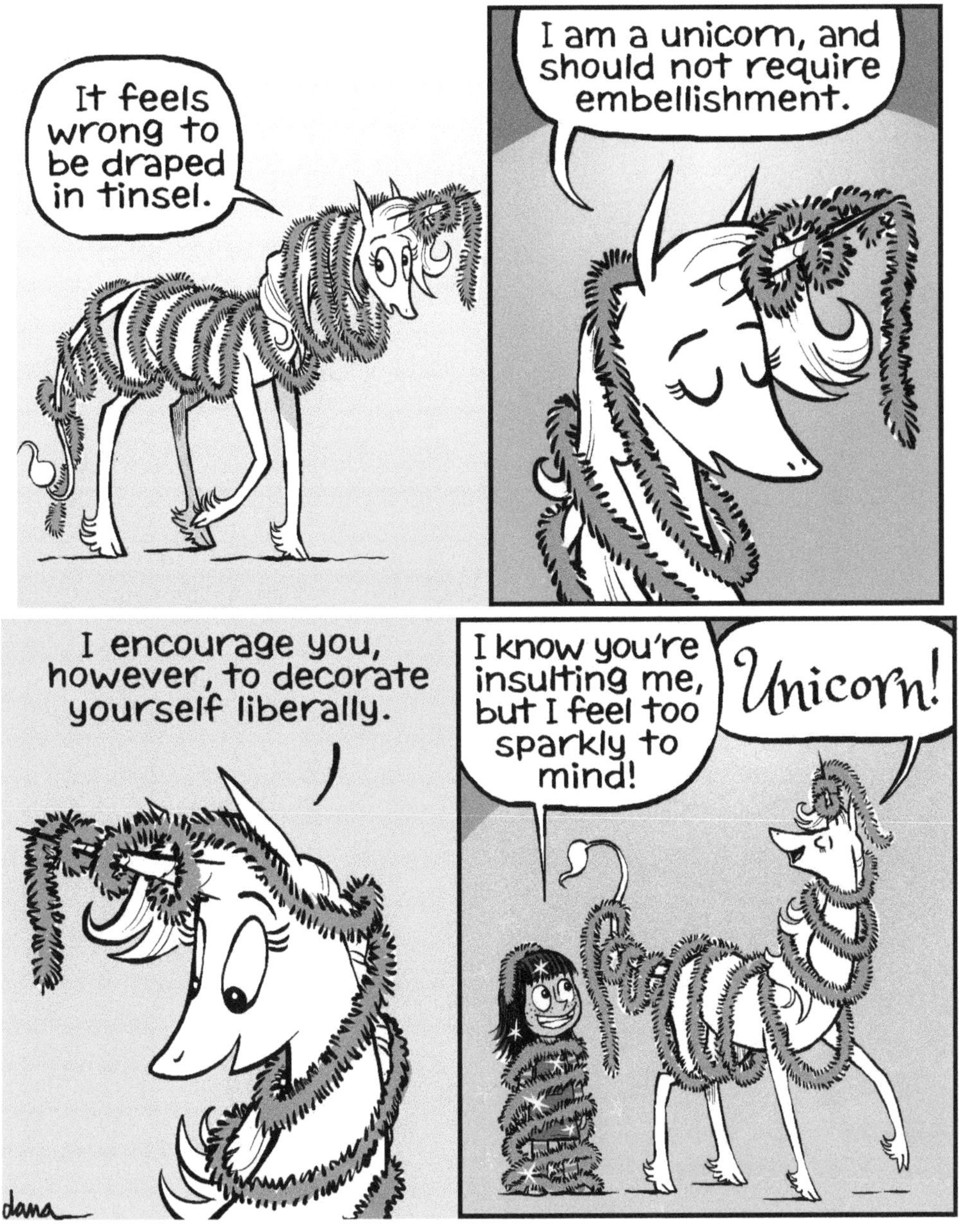
It feels wrong to be draped in tinsel.
I am a unicorn, and should not require embellishment.
I encourage you, however, to decorate yourself liberally.
I know you're insulting me, but I feel too sparkly to mind!
Unicorn!
dana

This is my **gift** to you, tree.

I will allow you to be the sparkliest thing in this room for the holiday season.

I know it is temporary, and soon I shall regain my distinction as the SPARKLIEST.

Are you and the tree having a nice conversation?

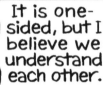

It is one-sided, but I believe we understand each other.

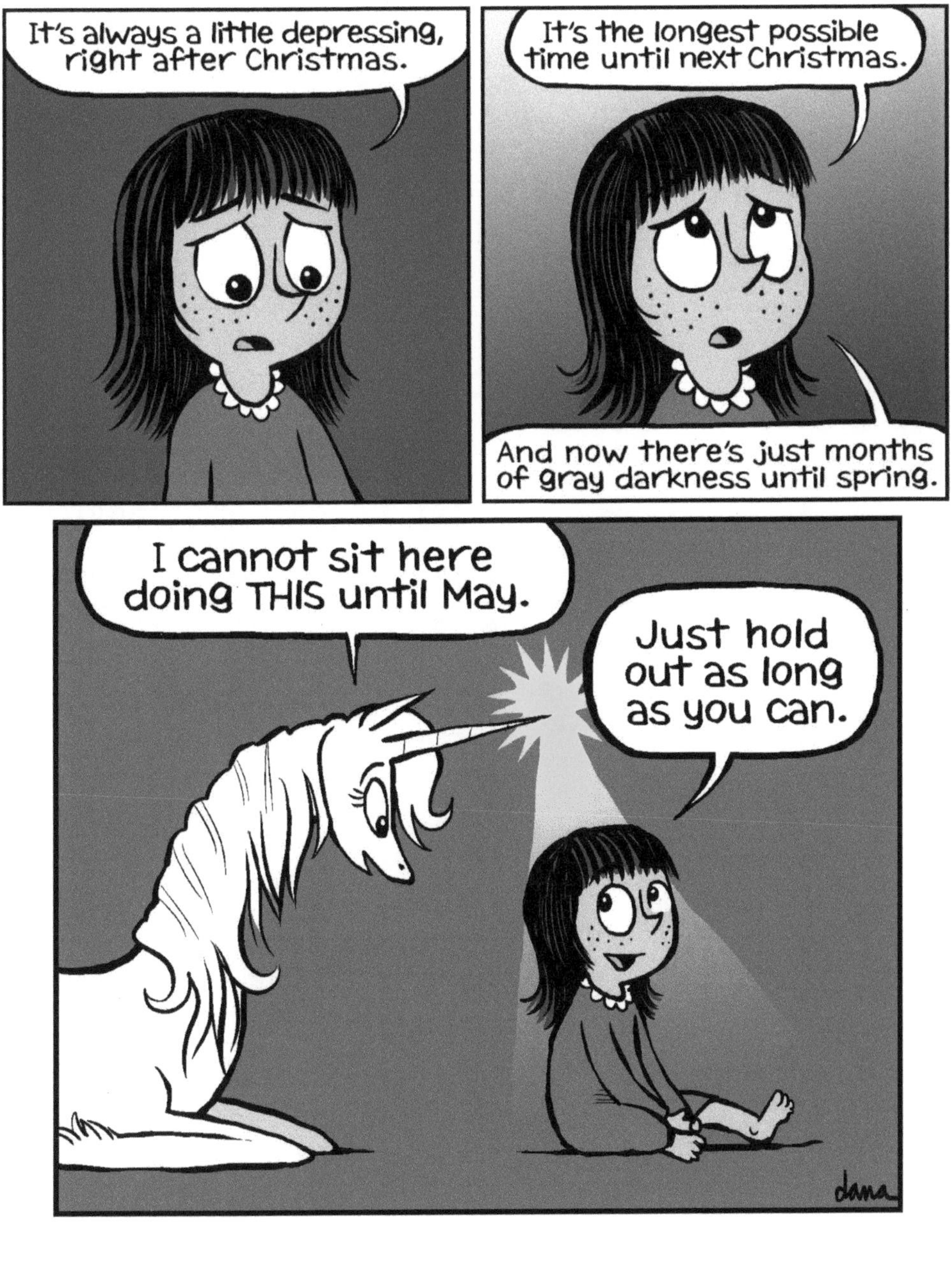
It's always a little depressing, right after Christmas.
It's the longest possible time until next Christmas.
And now there's just months of gray darkness until spring.
I cannot sit here doing THIS until May.
Just hold out as long as you can.
dana

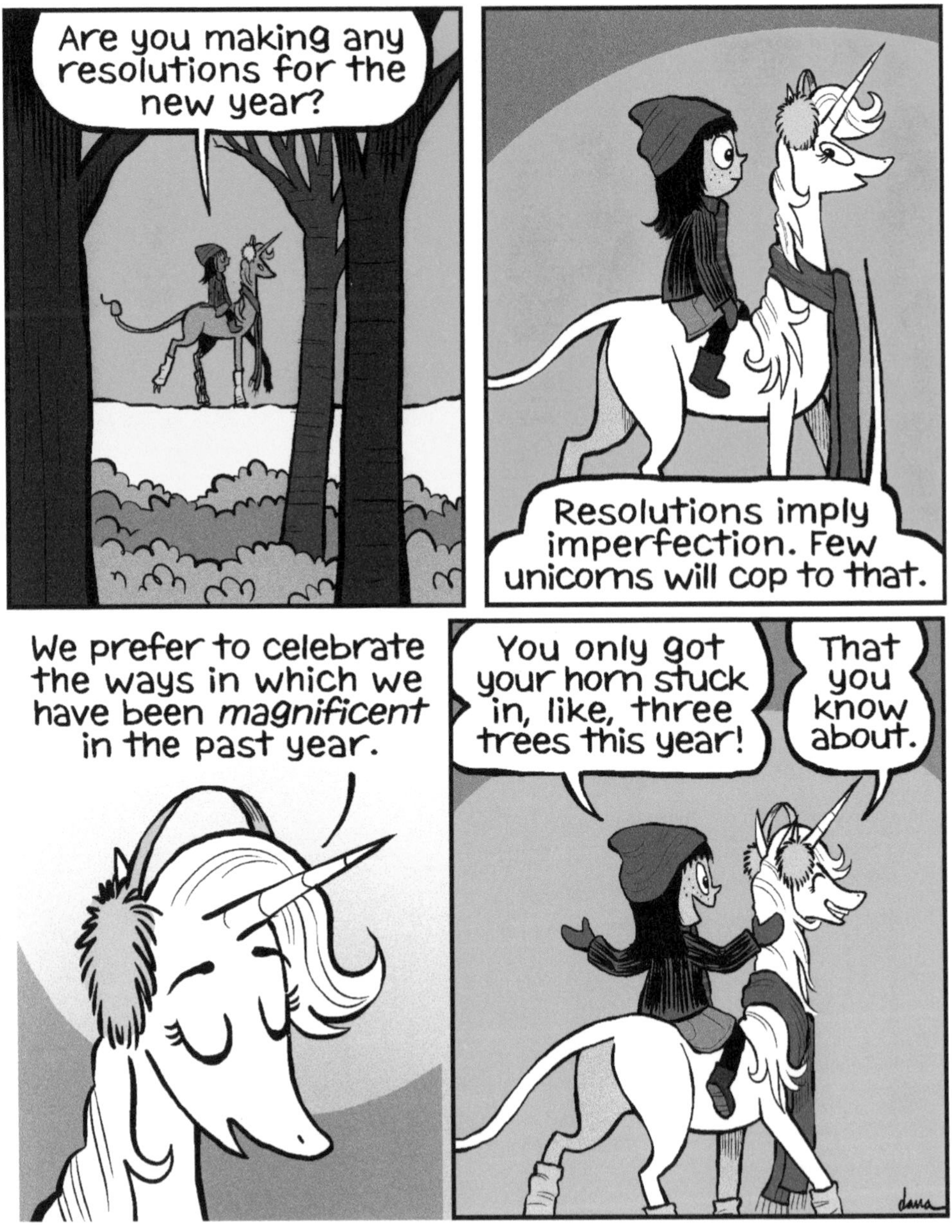
Are you making any resolutions for the new year?
Resolutions imply imperfection. Few unicorns will cop to that.
We prefer to celebrate the ways in which we have been *magnificent* in the past year.
You only got your horn stuck in, like, three trees this year!
That you know about.
dana

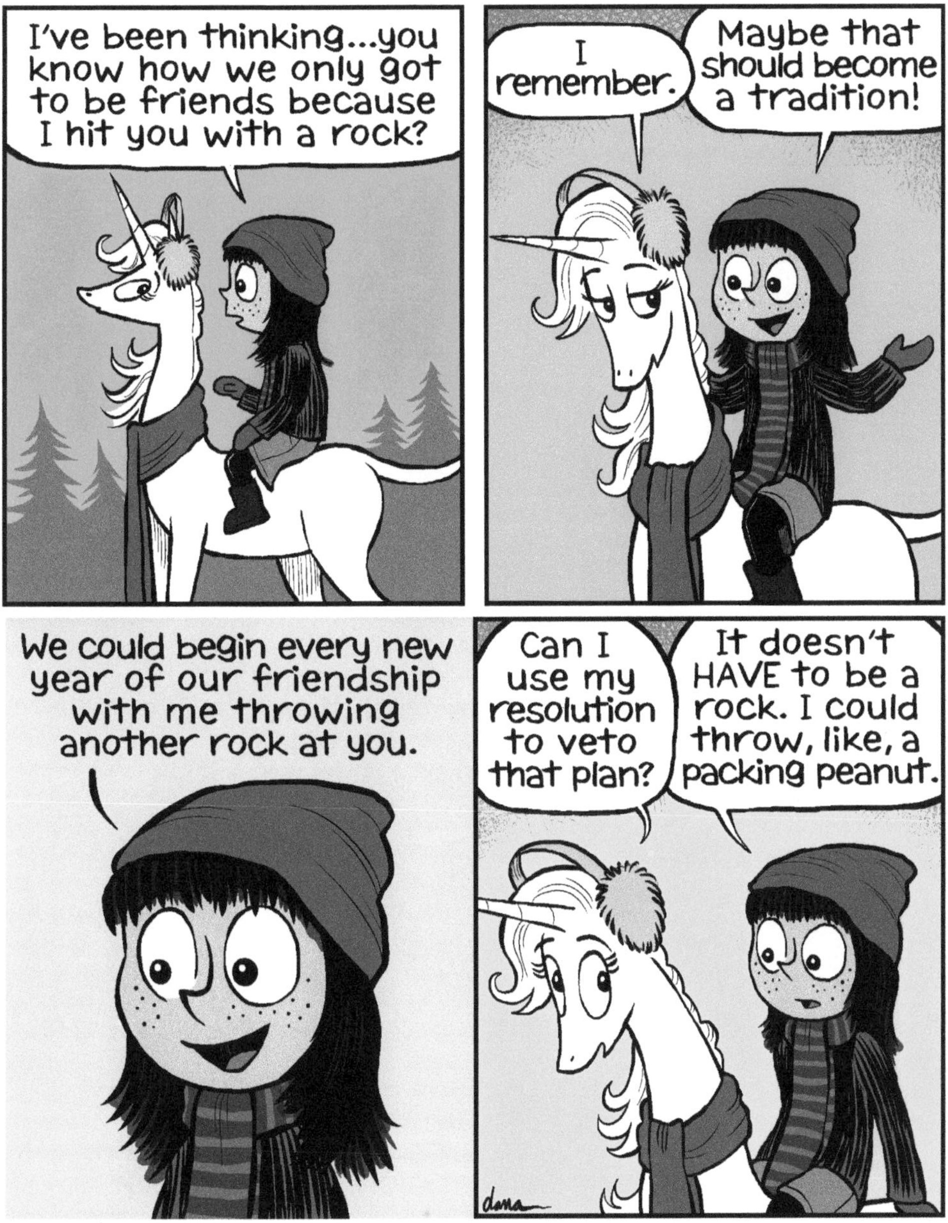
I've been thinking...you know how we only got to be friends because I hit you with a rock?
I remember.
Maybe that should become a tradition!
We could begin every new year of our friendship with me throwing another rock at you.
Can I use my resolution to veto that plan?
It doesn't HAVE to be a rock. I could throw, like, a packing peanut.
dana

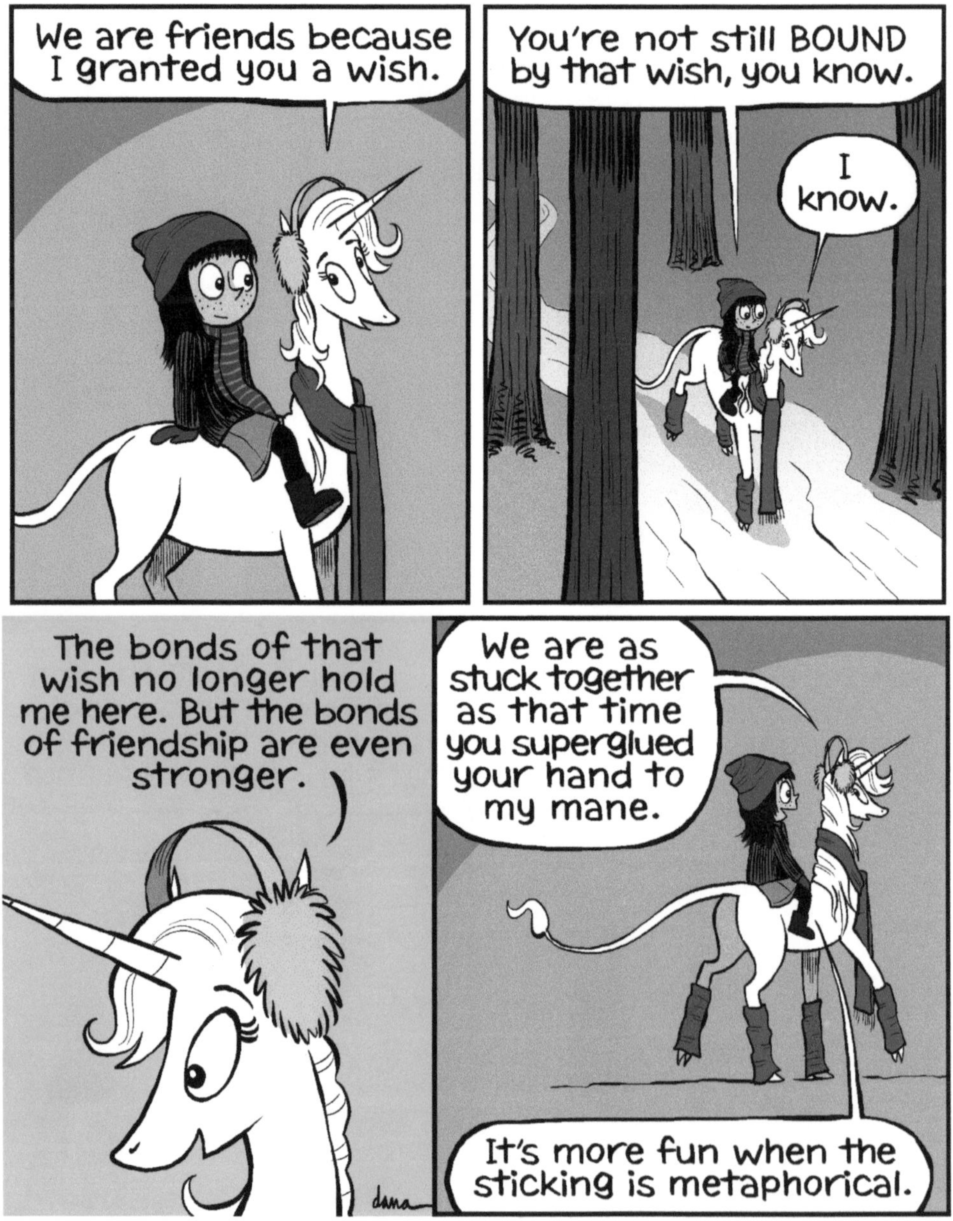
We are friends because I granted you a wish.
You're not still BOUND by that wish, you know.
I know.
The bonds of that wish no longer hold me here. But the bonds of friendship are even stronger.
We are as stuck together as that time you superglued your hand to my mane.
It's more fun when the sticking is metaphorical.
dana

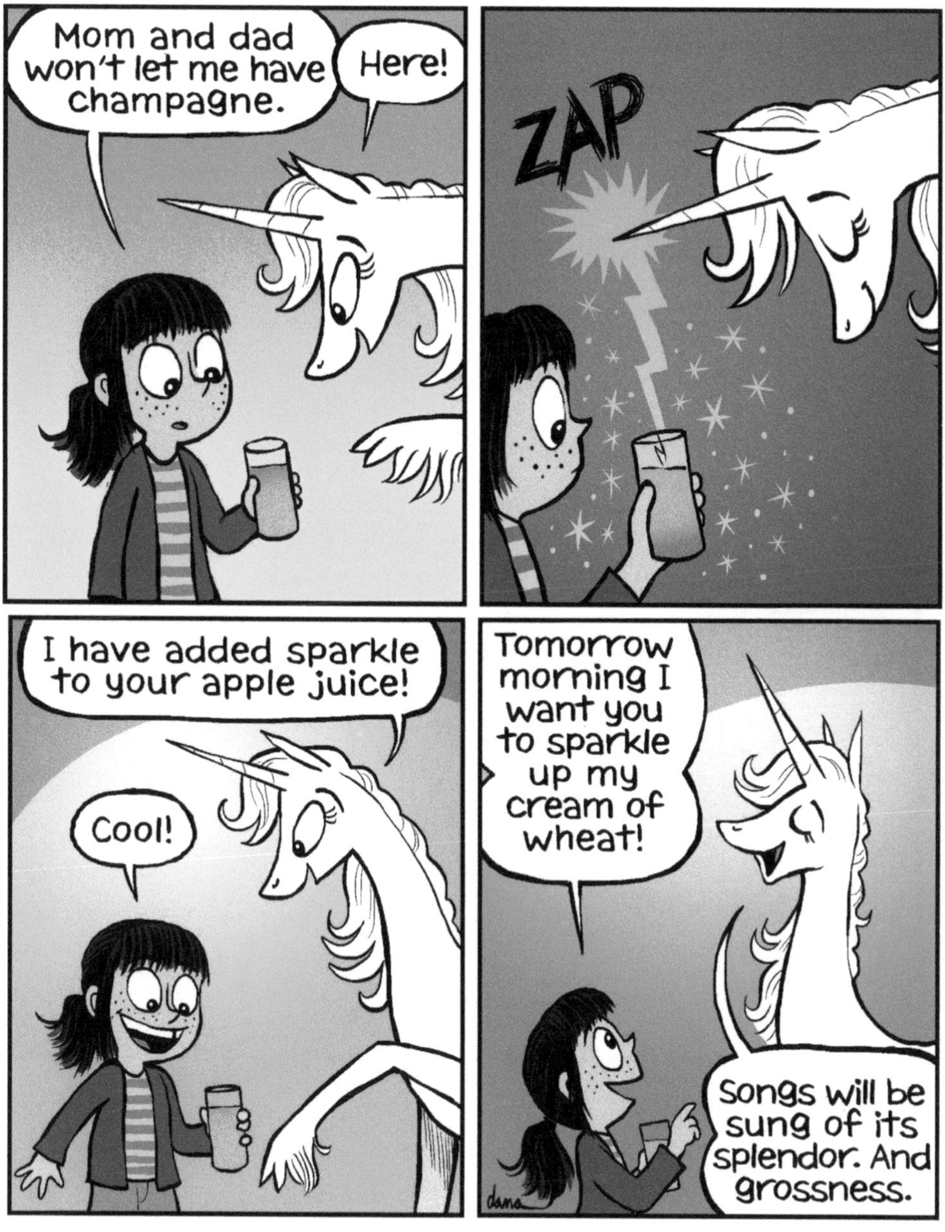
Mom and dad won't let me have champagne.
Here!
ZAP
I have added sparkle to your apple juice!
Cool!
Tomorrow morning I want you to sparkle up my cream of wheat!
Songs will be sung of its splendor. And grossness.
dana

My best friend lets me sit on her
As we explore the wood
From high atop a unicorn
The world looks pretty good.

Another year has come and gone
And I was seldom bored
'Cause everything is magic now
And this year there'll be more.

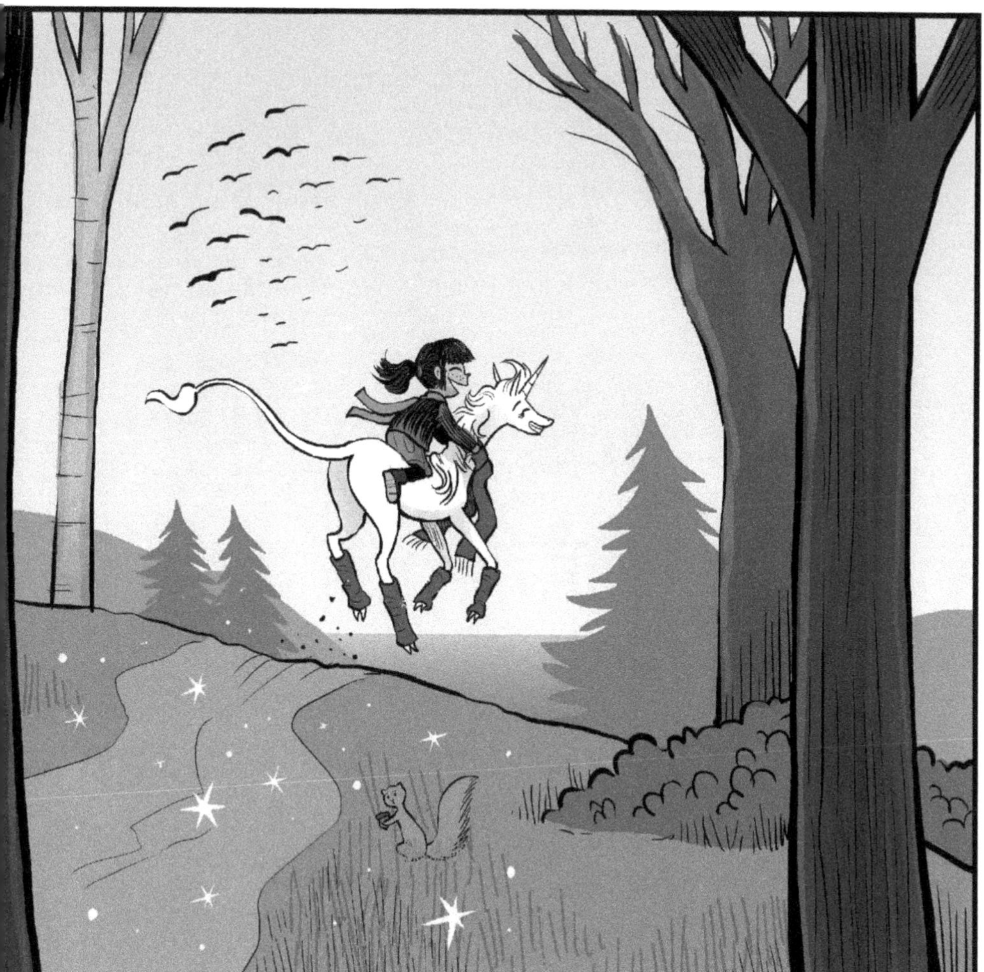

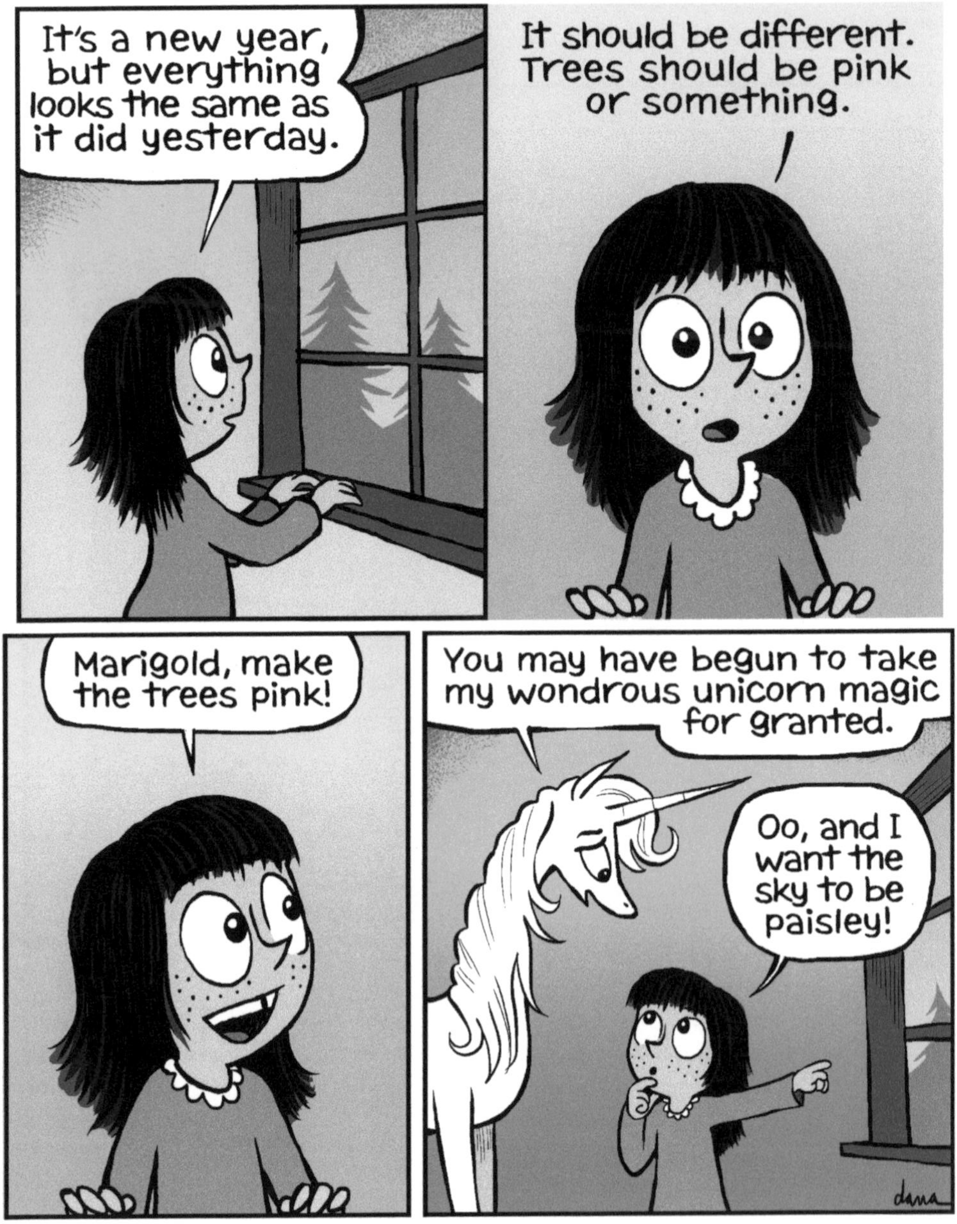
It's a new year, but everything looks the same as it did yesterday.
It should be different. Trees should be pink or something.
Marigold, make the trees pink!
You may have begun to take my wondrous unicorn magic for granted.
Oo, and I want the sky to be paisley!
dana

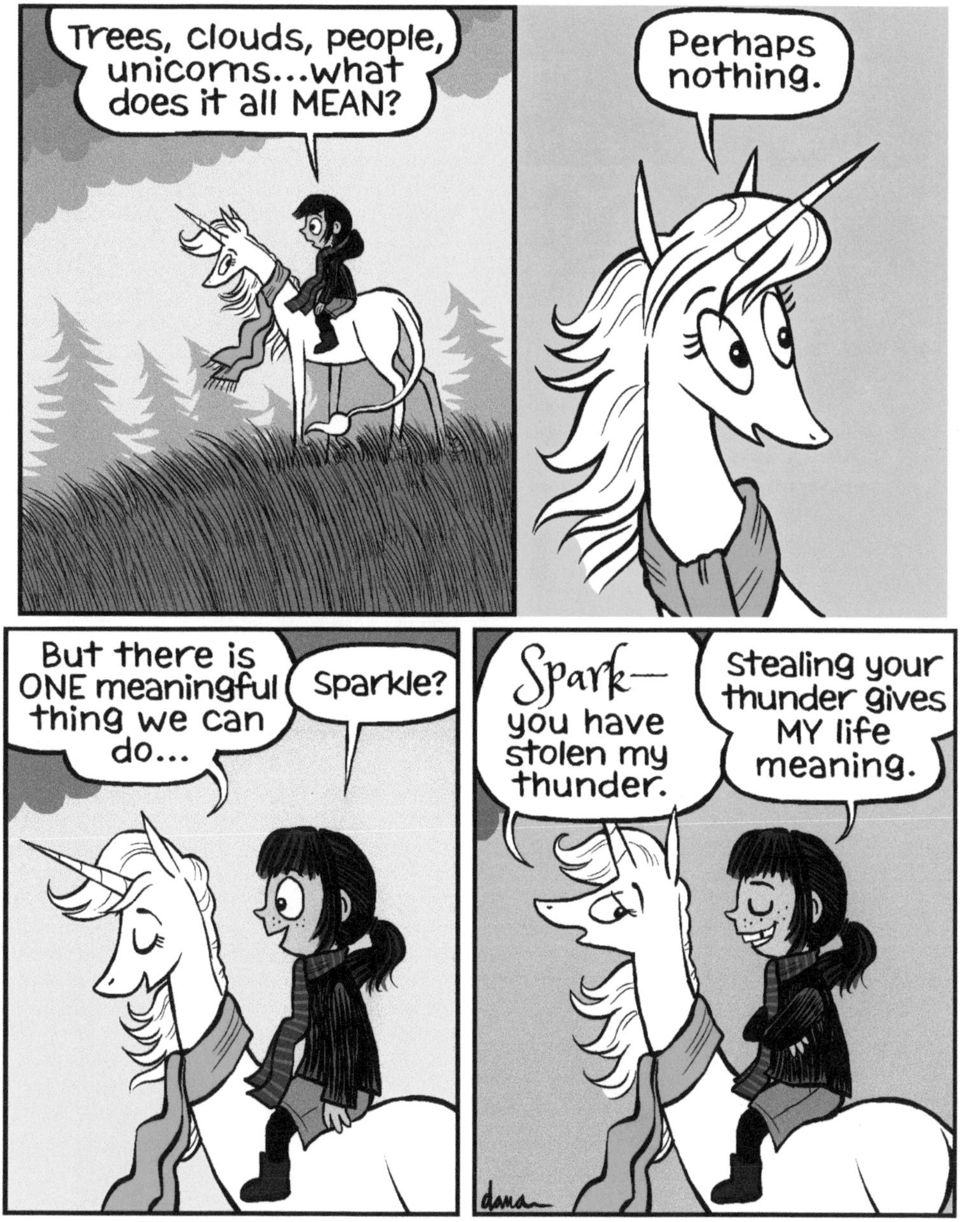
Trees, clouds, people, unicorns...what does it all MEAN?
Perhaps nothing.
But there is ONE meaningful thing we can do...
Sparkle?
Spark—you have stolen my thunder.
Stealing your thunder gives MY life meaning.
dana

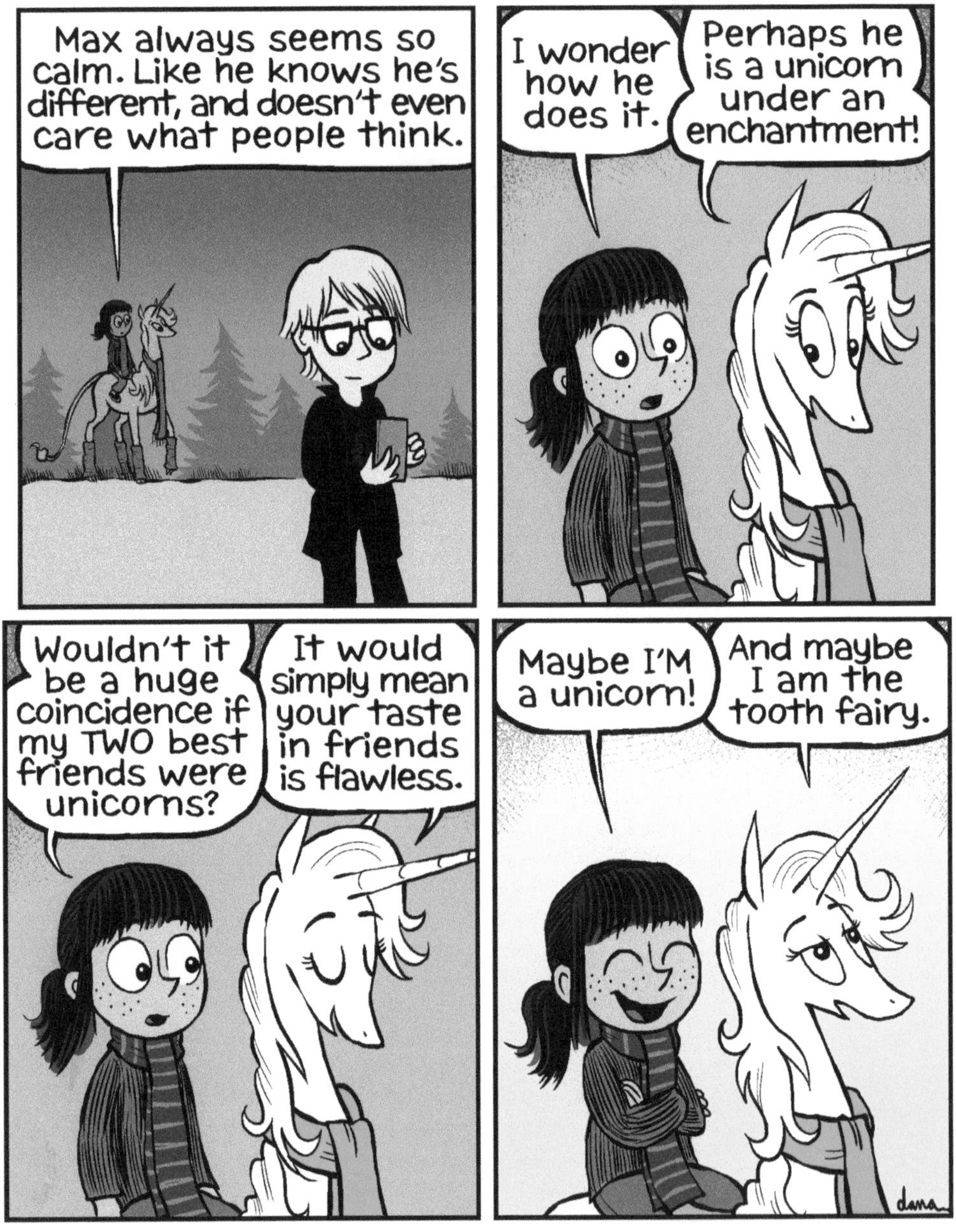
Max always seems so calm. Like he knows he's different, and doesn't even care what people think.
I wonder how he does it.
Perhaps he is a unicorn under an enchantment!
Wouldn't it be a huge coincidence if my TWO best friends were unicorns?
It would simply mean your taste in friends is flawless.
Maybe I'M a unicorn!
And maybe I am the tooth fairy.
dana

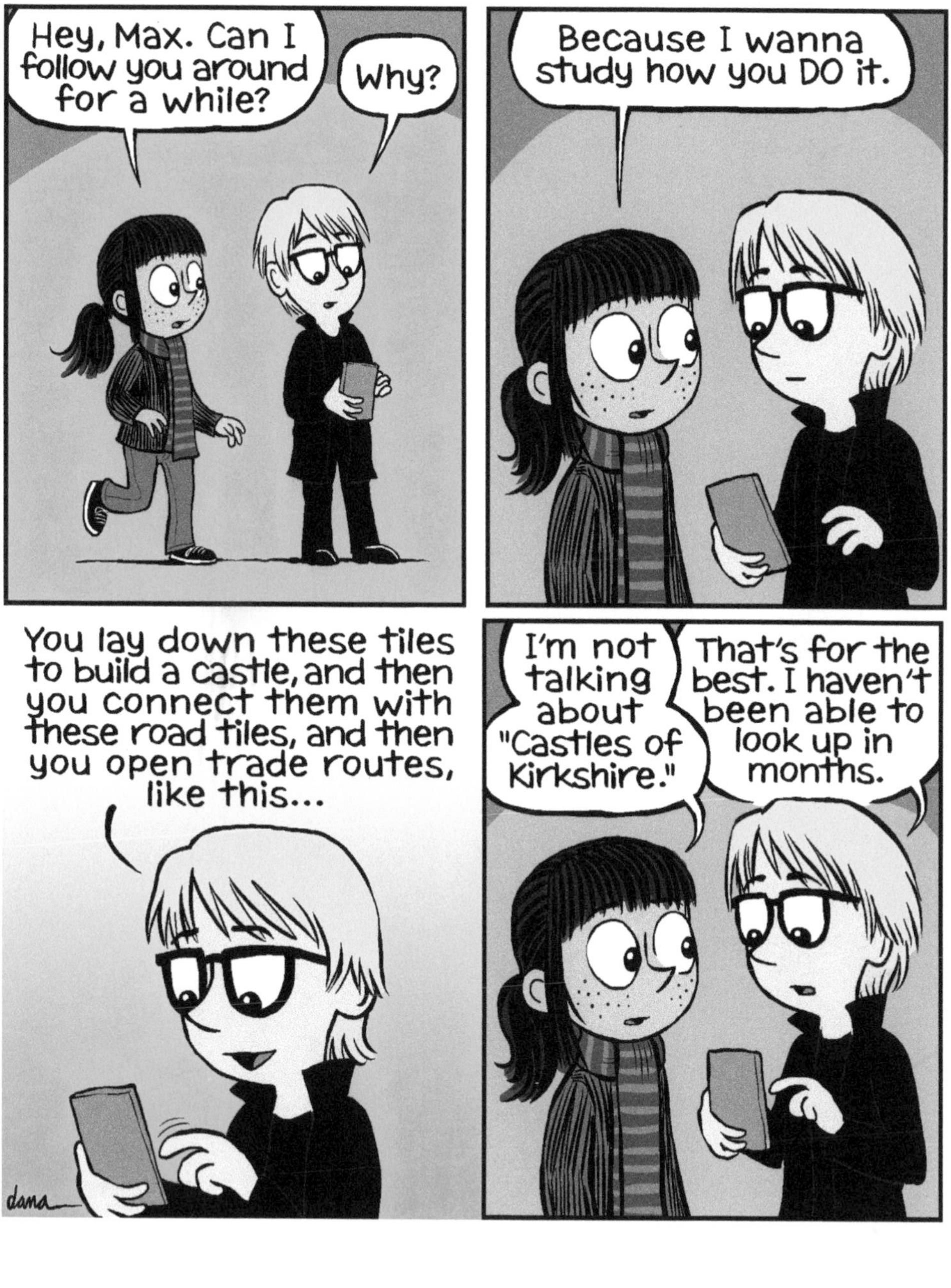
Hey, Max. Can I follow you around for a while?
Why?
Because I wanna study how you DO it.
You lay down these tiles to build a castle, and then you connect them with these road tiles, and then you open trade routes, like this...
I'm not talking about "Castles of Kirkshire."
That's for the best. I haven't been able to look up in months.
dana

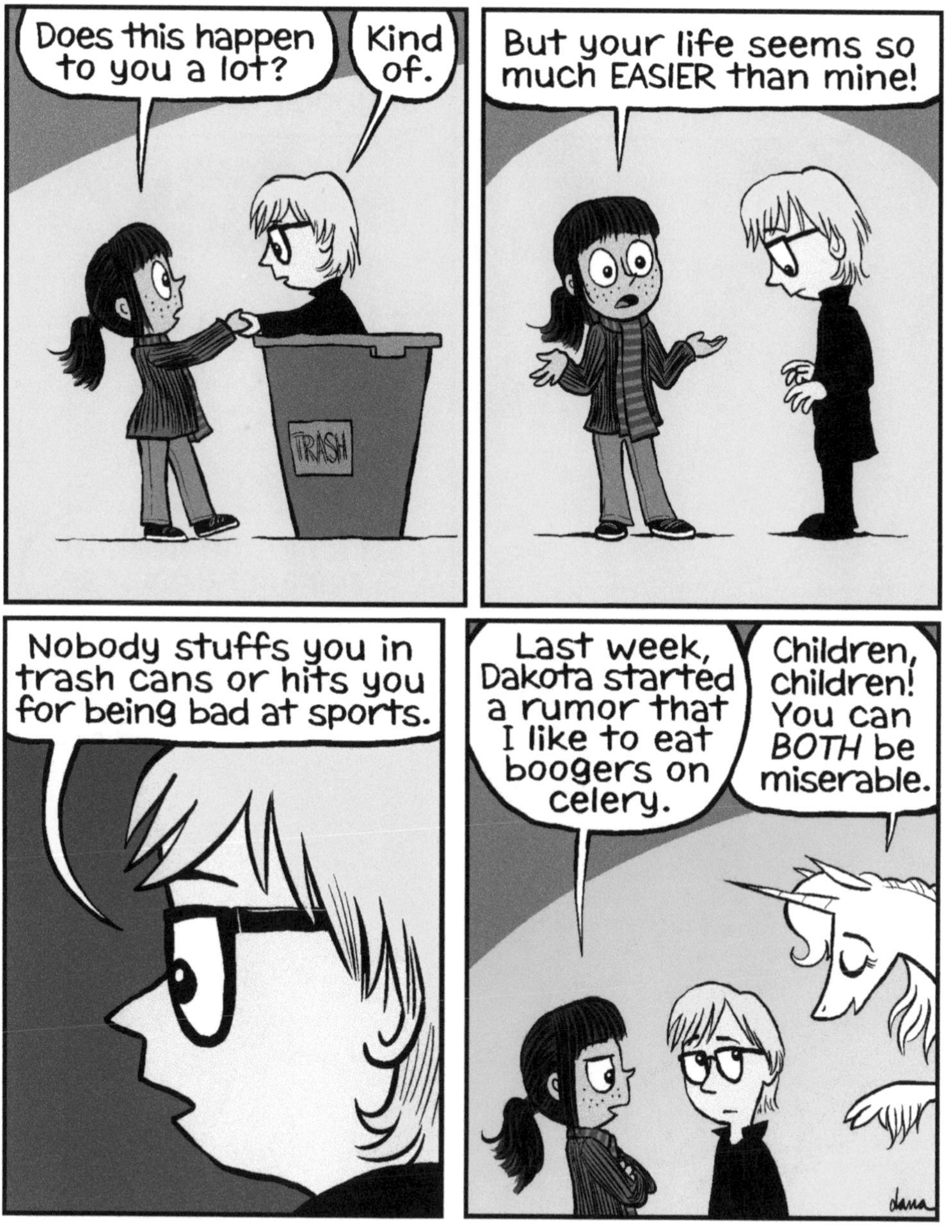
Does this happen to you a lot?
Kind of.
TRASH
But your life seems so much EASIER than mine!
Nobody stuffs you in trash cans or hits you for being bad at sports.
Last week, Dakota started a rumor that I like to eat boogers on celery.
Children, children! You can *BOTH* be miserable.
dana

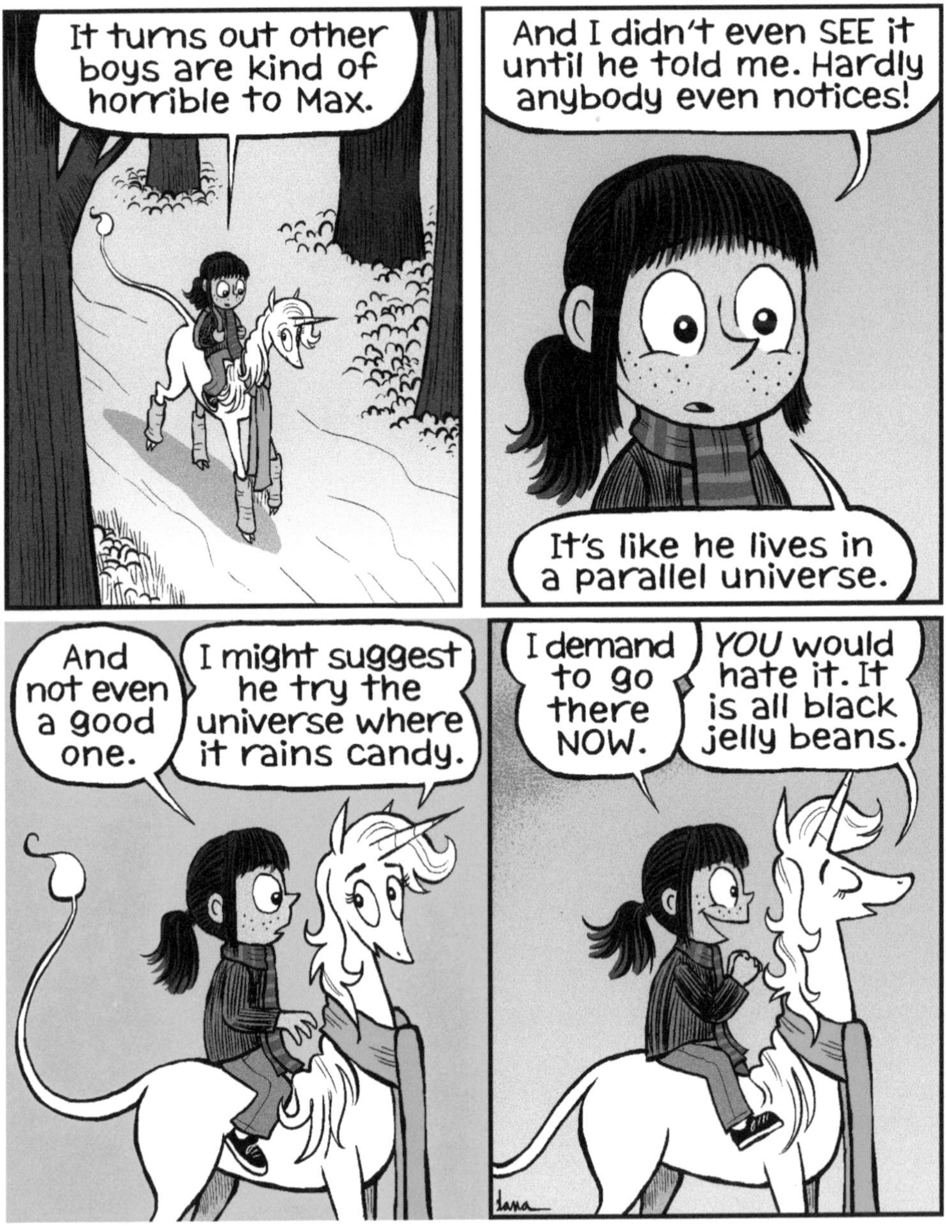
It turns out other boys are kind of horrible to Max.
And I didn't even SEE it until he told me. Hardly anybody even notices!
It's like he lives in a parallel universe.
And not even a good one.
I might suggest he try the universe where it rains candy.
I demand to go there NOW.
YOU would hate it. It is all black jelly beans.

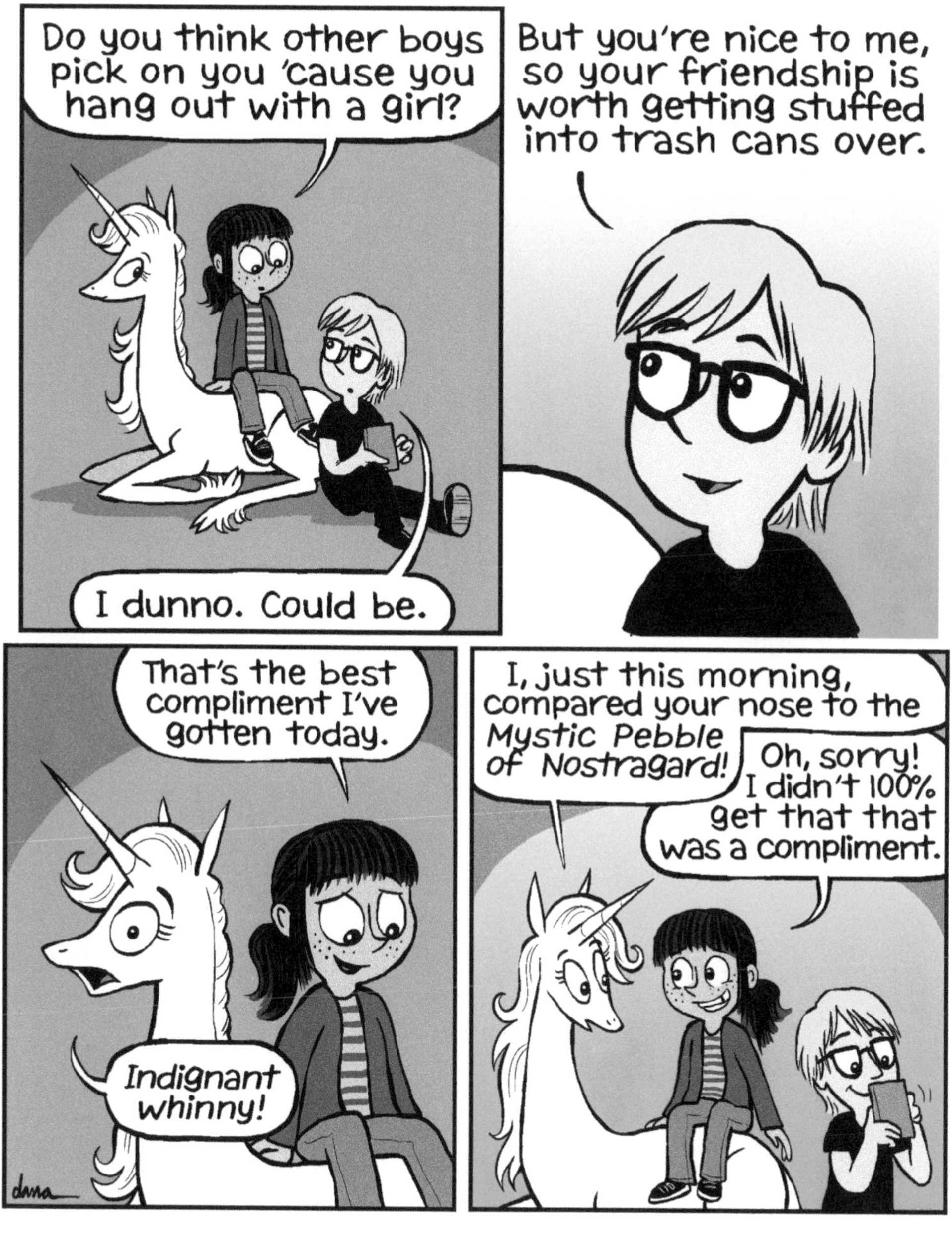
Do you think other boys pick on you 'cause you hang out with a girl?
I dunno. Could be.
But you're nice to me, so your friendship is worth getting stuffed into trash cans over.
That's the best compliment I've gotten today.
Indignant whinny!
I, just this morning, compared your nose to the *Mystic Pebble of Nostragard!*
Oh, sorry! I didn't 100% get that that was a compliment.

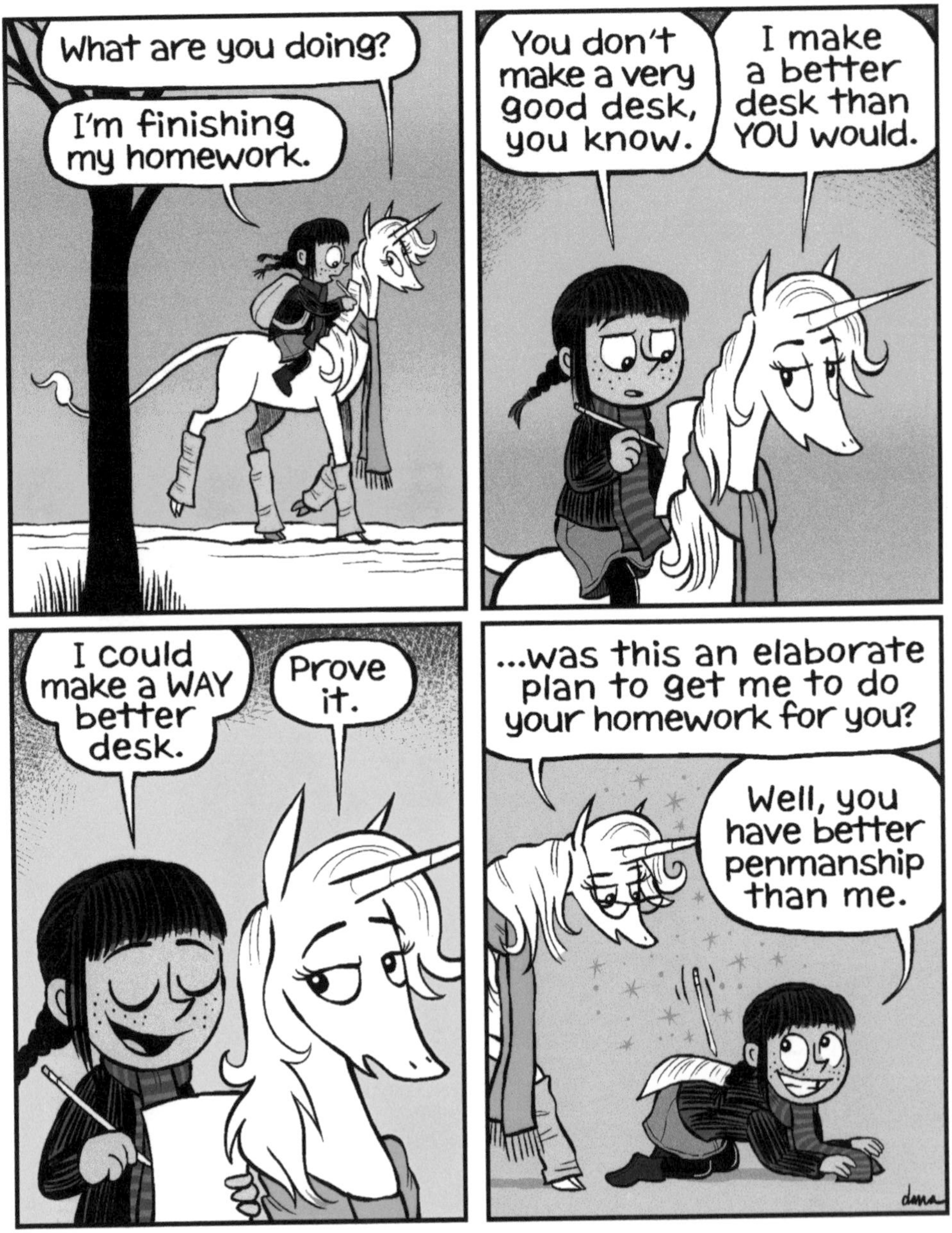
What are you doing?
I'm finishing my homework.
You don't make a very good desk, you know.
I make a better desk than YOU would.
I could make a WAY better desk.
Prove it.
...was this an elaborate plan to get me to do your homework for you?
Well, you have better penmanship than me.
dana

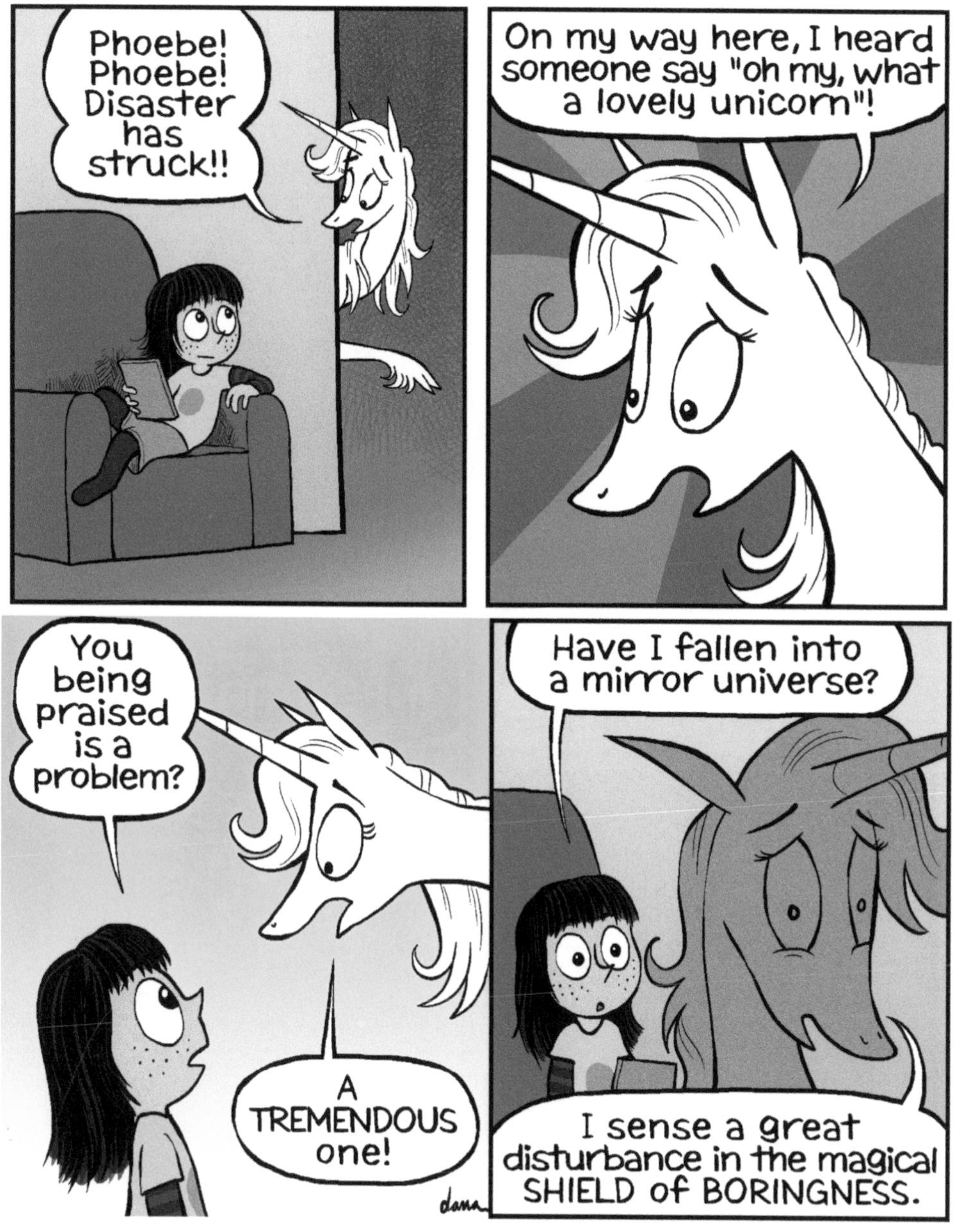
Phoebe! Phoebe! Disaster has struck!!
On my way here, I heard someone say "oh my, what a lovely unicorn"!
You being praised is a problem?
A TREMENDOUS one!
Have I fallen into a mirror universe?
I sense a great disturbance in the magical SHIELD of BORINGNESS.
dana

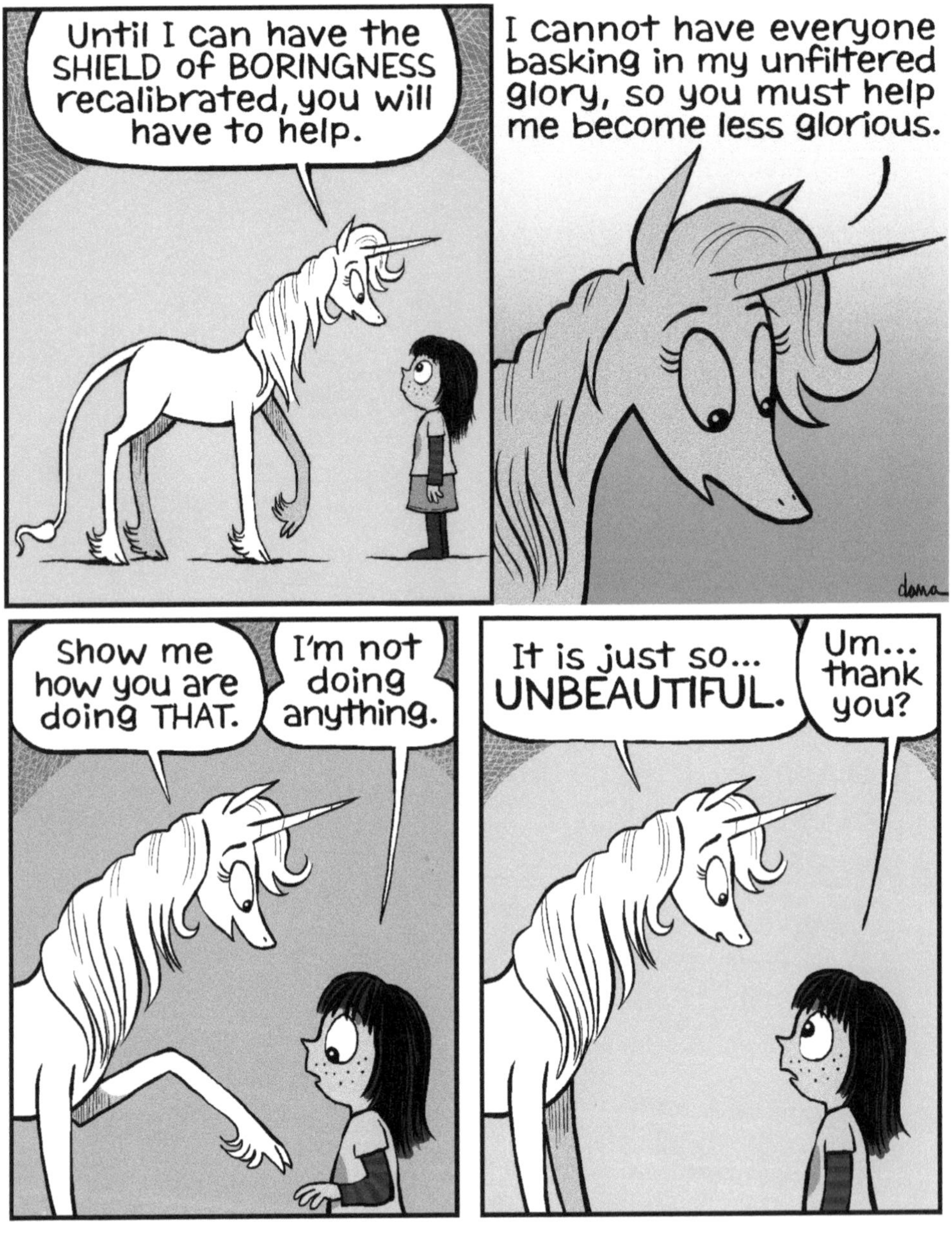
Until I can have the SHIELD of BORINGNESS recalibrated, you will have to help.
I cannot have everyone basking in my unfiltered glory, so you must help me become less glorious.
dana
Show me how you are doing THAT.
I'm not doing anything.
It is just so... UNBEAUTIFUL.
Um... thank you?

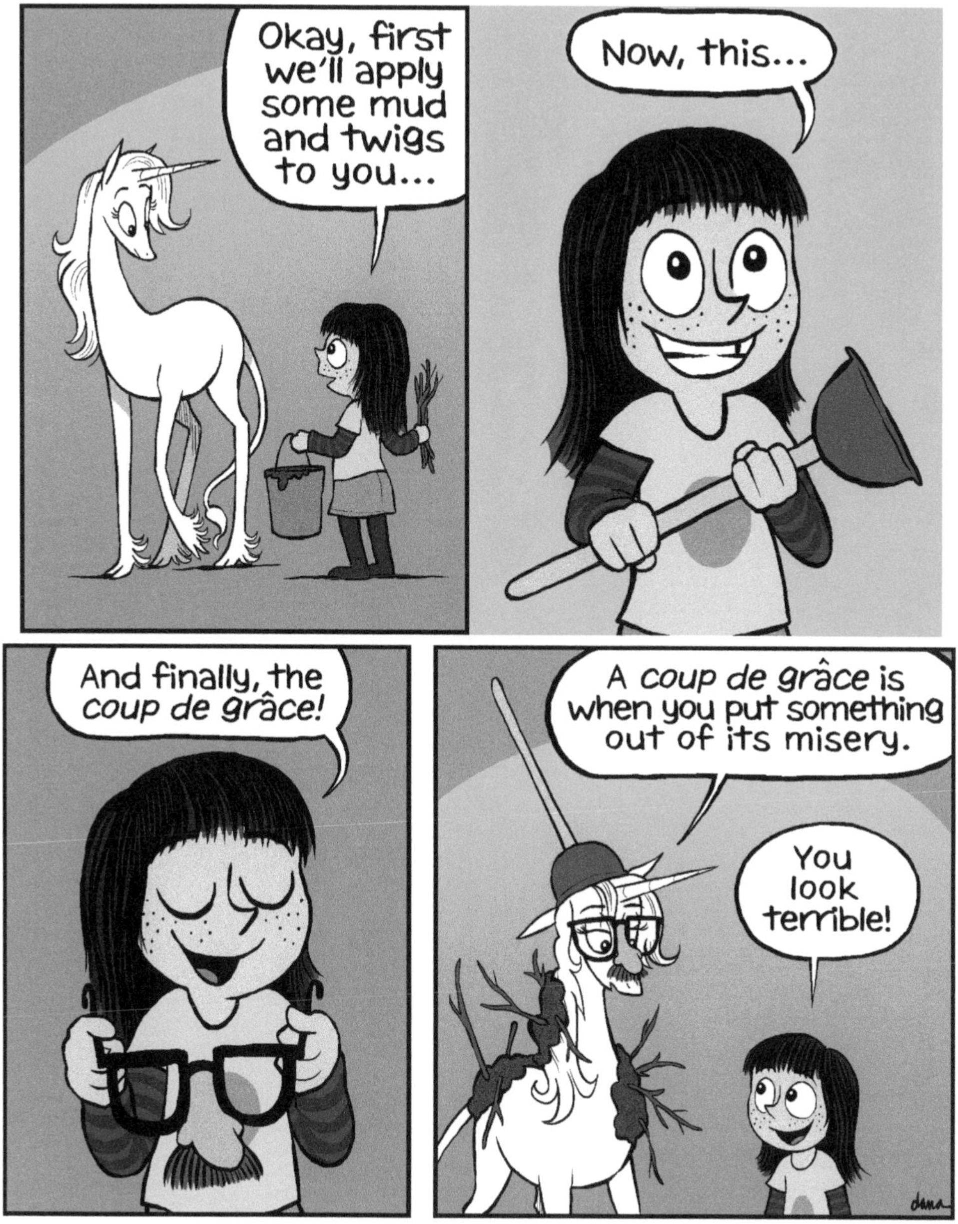
Okay, first we'll apply some mud and twigs to you...
Now, this...
And finally, the *coup de grâce!*
A *coup de grâce* is when you put something out of its misery.
You look terrible!
dana

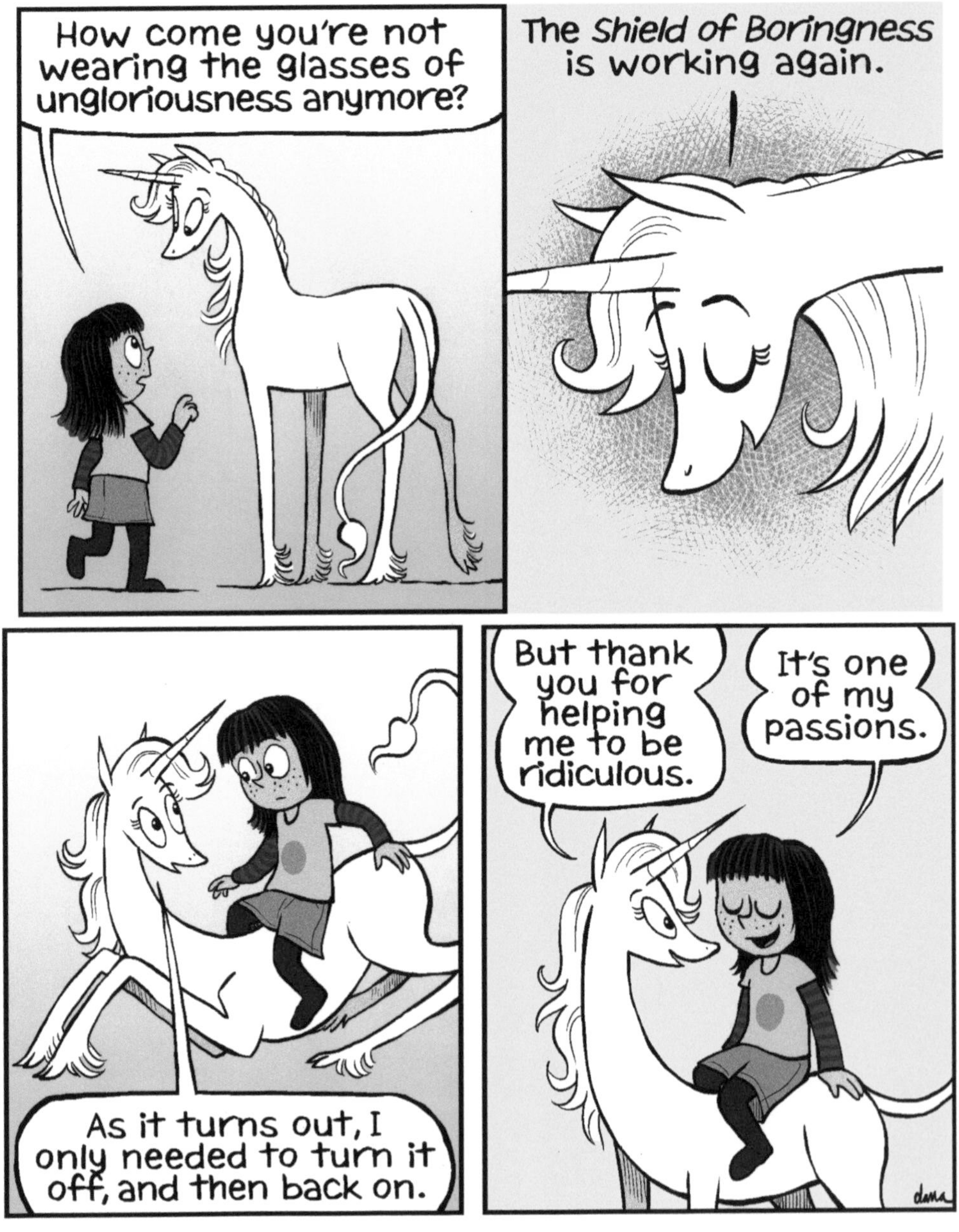
How come you're not wearing the glasses of ungloriousness anymore?
The *Shield of Boringness* is working again.
As it turns out, I only needed to turn it off, and then back on.
But thank you for helping me to be ridiculous.
It's one of my passions.
dana

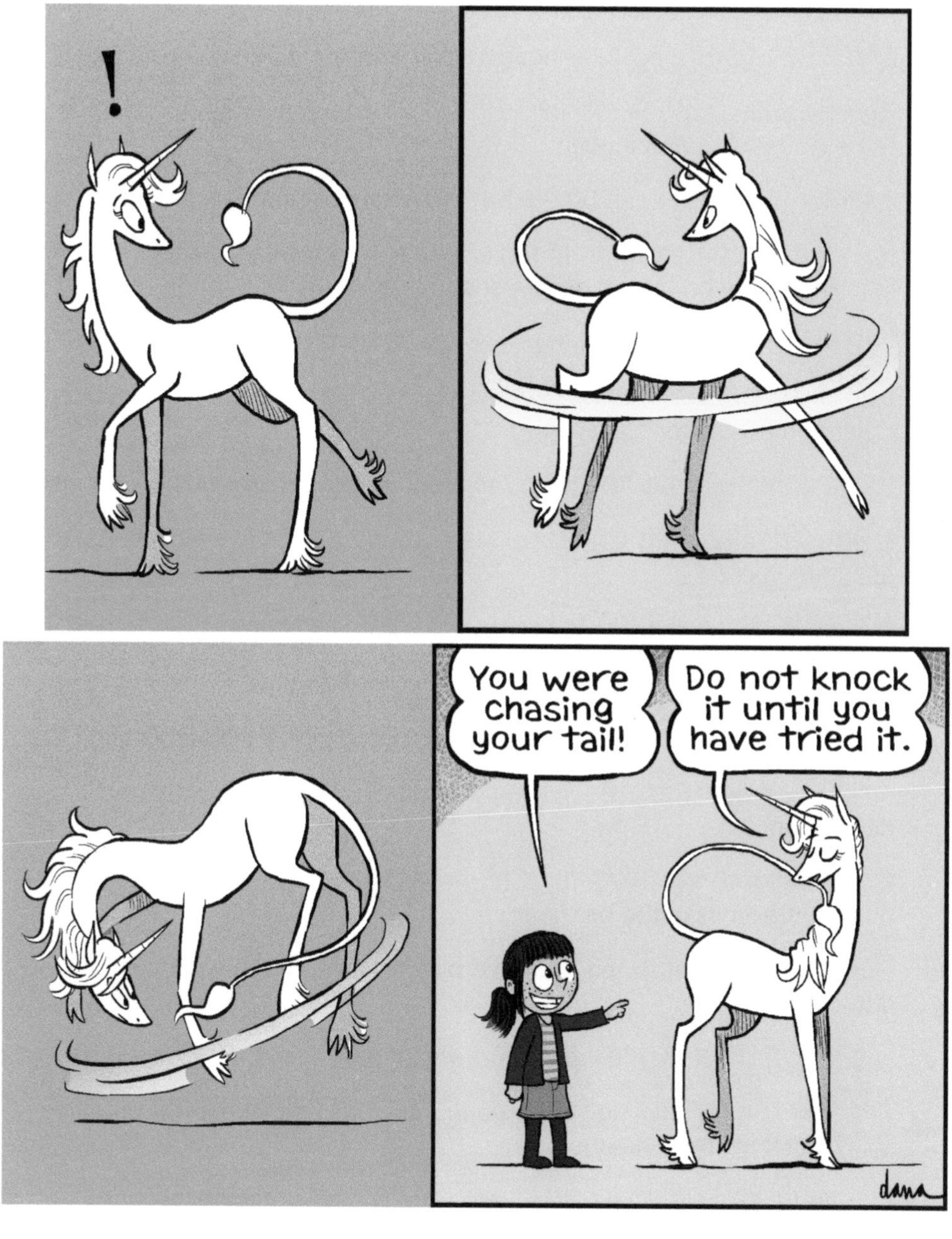
!
You were chasing your tail!
Do not knock it until you have tried it.
dana

More
TO EXPLORE!
A special section featuring
words to learn!

# GLOSSARY

**abode (uh-bode):** pg. 62 — noun / a place where a person lives; home

**abomination (uh-bom-uh-nay-shun):** pg. 98 — noun / something that is greatly disliked or loathed

**askew (uh-skyoo):** pg. 60 — adverb / out of position

**battering ram (ba-ter-ing ram):** pg. 84 — noun / an ancient military machine with a horizontal beam used to beat down walls, gates, etc.

**bestower (bee-stoe-ur):** pg. 140 — noun / gift giver

**compensated (kom-pun-sayt-ud):** pg. 11 — verb / made a payment in order to make up for something

**conjure (kon-jer):** pg. 70 — verb / to produce or bring into being by magic

**contention (kun-ten-shun):** pg. 119 — noun / a point used in a debate or an argument

**countenance (koun-tun-unce):** pg. 16 — verb / to approve or support

**debacle (duh-bah-kul):** pg. 141 — noun / total failure

**dirge (durj):** pg. 109 — noun / a mournful sound like a funeral song

**embellishment (em-bel-ish-munt):** pg. 149 — noun / ornament or decoration

**extraterrestrial (ek-struh-tuh-res-tree-ul):** pg. 45 — adjective / outside the limits of the earth

**flaunting (flont-ing):** pg. 115 — verb / conspicuously displaying; attracting attention

**frolicking (frol-ik-ing):** pg. 106 — verb / playing merrily

**grackle (grak-uhl):** pg. 103 — noun / any of a type of blackbirds with shiny black plumage (feathers)

**haggled (hag-uhld):** pg. 30 — verb / bargained; wrangled, especially over a price

**hypothetically** (hi-puh-thet-i-kuh-lee): pg. 133 – adverb / supposedly

**liberally** (lib-er-uhl-ee): pg. 149 – adverb / freely; abundantly

**metaphorical** (met-uh-fore-i-kuhl): pg. 154 – adjective / something used in a way to represent something else

**notarized** (noe-tih-rized): pg. 48 – verb / certified a document through a notary public

**notary** (noe-tih-ree): pg. 48 – noun / a person authorized to authenticate contracts and other legal documents

**ornery** (ore-nuh-ree): pg. 127 – adjective / unpleasant; cranky

**ostentatious** (os-ten-tay-shus): pg. 62, 115 – adjective / showing off wealth or treasure to make people envious; flashy or showy

**paisley** (payz-lee): pg. 158 – adjective / covered in a pattern of colorful, curvy designs

**pandering** (pan-der-ing): pg. 83 – verb / doing or saying what someone wants in order to please them

**Ph.D.** (pee-aich-dee): pg. 43 – abbreviation / Doctor of Philosophy; the highest academic degree awarded by universities

**pixelated** (pik-suh-layt-ed): pg. 84 – adjective / displayed in a way that individual pixels of a computer graphic are visible

**poise** (poiz): pg. 107 – noun / a dignified manner

**recalibrated** (ree-kal-uh-bray-ted): pg. 168 – verb / readjusted something for a particular function

**reluctant** (ree-luck-tunt): pg. 129 – adjective / unwilling; disinclined

**repository** (re-pos-it-or-ee): pg. 19 – noun / a place where a large amount of something is stored (like a warehouse, library, or store)

**résumé** (rez-oo-may): pg. 26 – noun / a brief written account of personal qualifications and experience, prepared by someone applying for a job

**sophisticated** (suh-fiss-tuh-kay-ted): pg. 66 – adjective / refined; worldly

**thesis (thee-sis):** pg. 43 — noun / a scholarly paper prepared with original research to prove a specific view

**touché (too-shay):** pg. 82 — interjection / an expression used to acknowledge something true, funny, or clever

**tribbles (trib-ulz):** pg. 59 — noun / fictional alien species in the *Star Trek* universe

**unionize (yoon-yuh-nize):** pg. 11 — verb / to organize into a labor union to protect workers' rights

***Phoebe and Her Unicorn*** is distributed internationally by Andrews McMeel Syndication.



Andrews McMeel Publishing
a division of Andrews McMeel Universal
1130 Walnut Street, Kansas City, Missouri 64106

www.andrewsmcmeel.com

ISBN: 978-1-4494-9506-0

Library of Congress Control Number: 2017952108

**ATTENTION: SCHOOLS AND BUSINESSES**

Andrews McMeel books are available at quantity discounts with bulk purchase for educational, business, or sales promotional use. For information, please e-mail the Andrews McMeel Publishing Special Sales Department: specialsales@amuniversal.com.

# Check out more *Phoebe and Her Unicorn*

Unicorn on a Roll
Another Phoebe and her Unicorn Adventure
Dana Simpson

Unicorn vs. Goblins
Another Phoebe and her Unicorn Adventure
Dana Simpson

Razzle Dazzle Unicorn
Another Phoebe and her Unicorn Adventure
Dana Simpson

Unicorn Crossing
Another Phoebe and her Unicorn Adventure
Dana Simpson

Phoebe and Her Unicorn in
The Magic Storm
Dana Simpson

Rainy Day Unicorn fun
140 Magical Puzzles
A Phoebe and her Unicorn Activity Book
Dana Simpson

## If you like Phoebe, look for these books!

Anne of Green Gables
a graphic novel

the Pinkaboos
BITTERLY AND THE GIANT PROBLEM
Jake and Laura Gosselin

WALLACE the BRAVE
Will Henry

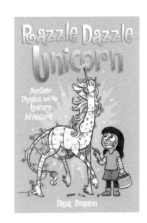

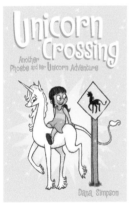

CPSIA information can be obtained
at www.ICGtesting.com
Printed in the USA
LVHW071700070421
683734LV00012B/343